# You Were Meant for Me

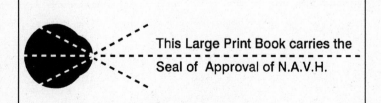

This Large Print Book carries the
Seal of Approval of N.A.V.H.

# You Were Meant for Me

Yona Zeldis McDonough

**THORNDIKE PRESS**
*A part of Gale, Cengage Learning*

GALE
CENGAGE Learning·

Farmington Hills, Mich • San Francisco • New York • Waterville, Maine
Meriden, Conn • Mason, Ohio • Chicago

GALE
CENGAGE Learning·

**LIBRARY OF CONGRESS CATALOGING-IN-PUBLICATION DATA**

McDonough, Yona Zeldis.
    You were meant for me / Yona Zeldis McDonough. — Large print edition.
    pages cm. — (Thorndike Press large print women's fiction.)
    ISBN 978-1-4104-7843-6 (hardcover) — ISBN 1-4104-7843-2 (hardcover)
    1. Single women—Fiction. 2. Foundlings—Fiction. 3. Foster parents—Fiction. 4. Birthparents—Fiction. 5. Large type books. 6. Domestic fiction. I. Title.
    PS3613.C39Y68 2015
    813'.6—dc23                                    2015000889

Published in 2015 by arrangement with NAL Signet, a member of Penguin Group (USA) LLC, a Penguin Random House Company

Printed in Mexico
1 2 3 4 5 6 7 19 18 17 16 15

To my dear friend Patricia Grossman,
for sharing the story that inspired this
novel

# ACKNOWLEDGMENTS

For sharing their intelligence, insight, and expertise, I would like to thank Sally Schloss, Sophia Seidner, Marian Thurm, and Dan Turbow. Special thanks go to my always patient but eagle-eyed editor, Tracy Bernstein, and to Judith Ehrlich, whose creativity, passion, and devotion make her a rare gem among agents.

She wove her way — dizzily, giddily even — along the deserted boardwalk. At this hour, everything was shuttered and still; the cold March wind gusted around her, whipping her hair — peroxided almost white, somewhat darker blond roots sprouting at the scalp — into a frenzy. After the hideous ordeal of the last few hours, she felt blissfully light and free, as if she might actually levitate. Of course, her recent chemical infusion — chemical infusion, she liked the sound of that phrase and congratulated herself on having come up with it — was contributing to her euphoria. But that didn't matter. A high was a high was a high. So what if she ached in ways she had not known it was possible to ache or that blood was still oozing down the insides of her thighs? No one would ever know; that was all behind her now.

She touched her fingers to the metal railing, glazed and slick from the rain that had only just stopped falling. But it was cold, so she pulled her hand away and kept moving. Bits of trash — grease-filmed food wrappers, empty soda cups — were lifted in the air when the wind blew and then dropped down again. She came to a bench on which sat a wet paper bag, its red and white stripes spotlighted by the streetlamp above. Reaching for the bag, she opened it to find the remains of someone's meal: bacon cheeseburger, French fries in a sticky pool of ketchup. Suddenly, she was ravenous. When was the last time she had eaten? She flopped down on the bench and devoured the food. Had anything ever tasted so good? When it was gone, she was still hungry and began to look around. A brimming garbage can stood nearby, and right on top, as if waiting for her, was a brown bag, this one not even wet, precariously perched on the mound. Inside she found an almost-full container of coffee, cold, of course, but so what? It was light, sweet, and tasted like pure milky heaven as it went down. Next to that was an untouched jelly doughnut. She inhaled it and then licked her fingers, the mingled taste of salt, oil, and powdered sugar unimaginably delicious.

She slowed when she came to an opening

in the railing. Beyond that opening lay the empty beach. How desolate it looked. And how beautiful. Veering onto the sand, which was packed and hard from the rain, she made her way toward the water's edge. The black, foam-tipped waves rose, crested, and crashed onto the shore, wetting the tips of her boots and spraying her shins.

She smiled; the sea was playing with her, inviting her to play back. Humming a little, she danced around the shoreline, feet getting wetter and wetter, until she knelt, unzipped her boots, and then kicked them off entirely. The humming stopped. There was the cold, stinging shock of the water and coarse, gritty sand, but it was a good cold, a bracing, cleansing cold.

She lifted her arms to the sky. Her hands were hidden by the sleeves of her purple down coat; the coat, which she'd spied hanging from a hook in a restaurant and helped herself to, was way too big for her, but she had been drawn by the color — lurid, hideous even — and wore it anyway. She wished she still had that other coat, the camel hair with the fitted princess seams, velvet collar, and buttons like pieces of melted butterscotch. Where was it now anyway? She had thought it prissy at the time, but now she regretted its loss. The luxurious softness of it. The warmth.

A big wave came and soaked her to the waist. The sea was getting more insistent now, its call more urgent. Come in, it seemed to say. Come in. She waded farther out. The cold was punishing, but also invigorating; she welcomed it like purification, a baptism. Infants were baptized. . . . No. Don't think of that. Don't. But thought was stubborn, and she thrashed around in the water, trying to escape it. The next wave swelled. This one was the biggest of all, rising in a great, undulant curve. It lifted her high before it broke — and then sucked her cleanly under.

# ONE

The supposedly hip place in Midtown was exactly the sort of place Miranda Berenzweig hated: cavernous, dim, and ear-splittingly loud. On one side of the room was a long, sleek bar made of highly polished black marble; on the other, a massive wall of water that rose from the floor like a tsunami. But since Bea was not only a hostess here but also dating the owner, their girl group had been lured by the promise of free food and drink. And look, here was Bea coming toward her.

"Hey," she said and kissed Miranda on each cheek. "You're the last one to arrive; everyone else is already ensconced. Follow me." Miranda was happy to do exactly that; she needed a guide in this latter-day Hades. The percussive beat from the music reverberated in the cavity of her chest and the crush of bodies thwarted her at every turn. But Bea seemed unfazed. Up a flight of black marble steps whose wrought-iron railing pulsated with clusters of tiny white lights and down a short hall to a dark paneled door, which Bea pulled open with a flourish. "The VIP lounge," she said. "Welcome!"

"We were getting worried about you," Courtney said. She was five-eleven, and her sleek blond head towered above everyone else's at the table.

"I was stuck at the office," Miranda said, shrugging off her coat and sliding into the tufted velvet banquette. "You didn't start without me, did you?"

"Of course not," said Lauren, who looked at Bea. "You'll be able to join us too? Even though you're working?"

"My shift is just about to end," Bea said.

Miranda had known Bea, along with Courtney and Lauren, since they had been freshmen at Bennington, and they still met every month or so to catch up on one another's lives. Tonight Miranda had a piece of good news to share — her first in a while — and when Bea sat down, a tray of pale green appletinis following in her wake, she dove right in.

"You're looking at the new online food editor of *Domestic Goddess,*" she announced. "We're revamping the Web site and I'll be responsible for all the food-related content."

"Does this mean you won't be handling the print edition anymore?" asked Lauren.

"No. The new job is in addition to, not instead of. So it's a bump up." Miranda took a sip of her drink — it was perfectly rendered — and smiled.

"Does it come with a raise?" Trust Courtney to bring up the subject of money.

"It most certainly does." Miranda took a celebratory sip. Ooh, it was *good.* "A generous one."

"Well, it's high time," said Courtney, who didn't so much sip as gulp from her glass. "You can finally stop living like a church mouse. Maybe you'll even move to Manhattan. You're not doing yourself any good out in the hinterlands."

Miranda went still. That was not a very tactful — or accurate — thing to say. She was not poor; she was *frugal,* which was an entirely different thing. She was diligent about putting money away for the proverbial rainy day, a concept Courtney, with her penchant for Chanel and Christian Louboutin, did not understand. Of course, Courtney was the accessories editor at *Soigné* magazine; she would claim her indulgences were necessities. "I love Brooklyn," she said.

"And you have such a great apartment,

15

right near the park and all," Bea, ever loyal, added.

"It *is* a nice apartment," Courtney conceded. "But it's just so far from everything."

"Not the things that matter to me," Miranda said quietly. But the conversation was already moving on, and everyone was congratulating Bea, who'd announced that she was now one of two finalists vying for the part of Maggie in an out-of-town production of *Cat on a Hot Tin Roof*. Then Lauren told everyone how her youngest child, Max, had just been admitted to a highly regarded pre-K and they all toasted that with another round. Along with the drinks, platters of grilled shrimp, empanadas, and spicy, translucent noodles arrived.

"Here's to finger painting!" sang out Bea.

Then it was Courtney's turn. Miranda was seized with the small, petty hope that Courtney's news did not involve her job; Courtney definitely had the more high-profile position — everyone knew *Soigné* — and she did not want her own promotion to be upstaged. There had always been a little thread of competition woven into her friendship with Courtney, something not present in her feelings for Bea or Lauren. But Courtney could also be her biggest booster, and it had been through a connection of

16

Courtney's that Miranda had landed at *Domestic Goddess.*

"Harris proposed!" Courtney sang out. "We're getting married!"

"That's wonderful!" Lauren and Bea started to clap.

"Mazel tov." Miranda tried to sound genuine though she thought Harris, a pedantic lawyer with a receding hairline and a premature paunch, was hardly a prize.

"Now you're the only one who's unattached," said Courtney to Miranda. "Girls, we have to find someone for Miranda. She's too special to remain on the vine. Maybe Harris has a friend. I'm going to ask."

Miranda, stung, said nothing. So what if she was single midway into her thirties? Was that a deficiency? A crime? "No Ivy League lawyers for me," she said, striving to keep her tone light. Harris had gone to Harvard, a fact he managed to work into all conversations, even ones that were ostensibly about the weather.

"What's wrong with lawyers?" Courtney said. They had moved on to White Russians — sprinkled with pulverized chocolate and dusted with nutmeg — which Bea said were the bar's signature libation. "Harris says that the law is the most stimulating intellectual pursuit he can imagine."

17

*Then his imagination must be pretty small,* thought Miranda.

"And that the people he met at Harvard —"

"I didn't say there was anything *wrong* with lawyers," Miranda interrupted. *Now he has* her *doing it too!* "I'm just looking for someone with, oh, I don't know, a more artistic bent."

"You mean some out-of-work painter who'll sponge off you for months before he maxes out your credit cards and moves on to a twenty-five-year-old?" said Courtney.

*"That,"* said Bea in a gentle but reproving tone, "isn't necessary. Or nice."

Miranda pushed her glass away. Ordinarily she loved White Russians, but suddenly the sweetness was nauseating; she thought she might be sick. Did Courtney need to dredge all that up *now*? And anyway, she was exaggerating. When Luke had gotten fired from his carpentry job, Miranda had offered to stake his purchase of art supplies so that he could keep on painting. But he was still morose and moody and she'd encouraged him to treat himself: expensive lunches, a new Italian suit from Barneys. But he'd hardly maxed out her card. Anyway, she had paid off the sizable AmEx bill, and her heart, though still bruised, was nonetheless on the pitted and rubble-strewn road to recovery.

"God, you're treating Miranda like she's made of glass or something." Courtney put a hand on Miranda's arm. "You know that I'm just concerned about you. We *all* are."

"Not necessary. I'm fine." Miranda stood up and brushed at her dark skirt, as if to wipe the lie away. Thanks to Bea's largesse, she was past her limit, and she swayed slightly on her feet. Better go home before she said something she'd regret.

Her standing up seemed to give the cue to Lauren and Courtney; the three women jostled their way through the still-crowded front room and out into the raw March night. Lauren and Courtney both lived uptown, and they headed off in the other direction. Bea and her manager boyfriend were still at the bar, which did not close until four a.m.

Miranda was alone. It was late, she was exhausted, and it had started to rain. To hell with being frugal; she was taking a taxi home. Raising her arm, she stepped off the curb to hail one.

But it seemed there was not a single available cab to be had in the entire city. After twenty minutes of watching taxi after taxi whoosh down the slick streets, she gave up and trudged toward the subway station on Forty-second Street. The platform was as full as if it had been the morning rush. Two musicians — a drummer and a guitarist — were at either end; the drummer, beating on several inverted plastic containers, was particularly good. A gaggle of teenage girls preened for the boys nearby. A large Hispanic family occupied an entire bench, and a couple leaning against a metal support kissed languorously.

Miranda turned away. It was just over eight months since Luke had packed up the toothbrush, the sketchbooks, the paint-flecked flannels, and the jeans bleached to that enviable state of softened whiteness he had left in her apartment. Over eight months since he'd told her that he'd decided to leave New York entirely and move to Berlin. "It's got a totally happening art scene," he'd said. "Really stimulating." She hadn't known until after he'd gone that some of the stimulation was being provided by an adorable, twentysomething German girl he'd picked up at a gallery in Chelsea and had been seeing behind Miranda's back.

The lovers were still kissing; the man's fingers wound through his girlfriend's hair in an intimate, caressing gesture. Miranda did not want to see any more, so she walked down the platform. At the far end, under the stairs, was a huddled mass. At first glance, it looked like a pile of old blankets, but the bare foot sticking out from one corner — dark, with thick, overgrown nails and leatherlike heels — made it clear that someone was sleeping underneath. Reaching into her wallet, she extracted a five and tucked it at the edge of the pile. She also set down the doggie bag of shrimp and noodles that Bea had sent her off with. Then the train pulled in — finally — and Miranda turned from the foot and the blankets. She found a seat and sank down gratefully.

Ordinarily, she was happy with her job, but today there'd been nothing but stress. The managing editor had gotten into a fight with the decorating editor during the weekly staff meeting, which seemed to put the entire office in a foul mood. Two of her writers had failed to deliver promised copy, and a very labor-intensive banana malted milk torte was knocked to the floor during a photo shoot. It had to be made all over again, which completely threw off the schedule, and Marvin, the art director, had one of his hissy fits when he found out.

Miranda had been looking forward to an evening with her friends. But Courtney's tactless comment had kind of ruined it for her; she felt flung right back in the misery that had been Luke. At least she could sleep in tomorrow. Her only commitment was not until four o'clock, when she'd agreed to meet Evan Zuckerbrot, the latest dish served up by eHarmony, for coffee. She had resisted signing up for eHarmony, but both Courtney and Lauren had been pestering her to *just do it.*

Miranda had succumbed, and even though she did not think Evan was that "someone special," she reasoned that an afternoon latte would not be all that much of a risk. The rocking of the train was making her sleepy; she rested her head against the wall and closed her eyes. *Just for a minute,* she thought. *Just one little minute.* When she opened her eyes, she was still sitting in the subway car, entirely alone and freezing. She leaped up in a panic. Clearly, she had slept right past her stop, and several stops after that; she'd come to the end of the line. The doors were open and the platform was elevated; that's why she was so cold. But where *was* she? Coney Island–Stillwell Avenue, that's where — at least according to the sign.

Well, she'd just have to get a train going back; she could forget about finding a cab out here.

Miranda stepped onto the platform. Even from up here, she could smell the sharp, salt-laced wind coming from the ocean. It was a good smell, actually — clean and bracing. But she had to get home. She felt nervous being out so late by herself, a feeling that intensified when she went down the stairs. There were no longer any token booths, of course; she could see the phantom spot where the booth had been, its ghostly perimeter still outlined on the floor, like something from a crime scene. There was not a soul in the station, and she was just about to sprint up the stairs to the other side when her attention was snagged by a neat, cream-colored bundle that sat right by the banister.

She paused. It looked harmless enough — a folded blanket or something — but in the post-9/11 world, she had to wonder. Could a bomb be concealed in those folds? How would she know, anyway? Did she even have a clue as to what a bomb looked like? While she was debating this, she saw something else even more startling: a tiny foot peeking out from one corner of the blanket. It flitted through her mind that this was the second bare foot she'd seen tonight. Only this one belonged to a doll.

A doll. Not too likely there was a bomb in there. Miranda could see the little toes, all five of them, lined up like tiny brown nuts. What a well-made thing.

Clean too. Why would someone have thrown it away? Then the foot *moved.* Miranda stopped, not sure she saw what she thought she saw. She was exhausted, disoriented, and possibly a little drunk. The foot was an exquisite creation, crafted from something so smooth and pliant that she could not guess what it might have been. But when it moved again — this time causing the blanket on top to stir ever so slightly — she knew that it was no mere simulation. The cold she had been feeling ever since she woke up seemed to gather speed and force; it shot right through her, like a bullet. Carefully, she lifted a corner of the blanket away.

There, wrapped in a surprisingly clean white towel and cushioned by the bottom part of the blanket, was an infant. No, not an infant, a *newborn,* with cocoa-colored skin, black hair plastered to its tiny skull, and eyes that were tightly shut against the harsh light of the subway station. *Oh. My. God.* Was it even *alive*? Should she touch it? She remained that way for several seconds until the infant opened its mouth in a yawn that seemed to devour its entire face. The eyelids fluttered briefly before closing again. Definitely alive!

The yawn propelled Miranda into action. She lifted up the tiny creature. Under the towel the infant was naked; the umbilical cord, tied in a crude, red knot, looked as if it had been sawed off, and there were reddish streaks on her body. Was the umbilical cord infected or was it supposed to be that way? Miranda had no idea but wished she had some antibiotic ointment. Avoiding the red protuberance, she shifted the baby gingerly in her arms. Around one wrist was a bracelet; the small pink glass beads were interspersed with white ones whose black letters spelled out BABY GIRL. Someone had cared enough to place that bracelet on her wrist; was it the same person who had left her here in the station? Miranda wrapped the blanket around the infant's body. But that didn't seem sufficient, so she opened her coat and positioned her close to her own body. That ought to keep her warm. Or at least warmer.

The station was still empty. What should she do? There was an app on her phone that would help her locate a police station. But she did not want to be walking around here in this strange neighborhood by herself. No,

25

she'd rather head for the station house back in Park Slope. She waited downstairs for the train; it would be warmer than the windy platform. When she heard it arriving, she hurried up the stairs and got in as soon as the doors parted.

As the train chugged along, it occurred to her that the infant might be hungry or thirsty. Hungry she could not fix. But she had a bottle of water in her bag; also hand sanitizer, which she wished she had thought to use earlier. Damn! Gripping the tiny body under one arm, she managed to squirt the green gel over both hands and rub furiously. Then she wet her fingers with the water and held them to the infant's lips. She opened her mouth and began to suck. Tears welled in Miranda's eyes. She was thirsty, poor little thing. Naked, abandoned in a subway station, and thirsty too — the final and crowning indignity in a brand-new life that so far seemed comprised of nothing but.

When they reached their stop, Miranda made her way through the dark streets toward the police station. At least the rain had tapered off. Against her body, the infant felt warm and animate. Miranda was keenly aware of her breath, in and out, in and out. The rhythm calmed her.

26

Yanking open the heavy doors to the station house, she stepped inside. A bored-looking officer behind a bulletproof shield was leafing through a copy of the *New York Post;* two other officers — one pale and seemingly squeezed into a uniform that was a size or two too small, the other as brown as the baby Miranda held close to her heart — were chatting in low voices. Above, the fluorescent light buzzed like a frantic insect. The cop reading the paper finally glanced up. He looked not at Miranda, but straight through her. "Can I help you?" he said in a tone that suggested he would sooner endure a colonoscopy, a root canal, *and* a tax audit — simultaneously.

"Look," she said urgently, opening her coat to reveal the infant in its makeshift swaddling. "Look what I just found!"

# Two

"You thought it was a *doll*?" Courtney leaned over to reach for one of the cookies Miranda had baked — there were snickerdoodles, gingersnaps, and chocolate chip. The three of them were gathered in Miranda's apartment on President Street. Bea would be here any minute; she promised to come in time for the local news broadcast that would be airing at five o'clock.

"The most lifelike doll I had ever seen," Miranda said. She had canceled — well, all right, *postponed* — her meeting with Evan; she had been up most of the night and had slept virtually all day to compensate. Now her friends had come over to hear the story directly from her and to watch the news clip. "Also, I was still a bit looped and I wasn't sure what I was looking at."

"I would have been frightened," Lauren said.

"Of what?" Miranda was about to reach

for a cookie too but then stopped. She had three cake recipes she had to bake — and taste — this week; winter pounds were so easy to pack on, so hard to take off. Besides, it was the baking as much as the eating that appealed to her. She loved the visual and at times almost sensual interplay of ingredients, colors, and textures: the dense, golden clay of batter punctuated by the dark bits of chocolate, the pungent, earthy drip of molasses, the powdery loft of flour hitting the bowl.

"That something would happen to the baby while you were holding it. What if she had died while you were carrying her on the subway? The police might have charged you."

"I never even thought of that," Miranda said. She was still remembering the feeling of the infant pressed so close to her; they seemed to fit, like puzzle pieces, so neatly together. Is this what new mothers experienced when their babies were handed to them? Well, not *that* infant's mother; clearly she had not felt that sense of completion when holding her baby. But Miranda was more sympathetic — and even curious — than judgmental. What could have driven her to do such a thing? What impossible place — all other options exhausted, rejected, used up — had she reached to make her decision? The blanket and the bracelet showed she had made some effort. Though leaving the baby in a subway station . . . well, it was pretty hard to put any positive spin on that.

The bell rang, and there was Bea, corkscrew curls massing around her face, running up the stairs. "Hell-o!" she said, plopping down on Miranda's rug with a big shopping bag from Duane Reade. "I brought provisions!"

"Let me see," said Courtney, peering into the bag. "Chips, pretzels, macadamia nuts, chocolate . . ." She looked up at Bea. "Is there anything you *didn't* buy?"

"Well, we're going to watch the news; I figured we'd need fortification."

"Bea, the clip is going to last, like, three minutes," Courtney said. "This isn't exactly a double feature."

"And I made cookies," Miranda added.

"You always make cookies!" said Bea. "But doesn't watching TV make you hungry?" She reached for a bag of chips and opened it in a single, deft stroke.

"Look, it's going to start!" Lauren said, squeezing Miranda's arm. "Turn the sound on."

The reporter, a tall, glib guy who re-

30

sembled a Ken doll, shoved the microphone in her face. "We're here, live in Brooklyn at the Seventy-eighth Precinct with Amanda Berenzweig —"

"Miranda," her on-air incarnation corrected.

"Excuse me?" Patter interrupted, Ken looked baffled.

"Miranda, the name is *Miranda* Berenzweig."

"Of course it is," he said with his dazzling smile. "Now, can you tell us what happened, Ms. Berenzwig? Right from the beginning?"

"You didn't correct him that time," Courtney noted.

"I thought he might cry if I did."

"Shh," said Bea. "I can't hear."

The talking stopped, and Miranda settled back to watch her televised self explaining what had happened: falling asleep in the subway, waking in an unfamiliar station, the doll-that-turned-out-be-a-baby. Then the camera cut away to the baby herself — now cleaned up and wearing a little cap over her head. *If anyone has any information, please call* . . . flashed along the bottom of the screen. Then some more blather from Ken and the segment was over. A commercial for a new breakfast cereal chirped across the airwaves until Bea clicked the remote to

31

mute it.

"So what's going to happen to her now?" Lauren asked. Of the four friends, she was the only one with children.

"Foster care, I guess. Until someone claims her. *If* someone claims her," said Miranda.

"Someone will claim her," Lauren said as she buttoned her coat. "You wait."

The rest of them sat around discussing it after she had left. Bea had been right: they polished off the cookies, the chips, the nuts, the pretzels, and almost all the chocolate. "Who wants the last square?" Bea said. Miranda wavered and was glad when Courtney spoke up. When she and Bea got up to leave, Miranda gave them each a hug. She had even forgiven Courtney — sort of. "Thanks for coming," she said. "I was so glad you were here."

"Of course we were here," Bea said. "Where else would we be?"

Over the next couple of days, Miranda found herself thinking about the baby. She thought about her as she baked those three cakes and while she edited the two late articles that finally showed up days past their respective deadlines. She thought about the baby in the shower, when she went out for a run in Prospect Park, and when she worked her shift at the food co-op on Union Street.

She also thought about the baby's mother. She first pictured her as a teenager, petrified to tell her parents she was pregnant. Or maybe she was a drug addict or an alcoholic. Miranda remembered the blanket, the towel. Whoever she was, the mother had tried, sort of. But why the subway station and not a hospital or a police station?

There were no answers to these questions. But she might be able to find out more about the baby. She returned to the police station where she'd first brought her. The once-bored cop now greeted her like a long-lost cousin. "You!" he said, smile wide and welcoming. "You're the one who found the baby!"

She nodded, oddly pleased. "I am. And I was wondering what happened to her since then."

The officer was only too glad to fill her in. She got the address of family court and the name of the judge assigned to the case. The building, at 330 Jay Street, was not all that far from her office in downtown Manhattan. The next day, she made the trip and, after a few inquiries, found the courtroom she'd been looking for. The metal benches

33

just outside were packed, and the waiting sea of faces looked sad, angry, embittered, or a ravaged combination of all three. Miranda stepped inside the courtroom and slid into a seat at the back. Up front, Judge Deborah Waxman was presiding. She looked to be in her sixties, with frosted blond hair, frosted pink lip gloss, and frosted white nails — it was like she was sugarcoated. But nothing about her manner or voice was even remotely sweet. She cut through the whiny excuses, the meandering stories, the bluster and the rationalizations made by deadbeat dads and criminally negligent moms with the same brisk, impartial efficiency in a way that Miranda found intimidating but admirable. When she called a ten-minute recess, Miranda asked a court officer if she could approach the bench. The officer looked at the judge who looked at Miranda. She felt herself being intensely scrutinized and was relieved when the judge inclined her head in a small nod. She had passed.

"What can I do for you?" asked the judge.

Miranda knew she did not have much time. "I've come about the baby," she said. "The one who was found in the subway at Stillwell Avenue."

"Stable condition at a city hospital," the judge said succinctly. "When she's been thoroughly checked out, she'll be released."

"Where to?"

"Family services is arranging for a foster care placement. No one has claimed her, so she'll be put up for adoption." Judge Waxman looked down as if assessing the condition of her iridescent manicure. "Why do you want to know?"

"I'm the one who found her that night," Miranda said. "I brought her to the police."

"You did." It was a statement, not a question.

"Yes, Your Honor."

"That was a very kind thing to do." The judge brought her gaze up from her nails. Her small but intensely blue eyes seemed to be taking Miranda's measure.

"No, it wasn't," said Miranda, meeting that gaze full-on.

"You think it was *un*kind?" Judge Waxman sounded surprised.

"It was no more than decent," Miranda said. "And decent is not the same as kind. Decent is what anyone would have done."

"Not her mother," said the judge.

"No, well, I'm sure there's a story behind that. . . ."

"Isn't there always?" The judge glanced at her watch. "Recess is over," she said. "Thank you for coming, Ms. . . ."

"Berenzweig."

"Ms. Berenzweig. I'll see that the mayor's office sends you a citation or something."

"I don't want a citation," Miranda said.

"No? Then what do you want?" It was a challenge.

Miranda felt flustered. Did she even know? "Just to know that she's all right," she said.

As it turned out, that was not enough. Now that she knew the baby was being cared for, Miranda craved more information. She was such a thirsty baby. Would someone make sure she drank enough? What about a name? Names were so important; Miranda hoped she wasn't given one that was silly or demeaning.

Over the next week, Miranda returned to Judge Waxman's courtroom three more times. Each time, she waited patiently for a recess or a break and would listen to the update that Judge Waxman delivered in the same clipped tone. The baby was drinking formula. The baby had gained an ounce. There was some evidence of drugs — she would not specify — in her system, but they were minimal; it did not appear that her mother had been an addict. Miranda warmed to the woman, frosting and all. How would the judge have known these details unless she too had taken a special interest in the baby?

Then Judge Waxman told her that a foster care placement had been found for the baby; she would be leaving the hospital shortly.

"Would I be able to see her before they let her go?" Miranda asked.

"Whatever for?" Judge Waxman's brows, two thin, penciled arcs, rose high on her forehead.

"Just because. Maybe I could hold her. The nurses must be so busy; they might not have time."

"I've never had a request like that," said the judge. Miranda did not say anything; she just waited while those shrewd blue eyes did their work. "But I see no reason why you couldn't. Come back tomorrow; I'll give you the name of the facility and a letter allowing you to visit with her at the discretion of the nurses."

"Oh, thank you!" Miranda said. "Thank you so much!"

She walked out of the courthouse buoyant with anticipation, and after work spent an hour in Lolli's on Seventh Avenue, considering the relative merits of tiny sweaters, caps, dresses, and leggings. She spent way too much money, but rationalized her purchases

37

as charitable contributions.

The baby was being held at Kings County Hospital, on Clarkson Avenue; Miranda took the subway to the 627-bed facility (she had looked it up online) after she left work the next day. The two nurses on the neonatal ward were only too happy to indulge her. "Honey, you can hold her all night long if you want to," said one, her Caribbean accent giving the words a musical lilt.

"Do you know that someone found her in the subway?" said the other one.

"I know," Miranda said. "I was that someone."

"Lord, no!" said the nurse.

Miranda nodded and looked down at the baby. She was definitely heavier; Miranda felt she had her weight imprinted somewhere in her sense memory and she could discern the difference. Her skin tone had evened out and her dark eyes were open and fixed on Miranda's face. Did she remember the time they had spent together? Could she in some inchoate way *recognize* her?

Miranda spent the next two hours walking, rocking, and talking to the baby. She took scads of photos that she would later post to her Facebook page. The baby guzzled the bottle of formula that the nurses prepared, and she dozed peacefully as

Miranda toted her up and down the hospital corridor. During a diaper change, which the nurse showed Miranda how to execute, she blinked several times and kicked her tiny feet. As her hand closed around Miranda's extended finger, the force of her grip was a revelation.

When visiting hours ended, Miranda pulled herself away with the greatest reluctance. She went back the next night, this time with butterscotch blondies she had baked from an office recipe; the nurses tore into them eagerly. "For someone who had such a start, she's doing all right," said the one with the island accent. She bit into her blondie with evident delight.

"She's lucky you're the one who found her," said the other.

"Maybe I'm the lucky one," Miranda said, gazing down at the baby who was now wearing a knit dress adorned with rosebuds; Miranda had rubbed the cotton against her own cheek to test for softness when selecting it.

The following day, Miranda was back in Judge Waxman's courtroom. "The family that adopts her — they'll be thoroughly checked out, right?" she asked.

"Of course," said Judge Waxman. "We have our protocols, and they are strictly adhered to."

"Will they love her, though? How can your protocols determine that?"

Judge Waxman pursed her shiny lips in what looked like irritation. But when she spoke, it was with more gentleness than she had previously displayed. "What about *you*, Ms. Berenzweig?" she asked.

"Excuse me?"

"What about you as a prospective foster parent? With the goal of adoption?"

"Me?" Miranda's hopes lifted briefly at the thought before they came plummeting down again. How could she even consider adopting a baby? She had no husband, no boyfriend even, and an already-demanding job that was about to become even more demanding.

"Yes, you," Judge Waxman was saying. "I think you've demonstrated a remarkable attachment to this infant already. How many times have you been to see me about her? And how many times have you been to see *her*?"

"Well, she's such a darling little thing, and of course I was concerned about her, having found her and everything —" She was babbling, babbling like an incoherent fool. She took a deep, centering breath and began again. "Doesn't it all take time?" she said.

"Aren't there *protocols*?"

Again that shrewd, raking look from the judge. "Of course there are. But in cases of urgent need, and this certainly qualifies, I have ways of . . . expediting things when I need to. We could conduct a home visit, and if everything is found to be in order, we could place her with you and begin the adoption proceedings. It would take a few months, but in the meantime you'd be fostering her and getting to know her better."

*I already know her,* Miranda wanted to say. But that seemed, well, crazy. So she kept quiet.

"Why don't you sleep on it?" Judge Waxman asked. "Think it over. Talk to your family. Your friends. And give me your answer in the next few days."

Miranda nodded and left. Isn't this what she'd been hoping for, wishing for, in some way *scheming* for since the first time she'd shown up in front of Judge Waxman? Now that the offer was actually on the table, though, she was petrified, and she walked out of the building bathed in a pure, icy panic. Rather than take the subway, she decided to walk for a while; she needed to clear her head.

The day was sunny and not too cold; there

were lots of people on the pedestrian path of the Brooklyn Bridge. Miranda had to maneuver past power walkers, joggers, women with strollers, old couples with thick-soled shoes and Polar fleece jackets, and an excited, noisy bunch of school kids, all wearing identical neon orange vests. Below, the water shifted and sparkled; a flight of birds — she had not a clue as to what they were — sliced the sky above.

The new Web site about to launch at *Domestic Goddess* meant that in addition to her current workload, Miranda would now be overseeing all the online food content — more recipes that needed testing, more features that needed assigning, more deadline-averse writers. It was a step-up in responsibility, prestige, and scope. It would also mean a lot more work, especially in the beginning. How would she manage all that, on her own, with a brand-new baby? And the baby looked to be black. Maybe she would be better off with a different sort of family — a family with two parents, or a family in which at least one of them had skin her color.

Once across the bridge, Miranda walked west until she reached Greenwich Street and started heading uptown. Assuming she could clear the racial hurdle — Judge Wax-

42

man, after all, had not even raised the issue — could she afford to hire a sitter? Or would she need to resort to daycare? What would her father say? Her landlady and her colleagues at work? Her friends? She had a hunch that Courtney was going to rain right down all over her parade. What was it with her lately anyway? Was it just the engagement, or was it something deeper, more systemic?

Her father. She realized she hadn't talked to him for more than a week. But given the fog of dementia that enveloped him, it didn't seem to matter how often they spoke because he was not there when they did. Still, she had to try, and she took her phone from her purse. His caretaker, Eunice, answered, and after giving Miranda a brief update, she handed over the phone. "Nate, it's your daughter," Eunice was saying in the background. "Your daughter, Miranda — you remember?"

"Miranda?" her father said uncertainly. "Do I know you?"

"Of course you know me, Dad." She closed her eyes, just for a second, as if her sorrow were a visible thing she deliberately chose not to see. "I'm your daughter. Your girl."

"There are no girls here. No girls." His

voice quavered. "I like girls — little girls, big girls. Girls are very, very nice. I think I used to have a girl once. What happened to her?" Now he sounded ready to cry.

"Dad! You still do! I'm that girl — it's me, Miranda."

"You're not a girl," he chided. "No, no, no. And Miranda — that's not a girl's name. I would have called a girl Rosie or Posy. Maybe Polly. But never Miranda."

There was a silence during which Miranda swiped at her tear-filled eyes. She had come to the mini-freeway that was Canal Street and did not answer until she'd crossed safely to the other side. But when she attempted to prod her father's ruined memory again, it was Eunice who replied. "He's having a bad day."

"I can tell."

"Some days he knows your name and everything. He remembers where you live and when you're coming to visit."

"But not today."

"Not today," Eunice said. "Why don't you try again tomorrow?"

"I will." She put the phone back in her purse and descended the stairs to the subway station. While on the train, Miranda took unsentimental stock of her life: eight years at a good job and a recent promotion, a nice apartment, money from both her salary and a small inheritance from her grandmother, a father sinking deeper into the oblivion of his disease. Good friends, no boyfriend, and apart from a date with a man she'd never actually met, none on the horizon either.

She had not been thinking about having a child when she first happened on the abandoned baby on the platform. But once she'd seen her, held her, everything changed. The very act of finding her seemed significant, so by extension, all the events leading up to it — falling asleep and missing her stop, waking up in *that* particular station, passing by *that* spot at exactly *that* moment — glowed with significance too. She'd found a baby. How not to believe that in some way that baby was meant — even fated — for her?

But was she equal to the job? Growing up, Miranda had not been especially close to her own mother. Her strongest bond had been with her father. Then she'd gone through that typical rebellious phase in her teen years, and before she'd ever had a chance to circle back and know or understand her in any more adult way, her mother had gotten sick. And died. Yet these last few weeks had opened new possibilities, new

45

horizons. Maybe she *did* have it in her to do it all differently, to form the kind of attachment that she had longed for in her own childhood. At the very least, she wanted to try.

Suddenly she felt energized and, when she reached the *Domestic Goddess* office on West Fourteenth Street, Miranda bypassed the elevator and took the stairs to the fifth floor. She wasn't even winded when she arrived. No, she was pumped, primed, and ready for the biggest challenge she'd ever faced. She'd sleep on it, of course. And then if she felt like this — so certain, so committed, so excited — tomorrow, she would contact Judge Waxman to tell her the answer was yes.

# THREE

Bea and Lauren showed up the following Sunday morning to help her prepare for the upcoming inspection from Child Welfare Services. Bea was organized and unsentimental, ruthlessly jettisoning yellowed plastic containers, wire hangers, and the broken sewing machine Miranda had lugged in from the street a decade ago and never had fixed. Lauren, by virtue of the fact that she had kids, could be counted on to spot hazards that posed a threat to child safety. Courtney was ring shopping with the insufferable Harris but said she would try to stop by later. As Miranda had intuited, she was the only one who seemed less than enthusiastic about the plan. Miranda brushed her concerns away; Bea and Lauren were right there with her.

By the end of the day, Miranda's sunny top-floor apartment was in peak condition. Unworn clothes were bagged and prepped for the Goodwill truck, and weeded-out books for the library. Clutter and old papers had been tossed, filed, or recycled. And the place was squeaky clean, from top to bottom, inside and out. When Miranda had tried to shove some of her knitting supplies into a closet — everyone at *Domestic Goddess,* even Martin, had taken a knitting pledge — Bea had nixed the idea. "They're going to look in the closets," she said. "And in the medicine chest, kitchen cabinets — everywhere."

"Does that mean I have to give up knitting?" Miranda said. She had hardly gotten started.

"No. We just have to turn your stuff" — she gestured to the skeins of yarn — "into decor." To that end, she repurposed a basket Miranda had been planning to dump and artfully arranged the yarn into a display of pleasing textures and colors. The needles she gave to Miranda. "High up for these. Top shelf."

"But it makes more sense to keep them with the yarn."

"Are you kidding?" Lauren said. "She's right — knitting needles could be *lethal* weapons. Get them out of sight. Now."

Miranda meekly complied. Then she ordered pizza and opened a bottle of wine

48

while they waited for it to arrive. Glass in hand, she looked around at her reconfigured apartment. The desk had been moved into the living room; she'd been persuaded to part with a poorly made bookcase, as well as many of the books in it, to make more room. "But not these; these are special." Miranda stood protectively in front of a pile she'd saved from the discards.

"They look like kids' books anyway," said Lauren.

"They are." Miranda picked up a copy of *The Poky Little Puppy,* which had been published in 1942. "They're all old, though. Some were mine when I was little; my mother had saved them. After she died, I couldn't bring myself to get rid of them. And when I'd see an old book I liked at a sale or a flea market, I'd buy it. I didn't really think of it as collecting until about five years in."

Lauren knelt in front of the pile. "*Alice's Adventures in Wonderland. The Velveteen Rabbit. A Child's Book of Fairy Tales* — look at these illustrations; they're wonderful."

"Those are by Arthur Rackham. He's one of my favorites."

"You'll have such fun reading these together." Bea was looking at *Noël for Jeanne-Marie;* one of the central characters was a sheep named Patapon. "She'll have a ready-made library when she gets here."

"You mean *if* she gets here." Miranda sneezed; some of those books hadn't been touched in a long while and were dusty. "It's not a sure thing yet." She reached for a cloth and dusted off Joan Walsh Anglund's *A Child's Year.* This was one of the books she had owned and loved; her name, written in red crayon, was still on the inside cover. Maybe there would be another name added to this book one day — the name of the little girl she hoped would come to live with her.

Miranda began stacking the books in the closet. She could have used that bookcase she was about to jettison, but she needed the space for something even more essential — the crib that Lauren's babies had used, rescued from its basement limbo, re-assembled, and wiped down thoroughly with non-toxic cleanser. "I'll give it back to you when she's through with it," Miranda had said.

"Not necessary. The shop is closed; I'm done." Lauren patted her midsection for emphasis.

Everything else in what had been the tiny study was left pretty much intact: the small armchair she had used for reading would be perfect for feeding the baby; the pine cupboard that had contained recipes, clippings, and back issues of *Domestic Goddess* had been emptied in preparation for the baby's clothes. The artwork on the walls — a poster of a still life by Matisse, another of musicians by Picasso, an oddball painting of an owl picked up at a local stoop sale — all seemed perfectly appropriate for the baby's eyes.

*The baby. My baby.* Every time she said or thought those words, they did not seem real. How would it feel to move from a single state to a coupled one? For even though people talked about single moms so casually now, as if it were simply another lifestyle choice in an array of many possible choices, how could a mother ever be considered single? Didn't having a child preclude all sense of singleness? Didn't being a mother make you part of an indissoluble binary unit?

Her own mother had seemed to chafe at that connection; she was always urging Miranda to *go and play.* Her best friend in those years, Nancy Pace, had a mother who flopped down on the floor and embarked on marathon games of Candy Land, Monopoly, and Parcheesi with her daughter and her friends; they baked together and

51

Mrs. Pace had taught Nancy to sew on a Singer machine she set up on the kitchen table. Miranda had longed for that mother.

The downstairs bell buzzed. "Pizza," said Miranda.

"Good," said the ever-hungry Bea. "I'm famished."

But it wasn't the delivery guy after all. It was Courtney, all artlessly-artfully tousled blond hair and chic black coat.

"Did you get the ring?" asked Lauren eagerly.

"I want to see it," added Bea.

Courtney shook her head. "No. We didn't find it today. But look what we did find." She twisted her hair into an impromptu ponytail so that the small, flower-shaped earrings — diamonds and rubies from the look of them — that twinkled on her lobes were more visible.

"Nice!" said Bea.

"Are they real?" Lauren asked, getting closer.

Miranda stood back. She was ashamed of the small, hot rush of envy she suddenly felt. Courtney had been her roommate and best friend freshman year; Bea and Lauren joined them later. It was Courtney who had seen Miranda through numerous all-nighters, boyfriends, and breakups, dreary jobs, and her mother's hideous death from colon cancer. But things had changed somehow, and she now seemed to regard Miranda with an annoying mixture of pity and disdain. The engagement had only made it worse. You'd think no one in the history of the world had ever planned a wedding before.

When Lauren and Bea finally stopped cooing over the earrings, Courtney looked around the apartment. "It looks great in here," she said approvingly. "I love what you've done."

"Thanks," Miranda said, relaxing a little. Maybe she was as guilty of overreacting to Courtney's comments as Courtney was guilty of obtuseness in making them. The two of them did go way back.

"You should bake something," said Lauren, who had recently purchased an apartment and was the veteran of a dozen or more open houses. "Use apples and cinnamon. And don't forget to have fresh flowers on the table, even if they're only a six-dollar bunch of tulips from the corner store."

"Are you staging Miranda's apartment?" Bea asked.

"Why not? It works with prospective buyers; I'll bet it will work with whoever they send tomorrow."

"I don't think you have to worry so much," said Courtney. She let her hair fall down again; the earrings disappeared. "It's just for a foster care placement. They won't be scrutinizing you so carefully."

There was an uncomfortable silence before Miranda spoke up. "Actually, that's not true. The foster care placement comes first, of course, but Judge Waxman considers it just a temporary stop on the road to adoption. And so do I."

"Miranda," said Courtney. "How do you think you're going to pull this off? I mean, your place is cute and all, but you can't seriously believe you can raise a child here." The patronizing tone was back at full blast.

"People do it with a lot less," said Bea.

"And Miranda could eventually move," Lauren pointed out. "Remember — promotion? Raise?"

"That's another thing," Courtney said. "How are you going to deal with all the pressure of a new job *and* a new baby? Even women who are married have trouble managing —"

"Maybe women who are married aren't as motivated as I am. I'm thirty-five, and I just broke up with my boyfriend. This may be my last chance to have a baby."

"Don't you think you're being a bit self-dramatizing? Irresponsible even?" Courtney pushed her hair back, and the earrings twinkled anew. "Maybe this is all a reaction to Luke and you need to slow down a little to think it over. Adopting a baby is a huge deal." She turned to Lauren. "Back me up here, would you? I mean, didn't we just have this conversation last night? You agreed with me then."

Miranda stared at Lauren, whose face had turned a damning shade of pink. So Courtney and Lauren had together decided that she was *self-dramatizing* and *irresponsible.*

"I'm sorry," Lauren said. "I do think Courtney has a point, but I'm behind you one hundred percent. We all are."

"Strange way to show it," said Miranda. Before Lauren could respond, the bell rang again. This time it was the pizza delivery, and Miranda spent several silent minutes putting the slices on plates and passing them around. They ate in awkward silence until Bea brought up some utterly lame-sounding new play she had seen. It was a transparent, if touching, diversionary ploy, but Miranda wanted Courtney — and all of them really — out of there *now.* Still, she managed to get through the next half hour, mechanically munching her pizza and even making comments about the play, which she had no intention of seeing. Finally, they all got up to leave. "Let us know how it goes," Bea said.

"We should talk," added Lauren, glancing at Courtney.

"Talk," Miranda said, averting her gaze. "Right."

The door closed behind them, and finally she was alone. She attacked the dirty plates and glasses and reduced the empty pizza box into a mangled but compact hunk of cardboard before depositing it in the trash. Only then did she permit herself to sink down into her sofa and succumb to the wretchedness she felt. She hadn't touched the edges of her own desperation about having a baby before; she hadn't let herself. But here it was; no escaping or looking away now. What she had said to Courtney was true: she might not get another chance.

Her phone sounded, and she reached for it; maybe Courtney or Lauren was calling to apologize; they certainly owed her an apology. But it was Evan Zuckerbrot, who had been more than understanding about the fact that she kept postponing their meeting.

"I'm so sorry I haven't gotten back to you," she said.

"No worries," he told her. "I wanted to

wish you luck. Tomorrow's the day that your place is being inspected, right?"

"Right," she said. How had he even remembered that?

"Are you nervous?"

"Very," she admitted.

"I would be too. If I were in your shoes, that is."

She was tempted to ask if he wanted kids, but since they hadn't even met yet, the question seemed presumptuous. "As soon as I get this over with, we'll make a date," she said.

"I'm looking forward to that," he said.

After they said good-bye, Miranda sat with the phone in hand. Luke had never been so up front or so open — not when they'd first met, not after they'd become lovers, not when they'd parted. She had liked that elusive quality of his — at first, anyway. But maybe it would be nice to date someone who just put himself out there and didn't feel the need to hide.

The next morning, Miranda woke at six o'clock even though the inspection was not scheduled until nine. She had taken a personal day, though she had not told Sallie Scott, the editor of *Domestic Goddess*, why. What if she was turned down? No point in bringing Sallie and possibly the rest of the staff in on her private life — at least not yet.

Miranda used the time to luxuriate in both her shower and her immaculate apartment. She knew that the brownstone itself would present well; her landlady, Mrs. Castiglione, spent an hour every morning polishing the banister and vacuuming and mopping the hallway and stairs. She even swept the stoop and the sidewalk out front; not a leaf or piece of trash escaped her vigilant broom.

Miranda changed three times before settling on something to wear. She wanted to seem grown-up but approachable, professional yet relaxed. Finally, she decided on black jeans — they were new and were especially well fitting — and a soft black sweater. Around her neck she wore a necklace of amber beads. She wanted something to liven up all that black, and she imagined the warm, golden color would be perceived as baby friendly.

Then she baked an apple cake from the *Domestic Goddess* archives. It was a dense, moist cake with chunks of fruit and a glaze made from reduced apple cider. Carefully, she dripped the warm liquid over the cake until it pooled in perfect puddles around the perimeter, and then she wiped away the excess with a moistened paper towel. This cake was ready for its close-up; even Marvin, as picky as they came, would have approved.

She had just set the cake on the table, next to the vase of purple tulips, when the bell rang. Showtime: the inspector was here. Instead of just buzzing her in, Miranda went downstairs to usher her up; she saw Mrs. Castiglione's head retreat back behind the double doors to her parlor floor. The landlady was well aware of Miranda's schedule and probably thought it odd that she would be at home and having visitors on a Monday morning. If the inspection went well and the baby actually came to live here, she would tell Mrs. Castiglione everything.

"Ms. Berenzweig?" A young black woman in a trim gray suit extended her hand. "I'm Joy Watkins." Miranda was disappointed; maybe Joy Watkins would not want to place the nonwhite baby in a white woman's care. Then she was ashamed of the racist thought; why should she have made any assumptions about how Joy Watkins would perceive or judge her?

"Please come upstairs," Miranda said, and together, they climbed to the third floor.

"No elevator," said Joy, who took out a notebook as soon as they got to the apartment.

59

"These old row houses don't have elevators. I'm used to it." Did she sound defensive? Hostile? Both?

"It might be hard for a child to climb all these stairs," Joy said.

"It's good exercise," Miranda offered hopefully. "Exercise is important."

"Very," said Joy, "especially given the alarming rise of childhood obesity."

"Oh, I'm just steps from Prospect Park," Miranda said, seizing the opportunity and running with it. "There are two playgrounds right nearby and a third over at Ninth Street. Lots of playground options in the neighborhood. Lots." Oh, the babbling again!

"I'd like to look around," Joy said, notebook at the ready. "Where should we start?"

Miranda took her around the apartment, trying to see it through her eyes. There were books — lots of them — on the shelves. A small flat-screen television. An upright piano that had been her mother's. "Do you play?" Joy wanted to know.

"I did," Miranda said truthfully. "I keep it more out of sentimental value. My mother loved to play." It was a sweet memory — her mother, leaning in toward the keys, a small private smile on her face. Miranda had always wished for greater musical aptitude, but the lessons were torture, the practicing almost as bad, and she had been so relieved when her mother finally agreed that she could stop.

Joy moved on, taking note of the soft rugs, the abundance of light and air. She made a cursory tour of Miranda's bedroom and spent more time in the baby's room, walking to the window and peering outside at the yard below. "Southern exposure," she said. Miranda nodded eagerly — wasn't this a real estate buzzword? — until she heard Joy's next words: "This room could get very hot. Do you have air-conditioning?"

"I have a ceiling fan," Miranda said lamely. "But I could easily put in a window unit here."

"And window guards too — you'll need them everywhere." Joy was busily writing in her notebook.

"Of course. I can have it done immediately."

They spent a few minutes in the bathroom; as Bea had predicted, Joy checked the medicine cabinet, where nothing more potent than Advil — in a childproof bottle! — was present. The kitchen too seemed to pass muster, though Joy declined an offer of apple cake with a curt little shake of her head. Miranda ardently hoped she did not think she was being bribed. Then Joy extended her hand and thanked Miranda for her time. "You'll be hearing from us," she said.

"When?" Miranda pinned all her hopes on that single word.

"It usually takes a month or so, but we've been told to expedite this placement, so you'll be hearing within a week."

Miranda said nothing. Judge Waxman had been telling the truth.

"We were looking at an April eighth placement, correct?"

Miranda nodded vigorously. She had filled out all the paperwork describing her childcare plans for the next few months. The baby's arrival would coincide with the start of her three-week vacation, time that had to be taken before the Web site launch. After that she would hire a nanny from a well-regarded agency whose name Lauren had given her; she already had three potential candidates.

Miranda accompanied Joy down the stairs and waited on the stoop until she had gone up the street and turned the corner. As soon as she stepped back inside the house, Mrs. Castiglione was there to meet her in the hall. She must have been listening. "Is everything all right, Miranda?" she asked.

"Everything's fine," Miranda assured her. She liked her landlady, but she was not ready to confide in her just yet; what if Joy Watkins decided this wasn't a suitable home for the baby? Sharing the story now would only amplify the disappointment later. No. She would keep her own counsel, at least for now.

But looking into Mrs. Castiglione's creased and worried face, she felt compelled to offer her something. "How about a piece of apple cake?" she said. "Just baked this morning. Wait here." And without waiting for a reply, she darted up the stairs to her kitchen, cut a generous slice, and eased it onto a plate before returning to the hallway.

Mrs. Castiglione looked down at the cake and back up at Miranda. "You're a nice girl," Mrs. Castiglione declared, as if she'd been pondering the issue for some time and had only just now come to her conclusion. "And nice things should happen to nice girls." Then she turned and went back into her own apartment.

Miranda watched her go, a slight, stooped figure with an impeccably shellacked silver beehive. Did becoming a mother to an abandoned infant found on a subway platform fall into Mrs. Castiglione's rubric of *nice things*?

# FOUR

Miranda stood outside the Swedish coffee bar, looking through the big window. Evan Zuckerbrot — she recognized him from his online photo — was sitting at a small wooden table, waiting for her. Or maybe the table wasn't small; it was that Evan was so *big.* The photo had managed to conceal that he was a beanpole of a guy, tall and somewhat gangly; his hands, wrapped around the white mug he held, were enormous. Other than that, he seemed attractive enough, at least from here. Was it his height that was somehow off-putting, or was she still not over Luke? She had an urge to turn and head for home; it would be easy enough to text him with some excuse. But she simply couldn't be that unkind to someone whose only fault, thus far, was being excessively tall. Forcing herself to smile like she meant it, she walked through the door.

"Miranda." He stood. "So nice to meet

you in person." He was easily six foot three. Or maybe four. In his huge hands, he held a bunch of daffodils and offered them to her.

"They're lovely; thank you," she said. She took them and tilted her head to look up at him. He had nice eyes, she decided — large and an unusual shade of deep bluish green. Nice smile too. "And thanks for coming to Park Slope."

"No problem." He sat down and she did the same; then he politely asked the waitress if he could have an extra glass of water for the flowers. "So they don't wilt before you get home." The waitress, no doubt charmed by his request, produced a vase rather than a glass, and as Miranda slipped the daffodils in, it occurred to her that in all their time together, Luke had *never* brought her flowers; he'd always assumed the cosseted role in their relationship — the sensitive artist whose talent needed nurturing and whose ego, bolstering. But Luke also had a lean, sinewy body that fit so perfectly against her own and a slow, maddening way of kissing that had left her breathless every time.

"You're even prettier than the picture you posted," Evan said after they had ordered.

What could she say to that? *You're even taller than yours?* She glanced across the room, and fortunately their coffees arrived at that very moment so she could occupy herself with depositing a couple of sugar cubes — brown, grainy, and oh so rustic, as was the trend these days — in her cup. "I don't take very good pictures," she finally said.

"That's because you haven't had the right photographer. The lighting in that photo was all wrong; it created shadows just where you don't want them."

"Maybe I should have hired you," she quipped.

"Or maybe not. If too many other guys had seen how attractive you are, I might not have gotten a chance."

For the next few minutes, they embarked on the obligatory fact-checking requisite to first dates: Evan was an only child, raised in East Meadow, Long Island. He'd been obsessed with cameras and taking pictures since childhood, and he'd gone to Pratt Institute, where he'd studied photography in a more serious way; now he was a professional who did mostly catalog and commercial work. "Mostly it's work to pay the bills, not to feed the soul, but I do some work of my own too." He held up a camera whose leather strap was on his shoulder. "Small format, black-and-white."

"Sounds intriguing." The camera looked

unfamiliar to her; she guessed it was not digital, but something older. "What do you photograph?"

"Whatever looks interesting. I can't predict exactly what it will be; that's why I keep the camera with me. I want to be ready in case the muse taps my shoulder."

Miranda had heard plenty about "the muse" from Luke, and the word set off warning bells; was he going to be another self-absorbed, entitled user of a guy? But she was getting ahead of herself.

"What about you?" he asked. "Your profile said you're a food editor. Did you go to cooking school? Train in Europe or something like that?"

"No. I grew up on the Upper West Side, but before my freshman year in high school, we moved to Larchmont. Then, in college, I did the usual liberal-arts kind of thing — heavy on the humanities, light on the math and science. No cooking, though."

"So what got you into food?"

"My mother."

"She was a good cook?"

Miranda laughed. "God, no! She hated to cook. Her motto was, *Why waste time making what you can buy or thaw?* Once, when I was in summer camp, I begged her to send me brownies. Not from a bakery, not from a store, but real, honest-to-God homemade brownies. The mother of one of my bunkmates used to send her care packages, and they always included brownies. I was so jealous."

"Did she do it?"

"Yes. I was so excited when I got the package. When I opened it, I found a box full of what were basically crumbs. She'd made the brownies from a mix, and they were so dry they crumbled in transit. I just threw them out. And never asked again."

"So you learned to cook to compensate?" He really did seem interested.

"Not exactly. She got sick when I was a freshman in college. Cancer. The chemo took away her appetite, and she totally lost interest in food. When I came home for the summer, I started playing around in the kitchen. I wanted to tempt her to eat. To live, I guess."

"Did it work?"

Miranda looked down into her coffee cup. "Sort of. I did get her to eat — for a while. But she died anyway."

"You were young to lose your mother," he said. "I'm sorry."

"I'm sorry I didn't get to know her better. That we weren't closer." She looked down at her coffee mug. What was she doing, going on about this now?

"How about you? Do you like to cook?" She was on a first date; she wanted to veer off the topic of her mother's death — now.

"Are you kidding? I eat out three times a week and order in the rest of the time."

Miranda was frankly disappointed by a guy who couldn't cook; Luke had often joined her in the kitchen, and preparing a meal was just one of the things they did well together. But Evan was already on to the next question. "So what's happening with that baby you found?"

She had only to hear the question before she took off nonstop for the next fifteen minutes, recounting the visit from Joy Watkins in considerable detail. When she finally came up for air, she realized that she might have blown this date entirely. Not so. Evan didn't seem in the least bit put off by her recitation. If anything, he seemed to be very engaged. "Do you have any pictures of her?" he wanted to know.

"Well, since you asked . . ." She pulled out her phone. There was the baby in the rosebud dress, as well as in the various sweaters and other garments Miranda had bought. He looked through them all before handing her back the phone. "What's her name?" he then asked.

"She doesn't have one yet. At the hospital they're calling her Baby Doe, which is kind of cute since she does have big, dark doe eyes."

"But you. What do you call her?"

"I haven't named her yet."

"Even in your own mind?"

Miranda shook her head. "I won't let myself until she's at home with me. I just don't want to be —"

"Disappointed. I get it."

The conversation hovered at a crossroads. Miranda knew she could have gone deeper and said more about how much she wanted this child and how crushed she would be if she did not get her. Instead, she opted for something less soul-baring and more neutral about a photography exhibition reviewed in the *New York Times;* had he seen it? It was all perfectly pleasant if not memorable; had she not been thinking so obsessively about the baby, she might have made more of an effort to connect.

When the check came, Evan insisted on paying. Then he lifted the flowers from their vase and gave them, dripping slightly, to Miranda. As she took them, he caught her hand and brought it to his lips for a kiss. "I hope you don't mind," he said. "I wanted to kiss you, but we're in a public place and all."

"I don't mind at all," she said. No one had ever used *that* move on her before; it was both goofy and charming. Luke never, ever would have done such a thing. It was too bad that she didn't feel more of a physical spark; Evan really was a nice guy.

They stood in front of the coffee bar saying good-bye — Evan was headed to the subway and Miranda, to take care of a few errands — when suddenly Evan bolted toward the curb. Miranda was too surprised to be offended; where was he going? When he darted into the street, the reason for his erratic behavior became clear. There was a little girl — a toddler really — alone in the crosswalk, and the driver in the oncoming car could not have seen her over the windshield. But Evan had, and he yanked her out of the way to safety. Then he frantically gestured for the driver to stop.

Miranda remained frozen in place while the rest of the scene erupted around her. The child had tumbled and rolled to the curb, where a woman, presumably her mother, fell over her, crying, "Haley, Haley, are you all right?" The driver honked furiously and then got out of the car; his face whitened when he saw what might have happened. Other cars stopped too; the honking and blaring intensified. Cell phones were whipped out; someone called 911.

Miranda's gaze remained fixed on the little girl. Her eyes were closed, and there was a vivid swipe of blood on her pale face. Then she opened her eyes, saw her mother, and began to wail. "Haley!" said the mother, who was weeping hysterically now. "Baby, you came back to me! You came back!" Someone comforted the mother, offering her something to drink, a coat to put over the child.

After a few minutes, an ambulance pulled up, and two EMTs hopped out. "Was she hit?" asked one. He had a crew cut and a pockmarked face.

"Not by the car," Evan said. He was still panting, and he wiped his forehead with the sleeve of his jacket. "But I had to shove her pretty hard to get her out of the way."

The EMT looked over at the girl, whose sobs had subsided. She was now whimpering in the circle of her mother's embrace. "She looks okay, but we'll take her to Methodist to have her checked out." He and his partner walked over. The mother got up from the pavement and allowed the EMTs to carry Haley to the ambulance. She was just about to climb in when she abruptly turned and ran up to Evan. "I can't even begin to thank you," she said, her voice cracking. "She would have been hit; you risked your *life* for her."

"He wasn't going that fast," Evan said. "I knew he'd stop."

"How could you know that?" she said. *"How?"* She hugged him fiercely before sprinting back to the waiting ambulance.

A small crowd had gathered. People were recounting what had happened to those who had not seen it. A couple of them pointed to Evan. "You were great, man," someone said.

"Yeah. You saved her."

"I think she'll be fine," Evan said. Miranda, who had by this time walked over to him, noticed how he deflected the attention from himself. "How about you?" he asked her. "You seem pretty shaken."

"I am," she said. "But you're not."

"I'm just glad it turned out the way it did." He bent over to pick up the flowers, which Miranda had somehow let drop. "We'll talk soon, then?"

"Soon," she echoed, and cradling the miraculously intact daffodils, turned and headed back to her apartment. Whatever errands she had planned could wait; right now, she had an urgent need to get home.

Meeting Evan had confused her. He was brave, modest, and heroic in a crisis. And before that, he'd been a lively and an interesting enough coffee date. He was *gallant;* that's what he was. But none of this added up to the mysterious alchemy of desire. He'd be a great friend, Miranda decided. Someone to talk to, to rely on. Maybe that's the way this could play out.

Once back at her brownstone, she saw that the mail was neatly gathered and left on the table in the front hall; Mrs. Castiglione did this without fail every day. Miranda sifted through the small pile: bill, Victoria's Secret catalog, and a credit card offer. There, at the very bottom, was what she had been alternately waiting for and dreading: the letter from the Administration for Children's Services.

All thoughts of Evan and his rightness/not rightness were immediately driven out by the faint roaring in her ears. Was she hearing the rush of her own blood? For the second time, the daffodils slipped from her grasp. They fell to the floor, and the rubber band holding them together snapped, strewing a cascade of bright yellow flowers all over the carpet. But Miranda barely registered their presence; she was focused entirely on the letter, whose envelope she tore in her haste to open it. *We are very pleased to tell you that you have been approved. . . .* She didn't read any more. She didn't need to. The sound in her ears had turned to a jubilant cheer. The baby — *her* baby — was coming home.

Still, when Evan called two days later, Miranda agreed to go out with him again. They met at the Brooklyn Academy of Music; there was a Charlie Chaplin festival in progress and they were going to see *City Lights.* Miranda was glad he'd suggested it. Charlie Chaplin was a favorite of hers, and apparently of his too. They sat very quietly in the theater, not touching or looking at each other — a good sign in Miranda's view. She could not abide people who talked or made any noise during a film — she was happy to spend an hour dissecting it later, but while she was watching, she wanted to lose herself completely.

Afterward, Evan insisted on escorting her home, and they walked along Brooklyn's Fifth Avenue, which had become an interesting mix of shops, bars, and restaurants in recent years. When they reached a café called the Chocolate Room, he turned to her. "Want to stop?"

"For chocolate? Always."

Sitting at the round, marble-topped table

over chocolate fondue, she told him about the baby who would soon be coming to live with her. He seemed really excited for her. Nice. A lot of men would have gone running for the hills at this point. Not Evan. "I want to meet her," he said.

"I'd like that," said Miranda. But because she didn't want to monopolize the conversation, she switched gears. "When did you discover Chaplin?"

"In high school. *The Gold Rush* was the first silent film I'd ever seen." He dipped a piece of pound cake into the dark, molten chocolate and then popped it in his mouth. "How about you?"

"I was ten. My father loved old movies, and we used to go to see them together."

"Did your mom go too?"

Miranda shook her head. "We did a lot of things without her. She always seemed kind of unhappy with my dad, especially after we left the city."

"Did he treat her badly or something?"

"Not from what I could tell." Miranda speared a hunk of pineapple with her fork and held it above the chocolate. "But it was always about his job — he was a lawyer — and it was a point of pride with him that his wife didn't have to work, which was sort of ironic because my mother really would have

76

preferred working."

"They sound kind of mismatched in that way."

"I suppose. There were some good times too. But I think he turned to me more, and then she resented that. . . ." She helped herself to another hunk of pineapple. "How about your parents?"

"They squabbled a lot but stuck together. Now they're out in Arizona. My mom doesn't much like it there, but it was my father's dream."

"Kind of like my mom in Larchmont. My father loved everything about it — his own house, a lawn, a backyard, eventually a pool. And my mom wanted none of it. She just saw it as oppressive; she never stopped talking about the apartment on West End Avenue where we used to live and how she wished we hadn't left. Suburbia was exile for her. Punishment even."

"Do you think boomer parents were happier or unhappier than their own parents?"

"That's hard to say. Maybe they expected more and so they were less satisfied with what they ended up with. My grandmother told me that she didn't love my grandfather when she married him but that she learned to love him. And she really did; they were very content."

"And how about you? Do you believe in love at first sight?"

Miranda thought about her first meeting with Luke, at a party, and yes, she'd been immediately and powerfully drawn to him. She remembered their first kiss, shared that same night on the terrace where he'd stepped out to smoke, and then realized Evan was still waiting for an answer. "I'd like to. But that kind of fireworks? They don't always last. Maybe the incremental approach is better."

Evan seemed to like that, because he smiled and impaled the last piece of fruit — a strawberry — on the plate, dipped it in the chocolate, and held out the fork so she could eat it. She leaned in and took a bite. But the strawberry was big and dropped off the fork, onto her mint green sweater — where it left a dark smear of chocolate — and landed on her plate. Miranda would have felt like a fool if Evan hadn't neatly speared it again and offered it to her. "Can't have you losing your berries," he said.

"Definitely not." She dabbed at her sweater with a wet napkin. She liked talking to Evan. Their conversation had an appealing reciprocity and elasticity; it was not exclusively about him.

When the check came, he insisted on paying it. And when his arm went casually around her shoulder on the walk back to her house, she welcomed its presence.

"That was fun," she said in front of the stoop. "Let's do it again soon."

"I'd really like that." He leaned down to cup her face in his two hands, and she stood on tiptoe for the kiss — very light, very sweet — that felt like the most natural move.

# FIVE

"Do you have enough diapers? Formula? Baby wipes?" Bea asked.

"I'm set on supplies," said Miranda. She patted the brand-new, quilted diaper bag that sat on her lap. "I've got two bottles in here — formula and sterilized water — and diapers, wipes, ointment, and a changing pad."

"It sounds like you've thought of everything," Bea said. They were on their way to pick up the baby; Bea, who owned a car, had offered to drive Miranda to the foster home where she had been placed until Miranda had been approved.

"Everything except what it's going to feel like when we're alone together for the first time. When it's just the two of us and she's really mine. I kept trying to imagine it, but I can't." She had just started her vacation, so at least she would have a chance to bond with the baby before she turned her over to the nanny.

"You'll be great," Bea said. "I know you will." She rested her hands on the wheel. Traffic on Eastern Parkway was stalled, and they weren't going anywhere for a while.

"Thanks for driving me," Miranda said; she'd said it before, but she thought it was worth repeating.

"You know I'm happy to do it."

They were quiet. Miranda wondered what, if anything, Bea had told Courtney and Lauren about this expedition. She was not speaking to either of them at the moment; in their last conversation, Courtney had said she was "too busy planning her wedding" to deal with Miranda's *Sturm und Drang.* But that was okay — Miranda did not want to deal with the bridezilla that seemed to have swallowed Courtney whole, so she supposed that made them even. Lauren was much more apologetic, but she too confessed that she had serious doubts about what Miranda was doing; Miranda resented her for siding with Courtney behind her back instead of being honest at the outset. It was all so junior high school, but Miranda couldn't help herself — she was just that vulnerable. This left her with Bea, who was staring at the back of the large truck in front of them as if the force of her gaze could make it move.

When the light finally changed and the truck veered off in a different direction, they continued on until they reached the address in Crown Heights. Bea waited in the car rather than try to find a parking space, and since Miranda had already filled out the paperwork the day before, all she had to do was go up to the apartment — 402, she had it memorized — to fetch the baby.

"She's had breakfast and is just waking up from her nap," said Mrs. Johnson, ushering her into the small but immaculate apartment. "I'll just go get her for you." Miranda nodded and looked around. The walls and all the surfaces were covered or crammed with framed photos of children at every stage of development: toddlers holding balloons and teddy bears nestled against grinning teens holding basketballs and diplomas. Surely all these children couldn't belong to Mrs. Johnson.

She appeared again, holding a bundle of pink fluffy cloth with a small face peeking out of the center. "Here she is," she said. "What a little love."

Reaching for the baby, Miranda was suddenly stricken. "Did you want to petition for adoption?" she asked. Mrs. Johnson appeared to be past sixty and so maybe not the best candidate, but she couldn't be sure.

"No," said Mrs. Johnson. "I've raised five of my own and fostered, oh, about twenty-five over the years." So that explained all the photos. "I'm just glad to see this one go to a good woman — and I can tell you're that woman." Miranda said nothing, but stared down at the tiny face. "Have you decided on a name?" Mrs. Johnson asked.

"Celeste." She'd decided to name the baby after her father's mother, hoping it might ignite a tiny flicker of memory in his mind, but so far that had not happened. Her father just mumbled the name a few times and then burst out, "I need an umbrella! Where's my umbrella?" That didn't matter now, though. Not with the pink-clad baby held tight against her chest. Celeste reached up from her cocoon and tugged a lock of Miranda's hair. Miranda inclined her head into the gesture.

"You'll be hearing from that case worker, Ms. Watkins, about the adoption proceedings," said Mrs. Johnson.

"Thank you," said Miranda, tearing up. She wanted to hug her, but it seemed logistically impossible with Celeste in her arms, so she settled for grasping the other woman's hand and bringing it to her cheek. "I'm more grateful than I can say." Mrs.

Johnson briefly pressed her hand on top of Miranda's. Celeste swiveled her head around to take them in — her eyes, Miranda noticed, were darker now — and then Miranda was down the hall, in the elevator, and out the door, to where Bea sat waiting.

"Let me see her," said Bea, setting aside the script she'd been studying. She got out to have a better look. Miranda was still clutching the baby, who had not yet made a sound. But the slam of the car door startled her and she uttered a short, urgent bleat.

"You scared her," Miranda said. She began a little jiggling motion in an effort to soothe her.

"Oh, I'm sorry, Celeste!" said Bea. Celeste quieted and looked up at Bea. But it was only the calm before the storm because she screwed up her face and opened her mouth to emit a series of staccato cries that seemed to ricochet off the surrounding buildings. "Jesus, did I do that?" said Bea, her hands fluttering uselessly in front of her.

"It doesn't matter," Miranda said nervously. "I've just got to get her to calm down. Mrs. Johnson said she ate, but maybe she's hungry. Or thirsty." She remembered how Celeste had eagerly accepted that water when she'd first found her. "Would you get me those bottles from the bag?"

But Celeste twisted away from both the formula and the water and continued to scream. Miranda's stomach coiled into a tight knot of fear. She didn't even have the baby home yet and already she'd run into her first crisis. Courtney was right — she wasn't equal to this. She knew nothing about infants. She was insane to have taken this on. She could feel herself starting to sweat, armpits pooling, blouse plastering itself to her skin like Saran Wrap. Someone in an apartment above opened a window and yelled, "Tell that kid to shut the hell up!"

"Now, that's helpful," said Bea. "Like you have a switch or something."

But the comment — and the string of curses that followed it — propelled Miranda into action. She hoisted Celeste, still screaming, a little higher on her chest and started walking away.

"Where are you going?" asked Bea.

"I'm going to walk her around the block." Miranda stopped. "Does that sound like a good idea?"

Bea considered. "Maybe you want to ask that foster mom for help. What's her name again?"

"Mrs. Johnson," said Miranda. "But I have to be able to figure this out on my own. I can't come over here every time the baby cries." She started walking again, picking up her pace.

"I'll follow you," said Bea, getting back in the car.

Miranda rounded the corner with the wailing baby in her arms. She'd heard that Crown Heights was beginning to gentrify, but she saw no evidence of that. Buildings, mostly small and brick or brownstone, were dilapidated, and graffiti ran riot over their facades. The trees all seemed stunted; amber and green beer bottles, many broken, lay in the gutter and strewn alongside doorways; and the one trash can she passed was overturned and lolling on its side. Throughout the walk, Celeste continued to scream.

"Don't cry," Miranda said. "Please, *please* don't cry." She could feel the heat emanating from the small body, and she loosened the blanket to give her more air. Bea honked the horn, and Miranda looked over. Thank God she was here — in her distress over Celeste, she'd almost forgotten about her.

"Do you want to get in?" Bea called over the sound of the crying. She stopped the car at the corner, and Miranda, who was fresh out of options, yanked open the door with a desperate gesture. Her hands shook a little, and she strapped Celeste into the car seat before sliding in next to her.

"There's something wrong with her." Miranda stroked Celeste's head. The baby's scalp was moist with exertion, and her black hair gleamed. "I should take her to a doctor. No — to the ER."

"Right. We'll go to Methodist," Bea said. "That's the closest."

Miranda fished a baby wipe out of the diaper bag and dabbed at Celeste's face, which was wet and mottled. There was much less traffic now and the car sped along Eastern Parkway. As it did, Celeste's cries began to soften and then diminish. By the time they passed the Brooklyn Museum, they had stopped entirely, and when Bea pulled up to the hospital on Seventh Avenue, Celeste was asleep.

"Look at that," said Bea. "Who knew that all it took was a little joy ride?"

"Who knew?" Miranda said weakly. Even though Celeste was now calmed, she still felt shaky. They drove back to President Street, where Miranda got out and carefully unstrapped the car seat, not wanting to wake Celeste. Then she hugged Bea goodbye.

"Call me later?" said Bea. "I want to hear how it's going."

"I will," Miranda said. Right now, she

could not wait to get upstairs to her apartment and *relax*. As she put the key in the lock, Mrs. Castiglione poked her head out of her door and then stepped out in the hallway to greet them. Thank God the baby was quiet now; she would have hated her landlady's introduction to her new daughter to have occurred thirty minutes ago.

"So here she is," said Mrs. Castiglione, peering down at the car seat that held the sleeping infant. "She's very small, isn't she?"

"The doctor says she's fine; she wasn't a preemie," Miranda said.

"My godson, Anthony, he was very small too. We called him Peanut. You'd never know it now, though."

Miranda had never met Anthony, but she'd seen his photograph in her landlady's apartment; he had the wide, powerful build of a linebacker.

"And you're calling her . . . ?"

"Celeste," Miranda said. "That was my grandmother's name."

"A lovely name," Mrs. Castiglione said. "And a lovely gesture. Your grandmother, may she rest in peace, would have been happy."

"I'd like to think so." Miranda's paternal grandmother had doted on her in the way her own mother had not.

"I know so," said Mrs. Castiglione firmly. She stepped back to allow Miranda to pass. "Please let me know if I can help in any way. I may not have raised any of my own, but I remember a thing or two from Anthony. Oh, he was a handful!"

"Thanks, Mrs. Castiglione," said Miranda. "I appreciate that." It was so clear she would have liked children of her own.

Although Miranda had wanted nothing more than to kick off her shoes and unwind in her apartment, Celeste wasn't having it. She woke up as soon as Miranda carried the car seat inside, and Miranda needed to change and feed her before she could even think of having any lunch herself. And when she did, it was just an apple, hastily devoured while she held Celeste tucked in the crook of her other arm; Celeste fussed when Miranda sat down with her, and the only way to keep her quiet was to remain standing. Miranda thought back to how calm Celeste had been in the hospital; what was different now?

Around four o'clock, Bea called to get an update, and at around five, there was a tap on the door. Miranda opened it to find Mrs. Castiglione with a casserole dish of what appeared to be baked ziti and meatballs. "It's hard to cook anything for yourself in the beginning," she explained. "I thought you might appreciate this."

"Thank you so much," Miranda said. Apart from that apple, she had not eaten since breakfast and was starved. Could she put the ziti on the counter and eat it, straight from the casserole dish, standing up? The aroma alone was making her swoon. If the ziti tasted anything like it smelled, she was going to get the recipe from Mrs. Castiglione and publish it in *Domestic Goddess.*

"Maybe you'd like me to hold her for you while you eat," Mrs. Castiglione offered.

"Would you? That would be great."

Mrs. Castiglione took Celeste in her arms and stood in the kitchen while Miranda tried not to wolf the food down too greedily. "This is so good; is there fennel seed in here along with oregano?"

"Yes." Mrs. Castiglione looked so pleased. "My nona's recipe." And she hadn't lost her touch with babies; every time Celeste looked cranky or was about to cry, Mrs. Castiglione made some subtle shift in position that seemed to forestall another outburst.

After she had eaten and Mrs. Castiglione left, Miranda felt confident enough to attempt giving Celeste a bath. She'd actually watched a YouTube video on the subject and had all the supplies on hand: ergonomically designed plastic baby tub, organically sourced baby wash, hooded towel, and non-talc powder. Miranda undressed her — the stump of the umbilical cord had healed by now — and held the naked baby in her arms before immersing her. Celeste's tiny lips formed a circle, like a Cheerio, when her body was submerged. Miranda tensed; the O looked like it might open wide, into a scream, but though Miranda braced herself for the storm, it did not come. Instead Celeste actually uttered a soft cooing sound and kicked her legs, froglike, in the water. The rest — the actual washing, drying, dressing — was relatively easy, and when Miranda finally put Celeste in her bassinet, strategically placed just inches from her own bed, she felt a sense of accomplishment that was nothing less than magnificent.

Although it was not even nine o'clock, she decided to go to sleep; it had been an exhausting day. Tomorrow Supah, the Thai nanny she'd hired, was coming over to meet Celeste and spend a little time with her. Miranda would not need her yet, but she thought it would be a good idea to introduce her into Celeste's life as soon as she could. It was only when she plugged her phone into the charger that she saw the two missed messages. One was from Evan. *Can't wait to meet the new baby,* he said. *Call me.* The other was an unfamiliar voice with a very familiar name. *Ms. Berenzweig, this is Geneva Bales. I saw the news bit about the baby you found on the subway and I was very taken with your story. I am wondering if we might meet. . . .*

Geneva Bales wrote a popular column, "Souls of a City," for the weekly magazine *Metro.* She had profiled the ninety-six-year-old proprietor of New York City's last surviving doll hospital, a firefighter who had risked his life to save a forty-pound boa constrictor trapped in a burning building, a young man who received his acceptance letter from Yale the day he buried his homeless, crack-addicted mother. She also weighed in on political figures, celebrities, and people in the news; you never quite knew what Geneva's take would be. You knew only that it would be quirky, interesting, and totally her own. And now she wanted to profile Miranda and Celeste.

She listened to the message in its entirety and then listened to it again. The accent was hard to place, the voice low and cultivated. Miranda got into bed and turned out the light. Even though Celeste was very close, the distance felt too great, and she carefully lifted her, still sleeping, out of the bassinet and positioned her into the comma of her own curled body.

It was flattering to be considered as the potential object of Geneva Bales's interest and gain, if only briefly, a moment in the sun. But once the story was made public, it would no longer be fully her own. And the attention might bring with it other, unintended consequences. She turned to the baby sleeping next to her. "What do *you* think we should do, Celeste?" she asked. Celeste took what seemed like an unusually deep breath, as if marshaling her thoughts. But all she did was exhale, her milky breath impossibly sweet on Miranda's cheek.

# Six

Miranda sat across from Geneva Bales in the charming back garden of a little Gramercy Park restaurant that even she, hard-core foodie that she was, had never heard of. Celeste had been home for almost three weeks; luckily, Supah was available to watch her for a couple of hours today. Miranda had been loath to leave her, but she reasoned that it was good preparation for her imminent return to work.

"So how are you managing?" Geneva dove right in. "It must be a big change. And so sudden."

"That's it!" Miranda leaned closer. "It's not just that I'm sleep deprived, that my life's been totally upended or all the other usual new-mother stuff; it's that there's been no time to prepare for any of it."

"Most women get their nine months, right? And adoptive mothers might get even longer because the waiting period can stretch on and on." Geneva's expression was warm and sympathetic.

"Exactly. I feel like I've been pushed onto a stage without having learned the lines or the blocking; I'm blinking into the footlights and hoping I can wing it."

"That's a lot of stress to shoulder, especially for one person."

"Well, yes, but it's worth it." Miranda suddenly pulled back. She hadn't even formally agreed to the interview yet, and here she was telling Geneva things she hadn't even fully articulated to herself.

"Of course it is," Geneva said. "But I'm sure you wonder where your old life has gone; it must be somewhat disorienting."

"That's true," Miranda conceded. "It's not only the taking care of her that's new and challenging; it's having to reconfigure everything else. No more stopping to see a movie on the way home from work, or meeting a friend for dinner without having made plans in advance. I used to be a member of a food co-op in Brooklyn; I'm putting that on hold for a while. Same with running in the park and my book club. Everything has narrowed down to a very fine point: Celeste. And once I go back to work, my job."

Geneva looked down at her lap, and Miranda realized she was taking notes on her phone. Really? She still had not said yes. Then Geneva looked back at her, her gaze frank and intent. "After I saw that little bit on the news about your story, I was very intrigued." She looked like she was in her early thirties, with brown hair cut into a crisp, chin-length bob and secured with a black velvet headband. Miranda thought it was a surprising choice; no one she knew wore headbands anymore — at least no one over the age of twelve.

"I'm flattered," Miranda said. "But I'm not one hundred percent sure that letting you do the piece is the best idea."

Their food had been served, and she took a bite of her sandwich — roasted red pepper, feta cheese, and spinach on sourdough — and then another, because it was so good. The shrimp-studded corn chowder that preceded it had been equally outstanding. How had this place eluded her radar?

"What are your reservations?" Geneva asked. "I'd like to address them. And hopefully lay them to rest."

"It's just that Celeste is still so new to me." When they had first spoken on the phone, Miranda had told Geneva that the adoption still wasn't even finalized yet. "I feel like I might be violating her privacy — even though she is just a baby." There was something else too, something she didn't want to tell Geneva. What if the story alerted someone to the baby, someone connected to her who had for some reason not yet stepped forward? Miranda knew she ought to want that for her — a reunion with her family. But she didn't.

"I understand," Geneva was saying. "But I see this piece as a celebration, not a violation. I'd want to celebrate her survival — and your role in it. After all, not only did you find her and bring her to the police, now you're about to adopt her. Not every Good Samaritan would go so far. In fact, I'd say almost none."

Miranda thought about that. She did like Geneva — both in print and in person. With her schoolgirl coif and quaintly old-fashioned clothes — prim white blouse, dirndl skirt, and flats — she exuded a refreshingly wholesome sincerity.

"You said you've read my column; you know how I do things. No one has ever complained about the way they've appeared in print."

"Well, I am a fan," said Miranda. By this time, the remains of their lunch had been cleared, replaced by a pot of tea, two bone china cups with matching saucers, and a plate of pastel-colored macarons.

"A little exposure could be a good thing," Geneva continued. "You'd be surprised how generous people can be when approached the right way."

"I wouldn't be doing it for that reason." Miranda reached for one of the macarons, and the feathery sweetness — coconut with a hint of lime — exploded on her tongue. "I have enough money to raise her." Though financial help would certainly be nice.

"I'm sure you do," Geneva said. "But everything is so expensive — schools, camps, lessons — and you'll want her to have opportunities, exposure to all kinds of things. It would be good to have some outside help if you can get it."

"That's all true," Miranda said. She was trying to make the macaron last, but knew she would succumb to at least *one* more. "You can do the piece without my co-operation, you know; it might not be the same, but enough of the facts are out there to make it feasible."

"I could but I won't," said Geneva. "That's just not who I am. If I don't earn your trust, then I won't go ahead with it." She lowered her eyes and sipped her tea.

Miranda raised her own cup to her lips. She was an odd one, this Geneva Bales. Charming. Intelligent. Low-key when it counted. But Miranda wasn't ready to commit — not yet anyway. "I appreciate that. And I'll keep all that in mind. I just need to think it over, that's all."

"Of course." Geneva signaled for the check. If she was disappointed not to have obtained Miranda's consent, she did not show it. "I'll be here. Just let me know."

Miranda was still on the fence about the profile the next day when she collected her mail from the hall table where Mrs. Castiglione had left it. She had stopped in the supermarket on the way home from work, and she put her bags down on her kitchen table while she sorted through the envelopes. There was one from the firm that managed her father's money; he'd given her power of attorney, so the statements now came to her. One of the bags contained a pint of ice cream, and she put it in the freezer before opening the letter. He'd lost money — again. It was the third time this year. She'd have to talk to his financial adviser to see about making some changes.

Miranda set the letter aside and began to put the rest of her groceries away. The nursing home where her father lived was expensive; he could easily go through his entire nest egg. She had never worried about this before, but now that she was poised on the cusp of adopting a baby, that fact had new and potentially alarming resonance. Maybe she would be wise to accept Geneva's offer — she might be glad of the help.

The next day, she called the number on Geneva's card. "I'm going to do it," she told her. "When do we start?"

"That's wonderful." Geneva had a low, controlled voice, but Miranda could still hear the pleasure that ran through it. "You won't be sorry," she said. "You have my word."

Later that same night, Miranda flopped down on her sofa, exhausted. Celeste just would not settle down, and Miranda had spent a solid hour trying to calm her; she'd fallen into a restless sleep. Silence reigned, but for how long?

She hadn't been here even a month, but already Miranda felt the enormity of the job she'd — willingly! eagerly! — signed on for. Yes, she wanted her. Yes, she was still in the throes of baby love. But it was hard — harder than anyone had told her it would be. Harder than she'd imagined.

What Miranda had described to Geneva Bales were only the most superficial aspects of how her world had shifted. She felt as if she'd fallen, Alice-like, right down the rabbit hole. Way up there was the life she used to lead; she saw it as if from a vast distance. Down here, in new-mommy-land, everything was different. Taking a shower, eating a meal, making a phone call, all things she had taken for granted, now had to be planned for, negotiated, and, if necessary, postponed. Or even abandoned. She, who had been the most avid of readers, had not even opened one of the new novels that sat in a pile near her bed. She could not even get through a newspaper, let alone the cooking and decorating magazines she subscribed to in order to remain current for her job. Her job. That was another thing. Here she was, struggling when she hadn't even gone back to work yet. How would she manage when she did?

Celeste had been asleep for about twenty minutes; how long before she was awake again? Miranda got up. She wanted just a brief distraction, a foray into the terrain she used to inhabit so thoughtlessly. She went over to her bookshelf and pulled out a thin, worn paperback. Yes. This was it.

Returning to the sofa, she sat down and propped her feet up on an ottoman she had recently purchased. The ottoman may have been new, but the hand-woven kilim that covered it was something Miranda had owned for years. She'd bought it in Turkey, on a trip she and Courtney had taken right after graduation. What fun they'd had, the two of them so young and clueless; how had they ever been that young? They'd explored the beaches and the temples, the markets and the cafés; they'd eagerly sampled the food, the wine. There had been fresh figs plucked from a tree in the courtyard of one restaurant, goat cheese made in the cellar of another.

The kilim had come from one of those dense, jostling marketplaces where animal carcasses hung from crude hooks, salt was sold from glittering heaps, and mounds of tarnished silver jewelry were piled right on the ground, waiting to be pawed through. Miranda had spied the kilim draped over the back of a donkey, and though it was torn and shredded in places, she had been drawn to its intense colors — vermilion, ochre, cobalt, forest green — and the almost geometric formality of its pattern. Courtney had urged her to buy it.

"What will I do with it?" Miranda had asked.

"Don't worry about that. You love it; that's the main thing. You'll figure out how to use it later."

Courtney had been right. The kilim was

the perfect thing with which to cover an ottoman. But she and Courtney were barely speaking now, and Miranda did not want to think about that trip.

Instead, she opened *Cat on a Hot Tin Roof,* the same play Bea was starring in and the same copy she'd owned in college, bought for her Modern Dramatic Literature course. That was the course in which she'd met Bea; they had read Ibsen and Chekhov, Strindberg and Ionesco. But Miranda's favorite playwright that semester had been Tennessee Williams, and she felt a deep and familiar connection as she turned the yellowed pages, several of them stained with what looked to be raspberry jam.

Had she not had Celeste, she would have flown to Oklahoma to see Bea play Maggie; right now, she couldn't even imagine getting into the city to see a New York production. Not that she wanted to change anything. But still. She smiled as she read the opening dialogue — Williams could be so funny.

Maggie was the Williams heroine she liked best. Unlike Blanche or Laura — fragile, broken creatures — Maggie was scrappy, a fighter and survivor. How interesting that she wanted to be pregnant with Brick's child when she disliked children so intensely. *No-neck monsters* was what she called her little nieces and nephews. And yet, how she pined. What did having a child mean to her? Was it proof of Brick's love? Was it a confirmation of her own womanhood? Or just the only way to secure her place in a family that did not fully accept her?

Miranda looked up. There were sounds — first rustling, then crying — coming from the other room. She put the book down. So much for parsing the meaning of the symbolic child; the real, live infant she had committed herself to needed her.

Celeste was crying, her fists clenched in tiny, tight balls. Her diaper was dry, so Miranda picked her up and began the pacing that often did the trick. When that failed, she tried rocking her. Celeste cried harder and twisted her face away from the bottle Miranda offered. Now what? It was late; she didn't want to take the baby out for a stroll at this hour. She touched the little cheek. Damp with tears and perspiration. Miranda felt sticky and hot too.

Suddenly, she knew what they both needed. She put Celeste back in the crib while she turned on the tap in the shower and shed her clothes. Then she undressed Celeste and stepped under the steady stream with the baby pressed against her naked skin. She kept her back to the spray and used her own body to shield Celeste. The warm, pulsating water created a fine mist on Celeste's hands and arms; she was intrigued and brought her hand to her mouth for an experimental lick. The crying stopped, and Miranda exhaled audibly. They remained under the water for a while, and when they stepped out, Miranda wrapped her baby in the large towel hanging on the back of the door. Celeste was calmer now. The crying, the fussiness — all gone. Miranda settled her back in the crib and then returned to her own bed. They both slept peacefully that night.

# Seven

Jared Masters stood on the corner of 117th Street and Lenox Avenue, lighting one of the elegant, gold-tipped Black Russian Sobranies that he'd recently started smoking. His clients Brandon and Isabel Clarke were late, but that was nothing new. Of the thirteen such appointments he'd had with the Clarkes, they had been late for all but one. Sometimes it was just ten minutes, but once they had kept him waiting more than an hour and had barely apologized when they finally showed up. He would have blown them off entirely — property up here in Harlem was selling briskly; he could have lived without their business — but he had a soft spot for Isabel, one of those fine-boned little blondes he'd had a taste for ever since he'd first encountered them in prep school. In fact, she reminded him of Carrie, the blonde to end all blondes; there was something about the eyes, or was it the mouth —

"Jared!"

He turned, and there Isabel was, actually hurrying down the street. Brandon lagged a few paces behind, gaze trained on the iPhone in his palm.

"Brunch ran late," she said, huffing adorably as she came up to him. "So sorry!" For a brief second, her hand — pale and splayed like a starfish — touched his chest. This gesture, combined with her uncharacteristic apology, melted any lingering annoyance.

"No sweat," he said, tossing the cigarette to the sidewalk and stubbing it out. "I really want to show you the place. I think you're going to like it."

Brandon caught up to Isabel and greeted Jared with that stupid fist bump white guys always seemed to think was necessary to demonstrate how cool they were, and the three of them walked down the block. "Take a look," Jared said, waving his hand at the newly restored facade. "Twenty feet wide, built in 1910, totally gutted in 2006. It's got central air, a washer and dryer in every unit, video intercom, and individual security systems."

"Nice!" said Isabel. She wore a sweater tied around her slim waist — the day had really warmed up — and some pale blue gauzy thing that made the outline of her small breasts plainly visible. That, plus the way the dress's thin straps kept slipping off her shoulders, was highly distracting. Forcing himself to look away, Jared lit another cigarette. Isabel turned to Brandon. "It's wider than the houses we've been seeing," she said. "It won't have that shoe-boxy feeling."

"Uh-huh." Brandon was still mesmerized by whatever was taking place on the screen.

"It gets even better. Let's go inside." Jared took one last drag on the barely smoked Sobranie, then led the way. He'd already sold a condo in this building — one of five — for a cool million two. Now he was determined to sell this one, a garden-floor duplex with a fully landscaped yard, to the Clarkes; he thought it had everything they were looking for.

"Great kitchen," Brandon said, running his hand along the granite counter.

"All the finishes are high end," Jared said. "Brazilian cherrywood cabinets, Sub-Zero fridge, Miele dishwasher."

"And look at the garden!" Isabel breathed. "Just think of the parties we could have here — they'd be legendary!" They all walked outside. The yard was looking especially spiffy; Jared had come over himself this morning to make sure that the leaves were all swept and that none of the neighbor-hood's legion of stray cats had left any unwanted deposits on the slate paving stones. Harlem was still oscillating between the old and the new, and sometimes bits of the former overlapped with the upscale aspirations of buildings like this one.

"You could plant bulbs out here, babe," said Brandon as he strolled around. "Tulips, daffodils, all that stuff you're so crazy about." His phone trilled and he answered immediately. "No," he said, frowning. "I *told* him that already. If I told him once, I told him *ten* times." He strode out of the yard and back into the house.

Isabel looked at her husband's retreating form and sighed. "It's hard to keep him on track," she said.

"Come on," Jared said tactfully. "Let me show you the upstairs. You'll love the master suite." There were two other bedrooms up there, and he knew from experience that since each had its flaws he should show them first. Then the master suite would look even better by comparison.

"Wow!" Isabel said. "It's gorgeous!"

She was right. The large, light room faced the back and the double-wide windows overlooked the yard. There was a mantel — purely ornamental but a nice touch just the same — and admirably restored herringbone wooden floors. The en suite bath was done up in marble and white subway tile; there were his-and-hers sinks and a freestanding tub. Isabel cooed and oohed as she touched this, inspected that. Jared watched as she primped in the large mirror over the sink, fussing with her hair and making a pretty pout at her reflection. For a brief but electrifying moment, their eyes met in the glass. Then he quickly looked away and walked out of the bathroom. Isabel followed a moment later.

Downstairs, Brandon was still on the phone. "The guy's a jerk," he was saying. "Total a-hole if you ask me."

"He's so busy all the time," she said apologetically. "But how can I complain when it's his hard work that's going to buy us" — she waved her arm to indicate the room — "something like this."

"Listen, if today's a bad day, we can schedule another viewing," Jared said. Damn, but he wanted *something* substantial out of this visit. Why couldn't Brandon put down the phone and pay attention?

"It won't be any different another day," Isabel said. "He's like this all the time. I swear, I once caught him looking at that thing when we were making love." Then she clamped one of those tiny hands of hers — he could see the megawatt diamond glittering on her finger — over her mouth like a small child. "I guess I shouldn't have said that."

"It's okay," Jared said. "I'm used to it. People are always telling Realtors stuff like that. We're like therapists. Or priests."

"I can see why," she said. "You really listen. And you don't pass judgment."

"I try." He moved toward the door, uneasy with the direction this conversation was heading. Jared liked the ladies and the ladies certainly liked him. But he never mixed business with pleasure. Especially *married* business.

Isabel was too quick for him. In seconds, she had crossed the room, reached up to pull his face down and close to hers. "Thank you," she said softly. Then she kissed him, her lips as light as a moth. Jared allowed his fingers to graze the skin of her bare shoulders before he stepped back. "Let's get Brandon and show him the master suite," he said. She seemed to recover quickly enough because she only nodded and followed him out.

On the way back to his apartment, Jared smoked yet another cigarette. So much for trying to quit. He didn't have another showing today, and he was annoyed by the way this one had gone down. He had not closed the deal on 117th Street; the Clarkes had said they needed to think about it some more. And then there was that kiss. Had there been something he'd done — a look, a tone of voice — that had given Isabel the invitation? But even if there had, how could he have helped it? He *was* attracted to her, and attraction was hard to mask, especially for him. *Everyone always be knowing your business,* he could hear his mother say. She was forever telling him that he needed to disguise his feelings better; she worried about what might happen to a black boy whose heart was not on his sleeve but plastered all over his face.

He walked first west and then downtown. The trees that lined the streets were having their brief, gaudy moment, and here and there a window box exploded with early spring flowers. The 'hood was looking good, which meant business was good too. Even though Harlem had become his turf, Jared had not actually grown up here, but in Queens, the only son of two solid, hard-working parents. His mother ladled out hot food in a school cafeteria and his father had been a motorman with the MTA. They had died, within eight months of each other, more than a decade ago, but at least they had lived to see him awarded the scholarship to Saint Crispin's Academy in Maine, and after that, the full ride at Haverford.

"I want you to go places," his mother had said, "but not forget where you came from." As if. Even all these years later, he could still remember the pressure of her hand placed on his forehead when he felt feverish, the aroma of her baked chicken and dumplings wafting through the hallway even before he got to the apartment, and the collection of hats, each one more wacky and embellished than the next, that she kept on wooden stands, ready for church. She'd been proud of him.

He wondered if she'd be so proud of him now. Yes, he was successful at his work, and he made good money at it too; he was considered up and coming in his world. He'd sweet-talked Athena, his boss at the agency, into offering internships to neighborhood kids who otherwise wouldn't have known how to even get near such opportunities, and he was personally overseeing two interns, Diego and Tiffany, right now. And he had plenty of friends, a great apartment; life was good. But while his work in real estate was lucrative, it wasn't what she'd had in mind for him. She would have been the lone black woman in America not made happy by Obama's election. *It could have been you,* she would have said. *It should have been you.* At thirty-three, he was unmarried and unattached; ever since Caroline's death, there had been no one special in his life. And even when she was alive, Carrie was not the kind of girl you brought home to meet your mother.

An ice-cream truck was parked on the corner of his block, and the kids in the neighborhood, a mix of black and increasingly white, were milling around as the lilting music from the parked truck pealed out into the spring air. Carrie would have insisted on stopping. She had a sweet tooth, that girl did, but she only liked the cheap stuff. The one time he'd bought her some fancy imported chocolates, she'd nibbled on a couple and left the box on the living room radiator in her apartment, where it had quickly turned into a molten, if costly, expanse of brown goo. So he'd taken to keeping his pockets filled with the crap she craved: SweeTarts, Skittles, Almond Joy bars, Hershey's Kisses. Her candy habit never seemed to catch up with her though; she was as delicate as a girl and had to buy her jeans in the kids' section of the Gap and have all her dresses — the skimpy little numbers she wore clubbing — taken in.

Thinking of her made him too restless to go home. He was meeting some people later, but a quick look at his watch confirmed that he had at least four hours to kill. He turned back around and headed uptown, to Minty's, one of his favorite uptown watering holes. Stepping in from the spring sunshine, he was momentarily blinded; when his vision cleared, he scanned the sparsely filled space with its portraits of famous abolitionists hanging over the bar. For as long as he'd been coming here, crepe paper chains in faded red, blue, and yellowed white had been draped limply over the frames and a boldly defaced Confederate flag had held pride of place on the wall. At the far end of the bar, seated almost directly under an outsized photograph of Harriet Tubman seated regally in a chair, was his boss and the agency's owner, Athena Neville. Minty's was just around the corner from the office, and they often came here together for a quick one after work; had he wanted to run into her?

"I'm assuming One Hundred Seventeenth Street was not a slam dunk," she said when he'd slid onto the stool beside her. "Or else I would have heard from you."

"They have to think it over," Jared said.

The bartender had brought a mug, but he sipped his beer directly from the bottle.

She considered the wine in her half-full glass. "What's your sense? Will they bite?"

"She's primed; she's ready," said Jared. *In more ways than one,* he thought but did not say. "He's the sticking point."

"Uh-huh." She took a sip from the glass. "How can we get him unstuck?"

Jared shook his head. "It just has to happen — or not — in its own time. You know that."

Athena's phone buzzed before she could reply. She was a good-looking woman, tall and full-bodied with hair that had been woven into an intricate series of narrow braids that articulated the shape of her skull. She wore a long, loose dress the color of a grasshopper, some chunky thing around her neck, and big gold hoops in her ears. His mother would have loved her. *Don't let this one get away,* she'd have said. *Smart, strong, and built for birthing babies. What more could you want?*

Jared shifted on the stool. Athena was a prize. She'd grown up in a Bronx project, gotten herself first to Stuyvesant High School, then to Smith — scholarship kid, just like him; she had opened her own boutique real-estate firm before she turned thirty. And he knew she liked him; she'd made it clear enough, though not so clear that they couldn't ignore the elephant in the room and carry on in a purely professional vein. There was nothing wrong with her, not one single thing, except she didn't make his heart stop, not the way those white princesses did. All those impossibly pretty princess girls, with their smooth hair and straight teeth, their cashmere sweaters, their white-girl ease in the world, finally culminating in the prettiest white-girl princess of them all: Caroline Alexa Highsmith.

Athena finished her call and laid her phone down on the bar. "You're right," she said, as though they hadn't been interrupted. "You're right, and that's what makes you such a good salesman. You know when to step back; you don't push."

"I was groomed by the best," he said, lifting the bottle in her direction.

"Flattery will get you everywhere." Athena signaled for the check. "What are you doing later?" She had taken out a small mirror and was using it to apply a deep, rich color — not unlike the wine she'd been drinking — to her generous lips.

"Meeting some people in Chelsea," he said, taking the last swig of his beer.

"I'm having a little thing at my place. Feel

free to drop by," she said. "Your friends too. There'll be plenty to eat and drink."

"Thanks." He pressed the cool bottle to his heated cheek. The air-conditioning had not been turned on, and the place felt stuffy. "Maybe I will," he said, knowing full well he wouldn't. No need to agitate that elephant. And then, to change the subject, he asked, "How's it going with Diego and Tiffany?"

"Tiffany is terrific; great choice. But Diego . . ." She had put her lipstick away and was signing the bill.

"What's going on?"

"Let's just say he has an attitude problem."

Jared thought about Diego, a handsome kid with black hair that was slicked back from his full, baby face and surprisingly light, hazel eyes. Those features could be door openers — if he bothered to try. Jared had seen the sullen looks, the slipshod work. Seen and tried to rationalize. "I'll talk to him, okay?"

"That would be a good idea," she said. "If he's going to stick around, he really needs to get with the program."

Outside, Jared said good-bye to Athena and hailed a taxi. The late-afternoon light was still rich and warm, but now he was eager to get home. He'd shower and rinse the disappointing day from his skin, and have a snack before heading out again. On the way up, he gathered his mail and took the elevator to the tenth floor. The apartment, tended to by his longtime housekeeper, was spotless. He left the mail on the table and did not look at it again until he was seated with a glass of cabernet, a wedge of Brie, and a handful of crackers in front of him.

Flipping through the new *Metro* magazine that was in the pile, he turned first to "Souls of a City," that column written by Geneva Bales; it was his favorite part of the magazine. Once, she profiled a woman who had designed the costumes for Arthur Mitchell's fledgling Dance Theatre of Harlem back in the 1970s; another time, she'd focused on a contemporary female rapper she'd discovered at an uptown club. This week's column was called "You Were Meant for Me," and it featured a white woman who'd found a black baby abandoned in a subway station and had decided to adopt her. Jared ate as he read the story. Then he checked out the photos. In one, the woman was shown holding the baby in front of the Park Slope house where she lived. The other was a close-up of the baby herself, her dark eyes wide for the camera, her expression unexpectedly serious. The caption said the baby had been found wrapped in a white towel and a blanket from the Cosmo Hotel.

Jared lit a cigarette. He knew the Cosmo quite well. It was in SoHo; he and Carrie used to party at the hotel's posh rooftop bar and sometimes they'd even stayed over. They'd had some wild nights there. *Wild.* But that was before Carrie had gone off the deep end and he'd tried to break it off, before all the screaming and raging, the accusations that he was screwing around. When she had seen these tactics weren't working, she'd switched gears: She was going blind. She had cancer. AIDS. Cancer *and* AIDS. She would kill herself without him. She would kill *him.* Jared grew weary of the threats, the scenes. It wasn't that he didn't love her. But she was too much for him and he wanted out.

The Cosmo was actually where he had last seen her. It was early on a summer evening, before the crowds descended, and he'd gotten them a discreetly situated booth in the almost empty bar. Her dress, he remembered, had been made of some iridescent blue-black material; it shimmered when she leaned forward to pick up her drink or to reach out to touch his face. In his innocence

— read: stupidity — he had thought that meeting in a public place would prevent an outburst. Wrong, wrong, *wrong.* But he'd never imagined that he would be the one to hurl the opening salvo. When he'd told her that this was the very last time, that they were over, finished, done, she'd gone very still for several seconds.

"Why?" she finally asked.

"I think you know," he said.

"Because I'm crazy, right?" She fumbled in her purse for a cigarette, which she held, unlit, in her trembling hand.

"Not crazy, not exactly, but —"

"Delusional. Paranoid. Manic. I know all the code words."

"Carrie, I —"

"Don't bother," she said. "I've heard it all before. I know what you think, what everyone thinks — my family, my shrink. You're no different."

"What about your family? Can't they help?" He was curious; he knew she came from somewhere in North Carolina and that her family had some money. But that was all; she would not reveal details, and when he tried to press, she'd put him off.

"Never mind about them. It's you that I care about. You, me — and the baby."

"Baby?" he said. The glass of wine he was

drinking tasted like poison. She couldn't be telling the truth.

"Yes," she said, with a small, triumphant smile. "Baby. Yours and mine. She'll be so beautiful, with skin like café au lait and —"

"God*damn* it!" He stood and pushed the table away so sharply that his glass fell on its side, rolled to the floor, and shattered. Wine puddled around his feet. "You will not do this to me. You will *not.*"

"Jared? Aren't you happy?" She blinked rapidly, but the tears were gathering and falling anyway. "I'm happy. So happy! We'll be a family. Don't you see? A real family."

"I don't believe you," he said flatly. "It's just another one of your tricks. And it won't work."

The waiter came hurrying over. "Is everything all right?" he asked.

"Don't ask me," Jared spat. "Ask *her.*" Furious, he tossed some bills on the table and marched out.

She began stalking him after that — calls, texts, and e-mail. Once she'd left a rubber doll in a box by his office door; she'd taken a Sharpie and drawn fat, black tears on the doll's face. Luckily, he'd found and disposed of the whole mess before Athena saw it. He was torn about what to do: confront her again, call the police, or seek some kind of help for her. And then it stopped. Just like that. No more calls, no more texts, no more dolls. Relief overcame worry; he was just so grateful that she was out of his life.

Months went by, months in which he tried not to think about her. To worry about her. In late March, a detective from a precinct in Brooklyn came to see him at home. A female corpse had turned up on a beach in Coney Island; the corpse was barefoot but wearing an oversized purple coat. In the pocket of that coat, sealed in a ziplock bag and reinforced by duct tape, was a piece of paper that read: *Call Jared.* His phone number was underneath.

Jared had to make a trip to the morgue to identify her, a horrible moment he'd never, ever forget. Then he'd been interviewed by the detective; he was in too great a state of shock to understand that the police thought he might have had something to do with Carrie's death. It was only later, hours after he'd gotten home, that he realized he'd been under suspicion, even briefly.

But Carrie's death was not the sole reason for Jared's stunned condition during the questioning. The medical examiner had said there were indications that she might have recently given birth; she had been in the water for some time, so it was impossible to say for sure. But Jared knew. Knew and was devastated. She *had* been telling the truth that last night — she had. The baby, whose body had never washed up, had no doubt drowned with her. And it was his fault.

He thought about trying to contact her family, though he knew almost nothing about them — but to what end? *Hey, I got your daughter/sister/niece pregnant, but I broke up with her and she drowned.* No, he could not imagine a conversation like that. What good would it do, anyway? Caroline was gone, along with any baby she'd had. His mourning and his guilt? Those were private, not to be shared with — or expiated by — anyone else.

But now, staring at the magazine, he had to wonder. What if somehow the baby — *his* baby? — had not gone into the water with Carrie, but survived and somehow turned up in the subway station? *What if?* The thought was like a slap: sharp, startling, and once the shock had passed, galvanic. He ground out the cigarette and went into the small bedroom he used as a home office. After a few minutes of digging around on the top shelf of a closet, he found it — the scrapbook his mother had assembled, an encyclopedic and doting record of his earliest days. Here was the wristband he'd worn in the hospital, his baptismal certificate, and a list of every baby gift he'd received. And here was the photograph, with his own wide-eyed face staring out of the border. Jared looked from the photo in the scrapbook to the photo in the magazine and back again. *Was* he seeing what he thought he was seeing? Because in these two faces — dark, unsmiling, and separated by about three and a half decades — he could have sworn there was a resemblance.

He looked down at the bottom of the article. *Comments? Questions? Contact me at gbales@metromagnyc.com.* Comments? He had a few of those. Questions too. Carrying the magazine in one hand, Jared went over to his laptop, sat down, and immediately began to type.

After the first couple of sentences, the words stopped. What was he doing, anyway? If this baby was his . . . then what? Was he prepared to claim her, to raise her? He never thought about having kids other than in that general maybe-if-I-met-the-right-girl sort of way. And the girls — women — he went for didn't seem to be the marrying, baby-raising kind. He sat there for a few minutes; the minutes stretched into something closer to an hour. Then he looked at the photographs again. The faces still looked the same — at least to him. He put his fingers back on the keypad. Whatever happened, whatever came of it, he simply had to know.

# EIGHT

Evan Zuckerbrot maneuvered his shopping cart through the crowded aisles at Fairway. He saw Audrey a few feet ahead, palpating the melons for ripeness. *Tap, tap, tap,* went her busy fingers. *Tap, tap, tap.* "Found a good one," she said when he had caught up. "Catch." She raised the heavy, round fruit as if to lob it in his direction.

"You wouldn't," he said, immediately bringing his hands to his face. He felt like he'd spent his whole childhood in this defensive posture; he hated sports and viewed any oncoming balls as threats, not competitive opportunities.

"I would if you could actually *catch* it instead of cringing. You're a wuss, Evan." But she was smiling as she gently lowered the melon into his cart. "Now we should get some prosciutto."

"Whatever you say." Evan had planned a picnic with Miranda for the next day, and

127

Audrey, his oldest and closest friend, was helping him put the whole thing together.

"Yeah, if she's a foodie, she'll be into the melon and prosciutto thing. We just have to clean and slice it beforehand, that's all." She started walking toward the deli counter and Evan dutifully followed. He wanted this picnic to go well. No, he wanted it to be *perfect.* Since their initial meeting at the coffee shop, he and Miranda had gone on three dates. Well, the first of these was not even a real date; he'd just accompanied her to the opening of a ridiculously twee popcorn shop — wasabi-laced popcorn, cinnamon-and-cardamom-dusted popcorn — on Van Brunt Street because it was minutes from where he lived in Red Hook. The second had more substance to it. They had gone to the Museum of Modern Art and he'd led her through the photography gallery, spending a long time in front of his favorites — Robert Frank, Lee Friedlander, Diane Arbus, Garry Winogrand — explaining what it was he saw in those pictures, why they moved him. She'd seemed engaged and her reaction made him hopeful. The third, when they had gone to the movies, was the best of all; that was the night he'd first kissed her.

But all that was before her new daughter

had arrived. Celeste. Now that she was here, Miranda did not want to leave her any more than she had to. So Evan suggested this picnic in Prospect Park as a way for them to all spend time together. He knew that most guys wouldn't have been too thrilled to have a baby tag along on a date. But Evan had a soft spot for babies.

Audrey was considering the prosciutto selections at the deli counter now. "Imported costs about three times as much as domestic. But the imported is way better."

"She'll be able to taste the difference, won't she?" asked Evan. When Audrey nodded, he added, "Imported, then. Definitely imported."

"Next up: bread," said Audrey.

Evan hurried to keep up. That was so Audrey: she had a plan and she stuck to it. Just like always.

Audrey Zelkowitz had had the seat next to Evan Zuckerbrot in homeroom on the first day of high school; she'd kept that same seat all four years. Four years in which they had been best friends, confidants, soul mates — and for one brief night, lovers. It had happened after the prom. They had gone together, of course, and they had been deconstructing the evening in the apartment

129

— conveniently empty at the time — that her parents had built over the garage. Splayed out on the double bed with a bottle of vodka and a box of Entenmann's chocolate-frosted doughnuts, they talked and talked. Then had come a lull in the conversation. This had not bothered Evan; he and Audrey could be quiet together too. But when she turned to him and said, "Well, I guess we should do it," he had to wonder whether he had missed some essential link in the conversation.

"What are you talking about?" She did not answer, but stood up and began to unzip the tight, electric blue dress she wore. "You're kidding, right?" Evan knew that she — like him — was a virgin. "Or you're drunk." They had been sharing the vodka, and maybe she was more looped than he knew.

"No to both, actually." The dress was off now; she stood before him in her strapless white bra and white panties, her strong, athletic body — she swam, played basketball, softball, and ran track — looking both unfamiliar and unbelievably exciting.

"But, Audrey, this isn't us." Confusion and lust were arm wrestling in his brain, making it pound. And the boner pressing against the front of his rented tux pants wasn't making things any easier. "Is it?"

"It could be," she said, coming closer to him now. "It should be. I mean, you're my friend, Evan. My best friend. I love you and I trust you. And I don't want to go to college a virgin — do you?" He shook his head. "So why not . . . initiate each other?" She reached over and slid her arms around his neck. "Come on. It'll be good. I promise."

Evan needed no further coaxing. She was right. He didn't want to go off to college a virgin, and here she was, all smooth, sturdy limbs, ponytail unloosening and spilling glossy brown hair down around her shoulders. . . . But she had been wrong. It wasn't good. Not for him, not for her. It had been awkward, lonely, and kind of sad. He'd rolled away afterward, for once not having a thing in the world to say to her. She was crying and trying to hide it; he could tell by the small, snuffling sounds she made.

"I have to tell you something," she said, finally breaking the silence.

"What is it?" He propped himself on his elbow so he could look at her.

"I like girls."

"Well, duh. *You're* a girl."

"No, you don't get it. I like girls *that* way. I'm a . . . lesbian." She began to gather her hair back into its ponytail. "I knew I was

131

before we . . . before we did it, but I wasn't a hundred percent sure, and I thought that if it was okay between us, then maybe I was wrong." Her voice clotted with tears. "That's why it wasn't any good. I'm sorry. I used you. Can you ever forgive me?" She began to cry in earnest, noisy sobs, and she pressed her face into her hands to muffle them.

Evan took her into his arms. A lesbian! So that was it. There was nothing wrong with him. Nothing wrong with her either. They were just wrong for each other. He was so relieved he wanted to laugh. Or sing. "Hey," he said, squeezing her tight. "No biggie, okay?"

"You mean you're not mad?" She lifted her wet face to stare at him.

"Nope."

"And we're still friends?"

"Best friends," he said seriously. "Best friends forever."

In addition to the melon and prosciutto, Audrey steered him toward a baguette, two kinds of cheese, cherries, and some tiny little cookies that were covered in powdered sugar as well as bottled water and some fancy paper napkins and plates. Then she helped him lug everything back to his place.

"Text me to let me know how it went," she said. "And let me know if she says anything about the prosciutto." These days, Audrey's light brown hair was shorn down in a buzz cut, and her strong limbs had been embellished by the addition of several memorable tattoos. But she was still the Audrey he knew and loved; he gave her a bear hug and kissed her on both cheeks before they said good-bye.

The next day, Date Day, dawned perfectly blue and cloudless. Evan loaded up his car and drove to Park Slope to pick up Miranda and Celeste. He found them waiting downstairs by the curb, Miranda in a snugly fitting sundress with ladybugs all over it and a straw hat, and Celeste, strapped into a car seat, wearing a one-piece romper, pointing and flexing her bare toes in the air. "You look great," he said, allowing his gaze to roam over Miranda's creamy shoulders and lush body. He loved that she wasn't one of those skinny, breakable-looking women, all clavicles and jutting hip bones. No, she was as full and ripe as a peach. What was the name of the magazine she worked for? *Domestic Goddess*? It could have been coined for her.

He strapped the seat into the car and they took off for the park. Not that they couldn't have walked, but there was so much stuff to deal with — food, blanket, two diaper bags, stroller — that he thought it might be easier to drive. In keeping with the charmed spirit of the day, he found parking immediately, and they set out looking for a spot where they might spread out. As they walked, Evan imagined how they must look: a man, a woman, and a baby equaled a family in most people's eyes. But it was obvious that Celeste was not his child, or Miranda's either. Her dark skin set her apart, a distinct and different genetic code visible to the world. Well, they would think she was adopted, that's all. The reasons why could be many and varied; no one would guess the real truth.

It had been more than two years ago, when they'd both turned thirty-five, that Audrey had come over with a bottle of seriously good Scotch and made him a proposition. "I want a baby, Evan," she said. "And I want you to be the sperm donor." She took a long swig of her drink and waited.

"Whoa," he said. "That's some bomb you just detonated, you know. How am I supposed to feel about this?"

"That's what I want to find out," she said, nudging the glass she'd poured him in his direction. They'd spent the next two hours parsing the situation from every possible angle. She was getting older, with that damn biological clock ticking louder and louder in her head. Yes, she would have rather had a partner, but she'd just broken up with her last girlfriend and she was afraid she'd miss her chance if she didn't act now. As for going to some anonymous donor, why do that when she had him in her life? "You're like family to me, Ev," she said. "I'd be so thrilled if you'd be my baby's father."

"Donor is not the same as father," he pointed out. "And I do want to be someone's father — at least someday."

"This wouldn't mean that you couldn't. This is an *added to,* not an *instead of.* And you could be as involved in his or her life as you wanted. I'd leave that up to you."

In the end, he'd agreed, and when he asked how she wanted to handle the mechanics, she gave him the name of a clinic where he'd need to go once a month. The whole thing had been weird and a little distasteful — heading to the men's room with a stack of magazines and a collection jar, sheepishly bringing the sample up front, looking out at the sea of other guys in the waiting room, hanging out until it was their turn. This went on for nearly a year, a year in which Audrey did not become pregnant.

Finally, she went for an examination by a highly regarded Park Avenue specialist; he went along with her. When the exam was over, she walked into the waiting room and sat down next to him. Her expression was grim. "Are you all right?" he'd asked. Maybe there was something seriously wrong with her; maybe she was going to *die*.

"I'm fine," she said. "Totally fine. Everything is in good working order — great, in fact."

"So then why can't you . . . ?" He trailed off as the humiliating implication became clear. "It's me, right? *I'm* the problem." He felt a slow burn creeping up from his neck to his face.

"Oh, Ev," she said, and her eyes filled. "I'm so sorry. The doctor suggested that you have some tests to find out what's wrong." She leaned over to hug him, but he went rigid. Audrey was his best and oldest friend, but at the moment, he wanted to punch her. To think that he had been getting it up, month after month, to help her out and to learn that all this time, he'd been shooting nothing but blanks.

"It's not your fault," he said stiffly. "But if you don't mind, I'm going to leave now. I need to deal with this on my own." He had gotten totally shit-faced that night; he was so drunk he had no idea how he'd managed to get home. When he woke in the morning — the daylight stabbing his eyeballs, the sound of the water running in the kitchen a deafening roar — she was there, bringing him a cool compress, a glass of freshly squeezed OJ, and a couple of extra-strength Tylenol.

"Hey," she said. "How are you?"

"Terrible," he croaked in return. He accepted the juice and gel caps; the compress was soothing on his forehead. "How did you get in anyway?"

"I have your keys, remember? Or did all the booze kill the brain cells where that information was stored?"

It took a while, but they did get over it and were even able to laugh about it. Audrey met someone and fell in love; her new partner had three kids of her own and was not eager for more, so Audrey had not pressed it.

Evan had taken her advice and submitted himself to a battery of tests: semen analysis, scrotal ultrasound, transrectal ultrasound, postejaculation urinalysis along with hormonal and genetic screenings. He'd drawn the line at the testicular biopsy, but what the doctor had found was damning enough even without it.

"Some men have abnormalities in the morphology; that is the shape of their sperm. Others have it with the motility." He sighed and Evan braced himself. "In your case, there are significant issues with both."

"Kind of like a double whammy?" Evan had said.

"Kind of," the doctor agreed. "And to compound the problem, you also have an unusually low sperm count."

Evan just nodded. "I guess the chances of my having a kid of my own are not too great."

"When you're ready, you can start to explore other options," the doctor said, not unkindly.

"Such as?"

"Donor sperm. Or adoption."

Evan gathered up all the information the doctor had given him — leaflets and print-outs, a big fat study about the issue — and left the office. He'd never thought seriously about fathering kids until he found out he couldn't. The knowledge brought with it shame and a weird, twisty kind of despair he had never felt before. His biological stock had just seriously plummeted; who would want him now? He came to a garbage can on a street corner, where he deposited everything the doctor had given him. He never revealed what he'd found out about himself; apart from Audrey and the two doctors who'd examined them, no one else knew.

"How about over there?" Miranda asked, pointing to a spot on the Long Meadow. "Does that look good to you?" He nodded and went ahead a few steps so he could spread out the blanket. Then he turned to see Miranda struggling to wheel the stroller over the grass.

"Let me help," he said, pulling the stroller as she pushed. He looked down at Celeste, who was looking straight up at him. She seemed to like the swaying motion of the stroller, because she opened her mouth in a gummy grin; Evan's chest puffed slightly with pride that he'd helped elicit it.

When they were settled, Miranda lifted her out of the stroller and placed her down on the baby quilt she had brought in one of the bags. Celeste's dark eyes — more brown than blue, Evan noticed — were looking around. Twittering sparrows, a squirrel scampering up a tree, a little boy on a neighboring blanket with a big red ball — she seemed to be taking it all in quietly, reflectively even. "She likes it here," he said.

"I think you're right." Miranda leaned her

face down to the baby. "You like the park, don't you, baby girl?" Celeste cooed in response.

Evan began setting out the food. The plates Audrey had selected were blue and white; the fruit, bread, and cheese looked especially appetizing against them. He never would have thought of that, but when Miranda said, "Oh, this is so nice! Thanks for pulling it all together," he was glad Audrey had. They talked while they ate: how Evan liked living in Red Hook, the awkwardness of eHarmony, freelance work versus a steady job. Miranda said she was worried about leaving Celeste when she went back to work. And she was saddened by the present estrangement from her circle of close friends.

"What about Bea?" he asked, and he bit a cherry from its stem. "Didn't you say that she was really supportive?"

"Totally." Miranda helped herself to the prosciutto, which she deemed excellent. "But she got the part in that play she tried out for. She's in Oklahoma City for the next eight weeks."

"Bad timing," he commiserated.

"For me," she said. "It's a great break for her, though — leading lady for a change. But you know who called me? Geneva Bales

— she's the journalist who did that story for *Metro*."

"Really? What for?" He remembered what she had told him about the interview.

"That's what I was wondering. She said she just wanted to see how Celeste and I were doing."

"Did you get the feeling she wants to be friends?"

"Not exactly. It was like she was still acting like a reporter, even though the piece was finished. Lots of questions, you know? I thought it was kind of odd, but then she didn't call again, so I let it go." Miranda sighed and then took another slice of prosciutto. "This really is fabulous."

*Score one for Audrey,* Evan thought. He'd text her later. After they finished eating, he wiped the powdered sugar from his fingers and brought out his Leica.

"Is that the camera you use at work?" Miranda asked. She'd picked Celeste up and held her against her ladybugged front.

"No. That's strictly digital," he said. "This baby is from another era." He held it out so she could see.

"Nice design," she said.

"It's the best," he said. "Compact, light-weight, easy to handle. And no one has to know that you're using it. You can be invisible."

"What do you mean?" She shifted position as Celeste buried her face in her chest — rooting around for a nipple, no doubt.

"I'll show you." Evan raised the camera up in a casual, even nonchalant fashion; he didn't even seem to be looking in Miranda's direction. But all the while he was snapping away, the depression of the shutter making a slight, easy-to-miss sound. The light was perfect; no flash required. He must have shot a dozen frames: Celeste pressing against Miranda, Miranda smiling down at Celeste, Miranda bringing out the bottle of formula, Celeste's lips pursed in anticipation, the utter relaxation of her limbs as she began to suck, the rivulet of formula that dribbled down her chin, Miranda's hands as she gently wiped the small face clean.

"So you've been photographing us all this time?" Celeste had dozed off, and Miranda carefully settled her in the stroller to nap.

"Uh-huh. And you were hardly aware of it, right?"

"I get it," she said, smiling at him. "You want to disappear."

"Not permanently." He smiled back, cradling the camera in his hand. "Just while I'm shooting. Once I've developed the film and start looking at the contacts, I'm back on the scene again. It's pretty stressful, actually."

"Is it?" Miranda adjusted the canopy of the stroller so that Celeste was shaded as she slept.

"Very. While I'm working, I never know what I'm going to get — only what I think I'm going to get. Or hope. Or pray. With digital, you can see what you've done right away; with analog, you're working on pure faith."

"Pure faith as an operating principle sums up a lot of things, don't you think?"

"Can't disagree with that." He stood and began to gather up the used plates and napkins. "Do you want to walk for a while?" he asked. "It's such a nice day."

Now that the food was eaten, their load was lighter. Miranda stuffed the blanket into the basket under the stroller, and she and Evan each took a diaper bag as they made their way around the park. Celeste was just stirring as they came to the carousel.

"Should we take her for a ride?" Evan asked. He remembered coming here with a whole bunch of friends when he was at Pratt; the carousel had been pretty seedy back then, with missing or damaged animals. But it had clearly been restored, and today, the brightly painted horses bobbed gently as they spun on their circular path.

"Let's!" she said eagerly. Evan insisted on buying the tickets and looked around for the right horse. "How about that one?" He pointed to a pale, dappled gray with a salmon-colored saddle and green pennants circling the column of its neck. "Or that one there?" It was the color of a storm cloud and had its head down, as if about to charge.

"Maybe she's not ready for those yet," Miranda said. Evan felt like an idiot. He should have known that Celeste was too little for a moving animal. But Miranda didn't seem bothered by his response; she'd already started walking toward the carousel. "How about that?" She led the way to a dragon-shaped chariot, and Evan took a few pictures of the creature — scaled body, open mouth, wings poised for flight — before he joined her. Celeste, who'd still appeared a bit drowsy when they boarded, responded immediately to the lilting music as it began to play.

"She's dancing," Evan said as she squirmed and rocked.

"She is." Miranda kissed the top of her head. Then she turned to Evan. "Would you like to hold her?"

Evan said nothing, but opened his arms.

He'd been watching Celeste all day, capturing her small gestures and the nuances of her expression on film; but he had barely touched her, much less held her. She was so warm and animate in his arms — it was like her whole body was humming. He did not kiss her — that would have been presumptuous — but he did bring her close and dipped his head so he could inhale her baby smell: shampoo, soap, powder, and the faint whiff of ammonia; she probably needed to be changed. When he was younger, Evan had not thought much about kids. But being sterile suddenly felt like an unbearable loss. He was surprised — and horrified — that his eyes welled suddenly, and he turned away so Miranda would not see. Audrey was right. He was a wuss.

"Are you okay?" Miranda asked as the ride slowed.

So she *had* seen. "Hay fever," he lied.

They walked slowly back toward the car, Evan still carrying Celeste. She felt good in his arms, like a cat or the large rabbit — a Flemish Giant — he'd held once at a county fair. They stopped so Miranda could change Celeste's diaper and again for a Popsicle from a vendor just outside the park. Miranda let Celeste have a lick; she seemed surprised by the cold and sneezed several times, as if to clear her head. She dozed again as they drove down the hill and woke blinking and yawning when Evan pulled up in front of Miranda's house. He double-parked so he could help her up the stoop with the stroller and the rest of her stuff.

"This was the best day I've had in a long time. I love having her, but it's hard being on call twenty-four/seven. And it's not like I had much preparation for it. It all happened so suddenly. But today, well, Celeste didn't even cry *once,*" she said, looking up at him. "Do you know what a relief that is?" Her fingers knotted easily with his, and he responded by tightening his grasp. "She must have had a good day too; thank you so much for making it all happen."

"You're welcome." He was ready to kiss her, but then a honk from a car trying to pass made him look away.

"Maybe you should go." Her key was already out and she was opening her door.

"I'll text you," he called after her. And after he had moved his car so the driver behind him could get past, he stared at the closed door, hoping that the next time he was here, he'd be following her through it.

# NINE

While Geneva Bales was speaking intently into her iPhone, Jared sat across from her in the small but neatly organized cubicle. On the desk sat a tall vase filled with long-stemmed tulips: pink, red, and white. A MacBook Air was propped open in front of her; on the wall behind her was a bulletin board covered in photos, clippings, ticket stubs, menus, and even a few scraps of fabric. Geneva shot him a look that said, *Sorry to make you wait,* and then launched into a low volley of *um-hum, I see, of course, yes, yes, of course.* When she at last concluded the call, she reached over and took the hand Jared extended in both of hers. "Finally," she said. "I thought he would *never* stop talking."

"It's okay," Jared said. "I appreciate your willingness to see me on such short notice." He'd sent his e-mail only the day before, and she had responded within the hour.

"I'm fascinated by what you said, Mr. Masters. Absolutely fascinated. To think that the baby might be yours and that you made the connection because of the photographs. I mean, what are the odds?"

"The likeness was uncanny," he said. "Here. I want you to see for yourself." He pulled out the scrapbook along with the magazine and placed them side by side on the desk. Geneva took a pair of tortoiseshell glasses from a chain around her neck and studied the pair of images. "I can see what you mean," she said. "The two faces are remarkably similar."

"That's what I thought. But it doesn't hold up unless I have proof," he said. "I want to do a DNA test. It's the only way to know for sure."

"How did you plan on doing that?"

"I could go to Child Services. Get someone to order the test. But that seems so cold. Hostile even. I think it would be better to meet her first."

"And that's where I come in?"

He nodded. "I know it's a strange request, and probably not the sort of thing you've been asked before. But it was only because of your story that I was able to put the pieces together." More silence. "Please? I just have to find out if she's mine."

148

"I'd like to help you," she said finally. "But I'm not sure if I can."

"You can introduce me to her," Jared said.

"Introduce you?" Geneva was still wearing the glasses, and her finely arched brows rose above the frames. "To Miranda?" Jared nodded emphatically. "I don't know," she said, shaking her head. "I just don't know, Mr. Masters —"

"Call me Jared," he said quickly.

"Jared." She seemed to hold the name in her mouth like she was tasting it. "You still haven't convinced me. For one thing, I don't know her all that well."

"You've interviewed her, haven't you? Been to her place? Seen the baby?"

"Celeste. Yes."

"She trusts you," he said.

"All the more reason for me not to violate that trust. She might not want to meet you. She might find it upsetting. After all, you have no real proof. Only pictures. And a hunch."

"What if I told you who Celeste's mother was? Would that make a difference?"

"I'd like to know that." She took the glasses off and replaced them on the chain. "I'd like to know that very much."

"Her name was Caroline Highsmith. She was a beautiful girl. Beautiful — and

149

troubled."

"Troubled in what way?"

"I don't know the diagnosis. Maybe she was bipolar, manic — whatever they call it. She had these swings, you know? She could be ecstatic over the smallest thing — the shape of a cloud in the sky, finding a dollar bill in the street. But then she'd be so easily crushed too, like if they were out of her favorite flavor of ice cream at the super-market. And her temper . . ." He paused, remembering.

"When did you find out about the baby?" She had started typing something into her laptop then; at first Jared was affronted by her rudeness. Then he understood: she was taking notes.

"In September. The last night I saw her alive," he said. "We met for drinks. I had already decided to break up with her; she told me she was pregnant and I didn't believe her. I thought she was making it up — to trap me." He felt ashamed, but he pressed on. "Your article said the baby was born in March. And it was in late March that I found out Carrie had drowned. I also found out that there was some evidence she'd recently given birth. So at first I thought the baby — if there had been a baby — must have drowned with her. But when I read your story and I saw the picture, it started to come together." He took a deep, ragged breath. "The baby — my daughter — hadn't drowned at all. She'd been left in that subway station, and Miranda Berenzweig found her."

Geneva had not looked at him for the duration of this recitation; her fingers danced and skittered on the keyboard for several seconds, the light tap of her nails against the keys the only sound in the office. Finally, she got up and walked to the window. Outside, the Chrysler Building blazed in the sun.

"All right," she said, turning slowly around. "I'll phone her. Feel her out."

"So you *will* help me, then?" His face broke into a wide, tremulous smile.

"I can't promise anything. But I'll try. I'll contact Miranda Berenzweig for you. It has to be done with great tact and delicacy. If she says no, you'll have to go through the court system."

"She might say yes," Jared said.

"She might," Geneva agreed. She returned to the desk, sat down, and began typing again. Jared watched her for a moment. Did he or didn't he want Celeste to be his? If he didn't, why was he even putting himself through all this? But he didn't think he could tolerate not knowing for the rest of his life. "I'll be in touch when I've made contact with her," Geneva said, looking up from the keypad. Jared stood and extended his hand once more. But Geneva surprised him by coming around the desk and giving him a hug. The embrace was quick and almost businesslike, but for the briefest second, he was sure he'd felt the hammering of her heart. Or was it just his own?

That was on Friday. He spent the weekend second-guessing himself. When his phone buzzed early Monday morning, he panicked. He had set this thing in motion; was he ready for the consequences?

But when he answered, it was not the cool, melodious voice of Geneva Bales on the line. It was Isabel Clarke. Jared said hello and groped for a cigarette. When he found the pack, he lit up and inhaled deeply. That first drag of the day was always the best: a little bit harsh, a little bit biting. It was the drag that reminded you that what you were doing had real consequences.

"Did I wake you?" she said, her voice soft and breathy. Jared wondered idly what she was wearing. Or not wearing.

"I was up," he lied. "What's going on?"

"It's the apartment on One Hundred

Seventeenth Street. You haven't sold it, have you?"

"Not yet, though there's been some interest. . . ." Another lie, but damn it, she had woken him and he didn't want to be jerked around by her — again.

"Oh good! I think I persuaded Brandon. We're going to make an offer. But I just need to see it *one* more time. For ten minutes. Or even five. Can you set something up? Today?"

"Sure, I can." He sat up straight in bed, took another deep drag, and began mentally rearranging his schedule. "Let me see when I can get you in there," he said. "Call you back?"

"Call me back," she said. "I'll be waiting."

When Jared arrived at the building on 117th Street several hours later, Isabel was already there on the sidewalk. Now *that* was a first. "Thanks for doing this," she said, giving his arm a little squeeze. "I really appreciate it."

"No problem," he said. His skin tingled where she had touched him. "Is Brandon looking for a parking spot?" The Clarkes owned a sleek, bottle green Mercedes; he could imagine that Brandon Clarke licked it clean at night.

"Brandon's at the office," she said. "I'm

153

flying solo today."

Jared gave her a look, but she did not meet his eyes. *Uh-oh,* he thought. This was not good, no way, no how. This was trouble, with a capital T and underlined three times besides. But now that he was here, how to gracefully get out of it? *Isabel, you need a chaperone. Or a keeper. I won't show you the apartment until you produce one or the other. Now just turn around and take your sweet, hot little body home before I jump your bones on the living room floor.* Instead he said, "Where do you want to start?"

"In the garden," she said, and he led the way. Since he hadn't been expecting her, he hadn't gotten a chance to check things out back there. Fortunately, it didn't look too bad: no trash and only a few scattered leaves. But what was that? Leaving Isabel to bury her nose in some shrub, he went over to the far end of the yard to inspect. Cat food, that's what it was. Tiny, dry kibble in the shape of fish — like the cat knew or cared. Someone around here must have been setting it out. Cat kibble brought cats, and cats brought trouble: they howled, mated, fought, and crapped. Jared had nothing against pet cats, but he did not want strays in this yard — not when he wanted to get a million two for it.

Hastily, he began to scoop the kibble up with his hands and put it in his pockets; he'd dump it later. But as if summoned by his anxieties — or the promise of a handout — a large, orange cat appeared. He must have weighed fifteen pounds, with a massive, leonine head. One green eye took the measure of Jared; the other was swollen shut. Both his ears had lost their tips.

"Oh, look," Isabel said. "Isn't he magnificent? Here, puss." She knelt and extended a hand.

Magnificent was not the word Jared would have chosen. The cat made him nervous, and he wanted it gone. "Isabel, be careful. He's a stray."

"Aren't we all strays in one way or another?" she said. The cat padded over, and when she began to stroke him, a resonant purr rose up from the depths of his throat. "See?" She looked up at Jared. "There's nothing to worry about; he's a love."

From his vantage point above her, Jared could have looked directly down the gaping front of the loose little dress she wore, but he resolutely turned away and lit a cigarette.

The sound of her cry — pained, startled — caused him to whip back around. There was Isabel, hands pressed to her mouth, blood everywhere — hands, face, dripping down her neck. With a disgusted swish of his tale, the cat bounded off.

"What the hell happened?" said Jared.

"I don't even know!" she cried. "One minute he was purring and the next, he just flew at me! Oh, it hurts, Jared. It hurts so much!"

"Okay. Okay. Try to calm down," he said. "Take your hands away. I want to see how bad it is."

Isabel's gore-smeared hands dropped to her sides. Beneath the blood that covered the lower part of her face, Jared could see where the cat's claws had torn her upper lip; it curled away from her face in a weird, unnatural way, and he felt sick looking at it. "Come on," he said. "We've got to get you to the hospital." He considered his options. Call 911 and wait for an ambulance, or try getting a taxi? She was crying harder now, and he put his arm around her shoulders and hustled her back through the house. Whatever frisson there had been between them had completely evaporated; she was freaked out, and his only thought was to get her medical attention.

A yellow cab was just pulling up to the curb to discharge a passenger when they got to the street; they got in and Jared told the driver where they were headed. There had been a hand towel in the apartment's bathroom and he'd thought to grab it on the way out. Isabel pressed it to her face and whimpered softly beside him.

"Hey, is everything okay back there?" The driver's gaze sought Jared's in the rearview mirror.

"Everything's fine," Jared said. "We just need to get to the hospital —"

"She's not going to OD in my cab, is she? Because if she is, I'm going to let you out right here; I don't need that shit, man."

"She's not on drugs," Jared said coldly. "A cat clawed her lip, okay? Now, can you please hurry?" The cab surged ahead and, in minutes, had pulled up to the ER entrance of St. Luke's Hospital on Amsterdam Avenue. Jared paid the churlish driver — "I hope she didn't drip all over the backseat, man" — and ushered Isabel inside.

She closed her eyes and rested her head on his shoulder while they waited for her name to be called. He used the time to call Brandon but got his voice mail, so he left a message. It seemed like she might have fallen asleep, and he remained still, even though the position he was in was uncomfortable. And he was freezing too — it must have been sixty degrees in there. Jared was wishing he had a sweater or jacket when he heard Isabel say softly but distinctly, "I'm going to need stitches. Do you think they'll have a plastic surgeon here?"

So she wasn't asleep. "I'll bet they do, and if not, you can see one yourself tomorrow —"

He was interrupted by a woman in scrubs holding a clipboard, calling out, "Isabel Clarke?" Trailing the towel like a bloodied security blanket, Isabel got up and followed the scrubs past a pair of double doors.

Brandon phoned right after she'd gone. "A cat clawed her? Jesus! Where were you? At the Bronx Zoo?"

"No, One Hundred Seventeenth Street."

"Why were you on One Hundred Seventeenth Street?" Brandon sounded suspicious. Or was Jared projecting?

"Isabel wanted to take another look at that apartment. She said you were ready to make an offer."

"An offer? On that overpriced dump? Hell no!" Brandon made a peculiar noise that Jared realized was laughter. He'd never heard the guy laugh before; he thought maybe he didn't know how. "What made you think that?"

*Your scheming little wife,* Jared wished he could say. So they weren't going to make an offer; she just wanted to play patty-cake with him — first in the garden and then the bedroom. Jesus, but he was a total and complete idiot not to have seen this one coming. "Listen, she's in with the ER doctor now. How soon can you get here?"

"On my way," Brandon said.

Jared waited until Brandon arrived and he knew that Isabel was going to be all right. Turned out there was a plastic surgeon available, and the woman promised there would be almost no scarring at all. Jared was relieved to hear this; he somehow couldn't stand to think of Isabel's delicate features being marred.

He left the hospital and slowly walked back home. His Thomas Pink shirt — very expensive, and of course not on sale — was smeared with blood and there was blood on his hands and probably his face too. He wasn't going to risk an encounter with another potentially snotty cabdriver; the next one might see the gore and think he was a criminal, a murderer. Besides, he needed the air. It would help him decompress after the adrenaline-fueled trip to St. Luke's and the meat-locker chill of the waiting room. Brandon, when he arrived, had been his predictably entitled, asshole self. "That cat is a menace; I want it euthanized," he said. "And I want to sue."

"The cat is a stray; good luck finding it," Jared said. "And who are you planning on suing? The city of New York for hosting a killer feline?" Brandon had ignored him, looking around for a nurse he could bully. What was it with these guys? Did they think there was always someone to blame? That they were exempted from the kind of plain old bad luck that dogged most of the people on the planet?

It was after four when he finally got home. He shucked his clothes and left them in a sorry heap on the bedroom floor, then did forty quick chin-ups on the bar he'd installed in the doorway before heading for the shower. He was bloody, sweaty, and above all, burned; he wanted to scrub the whole it-sucked-from-the-start day from his skin. But the buzzing of his phone halted him in his tracks, and he answered with a quick "S'up?" sounding just like the kids he heard on the street.

"Jared?" asked Geneva Bales. "Miranda Berenzweig has agreed to meet you, but she's asking to have a lawyer present."

"Tell her I'll meet her anywhere, anytime," he said. "And she can have anyone there she likes — lawyer, judge, the mayor, hell, the governor if that helps. There's only one thing *I* want."

"What's that?" she asked.

"Tell her I want her to bring Celeste. I need to see her."

When Jared got off the phone, he walked over to the mirror and stared at himself. A *baby,* for Christ's sake. What the hell was he doing? Then he heard his mother's voice in his head, as clear as if she'd been standing next to him. *You're a man who was raised to do what's right,* she would have said. *You know what that is; now it's up to you to do it.*

# TEN

Miranda's hands were shaking — really, truly shaking — when she put down her phone. Geneva's words — that someone claiming to be Celeste's biological father had surfaced and wanted to meet them both — were so staggering and so awful that her whole body picked up the cue and began to shake along with her hands. This was exactly what she had feared when Geneva first proposed the idea of the profile; why had she let herself be seduced into allowing it?

Abruptly, she stood. There was a mountain of work awaiting her attention before she left the office: an article that needed a final edit, two layouts that needed her approval, an in-box brimming with e-mail she needed to read. But she couldn't deal with any of those things now; she had to escape, if only for a few minutes.

She was just about to head to the ladies' room when Marvin, the art director, came storming in. "Did you see this?" he hissed, waving something in her direction. Miranda reached out to take whatever "this" was. It turned out to be a glossy, high-res photograph of some very elaborate Christmas cakes — *bûche de Noël* was the proper term — made by a celebrity pastry chef whose work *Domestic Goddess* had featured in the past.

"They're gorgeous; readers love them." Miranda was not sure what the problem was; the chef was a boldface name, and it was a major coup that he'd agreed to the story.

"The cakes may be gorgeous, but he's a nightmare to work with!" Marvin said.

*And you're not?* Miranda wished she could snap back. Instead she said, "But this was all decided in the last staff meeting. Don't you remember?" Why did Marvin have to pick this minute to have his hissy fit? Now, along with the shaking, her head had started to throb.

"I must have been out that day. I never would have agreed to work with him again," Marvin huffed. "He is such a drama queen. And a control freak! He wants approval of every single photo — even the ones we're not going to use!"

"Our readers swoon for him, our advertisers adore him, and our publisher worships him; I'd call that win-win-win, Marvin."

"I guess I'm just the odd man out," Marvin said bitterly; he practically snatched the photo from Miranda's hands and turned to leave her office.

"Maybe he'll have mellowed a little," Miranda called out to his retreating back.

"And maybe hell will have frozen over."

Miranda waited a few seconds before darting to the ladies' room, where she locked herself into a stall. Pressing her hands against the gray, coated steel walls seemed to stop the shaking, but not the vile, sick feeling that rose up inside. Celeste's father wanted to see her, meet her. He'd found out about her through Geneva's story. . . . If only Miranda had not agreed to cooperate. If only!

The piece had garnered some nice attention, and just as Geneva had predicted, some offers of assistance too. A disposable diaper company sent her several free cases of their product, and a baby food company did the same. She'd received three substantial gift cards to baby stores, and the local Park Slope toy store had posted the article in the window — and sent a plush, stuffed kangaroo with its own baby tucked into the pocket. She wished she could give it all back.

But she was being selfish. If Celeste's father was out there, he deserved to meet her. Not just to meet but to claim her. It was his right — even if it was going to crack her heart right in two.

She emerged from the stall and washed her hands in the hottest water she could stand. Then she returned to her desk and plowed through the work that awaited her. Articles to edit, layouts, e-mail — check, check, check. The office was nearly empty; she and Marvin were the only people left, and when he too called out a cranky "Night," she was finally, blessedly alone. But now what? She wanted to get home to see Celeste as soon as possible, but she also had to make some plans for the meeting with Jared Masters. She'd told Geneva that she wanted a lawyer present, but it wasn't exactly like she had an attorney on retainer; she needed a referral. Her mind flashed to Courtney and the tedious Harris, but then, just as quickly, she discarded the idea. Courtney would not be of help to her now; instead she would only deluge Miranda in a torrent of I-told-you-so's.

Back home, she accepted Celeste from Supah's arms without even putting down her handbag. "How's my little sugar pop?" she crooned. "How's my baby girl?" Celeste nestled her head into the place beneath Miranda's chin as Miranda held her close and listened to Supah's account of her day. They'd gone for a walk in the morning, then home for lunch and a long nap. Yes, the diaper rash was looking better and she'd actually eaten all of her pureed carrots *and* the applesauce too. They went to the playground after lunch, where Supah tried pushing her on one of the baby swings. "She love that," she said, nodding for emphasis. "She no want to leave."

"Has she had her bath?" Miranda said over the top of Celeste's head.

Supah shook her head and reached for the baby. "I do it now."

"That's all right, Supah. I can handle it." And she could; she was less anxious about the day-to-day care now. Miranda carried Celeste to the door, where she said good night to the babysitter. Then she gathered the things she would need, filled the baby tub, undressed her daughter, and lowered her into the tub.

Her daughter. The words still felt new, even miraculous. She had not given birth to this baby, but after three months of living with her, Celeste felt indisputably, undeniably, hers. Only now someone had stepped forth to both dispute and deny. Someone who might have a deeper, more abiding claim. Miranda found that tears were slowly trickling down her cheeks as she swaddled Celeste in a hooded towel and brought her into her room to diaper and dress her for the night — a onesie in a calico print with a pair of spurs on the front and the words WORLD'S LITTLEST COWGIRL embroidered on the back. Bea had sent it from Oklahoma.

Miranda sat down in the rocking chair while Celeste had her last bottle of the night. How she had filled out since the first time Miranda saw her; her limbs were rounded and smooth, and her face was cherubic. The pediatrician said that any developmental issues they might have worried about looked nonexistent now. "You're doing a great job," she had told Miranda. "A splendid job." Miranda's tears, which she had not bothered wiping, were dripping down onto the front of the T-shirt she'd changed into; some of them landed on Celeste's head, creating a small, gleaming patch in the dark hair. Smoothing it away, Miranda continued to rock her until her eyes closed, her head lolled, and the nipple of the bottle slipped from between her lips.

Gently, she placed the baby in her crib and then allowed herself to go into the bathroom, close the door, and give in to the hot onrush of sobs she had been fighting ever since Geneva had called. But the sobs, though ravaging, were over soon. She didn't have time for them. A quick splash of cold water on her puffy face, an even quicker blot dry with a terry towel. Then she went in search of her phone.

Once it was in her hands, though, she was stumped. Who was it she planned to call? Not Courtney and not Lauren either. Bea was just too busy to be of any help. Forget about her father; she'd tried to explain that she was adopting a baby, but he kept getting the baby confused with a puppy he'd surprised her with for her seventh birthday. And when she'd brought Celeste for a visit, her father started shaking and shouting as soon as they walked into the room. He kept saying she was an alien sent to take over his brain; Miranda had had to leave within ten minutes of her arrival. No, her father was definitely out.

Evan? But weren't they a little too new for her to turn to him in a crisis? Besides, they weren't officially a couple. She hadn't even slept with him. Miranda scrolled through the contacts on her phone, looking for inspiration.

She found it too: Judge Waxman, whose courtroom she'd sat in and who had helped expedite the adoption proceedings. The judge had given Miranda her cell phone number, and Miranda did not hesitate to use it. And to her relief, Judge Waxman actually answered. There were voices in the background. Music too. The judge must have been out for the evening, but she patiently listened while Miranda told her about Jared Masters.

"He'll need to do the DNA test," the judge said. "Otherwise, there is absolutely no basis for his claim."

"Do I have to agree to that?" Miranda said.

"It's not your decision," answered Judge Waxman. "The court will insist."

Miranda knew that. Knew it and felt crushed by the knowledge. "Should I have a lawyer present when he comes to see me?"

"Only if the test establishes paternity and you plan to contest his claim on the child."

Miranda thanked her profusely for her time and said good night. If paternity was established and Jared Masters did turn out to be Celeste's father, she would fight like a tiger to keep her. What was his connection to her mother? *Who* was her mother? How was it that he hadn't known about her birth? She was four months old; why had he waited so long to come forward? Wasn't it in Celeste's best interests to remain with her? Miranda was determined to find out the answers to these questions, and she would use them to keep her baby, her darling girl.

On impulse, she picked up the phone again and punched in Evan's number. So what if they were new to each other? He was a good person; she could trust him. "Hey, how's it going?" He was clearly delighted to hear from her.

"Terrible," she said, and then told him the story.

"What a shock. No wonder you feel terrible."

"Terrible, awful, horrible . . ." She began to cry again, but softly; she did not want to wake Celeste.

"It's possible he's *not* her father, right?" Evan said.

"Right, but —"

"You won't know that until the test is done."

"No, I won't —"

"Don't see him." Evan's tone was decisive.

"What do you mean?"

"The guy who's come forward. Jared Masters?"

"But why not?"

"You'll just get upset before you need to get upset. Let them do the test; if he's really her dad, you can meet him then. Why put yourself through it beforehand?"

"You have a point." Miranda actually felt the anxiety, binding her chest like a vise, begin to ease. Evan was right. Why did she have to meet Jared at this point? She would cooperate fully by having Celeste's DNA tested, and then she would wait for the results before moving ahead. "I really don't want to meet him unless I have to," she said.

"So don't. Tell this Geneva person no."

"You know what? I will." Miranda heard Celeste whimpering in the next room. "Listen, I hear her, okay? I have to go. But thank you, Evan. Thank you so much." And she clicked off before he could reply.

Miranda hurried into the baby's room. The whimpering was sometimes, though not always, a prelude to those crying jags of hers; Miranda hoped she wasn't about to descend into one now. She scooped her baby up and flew her around in the air. Celeste's whimpers subsided. Then Miranda felt her diaper, noted it was wet, and brought her to the changing table she'd bought not long ago. Celeste kicked half-heartedly as she was diapered, but by the time Miranda brought her back to the rocking chair, she had fallen back to sleep. This time, Miranda did not transfer her to the crib. She felt she could not endure any separation at all; she brought Celeste into her own bed and spent the night in a light, hazy, half sleep, never entirely unaware of the baby by her side.

The lab was somewhere on Church Avenue, a neighborhood Miranda never frequented. But she was here today, sitting rigidly next to Evan — he'd insisted on coming with her — as he guided his car into a spot in front of a place offering Haitian jerk chicken and meat pies; any other time, she would have gone in to sample the cuisine and scope out possible story ideas. Instead, she glanced nervously at Celeste, who had reached down and managed to pull off one of her lace-trimmed white socks.

"They told me it wouldn't hurt," Miranda said. "I only asked about twenty times."

"I'm sure they were telling the truth," Evan said. "The swab, it's like a long Q-tip, right? And all they have to do is collect a tiny specimen from inside her cheek?"

Miranda didn't answer. Celeste had peeled off the other sock; she looked extremely pleased with herself.

"Come on," Evan said. "We should go in."

The lab was up a flight of stairs, and the waiting room was empty. "Why isn't anyone here?" Miranda said. "Maybe it has a bad reputation. We should go somewhere else."

"Miranda." Evan put his hand on her shoulder. "You're here; you have an appointment. You just need to get this over with, okay?"

He was right. And she found his presence comforting; she was grateful he had offered to come. Miranda went up to the desk to sign in: name, procedure sought, photo ID. The woman behind the desk glanced at the sheet and said, "I'll need the baby's birth certificate, as well."

Miranda was prepared for this and gave the woman the birth certificate Celeste had been issued in the hospital.

"There are no parents indicated here," the woman pointed out. "Who are her mother and father?"

"That's what I'm here to find out."

After she'd finished signing in, she sat down and waited. When her name was called, she left Evan with a stack of ancient *People* magazines while she took Celeste, still in her car seat, into the examination room. A perky, lab-coated nurse — she

173

looked so young — followed them in. "I'm Becky," she said, touching the tag pinned to her chest. "And I'll be collecting the sample." She opened a cupboard and stretched up to get something off a shelf; Miranda resisted her impulse to offer to reach it for her.

Becky finally succeeded in pulling down what she needed: the long, wooden swab whose sterile tip was covered by a cellophane wrapper. It was an innocent-enough-looking thing, but to Miranda, it looked like a weapon — threatening and dangerous.

"This is what I'll use to take the swab," Becky said. "But first I'll need this." She picked up a Polaroid camera. "Photo ID." Then she snapped a picture of Celeste and had Miranda sign and date the bottom.

"Has the father —" Miranda swallowed. "I mean, the man who claims to be the father, been here yet?" she asked.

Swab in hand, Becky was approaching Celeste, who began to fuss in the car seat. "Oh, he wouldn't have to come to this collection site; he might go to any of the other sites in the city; there are four or five."

"I see," said Miranda.

Becky was inches from Celeste's face, swab in hand. "Open up, sweetheart."

Celeste squirmed and punched the air with her fists. "You won't even feel it."

"Let me take her out of this." Miranda fumbled as she unbuckled the strap and shifted Celeste into her arms. Celeste stopped fussing and promptly buried her face in Miranda's neck.

"She'll need to open her mouth," Becky said.

"I know. I know. But I want it to be . . . gentle." Miranda slid her finger under Celeste's chin and began to tickle her. There was no reaction at first, but then Celeste turned and opened her mouth in delight. Becky seized the moment to slip the swab in; it was out again before Celeste even had time to register what had happened.

"Okeydoke," said Becky, who was busily wrapping the swab in a fresh covering.

"Is that all?" Miranda wanted desperately to be gone from this place.

"There's one more thing." Becky produced a printed form and an ink pad. "I need to stamp her."

Miranda watched while Becky pressed the sole of Celeste's foot first to the ink pad and then to the paper; Celeste did not seem to mind.

"Now we're done here." Becky waved the form in the air to dry the ink. "As soon as the father's results are in, you'll have a legal document establishing paternity in two days."

"If he *is* the father," Miranda said.

Becky looked up. "Oh, of course. If."

The next two days moved with excruciating slowness. Miranda decided to call Geneva; she found out that Jared Masters had provided his sample and would soon have the results. "What about her mother?" Miranda asked. "Did he tell you about her?"

"I think it would be better if he discussed that with you himself," said Geneva. "He's still asking to meet you; he thinks it might make things easier for you."

Easier? There was no *easier* in this situation. "I can't," she said.

"But if he turns out to be Celeste's father —"

"Then I'll meet him. I'll meet him because I'm going to fight him tooth and nail."

Miranda got off the phone after that. Her last words to Geneva sounded just like what she knew them to be: desperate and hollow. Her words carried no weight, even to her. She could fight, but she highly doubted she would win. If it turned out that Jared Masters was Celeste's biological father, blood — his blood — would trump everything, even that impossible, miraculous mo-

176

ment in the subway station when Miranda had looked down and seen the tiny foot peeking out from under the hotel blanket.

# ELEVEN

When she got home from work on Friday evening, Miranda saw the FedEx envelope immediately. Supah had gathered the mail and put it on the kitchen table; the envelope, with its distinctive blue and orange stripes, was on top. Immediately, she was on alert and remained that way as she listened to Supah's account of Celeste's day — they had gone to the pond in the park and watched people feeding the ducks; she had eaten pureed string beans for the first time — and locked the door behind her.

It was only then that she deposited Celeste in the new playpen she'd set up in the living room and sat down with the envelope. She held it in her hands for a moment before pulling the tear strip along the top. The last time she'd been waiting for a letter, the news had been good; she'd been approved for the adoption. Maybe she'd be lucky again. Maybe.

Miranda pulled the tear strip in one decisive, hope-against-hope movement. Inside, there was a letter and two genetic reports, one for Celeste and the other for Jared Masters. Sixteen markers had been tested for; sixteen opportunities to confirm or deny the biological connection. The numbers made no sense to Miranda; she turned to the letter instead. It was excruciatingly brief: the results of the DNA testing performed on the infant known as Celeste Berenzweig and Jared Masters *conclusively ascertained paternity.*

The phrase jumped out at her, hissing and jeering, and she let the report slip from her fingers. Celeste was gurgling quietly; there was a mobile suspended above her head, and her attention was riveted by the gently revolving parts. The baby had bonded with her; Miranda was certain of that. She cried when Miranda left; her face lit up when Miranda returned. The separation would be hard on her. Traumatic even. And how could Miranda even imagine a life without her? She couldn't — and she wouldn't have to. No, instead she'd flee — the city, the state, the country. She'd fly down to Texas, get a car, and from there go to Mexico. Living was cheap in Mexico, and the weather was good. She'd change her name, get a job teaching English so she could support Celeste.

As these plans tumbled around her mind, she got up and hurried to the closet in search of her suitcase. Yanking it down from the shelf, she set it on her bed and began tossing her clothes in randomly — panties, bras, a couple of pairs of jeans, some tops, the dress with the ladybugs on it — then she stopped. Stopped and bent over double, convulsed with both grief and the sheer, maddening futility of her plan. She could not give up her job and her home for a life on the run; she couldn't leave her father, her friends, the secure little world she had created for herself.

When she straightened up again, she shoved the suitcase out of the way. She had to mobilize. There were calls to make: Geneva, Bea, Evan, and maybe even Lauren. Not Courtney; she was not ready to go there yet. But the first three calls went straight to voice mail; Lauren was the only one who picked up.

"You mean he surfaced because of the article in that magazine?" Lauren said when Miranda had finished telling the story. "You must be so upset."

"Upset doesn't even begin to describe it," Miranda said. "But I'm not giving her up without a fight. No, not a fight. A full-blown war. I found her, I love her, and no matter who her biological parents might be, she is really and truly mine." Lauren was silent. "Why aren't you saying anything? You don't think I should fight to keep her?"

"It's not that," Lauren said. "I'm thinking that you should call Courtney and have her talk to Harris. He'll know the right person to help you — and God knows, Miranda, you are going to need all the help you can get."

Miranda did not reply. But she knew Lauren was right. She had not talked to Courtney in weeks. Or was it months? It didn't matter. She would call her as soon as she said good-bye to Lauren. She almost — *almost* — hoped Courtney would not answer; she would leave a message, Courtney would enlist Harris's help, and no words between them would need to be exchanged. Instead, Courtney answered immediately. Before any of the why-haven't-you-been-in-touch awkwardness could take hold, Miranda launched into her story, hardly giving Courtney a chance to say a word. All right, she was rude. She was desperate too, and desperation could do that to a person.

Courtney listened quietly. "Harris will know someone," she said when Miranda

181

paused. "The *right* someone. One of his classmates from Harvard."

"I appreciate that," Miranda said. Of course the *H* word had been lobbed in her direction; what did she expect? "Thank you."

"How are you holding up, anyway? You never call."

"I was doing fine until this happened," said Miranda. "And you know why I haven't been in touch."

There was a freighted silence on the other end. Then Courtney said, "Look, I know you're still mad, but I was just being honest with you; that's what friends, *real friends,* do for each other. You don't want honesty, though. You just want unqualified validation for what any sane person would say was a totally impractical — if not flat-out crazy — idea. Rah, rah, rah. A cheerleader."

"I wanted your support," Miranda said. "In fact, I was counting on it."

"You've always had that! But you want it on your terms."

"Isn't that what all of us want, Courtney? Are you any different?"

"I'd want you to tell me if you thought I was making a big mistake. And look — I was right."

"How can you say that?" The indignant

tone of Miranda's voice must have alarmed Celeste because she started whimpering. "Celeste is the single best thing that's ever happened to me." She scooped the baby up and began to walk her around the room.

"And if you lose her? Won't that be the worst?"

Miranda said nothing; the hot, stinging pain of those words rendered her momentarily incapable of a reply.

"Look, Miranda, I'm sorry. I don't want to fight with you, especially now —"

"Then don't," said Miranda, fighting the urge to weep. "Just ask Harris for a name. Please."

At 6:59 the next morning, Miranda called the child custody attorney whose name Harris had provided; Harris had primed him, so he took her call. "It doesn't look good," he told her. "In fact, it looks terrible. This is going to be a tough case, and frankly, I don't think I can win it."

"Would you be willing to try?" asked Miranda. She was holding the phone so tightly her hand cramped. Is this what she wanted, though? A bitter and contentious court battle? Could she stand it? Could she even afford it? This initial consultation was free — again, thanks to Harvard Harris —

but the rest of the countless billable hours would not be.

"If you really want to go ahead with it — yes. But you have to think about Celeste. The longer she's with you, the harder the separation will be for her. That's what I tell all my clients: think about the kid. Because, bottom line, that's who it's about." Although she didn't want to hear it, Miranda knew he was right.

"Well, what if I can prove I'm the more fit parent? I mean, where was he while the mother was giving birth and then *abandoning* their baby?"

"I don't think that's going to work. Unless there's some big, surprising skeleton in his closet. When Harris told me you'd be calling, I asked my assistant to do a little digging. Nothing extensive. Yet. But I wanted to get a sense of the legal landscape, so I'd know what we're up against. Masters — he checks out pretty well."

"He does?" Miranda's hopes were shrinking to a tiny little pinpoint.

"Good education, good job, nice apartment. He's demonstrated his interest in his community; he's a regular supporter of a few local charities. His paternity is undisputed. And he wants the baby."

*So do I,* Miranda wanted to say. The

suitcase she'd pulled down last night was still on the floor, her clothes a riotous jumble inside.

"There's something else I think you should know."

"What's that?" The tone of his voice put her on alert.

"What I'm about to share is confidential information. *Very* confidential. You can't tell anyone. And if you do, I'll be forced to deny everything." He paused, letting that sink in. "I can't give you her name; that would jeopardize my source. But I can tell you the baby's mother had some . . . issues."

"Issues?"

"She used drugs and alcohol, though not excessively. But there was mental instability. And her death may even have been a suicide."

"How could you find all this out?" Miranda was horrified. "And — so quickly?"

"Masters had to undergo a background check before the baby can be released to him; even though he's the biological father, that's standard procedure. There were questions about the identity of the baby's mother, and he was forthcoming. I have a contact in Children's Services; we go way back, and he was willing to do me a favor. A big favor."

"But — doesn't that help my case? Even a little? Isn't he guilty by association or something?" Miranda was frantically trying to process this information as well as figure out how it might affect the outcome.

"Not really. Because as detached as it sounds, that unstable mother is out of the picture." The lawyer paused as if to let Miranda speak, but she had nothing to say. "Let me know what you want to do."

"How long?"

"Excuse me?"

"How long do I have to decide?" Miranda knew she had to get moving; Supah would be here in an hour and she was due at the office. Reaching into the suitcase, she plucked out clean underwear and a floral-printed linen blouse, the latter not *too* badly wrinkled.

"Have you heard from the father yet?"

"Not directly," she said, thinking of her own unwillingness to meet him.

"Well, you will," he said. "Take the week-end to think it over and let me know first thing Monday morning. Once they're set in motion, these cases tend to move pretty quickly."

"Monday morning," she repeated wood-enly. Then she said good-bye. For a few seconds she did not move. The enormity of what he had told her was devastating. But in some way, it was not surprising. This unknown woman had somehow met and made a child with Jared Masters; she gave birth *and then left her infant in a subway station.* What had she expected the backstory to have been?

Then she snapped out of it. Although Celeste, miraculously, was still asleep — had she ever slept so late? — Miranda had to get moving. How she would get through the day with this decision weighing on her was anyone's guess.

She made it only until five o'clock, the strain of holding herself together was so intolerable. Heading down into the subway station, she thought about the evening and then the weekend with Celeste; what if it was their last one together? Miranda's eyes welled at the thought; she swiped at them impatiently. She had to focus, not wallow.

There was a long delay on the train, and by the time Miranda walked through the door, Celeste had been fed, bathed, and dressed in pink striped pajamas. She waved her arms in the air as if she were conducting a symphony; was she always so glad to see Miranda, or did she sense something was wrong?

"Hello, baby girl," Miranda cooed, taking

the baby in her arms. Celeste uttered a few soft, snuffling sounds of content.

"She roll over today," Supah reported proudly. "First time."

"Oh!" said Miranda, gazing into Celeste's face. "Who's a big girl now?" She was rewarded with Celeste's wet, gummy grin. But wait — was that tiny bump the beginning of her first tooth, pushing its bony way to the surface?

When Supah left, Miranda washed her hands and gently rubbed a finger over the protrusion on Celeste's gum. It was hard and just the slightest bit sharp: yes, a tooth. Would Celeste even be here when it finally broke through? Oh God, if she were to lose her now, she couldn't bear it; she really couldn't. But she would not let herself think this way; she would *not.* Instead, she spent the next hour getting Celeste ready for bed: changing, final bottle, rocking, before setting her gently down in her crib. Miranda waited to see if she was really asleep; Celeste's tiny snore let her know she was.

Then she sat down at her laptop and began to write. She began with the story of finding Celeste, the trip to the police, the subsequent visits to Judge Waxman's courtroom. What began slowly, haltingly, soon turned into an avalanche of words, the words she hoped would plead her case so convincingly and eloquently that everyone would see that of course Celeste belonged with her.

But once she had finished, the urgency that had propelled her suddenly drained, sucked cleanly away. Even if she could convince a judge to let her keep Celeste, should she? This was her *father* who had come to claim her; why did she think her claim trumped his? It was hubris on her part, monumental and ugly.

And what would happen to Celeste during a court battle? Miranda doubted she'd be allowed to keep her. Maybe Celeste would go into foster care until the case was decided — another disruption to her brand-new life.

The sound of her phone startled her, and she regarded it with a kind of primal suspicion, as if the caller might say he was on the way now, this minute, to come and get Celeste. But no; it was Evan's number she recognized. When she answered, tears of relief were coating her cheeks.

"I'm sorry I took so long to get back to you," he said. "I had this insane shoot in Connecticut that ran over, and then I left my phone at the studio and they had to messenger it to me." Miranda could not speak; the tears were dripping down her face, onto the keyboard. "Hey," he said. "Are you all right?"

"No," she said. "I'm not."

"I'm coming over," said Evan. "Now. So just sit tight, okay?"

And although she knew Evan could not see her, Miranda's head bobbed in grateful assent. He was there within the half hour.

"Have you eaten?" Miranda had skipped dinner entirely, and suddenly she felt starved.

"Not really."

"Good. I'll fix us something."

He sat in her kitchen while she opened the fridge, cracked eggs and grated cheese. But the omelets she slid onto the plates were leathery and tough; the bread she'd toasted was burned.

"I'm sorry." She stared at the unappetizing meal she'd assembled. "I guess I'm having an off night."

"Everyone has an off night sometimes."

"Don't tell them at work, okay? I'm supposed to be one of the *Domestic Goddess*'s acolytes; I can't have this getting around."

"Your secret is safe with me." Evan got up and took the plates over to the trash. "Okay?" he asked, and when she nodded, he scraped everything into the garbage pail.

"Now, how about I order something for us? My treat?"

"Okay," she said. She felt so comforted by him; he really did know how to say the right thing. She wished she could tell him about what the lawyer had said. But she remembered the warning and kept silent. Instead, as she dug into the bacon cheeseburger, onion rings, and milk shake — he'd called it a throw-back-to-high-school meal — she allowed herself to be mollified just the smallest bit. Not that the situation with Celeste looked any more hopeful. But Miranda felt that at the very least, she had an ally and, if necessary, a shoulder to cry on.

It was past eleven when Evan got up, said good night, and headed for the door. So he wasn't going to make a move; she was not sure if she felt relieved or disappointed. Then a noise from the other room distracted her. "Celeste," she said, hurrying toward the baby. "Don't leave yet; I'll be right back."

Celeste was awake in her crib, not crying but making those preliminary-to-the-squall sounds. Miranda scooped her up for a quick diaper check. Soaked. She changed Celeste's diaper, and since the pajamas had gotten wet, changed those too. Then she settled her back in the crib on her side and rubbed a spot between her little baby shoulder blades; this had worked in the past and it seemed to be working now. Celeste's eyelids dropped and her body relaxed as she eased into sleep.

As she soothed the baby, Miranda was aware of Evan's presence in the other room. She had to ask herself why she had let him come over. She wanted his company — for moral support, for a willing ear. But it was late, and the evening's conclusion was an unanswered question. Did she want him to stay the night? Certainly, that's the way things were heading with them, and the idea was not unappealing. She liked him — a lot. And his tall, lanky frame had kind of grown on her. Also, those eyes. Still, she was too upset about the likelihood of losing Celeste to know what she really wanted.

Miranda suspended the rubbing and waited a few seconds. Asleep. She kept her eyes on the baby as she backed up toward the doorway. Then she jumped slightly — Evan was right there. They went back into the other room.

"Everything all right?" he said.

"Fine. Just a diaper change and back to sleep."

"Okay. I'll be going then."

"Don't." There. She'd said it.

"Are you sure?" he asked.

"Very." She walked over to where he stood and tilted her face up for a kiss. He kissed her back with such passion that she felt her own desire rise to meet it. It had been more than a year since she'd been with anyone — a long time.

They stood kissing for a while until Miranda saw that she would have to be the one to move things along. Gently she pulled away and led him toward her bedroom. "We'll be more comfortable in here."

Fortunately, the bed was made — some mornings there just wasn't enough time — and when they sank down onto it, Evan seemed less tall and more graceful. She let him undress her, which he did slowly, with something approaching reverence. "Your skin is so soft," he murmured into her ear. "So soft and so luscious."

When he took off his clothes, she discovered, with pleasure, that he was more muscled than she would have guessed. His long legs with their taut thighs and calves had been honed to precision by cycling, running, and who knew what else.

They got off to a slow start — there was the unfamiliarity of a new body, with new textures and tastes, and a certain hesitance about him that Miranda found endearing. But as they relaxed, his shyness dropped away and he moved with more confidence. Later, he did not want to roll over and go to sleep but kept her close, in the enveloping circle of his arm. "I'm glad you stayed," she whispered. And it was true.

# TWELVE

Evan sat up, momentarily confused about where he was. Then he remembered. It was Saturday morning, and he was in Miranda's apartment. Miranda's *bed.* He'd come over intending only to offer what comfort and support he could — and then leave. She was the one who'd asked him to stay.

"Are you sure?" he had said. God knew he wanted to, but he wouldn't have taken advantage of her vulnerability; he just wasn't made that way.

"Very." She came close and tilted her face up; her kiss was filled with such heat and longing. He knew it wasn't just for him — it was for everything she wanted, everything she now stood to lose. He didn't care about her reasons, though. She wanted him to stay and that was enough.

Evan looked around. He didn't see her, but he heard her in the other room, and a minute later, she appeared in the doorway, wearing a thin robe from which her unbelievable skin just seemed to pour. Celeste was in her arms. The baby's dark hair stood up in points on her head, and her tiny mouth was open in a big yawn.

"Good morning," she said. "Would you like some coffee?"

"Coffee would be great." He spied his clothes a few feet away on the floor; should he reach for them?

"Can you hold her? I'll get it going."

*But I'm naked,* he wanted to say. *Naked and in love.* Instead, he took the baby, who reached up to swipe at his nose. Gingerly, he set her on the bed and, keeping one hand on her — hadn't Miranda said she'd turned over for the first time yesterday? — managed to scoot his clothes close enough so that he could reach down to get them. He was dressed when Miranda called out, "Coffee's ready."

"Hear that?" He picked Celeste up in his arms and walked toward the kitchen. "Coffee."

The table was set with two simple white bowls filled with what appeared to be café au lait. "I didn't ask you how you liked it," she said. "Maybe you want sugar?"

"No sugar." He was waiting for her to say something — anything — about last night.

When she didn't, he felt compelled to add, "And I think you know *just* how I liked it."

She laughed and came over to put a hand on his cheek. "I liked it too. Very much."

Evan could hardly contain his smile as he looked down at the bowl she'd prepared for him; milk had been artfully swirled and a dusting of cinnamon sat on the surface. "It's perfect." He looked up again and handed Celeste to Miranda before sitting down.

Miranda balanced Celeste on her lap while she sipped from her own bowl. "You're pretty good at that," he said.

"Practice." She looked sad. "Though it all may end up being for nothing."

"Don't say that," he said. "You can't afford to let yourself think that way."

She nodded and took another sip. Then she nudged a plate in his direction. "Scones," she said.

Evan took a bite; it was flaky, buttery, and moist. He tasted — what? — flecks of orange peel and something sweet and chewy: dried cherries. "Where did you ever get these?" he asked.

"I made them."

"When?" Was she a magician, or had she gotten up in the middle of night?

"A month or so ago. I froze a batch."

Evan kept eating until the scone was gone,

and he hungrily eyed another.

"Go ahead," she said.

"But you haven't had one."

"I will. I'm just going to get Celeste her breakfast." And after settling her in the high chair, Miranda got up to prepare her daughter's meal.

"Have you thought any more about what you plan to do?" He wasn't sure he should be bringing this up, but it was too big an issue to just ignore. "Are you going to fight to keep her?"

"At first I thought I would do anything; I wouldn't stop until every option had been exhausted. But I've changed my mind."

"You have?" He put down the scone. "Why?"

"Because her father wants her. And if he wants her, and can make a home for her, then that's where she belongs."

Evan didn't know what to say. Last night she had seemed so fragile, practically melting into his arms. Today she was made of steel.

He watched as she began spooning cereal into Celeste's mouth. Celeste smacked her lips and smiled; when Miranda turned to reach for a scone, she plunged her hand into the bowl and smeared the gooey stuff all over her face.

"Celeste!" Miranda was laughing; it was good to see her laugh. But then he saw the tears on her cheeks.

After Celeste had been bathed and changed, Evan stood at the door to say good-bye. Miranda had gotten dressed, in something brilliantly red and gauzy; on her feet she wore purple flip-flops. He liked all that color, just the way he liked her skin and that perfume she wore, plum and honeysuckle — he'd seen the bottle sitting on her dresser. "I'll call you," he said, dipping his head to kiss her.

"Thank you, Evan — for everything." She looked so serious, it scared him; he could sense she was heading for a bad fall and he just hoped he'd be able to catch her.

He spent the remainder of the day in his Red Hook loft, catching up on e-mail, doing laundry, and developing film. It was a familiar, and even soothing, process: placing the metal reels into the developing tank, drying and cutting the developed strips of film before slipping them into their glassine envelopes. Then the printing, in rows, onto sheets of eight-by-ten paper, followed by the poring over the tiny black-and-white images with a magnifying glass, a red grease pencil, and a bottle of beer.

This last part was the most tedious,

especially when he knew that it all could have been accomplished so much more easily and efficiently with images enlarged and splashed all over his twenty-seven-inch iMac screen. But digital was digital and analog was analog; the two could not be compared. Evan had no case against digital; for commercial work, it was the perfect vehicle. What he was doing on his own time was different, and he was willing to put up with the inconvenience to get what he wanted. The thousand and one subtle tonalities that existed between the poles of black and white, for instance, or the way light could not only illuminate form but also create meaning. It was after midnight when he went to bed, leaving two empty beer bottles beside the pile of marked-up contact sheets and the worn-down nub of the grease pencil.

The next day, Evan met Audrey for their standing first-Sunday-of-the-month brunch date. Because the day was so beautiful — a surprisingly cool morning for late July, with a breeze coming off the water — they bought food at Fairway and rode their bikes along the path that snaked past IKEA before settling on a bench to eat. Sun glinted off the water — he'd just learned it was the Erie Basin — and overhead, a few opportunistic gulls circled.

"So I spent the night with her." He unwrapped his egg and cheese on a roll; it looked good, but he was thinking of that orange-and-cherry inflected scone. "Miranda."

"And that's all you're going to say? It's not like you to be withholding, Evan. Not like you at all." Audrey began eating her bagel; on the bench beside her, a container of coffee wafted a wisp of steam.

"It was pretty amazing."

"She's that into you?" Audrey gave him a probing look.

"I'm that into *her.*" Damn, she knew him so well.

"That's a start." Audrey blew on her coffee. "But it's got to work both ways, Ev. You *know* that."

Yeah, he did know that. But it was his weakness — virtue? — to be the one who always wanted more from the relationship. How did that line from Auden go? *If equal affection cannot be/let the more loving one be me.* Besides, that had not always been true: Margo, the woman he'd spent a good part of his twenties with, was a case in point. "She's into me too. It's just that it's complicated."

Audrey raised a pierced eyebrow. "What's

that supposed to mean?"

He filled her in on how Celeste's father had surfaced and was planning to claim the baby.

"That's going to be rough," said Audrey. "Are you sure she's ready for a relationship at this point?"

"She's going to need someone. I want to be there for her."

"Evan. Will you listen to yourself? That is *not* a good basis for getting together with someone."

"Oh no? I think it's an excellent basis, in fact. Shows my true colors. And hers."

Audrey wadded up the foil from her bagel and stuffed it into her empty coffee cup. "Is this by any chance about the baby?"

"What are you talking about?" He knew damn well what she was talking about though. Knew and did not like it a bit.

"Since you're not about to be fathering any kids yourself, you want to latch onto this woman who has one. You have to admit it's pretty convenient — a ready-made family."

"You've got it all wrong. It's not like that." He stood and pitched his wrapper and hers into a nearby trash can. "Now, can we get back on those bikes and ride?"

Audrey stood too and, shading her eyes

against the sun, looked up at him. "When you change the subject like that, I know it means I'm right."

"Whatever," he said, and draping his arm across her shoulder, propelled her toward their waiting bicycles.

Later that evening, after a dinner of mediocre take-out food, Evan went into the darkroom to make work prints, expertly pouring the developer, stop bath, and fixing agent into the stainless-steel trays. Then he set up the first negative in the carrier and slid it into the enlarger. The safelight, a lambent, golden moon, hung in a corner of the darkroom. He made the exposures on the Ilford enlarging paper he bought in bulk, put the exposed paper into a lightproof box so he could develop the sheets all together when the exposures were done. Each roll of film had thirty-six exposures; he was lucky if he found two or three decent pictures on a roll. Tonight, the five rolls had yielded fourteen pictures, which seemed like pretty terrible odds. But he liked to tell people it was like playing baseball: for every home run that sent the fans into a frenzy, Rodriguez or Jeter had to hit dozens of pop-ups, foul balls, and fly outs.

As he worked, he remembered Margo. It was funny how he hadn't thought of her in such a long time, and yet since his conversation with Audrey this morning, she'd been on his mind all day. She was a sweet woman: mild to the point of meekness, her plumpness a cause of constant concern — to her, not to him.

She had fairly worshipped Evan and deferred to his taste about music, movies, books, politics — pretty much everything. He'd found it flattering it first, but it soon grew tiring and finally annoying. He didn't want a woman who didn't know what she wanted, and he thought it was kinder to end things between them than to allow annoyance to turn into contempt.

Now came the part Evan liked best: immersing the exposed sheets into the developer and watching the images coalesce before his eyes. Here was Celeste with oatmeal coating her cheeks; here she was in the park with Miranda. He studied the pictures, noting a gesture he liked here, a visual echo there. The final work print he pulled from the fixative was the one he'd taken of Miranda last night while she slept. He'd gotten up to go to the bathroom, and when he returned to bed, he was struck by how the streetlight, filtered through a lace curtain, had made a pattern on her body. Her naked shoulder and the top of her ample breasts were imprinted with a delicate scrim of lace flowers; he thought the effect was pure magic and he'd groped through the unfamiliar apartment in search of his camera. But maybe she wouldn't like that he'd taken the photo of her without her consent, and he decided he would not show it to her — at least not yet.

When he emerged from the darkroom into the light, he had that sensation, familiar by now, of having been away a long time; it always took him a few minutes to reorient. Although the loft had air-conditioning, he put it on only when the temperature climbed into three digits, so on this temperate evening, the windows were open to the soft summer night. He wandered over to one and eased himself out onto the fire escape, his urban, workingman's version of a terrace. Seated on the metal slats, he tried calling Miranda but she did not answer. Tomorrow she would give the lawyer her decision, so he left what he hoped was an encouraging message and put the phone away. He went to sleep with his face pressed into the T-shirt he'd worn to her place; it still held the traces of that intoxicating fragrance she'd been wearing.

The next morning, Evan was up by six and out the door before seven. There was a big shoot in Chelsea for a mail-order catalog — despite the day's heat, the models were tricked out in ski parkas, snow boots, mittens, and mufflers — followed by still another shoot all the way uptown, in Fort Tryon Park, with the Cloisters as the backdrop. But the mail-order shoot ran over because of some technical problems. Then the traffic going uptown was horrendous, so he was late to the second shoot, which nearly got him fired from the job on the spot. He probably shouldn't have agreed to the two shoots in a single day, but he knew work came when it came, not when he asked for it, so he had said yes. It was after seven when he finally made it back to Red Hook. He was totally fried and wanted nothing more than a meal in front of the game, to have a beer, and go to bed. Too tired to even consult a take-out menu, he'd pull something from the stockpile in the freezer and nuke it. Then he remembered: Miranda. She must have called the lawyer by now; what had happened? He really needed to know.

But for the second time, she didn't answer. Evan collected his mail and trudged upstairs. What mystery dish would the freezer yield? Maybe some leftover pizza or a taco if he was lucky. Leaving his camera bag and the mail on the table, he inspected the offerings. And look. There was a whole package of frozen dumplings — score.

While he waited for them to heat, he began to flip through the *Metro* magazine that was in the heap. He turned to the last page, to read the "Soul of the City" column written by Geneva Bales. She had featured Miranda and Celeste in that column a while back. Miranda had shown it to him. And look — there was another baby's picture in the column this week. No, wait. Not another baby. It was Celeste. *Celeste!* What the hell was going on? The timer on the microwave pinged, but he paid it no attention as his eyes scanned the words on the page in front of him.

### Lost and Found

Some months ago, I reported on a most startling incident that happened in our fair city. A newborn was found in a subway station in Coney Island and the Good Samaritan who found her, Miranda Berenzweig, had begun adoption proceedings. I covered their early days together, the mother and child who'd come together by chance and were building a new life in tandem. But now, in a series of events far too unbelievable to have ever been invented, I learned that my story provided the clue that led the baby's father — her real and true parent — to come forth to claim her; it is his remarkable and tragic tale that I want to tell this week. . . .

Evan read the column from start to finish; then he read it again. There was a reference to the baby's mother; according to Geneva, she had "died under tragic circumstances," though what those circumstances were was not described. But the rest of it — what the fuck?

Miranda had told him that Geneva Bales had been sensitive and respectful throughout the whole process of writing the piece. So why had she written *this*? Was she using Miranda and Celeste in some weird way, to further some impossible-to-decipher plan of her own? What kind of person was she anyway?

Ignoring the cooling dumplings that sat in the microwave, Evan tried Miranda again. The phone rang once, twice — Jesus, he really hoped it didn't go to voice mail this time — and then she picked up. "Listen," he said. "There's something you need to know."

Miranda listened to what Evan had to say;

208

she did not interrupt him and she did not offer any comment. Finally he had to ask, "So what do you *think*?"

"About Geneva? I don't have any clue about why she would do a complete turn-around like that."

"I just don't get it," he said.

"Neither do I. But I can't even think about her, or her motives, now. I'm going to lose Celeste. Don't you see? Jared Masters is going to take her away from me."

# THIRTEEN

Hot, sweaty, and above all frustrated, Jared unknotted his tie and threw it on his bed, where it landed on top of the two other ties, shirt, and now-wrinkled seersucker jacket he'd already had on — and rejected. He'd changed three times; what was wrong with him? It wasn't like he had to impress anyone. The DNA test had conclusively proved that the baby girl was his, and the background check had gone smoothly. Now he was on his way to bring her home.

He looked at the pile of clothes on his bed with disgust. The weather report said the high today would be ninety-two. He didn't have to wear a tie at all. No jacket either. He glanced down at his crisply pressed blue shirt and khakis; he looked fine. He *was* fine. Just nervous, that was all.

When the results of the DNA test had confirmed his paternity, he'd kind of freaked out. Yes, he wanted to see his little girl and do right by her, but was he up to the job? He couldn't ask his black friends — Gabe or Tyrell, Shawn or Darius — because he knew they would have told him he was an idiot to have even asked for the test in the first place. A single dude raising a kid on his own — why? And he was ashamed to ask the white friends he knew from his prep school or college days; he did not want them to think he was conforming to some racial stereotype, fathering a child he knew nothing about.

But he'd decided to ask Athena, whose opinion he really did respect. And if he went through with this, he'd need her to cut him some slack at work too. So for all kinds of reasons, he realized it would be good to have a sit-down with his boss.

Jared had pulled some strings to book a table at Ambrose, one of Harlem's hippest new restaurants, ordered a very expensive bottle of wine that wasn't even on the wine list, and launched into the story. Athena sat quietly sipping from her glass until he'd come to the part about the test results.

"You're one hundred percent sure that she's yours?"

Jared nodded; he still wasn't sure whether he was elated or devastated by the news.

"And her mother was that skinny little

blonde you used to bring around?"

He nodded again; he'd brought Caroline to Athena's holiday party one year, and she'd met him at the office a few times.

"I could tell she was trouble," said Athena. "From the get-go."

Jared shifted miserably in his seat. Why had he thought Athena could help him? She'd been jealous of Caroline. He could have predicted that one. But he didn't have anywhere else to turn, so he took a tentative sip of his own wine — not as good as it should have been given what it cost — and waited.

"I don't see you as dad material," Athena said. "Not at all."

"So you think I should let this white woman keep her?"

"Her mother was a white woman," Athena said. "You have a thing for white women, remember?" She drained her glass, and he quickly moved to refill it. "But if she'd been around, you'd be raising this kid together, and there would be some kind of balance. If you leave her with . . ."

"Miranda," he supplied.

"She'll grow up with a white mom and only a white mom, and she won't have any balance. It will be one-sided. *Lopsided.* She won't know who she is, where she came from. Not really."

"So you think I should petition to take her. Keep her."

"She's yours, Jared. You didn't want it or even know it, but now that you do, there's no forgetting it. If you turn your back on her, you'll be ashamed of yourself. Maybe not today, maybe not tomorrow, but one day, the shame will come. Regret too. And when *that* happens, it's going to bury you."

Jared scooped up his keys, wallet, and shades before heading outside. It was hot as blazes, but thinking of Athena's words — *it's going to bury you* — he could remember the sick, icy dread he'd felt when she'd uttered them. She was right. He hadn't planned on being a dad, but that's what he was. Time to man up, face the music — or whatever the hell cliché fit.

The transfer was scheduled for noon at the family court building in Brooklyn; that's where Miranda Berenzweig had been ordered to surrender the baby. He would not be meeting her though. At first she had said yes, but then she'd done an about-face, insisting that the transfer be handled exclusively through the family court system; she would not be present. He was stung by the refusal — wasn't she even the least bit curious about him? — but he decided not to dwell on it. Things could have been way uglier between them; he was being let off easy and he knew it. Although Miranda had initially planned to fight for custody, in another abrupt turnaround, she had decided to give up the baby without going to court. Had she contested his claim, he would have almost assuredly won, but he would have paid heavily — in time, in anguish, and in money. Now he was freed from all of that. The baby — his baby — would be coming home today.

The morning was already oppressively hot. Jared headed for the downtown subway station, settling his shades over his eyes to protect against the glare. The platform was even hotter and more oppressive than the street, but the train came quickly and he gratefully stepped into the air-conditioned car. The one thing Miranda had agreed to — had actually suggested — was that he hire Supah, the nanny who'd been taking care of his daughter already. So there would be some continuity in her life. He'd also lined up a nighttime sitter, a Barnard student named Olivia, who lived nearby on 110th Street. She told him she was premed and wanted to become a pediatrician; how perfect was that? He did not expect to need her every night, but he did promise her work two or three nights a week.

"You're bringing home a brand-new baby girl and think you'll be stepping out three times a week?" said Athena when he told her about his plan.

"Is there a problem with that?" Jared bristled. Now that he'd confided in her, Athena had felt entitled to dispense her advice freely, whether he asked for it or not.

"It just seems like you might be wanting to spend your off hours getting to know her, that's all." She bustled back into her office; he scowled at her retreating form. But then he thought of how she'd helped him turn the small second bedroom in his apartment into a nursery, competently ordering all the furniture and equipment — who knew such a tiny person required so much *stuff*? — and his annoyance dissipated. She was a good person, a good woman. That he had about as much desire for her as he would have for a manatee was a source of ongoing disappointment — to both of them.

Walking from the subway station to the family court building on Jay Street, Jared felt the anxiety whirring around his head, a nasty, insistent buzz. He said he wanted this — he *did* want this — but what did he know about raising a baby? Not a damn thing. He hadn't even been able to settle on a name for her yet. Celeste, while pretty enough, was what Miranda had chosen. He thought he should start fresh, so it was either going to be Lily, his mother's name, or Caroline, for the baby's own doomed mother. As he reached the elevator, the choice was obvious. He'd call her Lily Caroline Masters. Her initials would be LCM, and when she grew older, she'd have sheets or fancy stationery with this monogram; his mother would have approved. The decision seemed to calm him, and when he went first down the hall and then around a corner to the room whose number he'd been given, he felt a fluttering of something like anticipation as he laid his hand on the knob.

Her face. Jared could not stop looking at his daughter's face. After meeting the judge and the caseworker and signing a shitload of papers — so many that his hand began to ache — he strapped her into the car seat that Miranda Berenzweig had not wanted back, and took her in a taxi uptown. The baby's large brown eyes looked steadily into his, and he found he was transfixed, drawn into the gravitational pull of that gaze. Her face did not look like the face he'd first seen in the photograph anymore. She did not look like him, or Caroline, or anyone else he could point to. Instead she was entirely herself: a stranger, although not entirely strange.

There was traffic on the West Side Highway, and as the taxi moved along in syncopated lurches, the baby squirmed and began to make small sounds of irritation — *Eh, eh, eh.* "It's okay, Lily," he said and gave her his finger to hold. "We'll be going soon." Clinging to his finger, she quieted. Then the traffic eased and the taxi was able to move faster, shooting up past the familiar streets: Seventy-second, Seventy-ninth, Eighty-sixth. Lily opened her mouth in a wide, excited grin, and she kicked her feet furiously. "Speed demon," he said and placed a hand on her head. Her hair was black, but as silky as her mother's had been.

The sense memory of Caroline was suddenly all over him, crowding out everything else in the cab. She'd had such lovely hair, fine and glistening in the light, or falling in tendrils around her face when she pinned it up. Then there was the powdery smell of her, combined with the faintly citrus scent of whatever perfume she wore. The feel of her nestled within the protective curve of his arm, his hand big enough to span her throat. Her mouth, and the sticky, slightly strawberry taste of her lip gloss, her girlish body, so lithe and lively under his. Her tiny, perfect breasts, the faint line of down that ran along her torso to her pubic bone — the memories were an ambush, an assault. And then, as quickly as they had enveloped him, they were gone — thank Christ. The driver was turning into the exit lane and heading toward his apartment. "Hang tight," he said to Lily. "We're almost home."

He moved anxiously around the apartment, trying to get Lily settled. It felt a little weird to have a baby — especially his baby — in the place. She seemed okay. A little confused maybe, but she wasn't crying, not really. He carried her into the room that Athena had assembled: canopied white crib and matching dresser, pink and white curtains, sheets and quilt, rug shaped like a large pink and green bunny on the floor. *Eh, eh, eh,* said Lily. *Eh, eh, eh.* Jared felt a rising thrum of anxiety; it seemed that this was not a happy baby sound. Just as he was trying to figure out what he should be doing about it, the intercom sounded, and minutes later, Athena was at the door. She was wearing some voluminous caftan thing, trimmed in fringe, and long, dangling earrings.

"I thought you could use the welcome

wagon," she said. He saw then that her arms were laden with shopping bags; a couple were from the Fairway on 130th Street, and another from Bedelia's, an upscale baby shop in the neighborhood he'd never have even noticed had she not pointed it out.

"This is so nice of you." He followed her into the kitchen, where she began unpacking the bags.

"There's something else too." She gestured to the floor, where a bag from Barnes & Noble sat. "Open it." Inside were several parenting books. *Bonding with Baby. The First-Time Daddy's Manual. The Single Guy's Guide to Successful Fathering.*

Jared flipped through *The First-Time Daddy's Manual.* It seemed daunting. He closed the book. "Thanks. I'm sure I'll be needing these."

The intercom buzzed. "Are you expecting anyone else?" Athena asked. He shook his head when the buzzer sounded again. Jared poked his head out the window. There, on the street below, were Gabe, Tyrell, and Shawn; when he buzzed them in, he saw Darius was there too.

"What are you doing here?" Jared said as they trooped into the apartment. Lily took one look at Darius — who had a full beard — and started to wail.

"Athena told me and I told the guys. We just wanted to say hi to the new addition," said Shawn. "Jesus, she is loud!"

"Here, give her to me," Athena said.

Jared couldn't decide whether to be angry with Athena or grateful. Hell, it would have come out anyway. And he was glad to see his friends.

"The rest of you all know Athena, right?" Jared asked. They nodded. Athena smiled but focused on getting Lily to stop crying. She changed her, walked her, rocked her, and soon the wails turned to whimpers and then the whimpers trailed off. "I think she's asleep," Athena said. "But I can't be sure."

"Her eyes are closed," Jared said, flooding with relief. "Thanks. Thanks a lot."

His friends meanwhile had discovered the food Athena had brought and began setting it out on the table, along with a big sheet cake whose pale pink frosted surface was embellished with the words *World's Greatest Dad* in looping chocolate script. Gabe turned on the television and began channel surfing until he found a tennis match; when Lily woke up, the guys all took turns passing her around and the novelty alone seemed to stave off any further wailing.

They ate all the food, including the entire cake, and polished off two bottles of wine that Jared produced from a kitchen cabinet. He declined to have any himself — considering he was going to have to deal with Lily by himself later, it didn't seem like a good idea — but he was happy to be with his pals and was buoyed by their company. And it seemed like Gabe and Athena were really hitting it off; the two of them had moved off from the group, and Athena was looking at him with that bright, focused gaze that she tended to use on Jared. Why hadn't he thought of setting them up before?

It was after nine when everyone left. Athena had shown Jared how to change the baby, and tomorrow, Supah would be here, and she'd help him too. Maybe this dad thing would work out okay. Lily was already drowsy when Jared set her gently in the crib. She stretched her arms up, as if trying to touch the ruffled canopy over her head before curling onto her side to sleep. Jared left his door wide-open and the fresh-from-the-box baby monitor was set up right next to his bed, so that the sounds of Lily's breathing were amplified and piped into his sleeping brain.

When she awoke, crying, a few hours later, he was completely thrown. He stumbled toward the sound, and once he reached her room, he picked her up. Lily continued to cry. Jesus. What had Athena done earlier in the day to make this stop? He remembered how she rocked the baby, so he tried that. No good. So he started to walk with her, back and forth, back and forth. There, that seemed to be working. She was slowing down, getting quieter, but when he attempted to place her back in her crib, she instantly began to fuss.

Okay, he told himself. Okay. Just get a grip here. Maybe it was the diaper — yeah, that could be it. Tentatively, he put her on the changing table Athena had told him to order. But now how was he going to get the fresh diaper, wipes, and other stuff? So he picked her up and, holding her awkwardly with one hand, he assembled what he needed. Then he tried it again. The diaper was soaked, and he wrinkled his nose in aversion as he wadded it up and pushed it aside, to be dealt with later. He was a little clumsy in cleaning her up — he wanted to be thorough yet didn't want to be too rough or hurt her — but he managed to get the job done. Now came the diapering part.

He positioned the disposable diaper under her and attempted to fasten the self-adhesive tab. Only the protective layer on the peel-off strip would not peel off; he ended up ripping the tab off entirely, which meant he had to get *another* diaper and start again. Jesus. Despite the hum of the air conditioner, he'd started to sweat. But he managed to get the diaper, open it, and wrap it around his squirmy little girl. He did the pacing routine again; she fell asleep and this time stayed asleep when he put her into the crib.

Jared stood there watching her for a few seconds. This whole episode had taken about twenty minutes; was this what he had to look forward to every night, maybe multiple times a night? He was totally awake; there was no way he could get back to sleep now. He spied the books Athena had brought earlier, picked the top one off the pile, brought it to bed, and began to read. Eventually, he grew drowsy and put the book down beside him; he'd just drifted off to sleep when there it was: that staccato sound, *eh, eh, eh,* emanating from Lily's room. This time, he didn't even wait for the full-blown wailing to start; he hauled himself out of bed and trudged toward its origin.

# FOURTEEN

The first morning without Celeste, Miranda couldn't wait to get to work; she desperately wanted to believe that the familiar routine would distract and soothe her. But once she got there, she felt cut off from everything, her senses blunted or even warped, so the activity around her — phone calls, texts, e-mail, production meetings, manuscripts — seemed to be happening very far away; she could barely make out the voices. Finally, at the end of the day, she walked into the office of Sallie Scott, the longtime editor in chief of *Domestic Goddess,* and closed the door.

Sallie was sitting behind her desk — a four-foot, painted baroque extravagance she had paid a fortune for at auction — and looked up when Miranda came in. Her hairstyle, a vigorously hair-sprayed bubble, probably had not changed since Kennedy was in office, and her tailored suit, in ecru poplin, suggested a buttoned-up, rigid demeanor. But in Sallie's case, appearances were deceiving. Her brown eyes radiated concern, and she tactfully nudged the lacquer tissue box in Miranda's direction. "You look like hell," she said.

"I feel like hell too," Miranda said. "And I'm sorry, Sallie. I've been trying. I really have. It's just that —"

"You don't have to explain. I really do get it. Take some time off, all right?"

"But we're so busy now, between the Web site launch and the Christmas issue. And you know I've been trying to land Alan Richardson for an exclusive recipe; I'm almost there." If she could get Alan Richardson, or his partner, Karen Tack, the industry giants responsible for *Hello Cupcake,* to provide an over-the-top cupcake project for the magazine, it would be a real coup.

"I know," said Sallie, placing her hands, with their manicured geranium pink nails, on the desk. "You're a wreck, though. I can see it, and so can everyone else. You can stay in touch with the office and we'll muddle through until you come back."

"Well, maybe I should," Miranda said, both shamed and grateful. So everyone knew she was a mess? Well, why had she thought she could keep that hidden? "Thank you, Sallie."

"Don't mention it." Sallie's phone buzzed, but before she answered, she added, "I'm so sorry, Miranda. I know the loss has been . . . devastating."

Sallie's sympathetic words made the tears rise again, so Miranda just nodded and got out of there before she let loose.

Miranda went home and climbed into bed, where she pretty much remained for the next five days. Yes, she had abandoned her plan of fighting for Celeste. The baby should go to her father. But Miranda was still going to have to grieve her loss.

She used her laptop to watch one old movie after another, all of them frothy and insubstantial confections — Gene Kelly and Debbie Reynolds dancing with frantic energy, Fred Astaire whirling Ginger Rogers around in his arms. Every now and then, she looked at the upper-right-hand corner of the computer to check the time. It was noon; Celeste usually had lunch at noon and was down for a nap by twelve thirty. She was up by two o'clock and needed a diaper change and a bottle. The passing hours were nothing more than signposts to gauge Celeste's imagined movements: where she might be, what she might be doing. This was worse than when Luke left her; worse, even, than when her mother died.

Despite what Miranda had said to Sallie, she had not kept in touch with the office, or with anyone else either. She did not check her e-mail, though she occasionally glanced at her phone. In addition to calls from the office, there had been phone calls from Evan — several of these — and her friends, and although she knew she ought to return them, she did not. Eunice, her father's caregiver, had been trying to reach her and she ignored her too. When her landlady knocked on the door, Miranda just called out, "I'm fine, Mrs. Castiglione. Don't worry about me." She didn't say anything else, but waited until she heard the creak of Mrs. Castiglione's footsteps on the stairs as she went back down to her own apartment.

Miranda paused the movie and got up. Her appetite had left her, and she knew she must have lost several pounds over the last few days. The irony of this was not lost on her; she was always thinking she could stand to lose five or even ten pounds, but now that she had, she didn't even care. She was thirsty, though, and had to steel herself to walk into the kitchen; from the kitchen she could see the door to what had been Celeste's room. That door was closed, and everything that had belonged to her daughter was inside, including the play yard and the stroller.

Miranda knew she ought to go in and empty it out — surely many of the things inside could be donated to charity — but she could not bring herself to do it. The room had a force field around it and was walled off, like a crime scene, in her mind. She poured a glass of water from the pitcher in the refrigerator, went back to bed, and started the movie again.

Fred spun Ginger, whose long, diaphanous skirt fluttered as she twirled. Miranda let herself be lulled by the music and dancing; when it was over, she simply began another.

Then the knocking started again. "Mrs. Castiglione, you don't have to check on me. I'm all right. Really."

"It's not Mrs. Castiglione," said a voice from the other side of the door. "It's me."

"Bea!"

"Yes, and I flew all the way from Oklahoma, so you'd better open up."

Miranda got out of bed and quickly ran her hands through her hair, which she had not exactly bothered to brush or comb recently. Her clothes were none too fresh either, but there wasn't really anything she could do about that now.

When she opened the door, there was Bea, along with Lauren. At least Courtney wasn't with them; she didn't think she could face her now. Then she saw Mrs. Castiglione, hovering by the banister. "I hope you don't mind that I let your friends in, Miranda," said her landlady. "But I was worried about you. We all were."

Miranda took a step back to let them in. Now that they were here, she was just going to have to deal with them. "What about the play?" she said to Bea.

"Monday the theater's dark, remember? I'm only here for the night; I fly back tomorrow in time for the show."

"You didn't have to do this," Miranda said. But she was grateful that she had.

"Oh, yes, I did." She eyed her friend. "When was the last time you had a shower? Or ate anything, for that matter? You're looking thin."

Miranda looked down. Her pants *were* loose, and even her T-shirt suddenly seemed baggy.

"Why don't you take a shower and let me fix you something to eat," Lauren said, opening the fridge and the cabinets. "Except there's nothing in here."

"I haven't been food shopping," Miranda said. She was aware of the look that passed between Lauren and Bea.

"I can go now," said Lauren. "What do you want?"

"I want my baby girl!" Miranda covered her face with her hands, trying to hide from the words.

"I know you do." Bea moved closer to hug her, and Lauren joined in.

No one said anything for a moment, and Miranda just let herself be embraced.

"Who could have predicted that this would happen?" Bea broke the silence. "It's just such a strange coincidence — the father turning up like that."

"I should be happy for her." Miranda wiped her eyes. "I should be glad that her father found her and wants her. But I'm not. I'm not!" She started to cry again. Bea patted her back, and Lauren smoothed the hair away from her face.

After several minutes, Miranda wiped her eyes and looked at her friends. "I think I'll take a shower now." She went into the bathroom, stripped off her clothes, and turned on the faucet. It did feel good to let the warm water sluice over her hair and body. When she emerged, Lauren was back from the store. She'd brought a log of goat cheese and a baguette, a couple of ripe, Jersey tomatoes along with several plums and a box of cookies. Miranda looked down at the food Bea had assembled on the plate. It was good to eat something again, good to be with her friends.

Lauren didn't mention her kids once, and Bea told them funny stories about the production in Oklahoma: the time she mistook toothpaste for hair gel in the darkened wings and emerged on stage with her head coated in Crest; the stage manager who chewed cinnamon sticks in his effort to quit smoking. Before they left, Bea made her promise to check in the next day. "You can call in the morning," she said. "I'll be waiting." And she told Lauren she'd be in touch with her too. No one said a word about Courtney.

When she was alone again, Miranda contacted her office and then called Eunice to check in on her father; she told Eunice she would visit him over the weekend. At least she would not have to talk about Celeste; he would not even remember her. Her heart still felt like a piece of lunar rock — pocked, cold, dead — but something had shifted inside.

Early that evening, there was yet another knock at her door. She walked right over to open it, sure that Mrs. Castiglione would be there, bearing a plate of meatballs or ziti.

Miranda even smiled at the thought. But instead, Courtney was standing there; under her arm was Fluff, her five-pound, high-strung-to-the-point-of-hysteria Pomeranian.

"You came here with your dog?" Miranda liked dogs, but Fluff was an exception; the dog was a quivering mess much of the time and had a bark high-pitched enough to crack a wineglass.

"I didn't want to leave him at home; he gets on Harris's nerves."

Miranda could well understand why but thought better of saying so.

Meanwhile, Courtney was eyeing her appraisingly. "You've lost weight."

"I haven't been eating," said Miranda, aware that she was still barring the entrance.

"Well, you look terrific, though it's a hell of a way to go about it."

"It's not like I had a choice."

"I know," said Courtney. "That's why I came. Aren't you going to let me in?"

Reluctantly, Miranda stepped aside and allowed Courtney to come into the apartment. She set Fluff on the floor, and instantly, the dog began to bark.

"Is there any way to quiet him?" Miranda was worried about Mrs. Castiglione, who was no fan of dogs.

"Sorry." Courtney scooped the dog up;

the barking stopped as quickly as it had started. "He has separation anxiety, but he's fine if he's with me." Sitting down on the couch, Courtney settled the dog on her lap, where it appeared to be calm — at least for the moment. "Aaron told me you'd decided not to pursue the court case." Aaron was the lawyer Harris had recommended.

"He was very helpful," Miranda said. "Thank Harris for giving me his name." She waited. "And thank you too, Courtney."

Courtney shrugged. "It was the least I could do." She looked straight at Miranda. "He told me about that piece in *Metro,* the one that woman, Jennifer, or whatever her name is, wrote —"

"Geneva Bales, and she's not a woman; she's a viper! I wish I'd never met her. If only I hadn't agreed to the first profile, Jared Masters would never have known about Celeste. And the way she turned around and made him seem like some romantic, tragic hero! I can't even stand to think about it!" Miranda tried taking a slow, deep breath to calm herself; she'd been feeling okay for the last couple of hours, but this conversation was pulverizing her fragile equilibrium to so much dust.

"I know," Courtney said gently. "When I read it, I felt terrible for you, Miranda. I

really did." Miranda said nothing, so Courtney went on. "I know you think I've been
evil-bitch-friend for these last few months."

"You're the one who said it first. . . ."
Miranda crossed her arms over her chest.

"And maybe I am guilty of being an
emotional clod. I didn't realize how much
you wanted a baby."

"*I* didn't realize how much I wanted a
baby," Miranda said. "Not until I found her,
not until she was mine. And now . . ."

"Maybe it's not all over yet," Courtney
said. "Wouldn't her father let you see her
sometimes?"

"Maybe he would; he's asked to meet me.
More than once." Miranda used the front
of her shirt to blot her tears.

"So why don't you do it? It might be better than this. Right now it feels like she's
dead to you. She's dead and you're mourning her. But she's alive. Alive, well, and living uptown with her dad. You know, it's got
to be hard for him too. He wasn't expecting
a kid; now he's got one he has to raise all
by himself, no mom in the picture."

"He might have a girlfriend. . . ."

"The magazine piece said he was single."

Maybe Courtney had something there.
Miranda had been so adamant about refus-
ing to meet Celeste's father because she

thought it would bring her too much pain. But would it be any more painful than what she was now feeling? It was even possible it could be less. And the thought that she might see Celeste, hold her in her arms — Courtney was right. She was reacting as if Celeste had died. But she hadn't. She hadn't! This was the happiest thought she had had in days, if not weeks. And Courtney was the one who'd led her to it.

"I was pretty angry at you," she said. "I thought you were undermining me."

"I'm sorry, Miranda. Really and truly sorry." Courtney said nothing more, but used one hand to fiddle with her earring, twisting it around and around on her earlobe. The other hand remained on Fluff's shining, red-brown fur.

Miranda knew how difficult it was for her to say she was sorry — about anything. She'd always been this way. And she realized that Courtney's silence meant she was *nervous* — nervous that Miranda might not accept her apology.

"You said a lot of hurtful, callous things," Miranda began. "But I appreciate your coming here today; what you said about Celeste made me feel better. And you know what else? I've missed you." As soon as the words were out, Miranda knew they were true. Courtney, never a hugger, reached out and took her hand; they sat like that for several minutes. Fluff snorted, a tiny, contented canine snort. And later, after Courtney and the dog had left, Miranda had the best night of sleep she'd had since Celeste's father had surfaced.

Evan stood in the front of Miranda's door with a bunch of lush, apricot-colored roses in his arms. He'd stopped at Zuzu's Petals on Fifth Avenue to get them; unlike the dozen-roses-for-ten-bucks that were hawked at corner grocers all over the city, these flowers had a real scent and would not wilt the next day. Upset that he'd not been able to get in touch with Miranda, he'd biked over to Park Slope to check on her. But after three rings to her buzzer produced no results, he had to conclude that she was not there. Wait — wasn't that someone approaching from behind the lace curtain? The door opened, and he saw an elderly woman with thick glasses and a light scarf tied over the neatly coiffed mound of her silver hair.

"Are you looking for Miranda?" she asked.

"Yes, but it doesn't seem like she's home."

"She went back to work," the woman said. "And I'm glad. I was getting worried. But those friends of hers showed up last night, and I think that made her feel better. She's been so sad since the baby went away."

"So she's at the office?" said Evan. "Thanks for telling me." He looked at the flowers, which he'd had to balance very carefully on the handlebars of the bike.

"Would you like me to take those?" The woman's gaze followed his. "I'll put them in a vase and make sure she gets them as soon as she comes in."

"That'd be great," Evan said. "I really appreciate it." He handed her the flowers, but not before adjusting the bow on the pale green ribbon with which they had been tied. Then he went down the stairs, unlocked his bike, and pedaled back home. Until he heard from her, there was nothing else he could do.

A little after six o'clock, he was just beginning to consider his dinner options — frozen or takeout — when Miranda called. Finally. "You okay?" he said. "I haven't been able to reach you, and I was worried. Really worried." And hurt too, though he did not mention that.

"I'm sorry. I just didn't want to deal with anyone. I went into the office today though; I can't say I'm okay, exactly. But I'm functioning. You wouldn't believe how restorative a gift from the cupcake king can be."

"Cupcake king?" Evan did not follow.

"Alan Richardson. He's the man of the moment when it comes to novelty cupcakes, and I got him to agree to come up with an exclusive recipe that we'll feature in print and online too. My boss is over the moon."

"Must be some cupcake," he said.

"It will be. But why am I nattering on about this? Have you eaten yet?"

"No, I haven't, actually."

"Then why don't you come over here and I'll make us dinner? I bought some fresh basil on the way home and was planning on doing a pistachio pesto."

"I love pistachio pesto," he said even though he'd never even considered, much less eaten, such a thing.

"Good. See you soon?"

"Soon."

"Oh, Evan! I almost forgot! Those roses . . . They're extraordinary. Thank you so much for bringing them."

Evan knew she couldn't see him grinning. "Glad you liked them."

A little while later, Evan was once more locking his bike inside the gate at Miranda's house. He had not brought wine or anything to eat; she was such a foodie that he was afraid the wrong offering would humiliate him. But he did have another small gift for her; he'd debated about bringing it and then decided yes, it was the right time.

The pistachio pesto — green from the crushed basil leaves and rich from the crushed nuts — was delicious and there was plenty of crusty bread to sop up any that remained in his bowl. She followed that with a light salad and for dessert she poached plums and served them with whipped cream and a drizzle of melted dark chocolate; Evan could have easily licked the plate.

"Do you always eat like this?" he said.

"Pretty much. Though not lately — lately I haven't been able to eat much of anything."

"You've been taking it hard, haven't you? Losing Celeste?"

"I have." She had stopped eating and let her hands drop to her lap.

"I wish you had let me in. I might have helped."

She looked at him as if she was trying to decide whether this was true. "I appreciate that. But I just couldn't see anyone for a few days. Talking about it would have made it worse."

He didn't totally buy this; maybe she meant *talking about it to him,* but he didn't want to push it. "And now?"

"Now it's a little better. A little. I don't

feel so . . . shell-shocked. I'm functioning again. Sort of."

He suddenly wanted to kiss her then but thought he should wait for a signal. Maybe she was still too upset over Celeste to be in the mood. Hell, *he* was upset about Celeste. Instead, he helped her clear the table and load the dishwasher; when that was done, he was unsure about what his next move should be. He was not going to assume anything. Then he remembered the gift.

"I have something for you." He went to get it from his backpack.

Miranda took the flat package and tore off the dark green paper to reveal a wheat-colored linen album; he'd filled it with eight-by-ten prints he'd taken of her with Celeste, a dozen photographs in all.

She did not say anything as she slowly leafed through the pages. She stopped at one that showed Celeste in her bath, a crown of shampoo covering her head. The next one had been taken in Prospect Park; Celeste was on her back and Miranda was leaning over her, each of their faces mirroring the delight seen in the other. Evan grew anxious. He shouldn't have given it to her; maybe he'd only made things worse. Finally, she looked up.

"It's precious," she said. He could see her

trying not to cry. "Precious and beautiful and perfect." Then she set the album on the counter and opened her arms; Evan was across the room in seconds.

# FIFTEEN

It was a slow afternoon in July; Jared and Diego were the only ones left in the office. Jared was ready to head out soon too, but there were a couple of important calls he needed to make first. And while he was here, he could have Diego finish some filing that had been mounting up. Only where was the kid? Smoking weed in the men's room? Jared walked all through the office and did not see him. Had he left without signing out? He was getting school credit — not much, but still — for his work, and Jared needed to keep track of his hours.

He had just finished the first of the calls when he heard the door open.

"Diego? Can you come in here?"

Diego walked into Jared's cubicle with that sullen look on his face; he seemed never to be without it. "You need me?"

"That's the idea," Jared said. "I've got some filing for you to do."

Diego said nothing but took the stack of applications from Jared's hands.

Jared resisted the loud, exasperated sigh he was dying to expel and watched him go. Most of the interns had worked out pretty well — a couple had gotten real, paying jobs, and one had gone on to college. Tiffany was a perfect example. Whenever he ran an open house, he had Tiffany sit at the sign-in desk. The girl was pretty, polite, and had a nice way with the prospective buyers. Diego was another story. On the one occasion Jared had positioned him at the desk, he'd spent the whole time glued to his phone. No hello, no eye contact — he'd even forgotten to have some of the people sign in. The kid was a total washout.

"Get rid of him," Athena had said. "If you want this mentoring thing to work, he's got to meet you halfway."

But Jared did not want to give up on Diego. At least not yet. So he kept him in the office, where he could monitor him more closely. Diego did whatever clerical chores he was asked to do but without any sort of enthusiasm or even apparent interest. Still Jared had hopes of reaching the kid.

Diego walked — or more aptly *strutted* — back into Jared's cubicle. "Filing's all done.

Can I go now?"

"There's one more thing." Jared handed Diego another batch of applications.

"File these too?"

"No. Athena needs to see them first," Jared said. "Put them in a folder, write a note for her, and leave them on her desk, okay?"

"Sure," Diego said. And as he turned away, he added, "Whatever."

This time Jared did sigh — not that Diego appeared to notice. Maybe Athena was right about this one — he really was going nowhere. He thought about this as he made the second call, which took longer than he'd expected. While he was still on the phone, he got up and went quietly into Athena's office; he hated to think that he was spying on Diego, but he did want to make sure the applications were where they were supposed to be. Sure enough, they were. It was only Diego who was somewhere he shouldn't have been; he had opened Athena's top left-hand drawer, the one where the petty cash was kept. When he saw Jared, he slammed it shut in a hurry.

Jared ended his call. "How much?" he said.

"What are you talking about?" Diego looked nervous, though; in fact, he looked guilty as hell.

"How much did you take from the drawer, Diego?"

"Me? I never took nothing, not a cent." Indignation had replaced guilt.

"Really? Then what were you doing in there?"

"You told me to put the folder —"

"*On* the desk, not *in* it."

"What are you going to do? Frisk me? Or do a strip search — full body, cavity maybe?"

Jared walked over to the desk and brought his hand down hard on its surface. The resultant smack made Diego start a little. Good. Maybe he was getting somewhere. "Why would I frisk you?" he said. "Do you think being here is like being in jail? Punishment of some kind? Because if you do, you should just walk away. Walk away now, Diego. No one is making you stay. Certainly not me."

Diego stood there, nostrils flaring like a restive horse.

"What's eating you, anyway? Don't you like working here?"

"It's not so bad," Diego said. "At least *you're* not so bad."

"Who is, then?"

"All those white people coming through

here. They're the ones with attitude. They think they own the neighborhood. Hell, they think they own the world."

"And stealing from Athena is going to fix that?"

"I told you: I didn't take nothing. I —"

"Come on. Just drop the act, okay? I'm not going to ask you again how much you took; I'm going to walk out of here in a few minutes and just let you put whatever it was back."

"How do you know I won't just take it all and clear out? Never come back here."

"I don't," said Jared. "But I'm willing to take a chance." He let Diego process that and then added, "You didn't answer my question. How is stealing from Athena going to fix the white-people problem?"

"She's worse than they are! She's such an Oreo, acting all false and smiley with them. Makes me sick."

Oreo. Jared had heard that one for years, like he'd personally betrayed his people and his race by being smart, ambitious, and wanting to swim in a wider sea. "Sit down." He pointed toward one of the two chairs facing Athena's desk; Diego sat down and Jared sat next to him. "I don't know if white people *own* the world, but they have a lot of power, and if you want in, you have to play

246

nice. That's what Athena figured out. She's not an Oreo cookie, but she sure is a smart one. She's made something of herself. And you can too. Only you have to decide you're going to join the party — not spit on it." Jared got up. "I'm going back to my office. You can do the right thing. Or not. It's up to you, Diego. It always is."

Jared sat quietly at his desk. He was not going to check Athena's petty cash; he had no idea how much she kept in there on any given day, so he wouldn't have been able to tell if Diego had put the money back or not. Anyway, if Diego decided to turn things around, it wasn't going to be because Jared had shamed or scared him into it; it would be because he wanted to. A little while later, Diego appeared before Jared yet again, this time with a sheet of lined paper in his hand. "I wrote a note to Athena," he said. "Want to see?"

Jared took it from him. Diego had gone through the applications himself and marked the ones he thought had red flags; he made an itemized list detailing each one and why. "She'll appreciate this," Jared said. "Good work." And for the first time in Jared's recollection, the kid smiled.

The sky was still light when Jared left the office and headed home. He walked quickly because he was planning on going out again tonight, only it was business, not pleasure, that was taking him away from Lily. The two of them had settled into a viable rhythm. Supah arrived five mornings a week to take care of her; he got home around six to take over. He'd feed and bathe his daughter and then sometimes Olivia would come over so he could go out for work or to meet friends. If he wanted to go somewhere straight from the office, he arranged it so that Olivia would arrive at the apartment just as Supah was getting ready to go; both of them had keys to his place, and the transitions had so far been pretty seamless.

Of course there were some bumps in the road to new fatherhood. That was normal, right? Lily could go off on these crying jags that went on for more than an hour. Was it gas? Colic? Missing Miranda Berenzweig? Damned if he could tell.

When this happened, it was like the subtly shifting pitch and tenor of her screams were being channeled directly to his brain and he felt ready to explode. The business of changing her diapers didn't get any less gross. Ditto dealing with her throwing up, which seemed to happen with some regularity. She might wake him four times during the night and then again at the crack of dawn. He was exhausted and losing weight — not that he needed to — and was starting to look pretty haggard. He hadn't given any thought to a vacation, and his love life had stopped dead in its tracks.

He wished he could connect Lily with the feelings he'd had for Caroline. They had met at a club, and their chemistry had been instant and explosive. Everything they did together had that impulsive, pushing-the-envelope kind of feel — driving to Atlantic City on a whim and spending the entire night in a casino, a midnight swim on a Montauk beach, blowing an entire paycheck at Saratoga.

Sometimes, just sometimes, when he walked into the room and Lily smiled at him, or pressed her tiny head against his chest, he'd feel the pull toward her and he'd get it — the connection, the love. But those moments were often obliterated by the daily grind of caring for her, a grind that was not shared with a woman he loved. With Lily's mother.

Jared let himself into the apartment, took Lily from Supah, and popped her into the high chair for her supper. Then it was a bath and pj's; he had no time to eat or even change. Tonight he was meeting with a skittish client who was teetering on the edge of making an offer on that garden apartment in the building on 117th Street.

Those apartments were *not* moving; it was like the incident with Isabel Clarke and that berserk cat had jinxed it and the apartments remained, unappreciated and unclaimed, on the market, which was really bad news. If a place sat around too long, prospective buyers began to wonder why, and soon the apartment developed what he privately thought of as bad buying juju. It was a real shame this little gem of a property had fallen victim to the syndrome, and he was hoping that the meeting tonight would turn things around.

The only trouble was that Olivia was late, damn it. He checked his watch and his phone as he impatiently waited for her; Lily was all ready to be put to bed, and he could tell she was tired — rubbing her eyes with her fists and opening her mouth in a series of luxurious yawns. He laid her in the crib and turned out the light; when he looked in on her again, she was asleep. But still no Olivia.

He had texted her three times without getting a reply; he was standing at the window, looking out at the street and willing her to appear, when his phone pinged with an incoming message. *Sorry I'm late. Be there in 5.*

Finally! But he still had to get out of here or he wasn't going to get there on time. Should he wait for Olivia or leave now? He darted into the baby's room to check on her; her little onesie-clad rump was in the air and her cheek was mashed against the sheet. She snored lightly. Olivia would be here any minute. And his client, a high-powered finance guy, was such a stickler; he knew that being even two minutes late might piss him off and ultimately screw up the sale. Jared decided to risk it. *Late. Have 2 leave now. Lily asleep. Just let yourself in. See u around 10,* he texted.

Then he was out the door. He hadn't gone a block when he stopped to text Olivia again. To his relief, she texted right back.

*Here now. Lily still asleep. Don't worry.*

Jared stared at the tiny letters before slipping the phone back in his pocket. Lily was fine, totally fine. Great. He had a good feeling, a *selling* feeling, about this showing, and he hurried down the subway steps, eager to meet his client.

# Sixteen

"It's the next exit," Miranda said to Evan. "The ramp comes up quickly, so you have to watch for it." She was sitting beside him in his Kia, on the way to the nursing home in Westchester to see her father. Once in a while she rented a Zipcar and drove up there herself; the rest of the time she took the train from Grand Central Terminal. But when she mentioned to Evan that she'd planned to visit this weekend, he'd volunteered to drive her.

"Got it," he said, glancing over in her direction. "It's really pretty close."

"It is," she agreed, letting her gaze drift out the window at the rush of passing roadside shrubbery. "I should get up to see him more often."

"Sounds like the visits are depressing."

"That," she said, turning back to him, "is an understatement. You'll see for yourself."

Evan found the ramp and they were off

the highway, heading onto the tree-lined streets. The nursing home was in the center of town, flanked by a frozen yogurt shop on one side and a sandwich shop on the other. On his better days, Miranda had taken her father to both, but that had not been for some time. In the last few months, he was reluctant to leave the building, even for a little stroll around the grounds. She didn't know what to expect today, or how her father would react to Evan. There was just no predicting.

Inside the nursing home it was warm and stuffy; although there must have been air-conditioning, most of the residents didn't like the cold. Miranda signed in and led Evan to the elevators, down the hall, and finally to her father's room. Only when she got there, it was empty. Her first response was alarm; had something happened? But they would have notified her. Leaving Evan looking out of the window, she went into the corridor to investigate. "He's in arts and crafts," said the desk attendant. "It's on the third floor. You can go down and stop in if you want."

"Thanks, but I'll just wait in his room." Miranda briefly tried to imagine what her father might be doing. Weaving loops of fabric into a potholder? Gluing tiles down to form a trivet? She decided it didn't matter. Anything that could release him, even temporarily, from the prison of his diseased mind would be a welcome distraction, and she did not want to interfere.

"He's in arts and crafts," she reported to Evan back in her father's room. Evan, who was holding his camera, nodded; he was photographing something outside in the street. Miranda settled in with a magazine to wait, but she had no concentration, even for the length of an article, and she kept checking her phone.

Earlier that morning she had left a message for Jared Masters, telling him she had changed her mind and asking if he would let her see Celeste. Even thinking of her baby girl (she would always, *always* think of Celeste as hers in some essential way) could bring on a storm of tears, but she remembered what Courtney had said: Celeste was alive, not dead. Mourning was not the operative mode here; negotiation and compromise were. Just because she'd surrendered custody didn't mean there was no place for her in Celeste's life. Maybe she could be a godmother of sorts — not too close to threaten Celeste's father or any woman who might come into his life, but not banished either. So she was keeping the phone close and was ready to pick up in an instant. Only Jared Masters had not called back.

Miranda heard voices in the hall, one fretful and petulant, the other soothing and calm. Aided by his walker, her father shuffled into the room. Eunice was right behind him. "Look who's here, Nate!" Eunice announced. "It's your daughter!"

Miranda saw her father look at her, but there was no recognition — at least none that she sparked. He seemed much more interested in Evan, who'd turned away from the window and was standing with his camera still in his hand.

"Norm!" The elation in his voice was unmistakable. "Norm, you old son of a gun! Where've you been keeping yourself? It's good to see you." He moved across the room — he was surprisingly quick for a man with a walker — until he reached Evan, whom he squeezed tightly in a bear hug.

Miranda could see Evan looking over the top of her father's head at her. "Norm?"

"His brother, Norman. He's been dead at least twenty years."

"Do I look like him?"

"Of course not," Miranda said.

"He's been having a bad day," said Eunice. "We had to leave arts and crafts early because he dumped all the buttons on the floor and threw glitter in someone's hair. And he used the f-word to the occupational therapist. Twice."

"Well, he looks happy now," Miranda said.

Her father had released Evan and stood grinning up at him. "How about a game, Norm? Pinochle? Scrabble? Checkers? You name it; I'm your man."

"I guess checkers would be okay," said Evan.

"I can get the checker board from the game room," Eunice said. "Be back in a jiff."

Miranda looked at Evan. "You don't mind?"

"Not a bit," he assured her.

Eunice returned with the game and set it up at a small table. The two men played three rounds; Nate won each time. He was exuberant in his victory, high-fiving Evan and Eunice. Miranda he ignored totally, even when she opened the tin of lime melt-aways — made from one of her favorite cookie recipes — and served them with the iced jasmine tea she'd brought in a large thermos.

"Excellent cookies, Norm!" said her father. Crumbs dotted his chin. "Where'd you get them?"

"Miranda baked them for you, Nate," said

Evan. "You know Miranda. She's your daughter."

"Daughter?" A scowl crossed Nate's face. "No daughters, no girls, and NO BABIES!" Suddenly he was shouting, and he spit the cookie out in apparent disgust.

"Nate, don't get yourself excited." Eunice was right there, hand pressed to his shoulder, voice gentle but firm. "And please don't spit."

Miranda just watched. Why had he said anything about babies? Babies had not been mentioned at all today. Not once. It meant he did remember something, he *did*. If only she could find a way to reach him. "You're right, Dad. No babies. No babies here; no babies anywhere." Her voice was reedy with sorrow.

"Baby, baby, bye-bye, baby." Her father turned the words into a song; his anger was gone as quickly as it had come. He took another cookie and offered it to her. "Have this. It's good."

"Thank you, Daddy," Miranda said, and ate it slowly, making it last as long as she could. Then she turned to Evan. "Time to go?"

"Time to go." Evan walked over to hug her father again.

"Don't be a stranger, Norm," Nate said as

he gazed up adoringly. "Next time, we'll play chess. A real intellectual game."

"We'll do that," Evan said.

She hugged her father before she left, but he did not react and his eyes remained fixed on Evan.

Miranda was mostly quiet on the drive back to Manhattan. Earlier in the day, Evan had mentioned stopping by a photography gallery on Orchard Street; she wasn't sure she'd be up for it, but when they got there, she decided that she would go in with him after all.

"I think you'll like the pictures." He locked the car doors. "The show is coming down tomorrow, and after that, the gallery will be closed until September, so this is my last chance to see it."

Miranda followed him inside. Large color photographs were strategically hung on the white walls. Many of them depicted a thirtyish woman, often with a child or two, though sometimes alone. The woman was very striking, with a mane of rippling hair, full mouth, and well-defined cheekbones. But there was nothing airbrushed about her looks, and some of the photographs showed her face in close-up, so that her pores or a thin film of sweat were quite visible. In one, she had the beginning of a blemish, red and angry, near her chin. And the pictures of the children, always the same two, were equally unsentimental: here was one of a small boy crying, a thin thread of mucus trailing from his nose, his face wet and smeared.

"Who is she?" Miranda asked as they moved around the gallery.

"Elinor Carucci," he said. "She's actually the photographer. She uses a tripod with a timer so she can be in the pictures as well as take them. What do you think?"

"I like them." She stopped in front of a photograph that showed the top part of a child's face and the bottom part of a woman's; the two faces were close together and the child's hand rested on her mother's cheek. "Do you?"

"I really do. Look at what she does here. You get just the girl's eyes, staring right out at you, but not her mouth or nose; the mother's face is also cut off, so you see the nose and mouth but not the eyes. It's like they're two parts of the same whole. And this gesture" — he pointed to the hand — "is so intimate. It's perfect. The child is reaching for her, caressing her, and claiming her, all at the same time."

"You see so much." Miranda loved how animated he was, how passionate.

"It's all in there; you just have to look."

Miranda lapsed into silence again on the drive home; the gallery had been a lovely respite, but being with her father always wore her out. And today was one of the worst visits. Even though she was glad he'd enjoyed Evan and the checkers, his inability to recognize her was excruciating. She knew it was not his fault; it was the damn disease, turning his brain into Swiss cheese. But still. And Jared Masters had not called back. Maybe he never would.

As they were crossing the Brooklyn Bridge, the lights of the city behind them and the vast river rippling out below, she blurted out, "I called Celeste's father."

"You did? What for?"

"I decided that I do want to meet him. No, that's not exactly right. I want to be able to see her. And if I want that, I have to meet him."

"I thought you had decided against it." He kept his eyes straight ahead on the road.

"That was before . . ." she said. "Now that Celeste is with him, it's the only way to have contact. And contact, even once in a while, is better than nothing at all."

"You're sure about this?"

"No, I'm not. I don't know how it will play out. Maybe he won't want me to see her on a regular basis. Maybe he'll get married and Celeste will have a new mother."

"What did he say?"

"So far — nothing. He hasn't called me back yet." Evan was quiet, so Miranda asked, "You don't think it's a good idea, do you?"

He didn't answer right away. "I just don't want you to get hurt. And from where I sit, that seems like a very likely possibility."

"I'm hurting now," she said quietly. "I'm dying, actually."

When Evan pulled up in front of Miranda's house, he offered to take her out to dinner. But she said that after taking her to Westchester, the very least she could do was to make a meal. It was too late to start shopping now, but she knew she could pull something together quickly, and a short while later, they were sitting down to a frittata made with cheese, red pepper, and zucchini; she had no lettuce but found carrots and red cabbage in her fridge, so she ran them through her food processor — the unexpected color combo was good — and topped them with olive oil, fresh lemon, and coarse crystals of sea salt.

"You can turn anything into a meal," he said. "You're a magician."

"Not anything," she said. "But after all

261

these years at the magazine, I do have a few tricks up my sleeve."

"What are the others? Can you whip up a ball gown? Knit?"

Miranda shook her head. "There are people in crafts that do that kind of thing. I can barely sew on a button, and forget about hems. Though we did all take a knitting pledge."

"Knitting pledge?"

"The crafts editor had this idea; she made us sit in a circle and taught us to knit. We did it, oh, five or six times, and we were supposed to keep it up. We were all making scarves, and she was going to feature them on the Web site."

"So how did it go?"

"Not too well. I hated knitting. I'm just not dexterous."

"With needles, maybe. But in the kitchen it's a different story."

"I told you how it was all because of my mother. I started with soups; she could keep them down. Then when she had sugar cravings, I started baking; I'd make cookies with crushed pecans or lemon zest. . . . She'd ask for them, even at the end, when she was too sick to eat anymore."

"So you've been feeding people ever since." Evan's plate was now clean; he'd eaten every bite.

"Habit," she said. "It dies hard. And anyway, I've made a career of it."

After they finished dinner, she washed out the food processor so she could use it to chop up the amaretto biscuits — they were a little stale — which she sprinkled over butter pecan ice cream. All the while, she kept her phone close at hand and visible.

"You're still waiting for that Masters guy to call you back," he said.

"I don't understand why I haven't heard from him. He seemed pretty eager to meet before. So I am wondering what might have changed."

"Geneva Bales," said Evan, using his spoon to scrape up the last of the ice cream.

"What are you talking about?"

"Maybe she said something to him, discouraged him from contacting you."

"But why?" Miranda said, and then realized how pointless her question was. Why had Geneva written so eloquently and movingly in praise of her adopting Celeste and then done a complete reversal, championing Jared's claim over her own? Was she just a journalist out for a story? Or was there something else going on?

"I don't know," said Evan. "I'm curious about her."

263

Miranda set her spoon down. She had not finished her ice cream, and it had pooled into a taffy-colored puddle at the bottom of her bowl. She glanced again at the silent phone. "So am I."

# SEVENTEEN

Evan spent the night with Miranda snuggled peaceably by his side. He didn't initiate sex; he sensed she was too preoccupied. But early the next morning — it was Saturday, and neither of them had to be at work — she surprised him by coming into the bedroom fresh from the shower and dropping her towel when she stood in front of him. "Are you in a hurry to leave?" she asked.

"No." He reached for her; beads of water still dotted her collarbone and throat. "No hurry at all."

Back in his own place, he sat down at his laptop and began Googling Jared Masters. He wanted to see what he could find out about the guy. Good education — private school in New England, followed by four years at Haverford and an MA in urban planning from Columbia. He now worked for a boutique real-estate company in Har-

lem and seemed to be on the rise profes-
sionally. He'd also been a soccer coach for
some uptown youth league, and more recently, he had started some kind of intern-
ship program for high school students at
the real-estate firm. Evan read about his
many accolades and the citation from the
principal, and there were several pictures of
him with the students, one of whom was
now at Princeton.

Masters was also a very social guy; Evan
found plenty of pictures of him at various
clubs and restaurants in the city as well as
out in the Hamptons. He was inevitably
with a woman — always white — of a kind
that Evan did not consider especially attractive but that he knew other people did:
blond, skinny, done to the nines.

After a while he switched to searching for
Geneva Bales. He couldn't help suspecting
she and Jared Masters had some kind of
connection, that it wasn't journalistic objec-
tivity that had made her take his side the
way she had.

The first things that came up were, predictably, the pieces she'd written for *Metro;*
the magazine archived them, and had he
wanted, he could have gone back over the
seven years' worth of columns that were
available online. There were references to

other pieces as well — a bunch from the *New York Times,* a couple from the *London Observer,* one from *Vogue,* and another from *Vanity Fair.* He found photos too, pictures taken at various New York social events: galas for the New York City Ballet and the New York Public Library, a garden party held by the Central Park Conservancy.

But none of this was illuminating or even very interesting. Geneva wrote well and often. Along with her column, she plied her trade at various high-profile publications, and she had a modest presence on the New York social scene. Evan wanted more. Who was she? Where had she come from? There was no mention of a personal life — no lover or spouse, no parents or children. Surely that information had to exist somewhere; he just had to persist and he would find it.

Around one o'clock, he got up and went into the kitchen for lunch. The refrigerator yielded a can of Coke, a desiccated lemon, and some leftovers from a Chinese take-out meal that had been none too appetizing even in its original incarnation. He pitched the sorry remains in the trash and sighed dramatically. In the past, he would have eaten the Chinese food without question or complaint. But spending time with Miranda had spoiled him.

Forget lunch. He popped the top on the soda can and reached for a bag of potato chips. Potatoes were vegetables, right? Back at the computer, he studied the Wikipedia entry for Geneva Bales.

She was born in 1971, raised in Asheville, North Carolina, graduated from Randolph Macon Woman's College in Virginia, and came to New York in the early 1990s. No mention of her family, but knowing her hometown was a useful start, and Randolph Macon might be a source too. Easy enough to calculate the year she graduated; there must be old yearbooks or other school publications. But he'd done enough for today. He needed to get out.

He brought his bike down and hopped on; he had no particular destination or goal. His only imperative was about speed: if he went too fast, he couldn't see what was around him. And seeing was what it was all about. He loved this time of year, this time of day. The shadows stretching and expanding and the sky taking on its warm, predusk glow. He'd ride for a while, stop to photograph some little incident, some bit of urban drama — *street theater* was his term for it — before getting back on the bike and pedaling on.

That night, he had dinner at the Tribeca loft Audrey shared with Gwen and Gwen's three kids. While both of them were lawyers, when it came to earning power, they were at opposite ends of the spectrum. Audrey counseled rape victims, and it seemed like half her work was pro bono; Gwen had made partner in a white-shoe firm on Park Avenue. It was Gwen's money that paid for the high-gloss loft on North Moore Street, with its seeming acres of highly polished wooden floors across which the kids ran, cartwheeled, and in the case of one of them, skateboarded.

"Dylan! Put that thing away before I take it away," Gwen scolded.

Dylan, an impish child with a halo of blond curls and pale blue eyes, said, "Okay, Mom," and then proceeded to skate down a long hall, out of his mother's range. Not that she would have noticed. Three kids were quite a handful, and dinner was an unruly, noisy affair. Gwen had ordered in — "I hope you like Japanese," she said — and somehow, amid the giggles, tossed napkins, and spilled juice, the food managed to make it to the table and everyone did eat. After they finished dessert — a store-bought, elaborate tiramisu for the adults, cannoli for the kids — the youngest of them, Emma, decided she liked Evan and climbed into his lap.

"Would you read me a story?" she said. "Please?"

"Sure," he said, shifting to accommodate her weight. She was as golden and curly haired as her brother, but her eyes were a darker, more somber shade of blue.

"You don't have to do that," Gwen said. "She can go play with her brothers."

"No, I want to," said Evan. He looked at Emma. "What story would you like?" She produced a book that seemed to be mostly about fairies and unicorns; pink and sparkles were the operative design elements. While he read, she relaxed against him and began to suck her thumb; when he finished — the fairies and the unicorns had retired to some magical, fairy-and-unicorn never-never land — she took her thumb out of her mouth and said simply, "Again." So Evan read it again, and then a third time. She was asleep before the fairies made their final flight home; Gwen came to lift her from his lap and take her to bed.

Audrey flopped down on the couch beside him; it was long, streamlined, and white, which seemed like a puzzling choice for a three-kid household, but it looked pristine, as if it had just been delivered from some very high-end showroom.

Audrey had told him Gwen had a house-keeper in several times a week and that no one was allowed to eat on it — ever.

"Thanks for being so sweet with her."

"She's adorable," he said. "A real doll."

"I can tell you miss that baby," said Audrey.

"I do, actually." His smile was slow and rueful. "Who'd have thought, right? I mean me, wanting a kid so much?"

Audrey leaned over to touch his cheek. "It'll happen for you, Ev," she said. "You wait and see. If not with Miranda, then with someone else."

"I don't want it to be with someone else; I think I love her." He had not actually said this out loud, and once he did, it seemed indisputably true.

"And does she think she loves you?"

When Evan did not reply, Audrey sighed.

"What's that supposed to mean?" he said.

"I just don't want you getting hurt," she said. "Is that so bad?"

"There's always a chance of getting hurt," he said. "No matter how it plays out."

"You seem more prone to it than most. Heart on your sleeve and all that."

"I like keeping it handy," he quipped. "You never know when you'll need it."

■ ■ ■ ■

When Evan got home, he was restless and unable to wind down, so he settled in with his laptop. Audrey and Gwen had sent him off with a cannoli-filled bag, and he absent-mindedly chewed on one as he continued his Google search, this time back through archives from the Asheville local news-papers. He stopped when he got to the wed-ding announcement for one Geneva High-smith; Geneva was not what you would call a common name. The groom's name was Preston Bales.

Okay, Bales he got. But what was it about the name Highsmith? He felt like he'd heard it before. As he continued to sift through the newspaper archives, looking for ad-ditional references, it hit him. Highsmith was the last name of the woman who had drowned — the woman who was Celeste's biological mother. Miranda had learned a little about her when Jared Masters first came on the scene. Was it just some crazy coincidence, or was there a connection between Geneva Bales — Geneva *Highsmith* Bales — and the woman who had died?

Fueled by his desire to find out, Evan kept looking. The papers yielded nothing more, but then he found an entry for a country club in North Carolina. The country club had a newsletter, and some patient, devoted club member had digitized all the old issues going back to 1952. He checked the date of the wedding announcement again and then went back to the issues that corresponded. Bingo. There, on page seven, was a wedding photograph of Geneva Highsmith and Preston Bales, each flanked by family members. To Geneva's left was Eloise Highsmith — Geneva's mother. And next to her was a slender, delicate-looking figure in an ice blue dress that seemed way too big on her. Her straight blond hair hung down past her shoulders. Caroline Alexa Highsmith. This twig of a girl was Geneva's sister — and Celeste's mother.

Evan stared at the screen. There it was, irrefutable proof of the connection between Geneva, Caroline, and the abandoned baby. Is this why Geneva had contacted Miranda in the first place? Did she know all along that the baby was her niece? Although it was after one a.m., he knew he would not be able to sleep until he got to the bottom of this, so he went into the kitchen to make himself coffee. He brought the steaming mug back to the computer and settled in. Then he began a new search — Geneva

Highsmith — and felt a small, electric jolt when the results began to load.

Miranda was surprised to hear from Evan early Sunday morning. He said he had something important to tell her. He couldn't do it over the phone, and it couldn't wait. He needed to see her immediately.

"All right, then," she said. "Just come over now." She decided to make a batch of scones for him. They were his favorite.

He seemed agitated when he arrived, and he didn't even react to the aroma wafting from the oven. Instead he reached into his backpack and pulled out a sheaf of papers. "It's Geneva Bales," he said. "Geneva Highsmith Bales. I found out who she is."

"What are you talking about?"

"Highsmith, don't you remember? Celeste's — I mean Lily's — mother was Caroline Highsmith, and Geneva is her older sister. Which means that Geneva is the baby's *aunt.*"

"I don't believe it."

"I didn't at first either. But I did a complete search and I found everything — all the documentation." He thrust the papers at her. "Here. Read for yourself."

Miranda's eyes traveled over what Evan had given her: printouts of newspaper clippings, photos, and a wedding announcement. She looked up at Evan. "Can it be true?"

"I know it is," he said. "But here's what I don't know. Was she aware of the connection? And if she was aware, how the hell did she ever figure it out?"

Miranda spent several seconds staring at the photograph. Yes, that was Geneva; she could recognize her easily. Her hair was even styled the same way, though she wasn't wearing a headband. Finally, she looked up at Evan. "Why did she come after me to do that story? And what did she want from me?" But of course Evan had no answer for that.

# EIGHTEEN

Jared sat at his office desk, straightening the already-straightened piles of papers, relocating his stapler and tape dispenser. The pencils in the pencil holder seemed a little dull; maybe he'd even sharpen a few before he left. And how about some filing? There was always something that needed to be filed, wasn't there? But he did neither of these things and instead sat there, hands open and still on the orderly surface.

He knew it was time to go home, but Jared was procrastinating. Tonight, he was the last one here; even Athena had gone, and the evening sky, glimpsed through the wide windows on the office's far wall, was turning lilac as it darkened. He'd called Supah to tell her he was going to be late, but still, this was really pushing it. He'd better leave — now.

Fortunately, the heat had abated a little bit and his walk home was not so bad. It

had been years since Jared had been in the
city in August for such a long, unbroken
stretch. He'd always managed to get away
— to the Hamptons, of course, but also to
the Cape or the Vineyard, where some of
his prep school and college friends had
places. But this year he'd canceled his plans
because he thought the disruption — new
surroundings, new babysitters — might not
be good for Lily. Now that he was stuck
here in the dog days, though, he was regret-
ting his decision. He felt trapped and
resentful.

Back at his apartment, he was relieved to
find that Supah had already put Lily to bed.
Having to deal with the baby as soon as he
walked through the door could be stressful.
Sometimes she was cranky, or she needed
to be changed. Once, she'd thrown up on a
really expensive Hermès tie; the stain had
not come out.

"Thanks for staying," he said as Supah
slung her bag over her shoulder.

"You welcome." She had her hand on the
doorknob. "I take Lily to the sprinkler
today. She no like."

"No?" Jared was surprised; didn't kids
love sprinklers? He sure had when he was
little.

"Water get in face. She cry."

"Okay, no sprinklers, then." Jared reached for his wallet. Usually he paid Supah on Friday, but tonight he slipped her a twenty. "Thanks. I know I've been keeping you a lot lately." She looked down at the crisp bill, surprised but clearly pleased too. Then she said good night and left.

Jared tiptoed in to peek at Lily. Asleep, though who knew for how long? She was teething now, and the pain would wake her — and therefore him — suddenly and jarringly. Those teething screams were something else. Just anticipating the next few hours, he poured himself a glass of wine. He remembered how he'd been afraid to have so much as a sip of the grape that first night; by now he'd realized that a little booze helped take the edge off, and, man, did he ever need that. He wished he could have a cigarette too, but he'd given up smoking — at least at home, and where else could you smoke these days? — in deference to Lily's little lungs.

Jared changed out of his work clothes into shorts and a T-shirt and then padded barefoot into the kitchen to see what he might have for dinner. And look at that — Supah had prepared a noodle dish and left it in the fridge for him. He was so hungry and worn-out that he didn't bother to heat it up. Even cold it was delicious, seasoned with coriander and some kind of spicy peanut sauce.

After he'd finished his dinner and the wine, he felt better. Had he been alone, he would have headed out — some of his favorite spots, like the Cosmo, were just getting going about now. But he wasn't alone; he was tethered to the baby asleep in the next room. He needed to get out more; he'd see if Olivia wanted to pick up any extra evening hours. Being a father was not the sum total of his identity. He was a guy, and guys had needs.

Not that he'd had much time to think about those needs lately. Since Lily's arrival, his libido had gone into the deep freeze. Not tonight though. That soft summer sky had stirred something in him. He was lonely; that's what it was. He was lonely and in need of some female company. He couldn't even rely on the steady beam of Athena's affection; now that she and Gabe were an item, she had turned her gaze elsewhere. To his surprise, he found that he missed her.

Jared channel surfed for a while, and when none of the hundred-plus channels engaged him, he turned the television off. Facebook was another downer; the first thing that popped up was a picture of Athena and Gabe, both in bathing suits, yukking it up at her place on Sag Harbor. She'd invited him to bring Lily and join them, but he'd declined, saying it was too much of a hassle to travel with a baby. This was only partially true. The real reason was that he didn't want to be around all that giddy, newly-in-love stuff. It made him feel like shit.

God, but he was one gloomy son of a bitch tonight! He had to shake this off *now;* nothing killed the interest of the ladies faster. The ladies, the ladies . . . When was the last time he'd even been interested in a lady? The image of Isabel Clarke popped into his head — not the last time he'd seen her in June, freaked out and bleeding from that bizarro cat attack, but before that, when she'd been all flirty and hot. How the hell was she anyway? Was her lip okay? Did she and her asshole of a husband ever find a new place? Without giving himself time to weigh the pros and cons — and knowing that if he did, the cons would win by a landslide — he called her. And just like that, she picked up.

"Long time!" she said. "Sorry I was such a mess that day."

"Are you kidding? It wasn't your fault. That cat was *crazy.* But are you all right

280

now? Did you have to have surgery?"

"I did, but I'm good as new," she said. "You can barely even see the scar."

"I'm so glad." It was true. Even if he hadn't been thinking about her, he was genuinely awash in relief to learn that her lovely face had not been marred. "So have you and Brandon found an apartment?"

"Not yet." She waited before speaking again. "Is that apartment on One Hundred Seventeenth Street still on the market?"

"As a matter of fact, it is." The finance guy had not made an offer. "But Brandon said he wasn't interested in that place —"

"He wasn't." Isabel's tone had taken on an edge. "*I* am. Kind of. I think."

Jared tried to make sense of this. Were they splitting up? "If you haven't found anything yet, maybe I could show you something else? I've gotten a couple of new listings that might be just your kind of thing."

"Could you?" she said in that little-girl voice of hers. "Would you?"

"Of course. When would you and Brandon like to meet?"

"Brandon's in London right now," she said. "On business."

"I see." He had to tread carefully here. But she was a big girl. She knew what she was doing. And so did he.

"Could we meet? For a drink or something? You could tell me about those listings."

"I'd be happy to," he said, trying to sound professional even though that was sure as hell not how he felt. "How's Thursday?" Today was only Monday; Thursday should be enough notice for Olivia. Thursday was *perfect.*

Jared was practically humming when he got off the phone. So a-hole Brandon was in London. Yippee. He hoped he was having a good time because Jared was looking forward to having a very good time with his wife.

Thursday he left work a little early so he could shower and change before heading out again. Lily was fussy when he got there; Supah had not been able to get her to take her afternoon nap. "She sleep good tonight," said Supah.

"I hope so," said Jared, thinking of the evening with Isabel.

Since Supah had not yet bathed or fed her, he decided he'd better do that before Olivia arrived. So he sat Lily in her high chair and attempted to feed her dinner, which came from tiny jars of strained chicken and rice, carrots, and applesauce. Usually Lily ate with appetite and enjoyment. But not tonight. She twisted her face away from every spoonful and even managed to push his hand out of the way, which lobbed a bright spray of pureed carrot all over the wall. While Jared was wiping it up, she overturned the dish containing the rest of the food onto the tray of the high chair and was happily slapping her hands in the resulting mess. When he tried to clean her hands, she ended up smearing both their faces with baby food. Baby food was dripping down from the tray onto the floor too.

Jared tried to keep his temper in check. She was a baby, after all. She didn't mean to be such a pain in the ass — even though that was exactly what she was. "I guess you're not hungry tonight," he said. "So we'll just skip dinner, okay?" He lifted her from the high chair and managed to get her undressed and into the plastic tub without too much hassle. But she splashed nearly half of the water onto the floor; when it mixed with the baby food — which he'd not had time to clean up — it made a nasty sludge that he really did not want to track all over this apartment. He couldn't clean it now, though, so he slipped off his shoes and did his best to avoid stepping in it.

Finally she was bathed, dried, and in pajamas; Jared, however, was sticky with exertion, stress, and baby food. He still had to get her to sleep and get himself cleaned up and presentable. He deposited her in her crib and then had to endure her crying while he attacked the worst of the kitchen. He steeled himself against it, and eventually, her cries tapered off. He popped his head in to check on her — she was asleep. Great. He was running behind and needed to shower before Olivia got here.

Twenty minutes later, he was dressed and ready to walk out the door. He hadn't given Lily her bottle because she was still asleep, but he'd tell Olivia to do it if she woke up. So where was she? He checked his watch and began to pace. He texted her and was reassured by her immediate answering text.

*Be there very soon. Sorreee!*

*No prob,* he texted. *Get here asap. Use yr key.*

He checked on Lily again. Still asleep. He didn't love the idea of leaving now, but he figured it would be all right. Lily hadn't had her nap, so she'd be out for a long while. And anyway, would it be so terrible if she cried for a couple of minutes before Olivia got here? Some people believed in the cry-it-out approach; he'd heard heated arguments in favor and against when he took Lily to the playground and hung out with the moms, nannies, and the occasional dad. And it did seem to work — when he'd left her crying in her crib tonight, she'd ended up falling asleep on her own.

These were the things he told himself as he let himself out of the apartment and hurried to the street. No subway tonight; he was meeting Isabel at a new place she'd wanted to try in Hell's Kitchen, and he was taking a cab. He was able to flag one down quickly, and once inside, he texted Olivia again. She didn't reply, but he'd try her as soon as he got downtown. *It'll be all right,* he told himself. *It'll be fine.* He had his iPad on his lap; he'd brought the new listings to show Isabel. He didn't think that was their real agenda; still, best to act as if.

The place Isabel had suggested was called Les Nuages, and it was packed. She was waiting for him up front, and as soon as he saw her, he forgot about texting Olivia and the listings on his iPad. He forgot about pretty much everything but the way she looked in that short, body-hugging black dress — what was all over it? fringe? feathers? — and those killer heels. Her legs — had he ever seen them before? — were terrific, and her bare, tanned shoulders were peeling slightly; he wished he could lick them. "I ordered for both of us," she said, gesturing to the bottle of champagne that sat chilling in an ice bucket in front of her on the bar. "But I asked them to wait until you got here before they uncorked it."

Champagne? So that's the way this was going down? "Well, what are we waiting for?" The bartender popped the cork, which shot off behind him, causing several onlookers to hoot in approval. Jared clinked his glass to Isabel's. "Let the good times roll." They polished off the bottle very quickly and then decided to head downtown, to Chelsea, to eat. They ended up at the Cosmo; Jared realized he had not been here since that last awful night with Caroline. He wanted to banish or, better still, obliterate the memory, so he immediately asked for a Scotch on the rocks. When it came, he drank it quickly, and then he and Isabel split a bottle of wine with dinner. Who even knew what they were eating? He was flying, feeling no pain, nothing but a ravening, need-it-bad, need-it-now kind of lust. Finally, the meal was over and they got into the elevator that would take them to their room; Jared still was known here, and he found his old privileged status was intact.

As soon as they were alone, the door shut smartly behind them and bolted, he was kissing her the way he'd been wanting to kiss her all night, pulling the skinny straps from her shoulders — Jesus, he tore one in his excitement to get her naked, but she didn't care a bit — and pushing her down on the wide, welcoming bed. He went wild when he saw the tan lines that encased her beautiful breasts — so small and perfect, the nipples as pink as gumdrops — and then ended above her ribs. Her white, lacy thong was no more than a scrap; he gently tugged it off with his teeth before touching the slick, salty place beneath it with his tongue. Her tanned thighs opened wider, and she grabbed his head, pulling him to her.

After they were done, Isabel produced a nice little bag of blow, and they did a couple of lines together. Then he scooped her up and carried her back to the bed. "Brandon could never go again," she said, arching her hips up to meet him.

"Brandon," he said as he thrust inside her, "is in merry old England. Cheerio!" And they both laughed so hard they nearly slid off the bed.

Jared must have fallen dead asleep after round two. He woke somewhere around dawn with a ferocious need to piss and a headache that felt like a two-ton truck barreling through his skull. Standing naked in the bathroom, he was disoriented, and for a moment he confused Isabel's sleeping form with Caroline's. Caroline! God, he'd missed her! Then it all came back to him: where he was, whom he was with. This was followed by the sickening realization that he had not gone home last night. Even worse — he'd never texted Olivia, the way he'd planned. Jesus Christ. Was Lily okay?

Coming out of the bathroom, he careened around, looking for his pants, which had ended up under the bed. He fumbled through the pocket, searching for his phone. When it was in his shaking palm, he saw that there were twenty text messages — maybe more — and as many missed calls. He was too freaked out to count any of them. The last one was from Athena, and it had come through just half an hour ago.

WHERE THE HELL ARE YOU?!!! LILY WAS ALONE ALL NIGHT. YOU'D BETTER GET YOUR ASS HOME RIGHT NOW!

Jared stared at the screen. How had Athena been dragged into this? What happened to Olivia? Was Lily all right? Galvanized by fear and guilt, he started yanking on his clothes. The activity woke Isabel, who let the sheet fall from her body as she rose to look at him. "What's your hurry? Come back to bed." She patted the place beside her invitingly.

"I'm sorry," he said. "I've got to go."

"Now? Is it me?"

"Hell no!" He knelt in front of her and traced her lips with his fingers. "You were amazing. You *are* amazing. But I can't stay."

"Why not?"

"It's my daughter." He shoved one foot into the shoe he'd found and started looking around for the other.

"Daughter! You didn't tell me you had a daughter." She sat up and pulled the sheet flat against her chest. "I didn't even know you were married."

"I'm not." When he saw her confused expression, he added, "It's a long story. And I'll tell it to you. Just not now."

She watched him in silence for a few seconds. "When will I see you again?"

"Soon," he said. "I promise." Though what the fuck was any promise from him worth? "You go back to sleep. I'll take care of the bill downstairs, so you don't have to worry about that."

"All right," she said. "If you say so . . ." She did not close her eyes, but remained propped up against the headboard, following him with her wary, alert gaze.

He left, not even bothering to check his

appearance in the mirror. Then he was in the lobby, swiping his credit card before stepping outside to hail a taxi. It was only minutes past dawn, and the just-risen sun had turned the sky a pale, cloud-streaked gold. Copies of the *New York Times* lay neatly coiled in their blue plastic sleeves, sparrows twittered decorously in front of a still-shuttered café, and an elderly woman walked a small white dog on a red leash. Everything seemed hopeful, decent, civilized — everything except Jared himself, a man who'd actually forgotten about his own flesh and blood, a man who'd left his baby girl by herself all night long.

# NINETEEN

Jared told the cabdriver to hurry; he was meeting Supah at the pediatrician's on Ninety-sixth Street. Athena had told him that Lily would not stop hiccupping — or crying — and so Supah had thought it prudent to take her to the doctor. Jared burned to think that this woman whom he paid had shown more concern for his child than he had.

When the cab pulled up in front of the building, Jared fairly shoved a wad of bills at the driver and told him to keep the change. He gave the receptionist his name; he could swear he saw her eyebrows rise right up to meet her hairline. Jesus. He was in for it now.

Inside the office, a tight-lipped Supah was holding Lily; Athena had already left for the office. Good. He knew she was going to rake him over the coals for this, and he was grateful for the reprieve. As it was, he had to listen to the doctor, an older black man with a nimbus of white at the sides of his mostly bald head, berate him for his conduct. "I can see that apart from that *inexplicable* lapse last night, she's been very well cared for and, I hope, well loved, so I'm not going to report you to the authorities — *this* time. But if there's ever even a whiff of something like this happening again" — he lowered his already deep baritone — "you can kiss your little angel good-bye."

Jared took his daughter. He was ready to hand Lily over to Supah so he could make amends with his boss; Supah had a different agenda.

"Doctor, he be right. I can no work for you, Mr. Jared," she said. "Not anymore." Her look was both stern and contemptuous.

"Lily needs you," he said. Begged. "Please don't punish her for what I did."

He sensed her hesitating and so he quickly went on. "I know I was an idiot last night, and I swear, nothing like that will *ever* happen again. But she trusts you. She *needs* you; please don't leave her."

Supah looked away from Jared at Lily, and he could see her expression soften. "Okay, I stay." She reached out to take Lily's hands in her own. "For her. For Lily girl."

Once Jared had sent them back home, he walked slowly to the office. He needed to calm down — he was sweating and his head was throbbing — before he faced the avenging angel that was Athena. He also needed to get in touch with Olivia; at least ten of those text messages had been from her. Hurrying to his apartment, she'd tripped on a curb and broken her ankle; she'd been whisked off to the emergency room, where she'd been stuck for the next several hours. "I tried calling you, Mr. Masters," she said again and again when they finally made contact. "But I couldn't reach you." No, she couldn't because he'd been too busy screwing Isabel Clarke and getting wasted.

Athena was waiting for him when he came in; apparently, Supah had phoned her when she'd gotten to the apartment and been unable to reach Jared. She ushered him right into her office and closed the door with somewhat more force than he thought necessary; the sound made his head throb an extra beat. "You could have lost her over this," she said. "Child services could have taken her away."

"I know," said Jared. "And maybe they'd be right."

"I hate to say it, Jared, but maybe she would have been better off with that woman who found her. I know I encouraged you to step forward and claim her. But now I'm thinking that the stress of it is too much for you. I mean, who walks out of an apartment and leaves a baby alone for five minutes, let alone the *entire night*?"

"You think I don't know this?" he said angrily. "You think I haven't thought the same thing myself?"

"So what are you going to do now?"

"Mind my p's and q's, as my mama would have said. Straighten up. Fly right. Become a contender for the Dad of the Year award." The thing he did not say was, *Call Miranda Berenzweig.* He had not told Athena about her message, the one in which she said she wanted to see him and was hoping to see Lily too. Would he get back to her so that they could talk?

Jesus, what piss-poor timing. A month ago, he'd wanted to meet Miranda, wanted her to understand who he was and why he'd come forward; he wanted her not to hate him. He would have let her see Lily; why not? She cared about his daughter, had formed a bond with her. He'd meant to call her back right away, but he'd just gotten busy. Now he couldn't even think of returning the call. He was too ashamed. So he left the message on his phone; he could not bring himself to delete it, but he couldn't bring himself to answer it either. Instead, he waited until he was out on the street, headed to an appointment, and called Isabel Clarke — he had a bunch of unanswered messages from her too.

"Are you all right?" Isabel picked up after the first ring. "And what about your daughter? That was a total surprise, Jared. I had no idea."

"Can you meet me?" he said. "I'll tell you everything, but I don't want to go into it on the phone."

"Brandon's back," she said. "I have to be . . . discreet."

"So do I, baby," he said, thinking of what Athena would say — and do — if she found out he was involved with a married client. "So do I."

They met several days later, ostensibly to see a penthouse apartment at 125 Central Park North. It was a recently constructed building, so it had plenty of amenities, like a private roof terrace, fitness center, lap pool, indoor parking, and a temperature-controlled wine cellar. The asking price was a hefty $2.049 million, which Jared thought was going to make the apartment too rich for Brandon's blood. But he also knew the guy would be impressed by all the bells and whistles.

Isabel showed up to the apartment wearing big black sunglasses and a broad-brimmed black straw hat that obscured much of her face; was she intentionally trying to assume a disguise? But she appeared as eager to see him as he was to see her, and they had a quickie in the master bedroom, though not, at his insistence, on the bed.

"How will anyone ever know?" she had said. "I'll remake it when we're done."

Jared was too spooked though, and instead they used the floor, where the sisal matting did a serious number on his knees. When they said good-bye, he pressed several glossy, stapled sheets about the building and the apartment into her hands and insisted she show the material to Brandon. "I'm just covering all our tracks," he said. "Trust me, okay?" But even though he was single, and ostensibly had less at stake here, he was jumpy for the rest of the day. What the hell was he doing, taking up with her? Like there weren't plenty of bodacious, badass single women out there?

It was after six o'clock when Jared got home one Friday evening in the waning days of August. He could barely meet Supah's eyes when he paid her and told her to have a nice weekend. After that conversation on the street, she had never again upbraided him or mentioned what had happened. Still, she *knew.*

The door closed quietly behind her, and then he was alone with his baby daughter for what promised to be two very long, hot days. Isabel told him she would be away this weekend, and he knew Athena and Gabe were off to Sag Harbor. His other buddies were away too. No one stuck around this late in the month. No one, that is, except him.

Damn. How had his life come to this? He remembered the rush of recognition when he first saw the photograph of Lily; that heady moment had since morphed into an endless treadmill of diapers, laundry, and sleep deprivation. It wasn't that he didn't love her. Of course he did. But he didn't think he could keep doing this. At least not like this and not by himself. Lily was quiet, occupied by chewing on a teething ring in her crib. He reached for his phone to make the call; Miranda Berenzweig wanted to meet him? Well, he wanted to meet her too. And there was no time like the present.

The next night, Jared was bustling around

his apartment in preparation for Miranda's visit. She'd been so eager to see Lily that she would have come last night, when he called. But he wanted a chance to pull the place — and himself — together. Earlier in the day, he'd buckled Lily into her stroller and walked over to Fairway, where he'd managed to grab a few things he could serve for dinner before Lily got too fussy. Then he spent the next hour at a playground, pushing her back and forth in a baby swing, which at least tired her out enough so that she fell asleep on the way home and stayed asleep for a while once they got there. The respite gave Jared a chance to shower, change, and set the table.

But when Lily woke up, he saw that the diaper had leaked. Damn, what was wrong with those things? They sure cost enough. She needed both a bath and a change of clothes, and the crib sheet had to be stripped and dumped in the wash too. He managed the bath okay. He'd gotten better at it, though when he looked down he saw his own shirt was wet and he'd need to change — again. Plus he had to find something for Lily to wear. He wanted Miranda to think he was taking good care of her.

He pawed through the stash of little dresses and outfits; the ones he thought looked best were in the wash, and when he pulled something out of the pile and attempted to put it on her, he realized it was too small. She was outgrowing her clothes and he'd need to replace them. What the hell did babies wear, anyway? And where was he supposed to go to get this stuff? He remembered Bedelia's, but he also remembered the price tags on a couple of the things Athena had brought. Sixty bucks for a dress that wasn't even going to fit her in a couple of months? Ridiculous. Anyway, he couldn't deal with any of this now, so he found some pajamas with a pattern of kittens on them — good enough.

The buzzer rang precisely at six p.m., and in his haste to answer it, Jared nearly tripped on Lily's playpen. But he caught himself at the last minute and scooped Lily up. "Here she comes," he said to her; she was already starting to fuss. "Here we go."

# TWENTY

Miranda took the three flights of stairs to Jared Masters's apartment with ease.

Since she had lost Lily, she'd stepped up her routine of jogging the loop around Prospect Park, either very early before she went into the office or in the pastel-colored evenings when she got home.

Her phone buzzed while she was climbing. Evan. They had been missing each other for a couple of days, but she really couldn't talk now. She'd connect with him later. Miranda was nervous about her visit with Masters; would he really consider letting her become a part of Lily's life on a regular basis? So much depended on this meeting. He had to see her as responsible and kind but not overbearing or intrusive. And if he perceived her as a threat, he might withdraw entirely.

The door was open and he was standing there with Lily in his arms. "Glad you could come," he said, extending one hand for her to shake. "It's really good to meet you."

"Good to meet you too." Even her eagerness to see Celeste did not prevent Miranda from registering how handsome Jared Masters was. She had seen the picture of him that accompanied Geneva's second piece. But that had not prepared her for the real thing — tall but not overly so, lean and muscled, with smooth brown skin the color of coffee beans or the best dark chocolate, and an intense, probing gaze. And oh, the smile, with those brilliant, lit-from-within white teeth. She actually felt flustered. *Get a grip,* she told herself sternly. This wasn't a date. Though she had the sudden, irrational wish that it was.

Then Lily turned at the sound of her voice and began an almost synchronized series of arm and leg movements. The spell cast by Jared was broken, and Miranda reached for the baby. "Oh, she's grown so much! Can I hold her?"

"Of course." Jared handed her over. There was an awkward pause, and then he said, "So please, sit down. We'll eat, right? And get to know each other?"

"I'd like that," she said. "I know how strange this is. . . . But we both have a connection to her. Yours is by blood, mine by pure happenstance."

She joined him at the table, where the food had been set out. "Has Lily eaten?" Jared shook his head no, and Miranda slid her into the high chair. "I could feed her if you want. Give you a little break."

"Sure. If you want." He spooned some pureed beef and sweet potato into a dish and warmed the food in the microwave. Lily opened her mouth wide for every spoonful, and when the food didn't seem to come fast enough, she lightly pounded her fists on the high chair's tray.

"No wonder she's been growing," Miranda said. "Look at her eat!" Her own food — some indifferently prepared chicken dish, bland vegetables — was not terribly interesting, and she ate only enough to be polite. She was much more interested in giving Lily her bottle, changing her diaper, and putting her to sleep, all of which Jared allowed with what seemed like relief.

While Miranda was in Lily's pink-and-white room, she could hear him clearing the table and loading the dishwasher. Finally, she went back into the living room, leaving Lily's door ajar. "I think she's down for a while," she said. "But I wanted to leave the door open just in case."

"Care for some more wine?" Jared said.

He'd poured from a bottle of white with dinner, but Miranda had not even finished her glass.

"That would be very nice. Thank you." She accepted the goblet and sat down on the couch. Not too near him though. Her own animal reaction to him was making her uncomfortable.

He sat down too and started playing with the stem of his goblet.

"I'm grateful that you agreed to let me come here." Miranda watched his fingers move up and down the glass stem; maybe he was as uncomfortable as she was, though she assumed the reasons were different.

"You know I offered to meet you early on," he quickly interjected. "But I get why you didn't want to."

"I was afraid," she said. "I couldn't even deal with the possibility that you might take her from me. And then when you did —"

Jared looked into the wine goblet. "I can imagine," he murmured.

"It was pretty terrible in the beginning — when she first left. But then a friend pointed out that I was mourning her even though she wasn't dead. That's when I began to think — to hope, I mean — that there might be some way I could be in her life. Not as her parent, of course." She stopped for a sip of wine and then another. "Or even as family. But as something. Because something really would be better than nothing at all."

"I don't see why we can't come to some arrangement about that," he said. "Maybe she could even spend the night with you sometimes. . . ."

"Really?" Did he mean it? That would be so wonderful.

"Yeah. Sure. Why not?" He took a sip of his wine. "And I haven't even thanked you yet." She must have looked puzzled, so he went on. "For finding her. For taking such good, good care of her."

"Finding her was the most extraordinary thing that's ever happened to me," said Miranda. "Think of it. In the course of your life, you might find money or jewelry or even a dog or a cat. But a baby? A newborn? What are the odds of that?"

"Not too likely," he agreed.

"Can I ask you something?"

"Shoot."

"You really didn't know anything about her? You had no idea you had a child?"

"None," he said.

"I was told that her mother was . . . unstable." The lawyer's warning had no weight, but she still wanted to be diplomatic.

"That," said Jared, "would be a serious

understatement. I loved Carrie, but I couldn't take it anymore. We parted on bad terms — really bad. I stopped hearing from her, and to be perfectly honest, I was relieved."

"So you didn't even suspect? Not a clue? Not a hint?"

Jared hesitated. "The last time I saw her, she told me she was pregnant. But I didn't believe her."

"Oh," said Miranda. "I see." The guilt he must have felt when he found out Caroline was telling the truth. And the shame.

"I know it sounds really shitty of me. But she had lied to me so many times. She said she had AIDS. Also cancer. And that she was going blind. So when she played the pregnant card, I thought it was just another ploy."

"How tragic," she said. "For her. For you. And for Lily."

He poured himself another glass of wine and refreshed Miranda's. "I was the one to identify her at the morgue. I don't know if she had family or where to even look for them. She never spoke about it, not even when I asked. When I found out that she might have given birth, I just assumed the baby had drowned with her. I didn't make the connection until I saw Geneva's piece."

Geneva. Miranda stiffened at the mention of the name. "Have you been in touch with her? Since then?"

"A couple of times, yeah. She said she wanted to keep tabs on us; she even mentioned doing some kind of follow-up."

Miranda thought about that. "Did you say yes?"

"Not in so many words," said Jared. "But I didn't say no. I mean, how could it hurt?"

Miranda debated whether she should tell him what she now knew about Geneva. Then she wondered whether he already *knew* — a very upsetting thought.

But if he didn't know, she wasn't ready to share it. At least not yet.

Jared refilled his glass and then leaned over to refill hers too. Miranda raised a hand in a gesture that said, *stop.* She was feeling a little tipsy but not that tipsy. She knew it was time to go. If she stayed, she might say — or even do — more than she wanted to. "That's enough for me. I'm going to be heading back now."

"How are you getting home?" he asked.

"Subway."

"Take a cab," he said, reaching for his wallet. "I insist." He handed her two twenties.

Miranda looked down at the bills and then up into his face. "It's not necessary."

"Yes, it is. Please, just take it."

Should she? Finally, she took the bills and tucked them into her wallet. Then she stood and smoothed down the front of her skirt. It was an innocent enough gesture; the skirt was wrinkled and sticking to the fronts of her thighs. But she was suddenly aware that he was watching her, and the air now seemed charged with unexpressed longing. Hers? His? She felt her cheeks go very hot. He stood too, and when she gave him a quick good-bye kiss, she wished that he would turn his face and she'd be kissing his lips instead. Oh, but it was really time to get out of here. "Thank you," she said. "For everything." And then, after a last peek into Lily's room, she left.

As she sat in the taxi heading home, Miranda thought about Jared. She had never thought he was a villain, but she had not expected their meeting to stir such a welter of emotions in her either: tenderness, sympathy, and, yes, desire. She believed him about Geneva; he had not known about her connection to Lily. Did he feel attracted to her? It had certainly seemed that way, especially when she got up to leave; she knew what that kind of look meant. Was this just about the most improbable wrinkle in an already highly improbable story? Adoptive mother meets biological father and falls madly in lust. . . . What if they actually got together? *What if?* They could be a family, the three of them — Jared, Lily, and Miranda. Wouldn't that be perfect? She allowed herself to linger on this fantasy; how could it hurt?

The cab stopped at a red light, and Miranda looked out the window in surprise. They were in Brooklyn already; she'd be home in a few minutes. She continued to think about Jared as she paid the fare, climbed the stairs to her apartment, and began getting ready for bed. It was only when the lights were out and she was falling sleep that she realized she'd been so preoccupied by her fantasies that she had not called Evan back.

# TWENTY-ONE

Miranda was still in bed when Courtney called. "What are you doing here?" she asked. "I thought you and Harris were going to Southhampton."

"We were. But there was a crisis at the office and he couldn't get away. Just as well; gives me time to do a little wedding shopping. Come with?"

"That depends." Miranda was grateful that her rough patch with Courtney seemed to have been smoothed over; she had even agreed to be one of the bridesmaids at the November wedding. But did she really want to spend the day at some massive bridal chain store, fighting her way through the trains, bustles, and veils? She did not. "Where are you going?"

"NoLIta," Courtney said. "Elizabeth Street, to be exact."

"What bridal shops are down there?"

"It's not a bridal shop. Her name is

Solange Repassier, and she does custom work — some bridal but other things too. Very understated, very chic. I think you would approve. And then we can get lunch down there. You can tell me all about seeing the baby. Please say yes."

Miranda hesitated. The sheets were smooth, the pillow soft. The late-summer sun dappled the parquet floor. She had been savoring last night's visit with Celeste — Lily — and replaying certain details in her mind. It had been such a sweet reunion. And if she handled things well, it could become a regular occurrence.

But she supposed it was time to get up. "All right," she said, warming to Courtney's idea. "It sounds like a plan." Somewhere in the back of her mind she remembered that she'd made tentative arrangements with Evan. He'd want to know about her meeting with Masters, and she wasn't sure she'd be able to lie. Better to put him off — at least temporarily.

The shop on Elizabeth Street was exactly as Courtney had described it. Not a bolt of lace in the place. No sequins or rhinestones or ruffles either. Instead, Courtney was able to consider a fitted strapless number with a skirt that belled out at the ankles, or another with a high waist, square neckline, and the simplest of lines; its only embellishment was the gleaming satin bow in the back. Miranda perched on a tiny gold chair and was offered a glass of prosecco and chocolate-dipped strawberries as she watched Courtney model the dresses. She was surprised — pleasantly — by the direction the wedding was heading, especially when Courtney said they had scaled the guest list way back. "We don't want it to feel like a mob scene," she said. "Harris and I both want something more intimate." *Score one for Harris,* thought Miranda as she nibbled on a strawberry. And the choice of venue truly shocked her: the Brooklyn Botanic Garden.

"Are you kidding me?" she said. "I thought you considered Brooklyn strictly second-rate."

"I never said that." Courtney was studying her reflection in the mirror. She had narrowed down the choices to two and was weighing their respective merits. "Anyway, it looks like the perfect place to have a wedding. The trees should just be turning color then; the Japanese maples will be scarlet."

"I'm aware of that," Miranda said. "I've seen them a few times."

Courtney was too caught up for the sarcasm to penetrate. A saleswoman appeared at Miranda's side to refill her wineglass.

"Perhaps you are in the wedding party? And would like to see a dress too?" She had a discernible French accent.

"Oh, that's such a good idea!" Courtney turned away from the mirror. "Why don't you try something on?"

"All right." Miranda set down the wine and stood up. She liked this place already, and when she began to try on the dresses — a sheath in burnt orange watered silk or moss green brocade, a scoop-necked dress with tiny accordion pleats all around — she liked it even better. These were bridesmaids dresses that went beyond the wedding day; she could imagine wearing any of them again.

Courtney decided to sleep on her choices, and they both thought Bea and Lauren should be there before any of the bridesmaids' dresses were selected. But it was altogether a satisfying outing, and Miranda was glad she'd come along.

The Butcher's Daughter, where they went for lunch, was almost empty, and Miranda gratefully sank into a seat at the scarred farmhouse table. Wine in the middle of the day was a sure way to get tipsy fast. She needed to eat and was glad when the waitress took their order right away.

"So now that we're sitting down, you can

tell me everything. Did you see her?" Courtney asked.

"I did; Jared Masters invited me for dinner last night. I got to hold her, feed her, and put her to sleep. It was hard." She paused for a drink of water. "But not as hard as I thought it would be. And you were right. It's better to have a little of her than none at all."

"What's he like?" Courtney had ordered a green juice made with algae, and she was sipping the vividly colored elixir through a straw.

"Nice. Kind of nervous." Miranda was careful at first. But she couldn't keep it in. "Also, one of the sexiest men I've ever laid eyes on."

"Where is that coming from? What about Evan?"

"Evan is a great guy and he'd be a wonderful father. He was so interested in Celeste — I mean Lily — right from the start."

"So where does Jared Masters fit in?"

"He doesn't. I just wasn't expecting him to be so good-looking. And he's also kind of modest and unassuming, like he's not entirely aware of how attractive he is. Which, of course, only makes him more attractive."

"Nothing happened, did it? Because if it did, that would be about the stupidest thing you ever did."

"No, of course not." Miranda remembered wishing Jared had kissed her. But he hadn't.

"Good!" A long pull on the straw and she had finished the drink. "So what did you talk about?"

"He told me about Lily's mother. She was a very troubled woman."

"Well, that's an understatement. She left her newborn baby in a subway station. I'd say nuts was more like it."

"He said that too, actually. Though not in those exact words."

The food arrived, and Miranda dug into her kale salad. This was a good, unpretentious little place; maybe she would suggest a small mention in the magazine.

"Do you think he'll let you see her again? Do you want to?"

"Yes and yes." Miranda looked around for the waitress. "Do you think I could get some balsamic vinegar?" she asked when the woman appeared at the table. Then she looked back at Courtney. "You haven't asked any more about Evan."

"All right. I'm asking now."

"I like him. I really do. He's incredibly sweet. Fun to be with. Supportive too."

"It sounds like there's a *but* ready to swing around the corner." Courtney devoured her melted cheese sandwich; bits of warm, gooey cheddar had oozed out the sides and onto her plate. She had one of those enviable metabolisms; even after a meal like this, she'd have no trouble fitting into her size-four wedding gown.

"Not really . . ." Miranda was hedging.

"Yes, really. I can tell. What is it? The sex? You're still comparing him to Luke-who-left-you-*and*-stole-your-money?"

"That's not it." At least about this Miranda was being truthful. She really had not been thinking about Luke or comparing Evan to him. If she did, Evan would come out way ahead. And it wasn't like she didn't enjoy the sex they had. "Maybe it's because I've never yearned for him. He's always been right there. And maybe, just maybe, there's something just the tiniest bit dull about that."

"So you're saying you preferred the seesaw of Luke."

"I didn't say that. I'm just commenting."

"Men like Luke are not worth your emotional investment. While Evan, well, he sounds like a keeper." Courtney had finished her sandwich and was now eating the jicama and apple slaw that had come with it.

"Oh, he is," she quickly agreed. So why

was the thought of kissing Jared Masters still buzzing, like a gnat, around the periphery of her brain?

Miranda did not get home until close to four o'clock, and when she checked her phone, she saw that Evan had texted her. Twice. Poked by guilt, she texted him back immediately. *I want to tell you about seeing Celeste/Lily. Come over for dinner and we'll talk.* Dinner meant staying the night; she hoped she could summon an enthusiastic enough response. She was willing to tell Courtney about her reaction to Jared, but she did not want to tell Evan. After all, what she thought and felt was her own business. A harmless fantasy. She was an adult, after all; she could control herself.

To compensate, Miranda went completely overboard with dinner. She grilled artichokes, made a salad of cold lobster meat, corn, and grape tomatoes, the small yellow and red flecks vibrant on their bed of greens. For dessert she baked a blueberry cobbler whose burst berries turned a dark and luscious purple that bubbled over the crust; she topped it with a silky crème anglaise speckled with the tiniest bits of pulverized vanilla bean.

Just when she was putting the finishing touches on the meal, she had a text from

Evan. *Just got word about a freelance job shooting a band in Williamsburg. Have to cancel tonight. Rain check?*

*Of course,* she texted back. *No worries.*

That she felt a flood of relief when she'd sent it was nobody's business but her own.

# TWENTY-TWO

It was late on the Thursday afternoon before Labor Day and the city had already begun its ritual emptying out. Traffic was light into Brooklyn, and Jared was able to find a spot practically in front of Miranda's house. He eased the car into the space before putting it in park and turning off the ignition. "We're here," he said to Lily, who was strapped into her car seat in the back. "Time to go and see Miranda." Unbuckling her from the seat, he wondered whether Lily would have any memory of this place; for the first several months of her life, it had been her home. But then he decided babies didn't remember stuff like that.

With a backpack over his shoulders, Lily in one arm, and a bag of her stuff in the other, he practically bounded up the stairs. He'd stay for a little while; he didn't want to seem rude. But then he'd be free, free as a bird. He was going to leave Lily with

Miranda for the weekend, while he headed out to Southampton, to stay at the house of Tripp Parris, an old buddy from his Haverford days. Tripp was going to be away, but he'd been happy to let Jared have the place for the weekend. "All I ask is that you keep it on the tame side," he'd said. "I remember what a party animal you were."

"Those days are long gone. I promise: no crowds," Jared said. "Just an intimate little dinner — or maybe drinks." But just how intimate was not something Jared thought he needed to share. Isabel Clarke was going to be in Southampton for the weekend. True, asshole Brandon would be there too, but they had already figured out a way around that inconvenient little fact. Isabel had scheduled a ninety-minute massage in town so there would be ninety sweet minutes alone in Tripp's well-appointed house, ninety minutes in which she could turn off her phone and not answer to anyone. The beauty of this plan was unassailable, and Jared congratulated himself mightily for coming up with it. Damn, he was good.

When Jared reached the landing, Miranda was standing at the open door to greet him. Her smile was both generous and tremulous at the same time; maybe that was what got to him.

"Who's my baby girl?" She reached for Lily.

"Thanks so much for doing this." He followed Miranda into the apartment and looked around. Not huge, but well laid out. Good light. Nice floors, lots of original details. He'd bet the landlady — it was always a landlady — lived downstairs and was either Italian or Irish. He knew the type — lived in the house for decades, maybe even born here. Stayed on after the kids had grown and the husband had died. Took great pride in the house: vacuumed the hallways, swept the stoop and even the sidewalk, taking the falling of the leaves every autumn as a personal affront.

"Look what I got for you," she said, slipping Lily into a bright blue plastic ring that was suspended from a doorframe. Inside the ring he saw a cloth seat and two holes to accommodate her legs. Her toes, in their pink socks, grazed the floor until she realized she could press off with the soles of her feet and set the thing bouncing. The sound of her laughter — resonant and surprisingly low — filled the room; Jared exchanged a smile with Miranda.

"It's called the Jolly Jumper," she explained. "The salesman at Toys 'R' Us said she would love it."

"Guess he was right." Jared watched as Lily bounced and chortled, chortled and bounced. Why hadn't he thought to buy her something like this?

"Do you want a drink of something before you go? I've got iced tea, but I could make lemonade too; I have lemons."

Jared glanced at his watch. She wasn't going to offer him booze, not when he was about to get on the road. But lemonade would be nice. He followed her into the kitchen, where she used a small handpress to squeeze the lemons. After a few deft movements, she had handed him the fresh, sweet-tart drink, which he sipped from a frosted glass she had pulled from the freezer.

"Damn good lemonade." He drained the glass and set it down on the counter.

"I could make you another one."

"Not necessary —"

"It's no trouble; here, I'll just refill your glass."

Jared drank the second glass more slowly and decided to stay while Miranda fed and bathed Lily. And then, once Lily was asleep in her crib, for the pizza topped with duck, fig, and goat cheese that Miranda was making for her own supper. He might even make better time if he went later.

"This is so good." He reached for another slice.

"Thanks. It's a recipe I'm considering for the magazine."

Jared nodded; his mouth was too full to reply. But he noticed her expression had changed and she now looked troubled. Anxious even.

"There's something I have to say to you." She was not eating.

He swallowed and then stopped eating too. "What?" he said. "Is something wrong?" For a few brief, crazy seconds, he decided that she had somehow found out about the night he had left Lily alone. The shame-soaked memory was not something he wanted to revisit; was she going to report him to Child Services?

"How well do you know Geneva Bales?"

"Geneva?" He was not expecting this. "I don't know. Not that well, I guess. She did that article, and then she called me a couple of times. Why?"

"Did it seem to you that she had a particular interest in Lily? An unusual, maybe even inappropriate interest?"

"I don't know what you're getting at."

"I'll show you." She got up from the table, and Jared could hear her opening and closing a drawer in the other room. She reappeared with a sheaf of papers, and without saying a word, placed them next to Jared's plate. On top was what looked like a wedding picture. Something about that slight, waiflike blonde looked familiar. Jesus — it was Carrie! He'd never seen her with her hair so long. Then he looked at the bride in the center. Geneva Highsmith Bales.

Jared put aside the photo and began to skim the material he'd been handed. When he was done, he looked up at Miranda. "Geneva is related to Carrie? And to Lily?"

"Sister." The word sounded strangled. "Aunt."

"Jesus." Jared put the papers down. His half-eaten slice of pizza remained on the plate; his appetite had vaporized. "Did she know?" Miranda shrugged. "And if she did, why? Why did she do this? It's so — perverse."

"Try manipulative. Or cruel?"

"It doesn't make sense." Jared looked down at the papers he still held; when he looked up, Miranda's cheeks were pale and her eyes had filled with tears.

"Hey." He got up and went over to put an arm around her. "It's all right. Really, it is." He had no idea what he was saying. What was all right? Lily? Miranda? But he felt the need to offer comfort. She turned her face and, still weeping, pressed it into his shirt; when he felt her shoulders shake slightly, it seemed like the most natural thing in the world for him to put the other arm around her too.

Holding her was so different; she was much fuller than the women who usually appealed to him. But the feeling of her breasts against his chest was arousing, and the way she smelled — of something sweet, something fruity — was arousing too. Her shoulders stopped trembling, and he thought her crying had tapered off. He tipped a finger under her chin to find out, and when she raised her face to look at him, he kissed her.

Jesus. Where had that come from? But she kissed him back, softly at first, and then with greater urgency. He moved his hands up to touch her hair. A sound from the other room made him freeze — Lily. "I'll go." She extricated herself from the embrace.

Standing by the window with Lily in her arms, Miranda tried to calm down. So she had been right: he felt something for her too. What was it, though? Just because she had been imagining that their coupling could result in a new configuration — mommy, daughter, baby daddy — didn't mean he was too. Maybe his desire was more specific — and more short-term. Yes, they wanted to sleep with each other. That was evident. But then what?

She didn't want a one-night stand with Jared, yet she couldn't imagine how it would play out between them if she gave in to her lust. Would it make seeing Lily easier — or awkward? And what about Evan? Was she ready to end it with him? Because that was exactly what she'd have to do. It was all so complicated. Maybe it would be better to walk back in there, finish the conversation about Geneva, and then tell him good night.

She sat down in the rocker. Gradually, the baby's whimpers dwindled and soon she was asleep again. Miranda's own heartbeat slowed, but when she saw Jared standing in the open doorway, it started to accelerate again. He said nothing but waited until Miranda set Lily down in the crib, and then they both went into the other room. He sat back down on the sofa. She remained standing.

"How did you find out about Geneva and Carrie?" he asked.

"I didn't." She sat down on the sofa too, but at its far end. "It was Evan. My boyfriend. He did a lot of research online and this was what he came up with." Her use of the word *boyfriend* was intentional.

"I still am not getting it. Did she know Lily was her niece?"

"I have no idea," she said. "But I feel so confused. Used, even." She was equally confused by her feelings for Jared. Sitting in the other room with Lily, it had seemed very clear what she needed to do. But now she felt herself drawn to him all over again.

Miranda leaned her head back against the couch and closed her eyes. Then, sensing that he had moved closer, she opened them again. He was looking at her with such a frank mixture of curiosity, surprise, and yes, desire. He wanted her too; it was that simple. He kissed her, and her mouth opened of its own accord. This was *stupid;* this was *wrong;* this would lead to nothing but trouble, and yet she let the kissing — heated, delicious — go on for several minutes. And when he moved his mouth down her throat and began to nibble, she allowed that to happen too. Tentatively, she touched his hair; it felt so soft and spongy under her fingers. It was only when he changed the pressure and the nibbling turned to a little nip that she shot up and away from him; her elbow inadvertently struck him in the eye.

"Oh God, did I hurt you?"

"No. I'm okay." He was cradling the upper part of his face with his hands.

"Let me get you some ice." Miranda fled to the kitchen and returned with several ice cubes wrapped in a clean dish towel.

He took the towel and pressed it to his eye. "Sorry if I misread the signals."

"You didn't misread them at all." She began to coil her long dark hair into a knot at the nape of her neck. "I find you unbelievably . . . attractive. But how could it ever work between us?" She shook her head, and the knot of hair loosened. "You'd better go. Now. Before we both regret that you came here."

"You're right." He handed her the damp towel and started looking for his backpack.

"Are you sure your eye is okay? You'll be able to drive?"

"I'm fine." He hoisted the backpack over his shoulders. "I'll call you when I get there. And I'll check in with you about Lily, okay?" He was at the door now. "Have a good weekend."

"You too." She did not get near enough for a kiss or even a hug, but waited, tensed, until she heard the front door of the house open and then close. Then Miranda walked into Lily's room and looked at the sleeping baby. Lily lay on her back, arms and legs spread wide, chest rising and falling peacefully. She needed adults who could — and would — take care of her. Not a pair of hormonally addled, overgrown teenagers succumbing to their lust. Still she stood there, letting herself mourn for the moment that she had pushed rudely away instead of grabbing with both hands. For the second time that night, the tears welled up in her eyes — and then spilled.

# TWENTY-THREE

Main Street in Southampton was hopping. Jared edged his way through the bustle, occasionally stopping to say hello to a client, an acquaintance, or an old school friend. Look — there was a woman he and Carrie had partied with way back when; he turned his face, hoping she wouldn't see him. He didn't want to be reminded of those crazy-ass nights and didn't want her to ask, *What ever happened to . . . ?* and have to spill the whole sorry tale. Or be forced to lie. God, sometimes this town was just too damn small.

He took a left and headed through the doors of Tutto il Giorno, one of his favorite hangouts. The manager remembered him, and even though he didn't have a reservation, she found him a decent table not *too* near the kitchen. He hadn't eaten much today and now he was *starved.* A menu appeared quickly, along with someone to take his drink order — he asked for a gin and tonic — and a basket of bread. He tore off a hunk and slathered it in butter and when it was gone, he tore off another.

The scene out here, especially on Labor Day weekend, was intense. Jared could do without the hordes, but he did like the stargazing. He saw Alec Baldwin holding court at one table, and was that Martha Stewart, looking seriously uptight, at another? He also spotted the usual assortment of anonymous stunners: impossibly young, impossibly beautiful models, pretty boys, and hangers-on.

Jared looked away and down at the menu; everything here was good, and he gave his order — the burrata, rigatoni, and braised asparagus — to the waiter without hesitating. Then he scanned the room again. Isabel had texted him to say that she and Brandon might be here for dinner, and though he had not spotted them when he walked in, he could see them now, wedged into a table for six with two couples he didn't recognize. He didn't want Brandon to see him, but he relished the idea of texting Isabel about their upcoming tryst with her husband sitting right by her side.

*Can't wait 4 tomorrow. What time is ur massage?*

Her response was a bummer:

*Road block. Brandon is going w/me. He arranged 4 a couples massage. Had to lie like mad; said that the original reservation was "lost."*

He tapped back, *What 2 do?*

*Hang on. Will find a way.*

He put the phone down. Damn. He'd gone through a lot of trouble — and expense — to arrange this weekend, and so far, it was not going well. Jared looked up as the waiter set down the creamy ball of the burrata, shining with oil and flecked with basil. He took a bite and was mollified — delicious. Then he flashed to Miranda. What a seriously stupid-ass move on his part. Last night, the idea of sleeping with her had seemed exciting, different, the crossing of some forbidden and tantalizing line. Today it seemed like nothing but trouble. He was relieved that she had pushed him away. At least one of them had been thinking clearly. He lifted his glass in a silent toast to her.

The burrata, once consumed, paved the way for the rigatoni with the spicy sausage and the crisp stalks of asparagus. Jared ate until he was sated and washed the meal down with a very good red wine. Across the room, Isabel threw back her head and laughed; Brandon put an arm casually around her shoulders and she leaned easily into the embrace. Transfixed, Jared watched while Brandon's hand moved lightly along Isabel's spine, touching the same delicate bones that he himself had touched.

Suddenly, his life seemed disgusting to him: sordid, small, pathetic. Here he was, alone in a sea of wealthy, white faces, congratulating himself for being the black dude slipping it to the wife of a white guy. But Brandon, cuckold that he was (and that was a good word, plucked from a Shakespeare seminar a hundred years ago, in college), was still Isabel's husband. He had a place, a claim, and a role. Whereas Jared had just about nothing. Just then, his phone pinged: a text from Isabel. *Meet me by the ladies' room door. Now.*

He didn't have to be asked again. She was already there by the time he made his way to the back of the crowded restaurant, and to his surprise, she yanked him inside the bathroom — it was a single, not multiple stalls — and shot the bolt home.

"You're nuts," he said, but he was excited. He *liked* his women a little nuts.

Instead of answering, she reached up and kissed him fiercely. He could taste the wine on her breath, and the feel of her perfect, braless breasts against his chest made him instantly hard. Why had he thought his life was pathetic? His life was *great*. She was so hot; *he* was hot. "When can you come over?" he said when she finally moved away.

"Late tomorrow afternoon," she said. "I'll tell him I'm meeting a girlfriend for a drink. He'll be so blissed out from the massage, he'll just want to go home and sleep."

"Okay," he said, nuzzling her tanned neck with its skein of thin, gold chains. "I'll be waiting."

The next morning, Jared peered into the nearly empty fridge. Clearly Tripp was no more interested in cooking than he was: Jared found an open bottle of white, jars that contained the desiccated remains of several imported mustards, and in the crisper, a dish of blueberries covered in so much white mold they looked like they'd been left out in the snow. He tossed them and headed over to the Golden Pear for breakfast; it was early, so he was not likely to run into anyone he knew. Wrong.

As soon as he sat down, Athena sailed into the restaurant with Gabe at her side. Of course he had to invite them to join him, and the solo meal he'd anticipated, with the paper, his phone, and fantasies of Isabel, was spoiled.

"I didn't know you'd be out here." Athena

settled herself in a chair and began checking out the menu. Gabe sat next to her, and after clasping Jared's hand in a hearty shake, his fingers sought Athena's and remained entwined with them.

"It was kind of last minute. I'm staying at my friend Tripp's; he's got a three bedroom that was just sitting empty." He looked at the menu too; he already knew what he wanted, but it was better than meeting her eyes. "And how come you're over in these parts? Isn't there a Golden Pear in Sag Harbor?"

"There is, but we like this one better." She gave Gabe's fingers a playful squeeze and he squeezed back. Clearly they were enjoying some kind of inside joke that he was not privy to.

Jared said nothing but continued to study the menu. Maybe he'd forgo the eggs and opt for oatmeal instead. Or maybe he'd just skip eating here altogether; he'd kind of lost his appetite. But Athena was still his boss and he didn't want to seem rude, so when the waitress came, he ordered the eggs; fortunately, the food came quickly.

"Where's Lily?" Athena asked between mouthfuls of French toast.

"Back in Brooklyn with Miranda Berenzweig." Jared remained hunkered over his eggs.

"Really? Why didn't you bring her out here with you?"

"I just wanted to relax and get away from everything." A stupid reply; the last two weeks in the office had been slow as shit and she knew it.

"Didn't you say the place has three bedrooms? You could have brought Lily *and* Miranda."

"Bring Miranda? Why would I do that? It's not like I'm dating her or anything." There was no way Athena could have known about the other night with Miranda, but he was feeling a little paranoid.

"No one said you were." Gabe buttered his bagel. "Athena was just making conversation."

Jared took a breath and then another. *Don't get riled,* he chided himself. *Don't.* "Yeah, I guess I could have done that. But I wasn't sure what my plans were, and honestly, I needed some time alone."

"Being a single dad isn't easy," said Athena.

"No, it isn't," he said gratefully. "It's been really tough, in fact."

"Let us know if we can help," said Gabe. "We could babysit." He turned to Athena.

"It would be fun, right?"

"It sure would." Athena polished off the last bit of French toast on her plate and then set down the fork; she always had been a fast eater.

"I may take you up on that." Jared looked around for the waitress, and when she appeared with the check, he took it before Athena or Gabe had a chance. "My treat," he insisted when Gabe suggested they split it. He had to leave them on a good note, a high note, and this seemed the easiest way.

After he'd begged off going to the beach and said good-bye to Athena and Gabe, Jared went back to Tripp's. The house was spacious enough to accommodate Lily and Miranda, but he was *not* having that; no way. Besides, the whole point of this visit was to hook up with Isabel. He checked his watch. It was only ten thirty; the day stretched long and lonely ahead of him.

But hey, that was no way to feel. Even if he wasn't keen on heading into town or the beach, there was plenty he could do here. Laps in the pool for instance. An hour with a tautly written thriller Tripp had left in one of the guestrooms and another on HuffPost.

Around noon, he picked up a sandwich in town and brought it back to the house so he could eat by the pool. It was nice out here — flagstone patio, red flowers in clay pots, green canvas umbrella shading the table. Tripp was in real estate too, though on the commercial end of things. He must be doing well to support this house. Jared had to wonder why he wasn't here this weekend; he was usually a fixture on the scene.

After he'd eaten, Jared had a nap, took a shower, and got dressed. He was about to pour himself a drink — Tripp kept the bar well stocked — when he heard the sound of a car pulling up outside. He walked away from the sound, into the kitchen. After a minute or so, there was a knock at the back door. "Well, hello." He pulled her inside and into his embrace.

"Hi, hi, hi," she said, kissing him, kicking off her very high-heeled sandals and running her hands through her hair — all at the same time. "I can't tell you what I had to do to get here."

"Brandon boy didn't want a postmassage snooze?" His hands roamed her body, encased in tight white jeans and a formfitting white top that had red stripes running across it.

"Oh, he wanted to go to bed all right — with me!" She stepped away from him and yanked the shirt off, tossing it to the floor;

337

it was almost immediately joined by her jeans. Underneath, she was stunningly, gorgeously naked. "I managed to put him off, but I don't have a lot of time."

"You mean after you leave me, you're going to screw him?" Jared was not sure if this thought excited or repelled him.

"When I'm with him, I might as well be asleep. That's how much I care about it." She was hurriedly unbuttoning his shirt, his shorts.

"And with me?" He was fishing, but he wanted to hear her say it.

"With you," she breathed close to his face, "I'm one thousand percent awake. Awake and *alive.*"

After that, they stopped talking and got to it: fast, furious, fantastic. When they were done, he collapsed alongside her, breathing hard. Her hair had gotten sweaty and was sticking in places to the sides of her face.

"You want a shower? Or a swim?" That pool was mighty inviting just about now.

"Mmm, that would be nice. But I don't have the time." She stood and began rooting around for her pants.

"How about tomorrow?" He sat up too and reached for his shorts. Since he planned to take another swim after she left, he didn't bother with his shirt.

"If I can," she said. "Brandon's making noises about some nature walk he wants to take in the morning. *Quel* snore."

"Text me." Jared stood and stretched. He felt better — about her, about himself, about everything. He was on his way into the kitchen for that drink — a vodka and something would hit the spot — when the front doorbell rang, loud and imperious.

"Did you invite someone else over?" said Isabel nervously. She was dressed and buckling one of the sandals.

"No," he said. "Maybe it's a neighbor. Or my boss, Athena. She's out here this weekend, and I told her where I was staying."

"Don't answer it," she said in a tight voice. "I'll just wait a few minutes and then go out the back."

"Okay," he said. "Good to play it safe."

The knocking continued and grew more insistent. "It's Brandon," she whispered. "I know it is."

"How did he know where you were?" He was whispering too.

"I guess he followed me. Jared, what am I going to do?"

Before he could answer, the knocking turned to pounding. "Isabel!" That was definitely Brandon's voice coming from the other side of the door. "Isabel, I know you're in there, so open up!"

"Hide!" she hissed at him. "Now!"

Jared looked at her; she was terrified and cowering. This was all *his* fault; he'd put her in this position. The self-disgust he'd felt at the restaurant last night came roaring back, shrieking and honking in his own ears; he seemed to hear it in concert with Brandon's shouts.

He didn't answer, but just walked quietly toward the pounding. Taking up with Isabel Clarke had not been a good idea, but he was deep in it now and he'd have to deal with the consequences. And maybe it was better this way — Isabel would have to make a choice: stay with her husband or leave him. No more hiding. That was over.

"Hey, Brandon," he said when he'd opened the door. "Maybe you should come in so we can talk about this."

"You!" Brandon spat. "I can't believe it. You're in here, screwing my wife no doubt, and you want to talk? What planet are you from? Do you really think I have anything to say to you?"

"Jared's right, Brandon. We really should talk. And he's part of the conversation."

"You're an idiot. You left our fucking car out front, Isabel. Parked right in front of the house. Did you *want* me to find you?"

"Maybe I did," she said tiredly. "Maybe I did."

"I don't think Isabel's been happy for a long time," Jared said. "That's why she got involved with me."

"What do you know about her, real-estate boy? What gives you the right to weigh in on whether my wife is happy or not?" He'd been pacing the room, ricocheting from window to door and back again, but he stopped to face Jared.

Something inside Jared went cold and glinting. He knew that tone all too well — he'd heard it at Saint Crispin's and later at Haverford. The tone let him know that the liberal we're-all-the-same, race-doesn't-matter mask had slipped, and underneath, the true face was revealed. That face and that tone were united in their derision: *No matter how many of our schools you attend, how many A's you get, or how many of our girls you bang, you'll never be one of us. Never.* "She wasn't happy in your bed, man. Not by a long shot." And he kind of smirked as he said it.

The punch, when it landed, took him totally by surprise. He'd been so smug, so damn pleased with himself for answering that white-guy sneer in kind, for *telling it like it is,* that he didn't even see Brandon's fist coil or his arm draw back. All he knew was the blow that exploded in his jaw, splitting his lip and sending waves of pain radiating through his head.

"Oh my God, you hit him! He's bleeding. He's bleeding!" Isabel rushed to his side.

"He's all right," Brandon said. "It's just his lip." But he didn't sound so sure.

"How do you know? Call nine-one-one. No — I will." She dove for her bag and began digging for the phone that was buried in it.

"Don't." Jared put his hand to his lip, which was dripping blood and starting to swell. And his head hurt like a bitch. But no teeth were loose, and he'd been in enough fights as a kid to know the damage here was minimal. He turned to Isabel. "I'm okay. Really. Why don't you go with Brandon? I don't think anyone feels like talking right now. I know I don't."

"Are you sure? I don't want to leave you." She was hovering anxiously, her small hands fluttering in front of her.

"I'm sure." He'd fished a handkerchief out of his pocket and used it to stanch the flow. Then he waited stoically while the two of them went to the door and quietly left. When he was alone, he went into the bathroom to survey the damage. The lip — fat, busted — looked like hell but would heal quickly. He went to the kitchen for ice to press against it and also to make that drink. After he'd finished it, he marched into the bedroom, lay down, and almost immediately fell into a deep, trancelike sleep. There were dreams — some of his mother, one of Carrie — and the perpetually startled cry of a bird in some neighboring yard wound in and out of them.

It wasn't even light when he awoke, but he bounded from the bed, a whirlwind of cleaning, straightening, tidying. Even though Tripp had said his housekeeper would be coming in, Jared stripped the mattress and made it up again with fresh sheets. He scoured the traces of blood still on the floor, washed the few glasses he'd used, and then tossed his stuff in his bag. He'd get coffee and breakfast on the road; right now, he just needed to get out of here.

The dark was lifting as he swung onto the Long Island Expressway. Sunday morning, and the outbound traffic was sparse — he'd make good time getting back to the city. What he'd do when he got there, though, was anyone's guess.

# Twenty-Four

The morning after Jared left, Miranda awoke to Lily's wailing, and all her efforts — changing her, rocking her, feeding her — did exactly nothing to help. It was like those early days, when the crying jags just went on and on. She steeled herself for a long, tense morning; somehow she'd have to cope. A tap on the door distracted her; Mrs. Castiglione had heard the cries. "You're sure she's not hungry? Or thirsty?" she asked.

"I tried feeding her and offering her a bottle." Miranda desperately jiggled the squalling baby in her arms. "Nothing worked."

"So you can't do anything to soothe her?"

"Maybe riding in a car." Miranda remembered that time when Bea was driving. "She seems to like the motion."

"We could call a car service." Mrs. Castiglione sounded doubtful.

344

"Or I could run with her."

"Wouldn't she be — heavy?"

Even through the wails, Miranda smiled. "I have Lauren's baby jogger. It's in the basement." And leaving Lily with a rather flustered Mrs. Castiglione, Miranda hurried down to get it.

Mrs. Castiglione followed her out to the street while Miranda brought Lily, still crying, downstairs. The day promised to be hot — the temperature was predicted to be in the high nineties — but Miranda didn't care. Between what had almost happened with Jared last night and the screaming baby this morning, she had to get out of her apartment. The run would do them both good. She slathered Lily with sunscreen and packed extra water bottles in the diaper bag before they set off for Prospect Park. She would have put a hat on her too, but when she tried, Lily twisted away and cried harder, so Miranda stuffed it in the already bulging diaper bag.

"Are you sure this is a good idea?" Mrs. Castiglione said anxiously. "It's going to be a scorcher."

"I'm ready for it." Miranda looked down at herself. There had been no opportunity to take a shower, and she had dressed hurriedly in a scoop-neck tank, shorts, and a baseball cap with a big visor. "We'll be fine."

Miranda started slowly; she'd used the baby jogger only a couple of times before, and maneuvering it took some getting used to. But soon she settled into a good, steady rhythm, and the sound her sneakers made on the jogging path — *clip-clop, clip-clop* — was calming. And it calmed Lily too. Pretty soon her cries had tapered off and Miranda stopped only once, to wipe her sticky, wet face, before continuing on. The park was sparsely populated at this hour, though as the day wore on, it would fill up with picnics, barbecues, cyclists, joggers, dog walkers, and skateboarders. There had been a lot of rain this summer, so the trees were still a vibrant summer green. Lily looked up, dark eyes focused on the canopy overhead.

*Clip-clop, clip-clop.* Miranda allowed herself to think of Jared, the way he had kissed her, the feel of his lips on her neck. One hand moved up to touch the place that he'd bitten, and the baby jogger veered off course; quickly she put her fingers firmly back on the handle. Sweat gathered at the base of her spine and under the baseball hat; the outpouring felt good, cleansing somehow. Soon she came to the carousel — not yet open — and sped up to get past it.

But the thoughts it sparked weren't so easily outpaced.

The last time she'd been here had been with Evan. Just thinking of him ambushed her with guilt. No, she had not actually, *technically,* cheated. But oh, how she had wanted to. Still, she hadn't. And it was action, not the heated realm of fantasy, that counted. She would call him as soon as she got home. Maybe they could take Lily somewhere this weekend. New playground? Zoo? He was so interested in the baby; that had been evident on their first date.

The more she thought about this outing — which was now growing more elaborate in her mind and included renting a rowboat — the better she liked it. She moved easily and effortlessly, running away from Jared, toward Evan and the easy, secure domesticity he offered.

Miranda slowed at the Third Street exit from the park and ran a baby wipe across her sweaty face. Then she refastened her ponytail, high on her neck, and started down the hill. Lily was dozing, and Miranda was already thinking about the baby's lunch and how they would spend the afternoon. So she was surprised — jolted really — when she found Evan sitting on the stoop of her house, his bicycle locked to the gate.

"Hey." He stood up, all six foot whatever of him, and grinned. "Did you forget?"

"Forget?" Clearly she *had* forgotten, but what?

"You asked me to come by today; I was going to help you with those books."

The books! In her ongoing quest for more space, Miranda had once again winnowed her personal library, and Evan was here to help her lug some of the boxes to the basement and others to the Housing Works store on Garfield Place. They had made the plan a few days ago, but it had completely flown from her mind.

"I'm so sorry!" Miranda hoped her memory lapse had not hurt his feelings. "I took Lily and went for a run; have you been here long?"

"Not too long." Evan looked down at Lily. "It's okay; we can go up and do it now."

"I can't believe I forgot. Everything's been so busy at work, and then Jared was coming by last night and I had to get everything ready for Cel— I mean Lily." She could not meet his eyes as she spoke but stared at the fraying laces of her sneakers.

"So she's here for the weekend? Jared Masters left her with you? You didn't mention it."

Just hearing Jared's name made Miranda's

heart skid, and she nodded, not trusting herself to say anything. Lily dozed on, and Miranda sat down on the stoop. After a second or two, Evan sat back down too.

"That's good. You'll get to see her from now on, right?" Again Miranda nodded. She was still feeling so awkward. But it would pass; she would make it pass. "What's he like, anyway?" The question was casual, almost an afterthought; he was now busy adjusting something on his ever-present camera.

"Who?" Miranda could hear the way her voice scaled up.

"Jared Masters," Evan said. "Who else?" He stopped whatever he had been doing to the camera. "Is something wrong? You seem kind of . . . uncomfortable. Upset."

"Upset? No, I'm not upset. I'm just —"

"What's that?" He was staring at her neck.

"What's what?" Her hand went to her throat; she was aware that her hair, gathered into its high ponytail, had left it bare. Oh God, had Jared left a *mark*?

"That." He gently pried her fingers away.

"I don't know what you're talking about."

"It looks like a hickey," he said. "Who did that to you? It wasn't me."

Miranda felt the flush begin at the crown of her head and descend over her forehead, cheeks, and chin like an ugly stain.

"It was Masters, wasn't it? That's why you're acting so weird. You let him screw you last night."

"I didn't *let* him do anything," Miranda flared.

"What, then? He *raped* you?"

"Are you crazy? No! You're distorting everything. He came over and, well, we kissed and —"

"And then you had sex with him."

"No, Evan. I did not have sex with him. Unless you consider kissing and this" — she touched her neck lightly — "sex. I was attracted to him and I —"

"Spare me." He crossed his arms tightly over his chest.

"Could you let me finish? Please? I didn't go through with it because I knew it wasn't right. Not for me, not for Lily — and not for you. I didn't want to hurt you, Evan. And so I didn't do it."

"Why would you expect me to believe you?"

"Because it's the truth." She looked at his hurt, angry face. How to explain what had happened last night? Did she start with the first time she'd laid eyes on Jared? The way she'd felt pulled into his orbit, revolving with an energy that wasn't entirely hers?

"He brought Lily over last night, and I told him about Geneva. I wanted to know if he'd had any clue about her relationship to Lily's mother."

"And did he?"

Miranda shook her head. "He was as surprised as we were. Then I started crying, and he put his arms around me — to comfort me; that was all. But it turned into something else and he kissed me."

"I'm not buying it. Not for a minute."

"What right do you have to interrogate me? To judge me?"

"Do you think I'm an idiot? That you can just lie to me and I'll swallow it? I'm supposed to sit back and say, 'Sure. Go ahead and sleep with him. I don't mind a bit. No sir. I'll just cheer you on. I'll just *applaud,* for fuck's sake.' " He got up, unlocked his bike, and pushed the kickstand savagely with his foot.

"Don't swear at me. I don't have to take this —"

"That's right. You don't have to take any of it. You don't have to take *me.*"

"Evan!" Miranda stood. "Please don't go! We can talk more about this. I think we *should* talk more; I never meant to hurt you."

"Jesus," he said. "I'd hate to see what

you'd do if you had." And he looped his long leg over the bike and pedaled away.

Miranda remained where she sat, waiting for the flush to subside and her breathing — she'd been practically panting — to return to normal. Had Mrs. Castiglione heard this conversation? A quick glance to the window, with its humming, outsized air conditioner, reassured her that she had not.

Then Lily woke up and began to squirm; Miranda instantly shifted into maternal mode, checking her diaper, offering water. It was only after Lily had guzzled nearly an entire bottle and then batted it away that Miranda realized how thirsty, no *parched,* she was. She took a long, cooling drink from the bottle she'd brought for herself. Better. Much better.

But when she got to her feet, she swayed slightly and the sidewalk tilted up at her in a new, perilous way. Evan was a good and decent man; in the months she'd known him, he'd been nothing but kind, protective, and caring. She had never been weak-in-the-knees in love with him; what they had was sweet but gentler. And then, just like that, she'd wrecked it.

But no. That wasn't fair. She hadn't slept with Jared. She'd stopped herself. She'd said no. The heat of the day pressed down on her as she locked the baby jogger to the fence — she'd put it away later — and picked Lily up. The stairs to her apartment suddenly felt so steep; every step was a supreme effort. What, oh what, had she done?

Evan pedaled demonically across the Brooklyn Bridge. He'd called Audrey, expecting her to be out in Sag Harbor, but to his amazement, she and Emma were still in the SoHo loft. "She's got some stomach bug," Audrey explained. "And she gets so carsick anyway, even with the Dramamine. I told Gwen to take the two other kids, and if Emma's better, I'll bring her out tomorrow."

Entering the loft, Evan carefully positioned his bicycle so that it did not touch the walls, which were as pristine as everything else in here. But when he went to sit down on the sofa, he noticed the faint, pinkish outline of a stain that had not been there before. "What happened?" he asked.

"Emma threw up," Audrey said. "I told Gwen a white sofa was a bad idea. She'll just have to deal."

"Where's Emma now?"

"Napping. The poor little thing is just worn-out." Audrey settled on the sofa next to him. "So what's going on? You said it was urgent."

"It's Miranda. She slept with Lily's father last night."

"She told you that?" Audrey looked incredulous.

"No. She claims she didn't. But there was a hickey on her neck as big as the state of Texas. And since I haven't been near her in a week, I knew it wasn't from me."

"Well, that stinks."

"It sure does." He leaned his head against the back of the sofa. It wasn't very comfortable.

"Evan, I have to say this, even though you are not going to like it."

"What?" He opened his eyes.

"Do you think that maybe, just maybe, she was giving you signals that she was not *the one*? Signals that you, with your tender, loopy, romantic-as-a-Hallmark-special heart, were hell-bent on not reading?"

"No!"

"Okay. Okay." Audrey raised her open palms in a gesture of surrender. "I just had to ask, you know? Because it is kind of a pattern with you."

"Well, it could be." He was not ready to concede entirely, but he lowered his voice. "And maybe there were signs, but I wasn't seeing them. I don't know." He looked at

Audrey beseechingly. "I thought we were getting somewhere. It's so easy being with her. She's smart. She's fun. She's a great cook. And that body . . ."

"You're in pretty deep," Audrey said. "So the question is, what do you want to do about it?"

"I'm not getting you."

"Can you forgive her?"

"Should I?"

"Only you know the answer to that." She turned in the direction of the doorway. There stood Emma, fists rubbing her eyes and blond curls a blurred halo. "Hi, sweet pea; come to Mama." Emma remained rooted where she stood, so Audrey got up and led her by the hand to the sofa. "Do you remember Evan? He read you the unicorn book."

Emma studied Evan for a moment before burying her face in Audrey's shoulder. "She's still sick," said Audrey. "Don't take it personally." But Evan did take it personally. And he took it even more personally when, a few minutes later, Emma disengaged herself from Audrey and like a nimble, blond monkey, climbed into his lap.

"I threw up on the couch," she said by way of greeting. "Mommy is going to be mad."

355

Evan patted the curls. "Maybe not," he said. "It wasn't your fault." His mind darted back to Miranda and Jared Masters. Had what happened been her fault? Maybe she'd been so caught up in having Lily back that she'd gotten confused. But then he remembered the large, plum-colored patch on her white skin. Masters had taken off her clothes, pushed her down on the bed, let his mouth travel all over her. . . . Evan practically had to shake himself to get the lacerating images out of his head. He turned to Audrey. "Is it too early in the day for a drink?" he asked. "It is a holiday weekend, after all."

"Have you eaten anything?" When Evan shook his head, she added, "Let's order in for brunch. There's a good Tex-Mex right around the corner; I can make the Bloody Marys while we wait for it to be delivered."

After a plate of huevos rancheros, tortillas, and slow-cooked salsa washed down by three strong and spicy Bloody Marys, the pain had receded — at least enough to get through the rest of the god-awful day. He didn't think he should bike back to Red Hook in that condition though, and his hand wasn't steady enough to use the camera that was always on his right shoulder. So after he left Audrey's, he ducked into the Angelika cinema on Houston Street, where he paid to sit through three different movies, though he didn't exactly watch any of them and fell asleep partway through the last. When he emerged, the sky was just starting to darken — despite the heat of the day, it was September, not July — and he splurged on a cab back to Red Hook. He'd need to get his bicycle from Audrey's, but that could wait until tomorrow; he'd moved it to a locked storage area and she'd given him a key.

Sitting in the backseat of the taxi, he glanced down at the cell phone he'd set on mute while he was in the movie theater. Just because he was drunk didn't mean he'd turned into the kind of jerk who ruined everyone else's movie-going experience with a chiming phone. He saw three voice mails and four texts — all from Miranda. Should he call her back? What would he say? He didn't know if he could or should forgive her; he didn't want to be her doormat. Reliable old Evan, you could wipe your feet all over him and he'd still flash you the welcome sign. He slipped the phone back in his pocket and told himself he would not take it out again until he got home.

The camera sat lightly on his shoulder; he let one hand rest possessively, even caressingly, across its top. This camera was the most stable and the most loyal thing in his life. Women? They couldn't be trusted. Work was what mattered; work was what endured. Outside the taxi window, he could see the faint ghost of the rising moon, a powdery disk in a salmon sky, and he forced himself to look at it, and not the screen of his phone, for the rest of the ride.

# TWENTY-FIVE

"Of course I'll take her." Miranda got up from her desk to close her office door. "You know I'm happy to do it. And you've cleared it with Supah?"

"She's totally fine with it." Jared must have been talking from some busy street corner; Miranda could hear a bus or a truck lumbering by.

"Perfect. When did you plan on dropping her off?" The idea that she would get a whole week — maybe even ten days! with Lily — made her want to skip around the office and hug everyone on the staff. Even Marvin.

"A week from today — next Monday."

"Monday is fine. Perfect, in fact." After they said good-bye, she sat looking at the closed office door. Well, that wasn't as bad as she had expected. Jared made no mention of that night when they'd nearly slept together and neither did she. Why would she? It was an incident best buried by both of them. Except that the fallout from that evening had cost her the relationship with Evan. She flamed, just thinking of him. He was so stubborn! So judgmental! But her anger was quickly replaced by remorse. Had she perhaps taken him for granted, just the slightest bit, and now she was missing him? Yes. She was.

But why was she dwelling on that? She had made the overture; now it was his turn. And anyway, Lily! Ten days! Where was Jared going? He'd been quite evasive in their conversation, and she hadn't been able to pin him down. Then there was still the Geneva connection. She was no closer to understanding that woman's motives than she had been when Evan first presented her with the facts.

A knock on the door halted the small tornado of her thoughts. "Miranda? Alan Richardson is here."

"Bring him right in," Miranda said. She'd been angling for this visit for months, and she wasn't about to spoil it; she'd have to deal with her personal life later.

Claudia opened the door and Alan Richardson came striding into Miranda's office with a flourish. "Cupcakes!" he announced. "Ready for the unveiling?"

"Of course!" Miranda moved aside some papers, and Alan set down the Tupperware cupcake holder. He and Miranda had been in steady communication about the exclusive cupcake he was creating for the Mother's Day issue of *Domestic Goddess.* But he hadn't wanted to share too many details, so she hadn't actually seen the cupcakes before; today was the big reveal. "Let me just get a few other people in here too." She buzzed Sallie and Marvin, and they all clustered around the desk as Alan took the lid off.

There sat twelve perfect pink and red cupcakes, nestled in red paper liners. They were iced with creamy white frosting and each decorated with a rose that had been fashioned from fruit chews that had been cut, shaped, and dipped in decorating sugar. Tiny green leaves — also fruit chews — peeked out from the petals. Clustered appealingly together, they looked like an edible bouquet.

"They're gorgeous," said Sallie. "Our readers will love them."

"We're going to do a link to a video showing how to make the roses," Miranda added. "And we're going to roll out the click-through feature on the recipe." The click through had been Miranda's idea; it would allow the online readers to click to products used in creating the cupcake — a silicon frosting spreader, nesting mixing bowls, rolling pin — and order them on the spot. The retailers had loved this idea — naturally — and ad sales were up as a result.

"I'm already imagining the layout," added Marvin. "Lush!"

"We'll do another batch for the shoot," Alan said. "I just wanted you to see them first. And taste them too."

"You don't need to ask twice!" Sallie began handing out the cupcakes. Miranda brought one out to the receptionist at the front desk, who actually squealed when it was placed in front of her. When Miranda returned, Sallie was halfway through her cupcake. "Great work," she said. "I think this is really going to be a hit."

Miranda reached for a cupcake and smiled. "Thanks. They're even better than I had hoped."

"Keep up the good work." Sallie finished eating and dabbed at her lips with the pink napkin Alan had brought. Then she turned to go back to her office. But Marvin, Claudia, and Alan were still enjoying the cupcakes — Marvin was in an atypically affable mood — and Miranda was tempted to take another; there were still three on the tray. It was a celebration, right? A small but satisfying professional triumph. Before she could reach for one, though, her cell phone buzzed. She hesitated; maybe she should let it go to voice mail. But what if Jared was calling?

Instead it was Eunice, calling from the nursing home. "You'd better come quickly," she said. "He's had a massive stroke, and they don't think he'll last long."

Miranda endured the fifty-minute ride up to Westchester in tense, wretched silence. When a woman sat down next to her on the train, she jumped up like she'd been singed. Her dread of what faced her made the company of someone — anyone — else intolerable; she had to change her seat. Once she arrived, she climbed into a taxi and used the ten-minute ride to prepare herself. *He may already be gone by the time you get there,* she kept saying to herself. The words were an inoculation. *It may already be over.*

But it wasn't. Her father was in the hospital wing attached to the home. When she walked into his room, his eyes were closed and his skin so translucent it seemed to be dissolving right in front of her. Eunice was seated at his bedside, a balled-up wad of tissues in her fist. "You can talk to the doctor if you want, but they said there's nothing they can do. His brain is too damaged. His heart too." Miranda looked at her father. No tubes, no wires, nothing at all. "He signed a *do not resuscitate* order, you know," Eunice added. Miranda nodded; she did know. There was another chair in the corner of the room, and she pulled it over toward the bed. Then she sat and waited.

From time to time, someone came in — a nurse, a doctor, an elderly rabbi who offered to sit with them — but Miranda remained focused on her father and only her father. Not this shrunken shell of a father though. No, she reached inside and brought out the memories, laying them all out before her like playing cards — a royal flush's worth. "Do you remember that summer on Cape Cod, Dad?" she said. "The waves were so big and gray; I asked you if they were dirty. You thought that was hilarious. And we ate fried clams at the little place we found — the one with the striped awnings and the lawn chairs? Mom didn't like it. She said it was tacky and she wouldn't go in. But we loved it. Remember? You do remember, don't you?"

Her father remained silent, breathing lightly. She tried again. "And what about when the skunk got into the cottage and we all ran out in our pajamas? Mom had that green goop all over her face and didn't want to go outside at first, so you carried her. She was laughing so hard you nearly dropped her." Miranda reached for her father's hand and squeezed it. He did not squeeze back. But he did not withdraw his hand either. Then his eyes opened and he saw her — really saw her. She could tell by the way he was looking at her. It was the way he used to look at her before . . . before all *this*. "Miranda," he said clearly. "Girl of mine." His lips moved in a strange grimace; Miranda gasped softly when she realized it was a smile.

"Daddy!"

His hand tightened around hers and his eyes closed again. He began to move, shaking and twisting that grew more and more agitated, almost violent. "What's happening?" she said to Eunice in a panicked voice. But she knew. Eunice hurried out to get a doctor.

Miranda was alone with her father — *this* father, the aged, ruined man, not the adored and adoring father of her girlhood. For a terrible few seconds his back arched, thrusting his chest forward and his hand, still in hers, squeezed tighter and tighter until he was hurting her. She did not remove her hand, but let it remain in that avid grip. Then all at once he let her go. His body sank back and his breathing grew slower and slower — until it stopped. By the time Eunice returned, a white-coated doctor hurrying in her wake, Miranda's father was dead.

They came, her good friends, cooing, tending, organizing. Bea, back from her out-of-town gig, Lauren, kids consigned to her husband's care, Courtney, wedding dresses and seating charts set temporarily aside. They helped her choose a funeral home, pack up what remained of her father's earthly possessions; they were there when the plain pine box was lowered into the ground and stood nearby when she let the first shovelful of dirt cascade down onto the casket, the sound unnaturally loud in her ears. They rode back with her in the black town car, set out the sandwiches and pastries she had ordered for the shivah. There was one large white box whose origin no one could figure out; inside were three dozen cupcakes, half covered in simple, dark chocolate swirls, the other half, vanilla, and a note from Alan Richardson: *So sorry for your loss.*

"At first I thought they might be from

Evan," Courtney said. "In fact, where is Evan? I was frankly kind of shocked that he wasn't at the cemetery."

"Evan and I are taking a little break." Miranda looked at the cupcakes, which Courtney had arranged on a tray; sending them was such a tasteful, thoughtful thing to have done. In fact, Evan didn't know about her father's death because she had not reached out to tell him.

"What are you talking about? You didn't tell me!"

It was true; Miranda had not told anyone about her night with Jared and the breakup with Evan; she was too ashamed. "I can't go into it now."

Courtney gave her that *what-bullshit-story-are-you-trying-to-put-over-on-me* look. "Does he know about your dad?" Miranda shook her head. "Because if he did, that might change things."

"No, it won't. He doesn't want to hear from me right now."

And then Courtney had to drop it because Miranda would not say anything more.

By Sunday evening, it was all over. Her father had been buried and she'd finished sitting shivah — she'd opted for an abbreviated, three-day version of the ritual. Bea and Courtney packed up what remained of the food, and Lauren cleaned the kitchen. They all hugged as they said good night in Miranda's doorway.

"Wait — forgot something," said Courtney, who darted back toward Miranda's bedroom. She stayed there for several minutes and emerged only after the others had gone.

"What did you forget?"

"Nothing. That was a ruse."

"A ruse?" asked Miranda.

"You're stonewalling me!" Courtney looked exasperated. "I feel like there's something you're not telling me."

"There's a lot I'm not telling you," said Miranda. "Pull up a chair and settle in." Courtney was right. She had been stonewalling her, but now she needed to unburden herself. She poured them each a glass of white and told Courtney about Geneva's relationship to Lily and then moved on to her unexpected encounter with Jared and Evan's subsequent discovery of it.

"You didn't actually sleep with him, did you?"

"I wanted to, but no, I didn't. Still, Evan doesn't believe me."

"What does he want — forensic proof?"

Miranda smiled. "Is that Harris talking?"

"I guess it is. I still think Evan would come

around if he knew about your dad." Courtney finished her wine and poured herself a
refill.

"I'm not so sure. And anyway, telling him
about my father would be manipulative."
Miranda paused. "Wouldn't it?"

"Not if you love him."

Miranda thought about that. "I do love
him but maybe not quite in the way he loves
me."

"Maybe he thinks whether you did or
didn't go all the way with Jared is beside
the point. Maybe what he feels — *knows* —
is that this guy floats your boat in a way
that he doesn't. And it hurts."

"You could be right. . . ."

"Listen, I believe that Jared Masters is
gorgeous, sexy, and makes your little heart
go pitter-patter. But do you think he's up
for being a part of your fantasy family?"

"I don't know. But Evan is." Miranda
contemplated the pale gold liquid in her
glass. "Of course, now I don't even have
Lily — at least not on a full-time basis."

"Would Evan care?" When Miranda shook
her head, Courtney said, "Call him. Soon."

"I'll think about it, okay? It's been a long
day."

Courtney got up from the table. "Of
course it has. You just lost your father. But

369

don't let Evan get lost too."

When she had gone, Miranda peeled off her clothes and left them in a trail as she made her way to the bathroom. She'd pick them up later, of course. But right now, she needed to immerse herself in a steaming tub, with the rest of that wineglass and a verbena-scented candle for company. Her breasts rose and bobbed on the water's surface. Oh, the heat felt so good, so comforting. "Here's to you, Daddy." She raised the glass. "Rest in peace."

Later, she wrapped herself in an ancient plaid robe she had plucked from his possessions. She'd also taken his Waterman fountain pen, a pair of silver cuff links, a green silk tie with a pattern of leaping fish, a box of his important papers, including his will, and the white, gold-embossed album that held her parents' wedding photos. She put it on the coffee table next to the linen-covered album Evan had made for her. He really had been attached to Lily; she might not find a man like that again so soon. Or ever. Maybe Courtney was right and she should try to contact him again. But she had tried reaching him. More than once. Wasn't it time for him to take a step in her direction now?

Seated on the sofa, she reached not for

the wedding album, but the other one, which held pictures of Lily. Yet instead of focusing on the baby in the pictures, Miranda was more aware of what she could not see: Evan, invisible behind the lens, absorbed in his task of seeing, of recording. What had she said to Courtney about never having yearned for him? Well, she was yearning now. Before she could change her mind, she reached for her phone and punched in his number. She waited tensely for a few seconds while it rang and then the call went to voice mail; Miranda hesitated but did not leave a message. If he wanted to talk to her, he'd call her back.

She put the phone down, trying to find some way, any way, to comfort herself. In the closet, she pawed around until she found her tattered copy of *The Best-Loved Doll.* How many times had she read this book or had it read to her? One hundred? Two hundred? More? The spine was fragile and some of the pages loose. But the story of the plain little doll who trumps all the others — even those who walk, talk, or had the most exquisite clothes — had an inevitable sense of rightness, and she read the words out loud as if Lily were in the room to hear them. Soon she would be.

Tomorrow she would see the baby girl

she'd found in that subway station, the girl who was, against all odds, meant for her. Supah had phoned earlier and would be bringing her in the morning. Miranda had asked for the day off, so they would be able to spend it together. And it was this thought she carried with her, like a precious vessel, as she lay down — fatherless as well as motherless now — and surrendered herself to sleep.

# Twenty-Six

The vast studio in Queens where Evan was shooting the pet supply catalog resembled Noah's ark: there were pairs of Siamese, Angora, and calico cats, along with pairs of Dalmatians, dachshunds, Scotties, poodles, and Pekinese. There were also several rodent duos: gerbils, hamsters, and black, lop-eared rabbits. There was even a pair of parrots, their feathers a blazing mix of teal blue, green, and red, squawking and spitting nutshells onto the floor of their cage. The only exceptions were a trio of affable mutts ("mixed breed" was the term of choice around here) and a single, sixty-pound bulldog, all jowls and wrinkles. "Can you bring the lights over here?" Nat, the art director, gestured to a spot near the windows. Evan picked up the light stands, each clamped to a tripod and tucked into its own soft box to better diffuse the light, and began arranging them in a loose circle. The

last tripod was wobbly, and when he attempted to adjust it, the bulb fell clean out
of the socket and crashed onto the floor.
The bulldog barked, a deep, gruff sound
that muted the string of curses Evan let
loose. Fuck. Shit. How had *that* happened?
He surveyed the wreckage — four hundred
bucks' worth of glinting shards — before
hurrying off to find a broom.

He managed to cut himself — twice —
while sweeping the glass and smeared blood
on the white no-seam paper he was using to
shoot the animals. But so what? One of the
Dalmatians peed on it, so he tore off the
soiled part and rolled down the paper — it
hung on a roll suspended by two hooks like
a giant toilet paper dispenser — and started
again. This time the other Dalmatian began
to chew on the edge of the no-seam, which
resulted in his vomiting up the chewed
paper in a frothy white puddle. Another
swath torn off and tossed.

"I thought you said this dog was well
trained." Nat turned to Bobbi, the animal
handler.

"The agent swore up and down he was
perfect." Bobbi was busy cleaning up the
mess the Dalmatian had made; Evan felt for
her.

"Perfect pain in the ass," sniffed Nat. He

looked back at Evan. "Let's try it again."

Six miserable hours later, Evan packed up his lights — now minus a bulb he'd have to replace — and the rest of his equipment. He couldn't wait to get out of there. True, he'd have to return tomorrow, but it would be without the animals. He would be shooting kibble and the rawhide chews, birdseed and catnip — a veritable piece of cake when compared with today. He'd have to leave early though. He needed to stop off at B&H Photo for that bulb.

Traffic was terrible getting back to Red Hook — of course; why wouldn't it be? — and he broke one of his cardinal rules about answering his phone while behind the wheel. It was not like he was driving; he was sitting. As soon as he started to move, he would hang up.

He recognized the number. "Hi, Mom."

"How are you? You didn't sound so good last time we talked. You had me worried."

"I'm fine. Really. Don't worry so much."

"Mothers worry," she said. "It's part of our job."

"How's Dad?" Evan tried to redirect the conversation.

"On the golf course. As usual."

"That's good. Isn't it?" Evan's parents had retired to Scottsdale, Arizona, a few years ago. Golf was a big part of the equation.

"If you call chasing a tiny ball with a skinny stick around a lawn good, then yes, I suppose so."

Evan waited a beat. The first two gambits had failed; what else could he trot out?

"How are you, Mom?" The traffic remained stagnant.

"It depends."

"On what?"

"You. A Jewish mother is only as happy —"

"As her least happy child." It was easy to finish the sentence; he'd heard it about a thousand times.

"Look, Evan, honey, I know you're disappointed about that girl you were dating, Melinda —"

"Miranda, and she's thirty-five, Mom. She's not a girl; she's a woman."

"Girl, woman — whatever. You don't have to jump down my throat; I'm just trying to help. Now, have you called Thea?"

Thea was the New York–based daughter of one of his mother's Scottsdale friends. "As a matter of fact, I did."

"And?" Her voice scaled up several decibels.

"And we're going out tonight. Okay? Are you happy now?"

"I'm happy if *you're* happy, darling. She's a wonderful girl. Woman. Tall — like you! Pretty. Whip smart. Oh, Evan, you'll love her."

Suddenly the car in front of him surged ahead, and Evan had to focus on driving. "Can't talk now, Mom. I'll call you soon."

Evan got home, showered, and changed into a fresh shirt and jeans. Which of them was more pathetic here? His mother, for still meddling in his love life? Or him for allowing it? But he'd been missing Miranda a lot and did not want to go back onto eHarmony — or any other online dating site — for fear of seeing her profile. And he was lonely. So he'd reluctantly taken the number his mother had provided and called Thea. They were meeting — for drinks, not dinner — at a place downtown. Drinks were good; if the date went well, you could extend it into dinner. If not, you could bail and not have invested an entire evening. He remembered these strategies from eHarmony, strategies he hadn't had to employ while he'd been seeing Miranda.

Evan walked into the bar three minutes before the appointed time of seven o'clock. He carried with him one long-stemmed red rose. He knew it was a cliché, but what the hell. It was a nice thing to do, and Evan prided himself on being a nice guy. *Too nice,* Audrey would have said.

At five past seven, Evan began to peruse the menu; at quarter past, he decided to order a drink. If she didn't get here by the time he finished it, he'd go. He'd tell his mother it hadn't worked out and he'd be off the hook. The waiter had just popped the top off the bottle of Heineken he'd ordered when a very tall, very slender woman approached his table.

"Evan?" She extended a hand and he took it. "Thea. So sorry I'm late!"

"That's okay." He stood and handed her the rose.

"How sweet!" She smiled at him and then touched a finger to the flower. "Thank you."

After she sat and ordered a beer — he always liked it when a woman drank beer — she filled him in about the rudiments of her life and asked him about his. She was divorced, worked in marketing and public relations, lived in the East Twenties. She was not his type physically — way too thin, with knobby wrists and thighs that hardly seemed wider than her calves. A beanpole. Skin and bones.

But when she regaled him about a recent trip she'd taken — on safari in Kenya — and compared notes on some of her favorite film directors — *Ingmar Bergman is one of my gods,* she'd said — he began to warm toward her. And though her body didn't appeal, her face did: greenish gold eyes, lots of tiny freckles peppering her cheeks and nose, thick, reddish brown hair cut in a choppy way; it kept falling in her eyes and he kept wanting to brush it away.

They decided to extend the drink into dinner and when they'd ordered, he asked her if she liked to cook.

"I don't cook," she said. "I burn."

He laughed but felt a funny little twist inside. Miranda. The scones, the pistachio pesto, the way she turned the humblest meal into a ceremony. But Miranda had betrayed him; he and Miranda were through.

"What about you? Do you like to cook?" Thea asked.

"About as much as you do," he replied.

Later, after dinner, he insisted on seeing her home. And when she turned to him at her door and gave him a soft, sweet kiss, he was pleasantly surprised. So she was not afraid to make the first move. Nice. Very nice. It was so easy to kiss her back, he thought as he moved into her arms. Easiest thing in the world.

The air, warm and moist as a steam bath,

was the first thing Jared noticed when he got off the tiny prop plane and walked across the tarmac. Tripp was waiting for him inside the terminal; no doubt he preferred the air-conditioning to the saturated heat outside.

"Hey, man." Tripp grasped his hand in a tight shake. "How was the flight?"

"Which one?" Jared had to change planes twice to get here.

Tripp laughed. "Yeah, this place is kind of off the radar."

"Way off." Jared picked up his bag. "I hope your car is right outside. I don't want to hike through the soup."

As Tripp drove and talked, Jared gazed out the window. Everything was so densely, almost surreally, green down here: even though it was mid-September, the trees were still in deep summer mode and dripping in kudzu; he saw lurid-colored flowers all over the place, not that he knew their names: orange, magenta, scarlet, yellow. He started seeing houses, just a few at first and pretty dilapidated, and then more and more. It sure as hell didn't look like the Hamptons, but at this point, Jared didn't care whether he ever saw the Hamptons again. Tripp's invitation to fly down to Louisiana to discuss a new business venture was perfect timing.

Finally, Tripp pulled into a town center. Or what once had been a town center. Four main streets led into an overgrown grassy circle; at the center of the circle was a statue of a rider whose horse was rearing back so far it was practically vertical. The rider himself was headless and he was also missing an arm.

When they parked and got out, Jared saw that most of the buildings — wooden, with nice ornamental detailing — were empty. The few that were occupied housed a liquor store, a couple of pawnshops, and a gun store.

"Where the hell are we?" Jared had only just gotten here, but he was ready to take off again.

"Welcome to Gilead," said Tripp. "Incorporated in 1836."

"And when was its demise? Not too long after, from the looks of things."

"I didn't bring you here to talk about that." Tripp looked around; clearly he saw something other than what Jared was seeing. "I brought you here to talk about its resurrection. And you're the guy to bring it back from the dead."

"Are you kidding? Even Jesus couldn't

bring this town back to life."

"I can't speak for Jesus," said Tripp, "but I have a lot of faith in you."

Jared had absolutely no faith in Tripp. But he followed him across the sorry-ass town square, past a ruined gazebo and more empty storefronts. They turned down a side street, and Tripp led the way into a luncheonette that, given the way the rest of the town looked, seemed surprisingly lively.

"Hey, Lulu," he called out. "This is the friend I was telling you about. And he's very hungry!"

A fortyish woman — her riotous dreadlocks were contained by a red bandana — poked her head from around a corner. When she saw Tripp, she came running over. "Good to see you!" She hugged him and then turned to Jared. "Welcome, stranger. Any friend of Tripp's is a friend of mine."

"He's no stranger, Lulu," said Tripp. "At least he won't be for long."

Lulu led them through the restaurant to a booth at the back. The place had a casual, funky vibe: walls painted china blue, lots of thrift store and paint-by-number art hanging on them. Mismatched chairs and napkins, empty soda bottles and jam jars filled with the same kinds of crazy flowers Jared had seen from the car. When they were seated, Lulu said, "The usual, Tripp?"

"The usual!" He looked at Jared. "Get ready to dine, my man. Get ready to *feast.*"

Tripp was not exaggerating. The food just kept coming. Gumbo and po'boys, pickled this and spicy that. Sweet potato fries, stewed tomatoes. Pecan pie with house-made ice cream. A bread pudding so light it almost levitated off the plate.

"How did you ever find this place?" Jared asked. He wasn't hungry anymore, but everything was so good he kept eating.

"I was in New Orleans and I read about it on some foodie blog. Drove sixty miles to get here. Then my damn car breaks down and I'm stuck. Stranded! But the meal I had here that first night made it worthwhile. And Lulu let me sleep in the apartment above the restaurant. She had it fixed up to rent, but as our little tour of the downtown might suggest, she didn't have a lot of takers."

"Yeah, I can see that she wouldn't." Jared helped himself to a bourbon-filled chocolate, compliments of the house.

"We got to talking about this town. What it had been and what it could be again. I made some calls, contacted some people. And I came back six, seven, eight times. Spoke to the town council — all of three people, one of whom hadn't left his house in a decade. I petitioned everyone I could think of to petition. Got some backers in New York to pony up some money; parlayed that into some government funds down here. We're right on the cusp, Jared. Right on the cusp. And I think you're the guy to bring us over."

"That's what you've been telling me. But you haven't explained exactly what or how."

"I wanted you to see it first. To get a feel for the place." Tripp moved his plate aside and planted his elbows on the table. "What I need is a facilitator. Someone who knows the real estate market, who understands how neighborhoods — and cities — evolve. You've got that degree in urban planning, right? Well, it's time to put it to use. Plus you're a born salesman; you've got the gift. And that's kind of what we need down here — someone with a gift, someone who can swim in more than one sea."

"So how do you envision it?"

"We're looking at a mixed-use model, some residential, some commercial, maybe even some light manufacturing. A new mix of small businesses, artists — because we know they can turn a neighborhood into gold — and cultural organizations. It's a mixed population here; there's a good balance of black and white; we don't want to lose that. But if this town is going to survive, it needs to change." He looked like a zealot as he outlined his plans.

"I've got funding. I've got tax incentives. I just need someone who can pull it all together. Match the right tenant or buyer with the right property for the right reasons. Keep an eye on the overall picture. Provide big-city expertise to a small-town venue. What do you say, Jared? You in?"

"I'm not sure." Jared looked away from Tripp and out the window. Across the street from Lulu's was the kind of grand old house that he'd always loved — three stories, wraparound porch, and a pair of weeping willows out front. Oval leaded-glass windows on the stairwells. He could see them from here. The house was a wreck, though. A disaster. But if he signed on with Tripp, maybe he'd be able to help bring it back. Or hell, even *live* in it. But in any case, he'd get to be a part of something good, something hopeful, something restorative, important, and maybe even noble. A thought from left field popped into his head: his *mother* would have been proud.

"I know it would mean a big change for you. Huge. You'd have to relocate down here — at least for a year or so. But I'd cover a

385

big chunk of your living costs — give you an apartment rent free; give you a salary too. You don't have to sell your New York place. You could rent it out for a while. See how you liked it."

"I'm interested. But there are other things I have to consider."

"Like . . ." Tripp had not moved his elbows from the table.

"Lily. My daughter. She's not even a year old."

Tripp's look was probing. "I heard something about that."

"It's a long story. Her mother died; I didn't even know about her. And then when I found out, I took her."

"That would be tough. If you take the job, you won't have a lot of time for her, especially without her mom in the picture. But I'm sure you can find a great nanny down here."

"Actually, I know someone. Someone who would be perfect, in fact." He thought instantly of Miranda, how happy this would make her. But what about him? Could he give up his daughter so easily? Should he?

"You do? That's great!" Tripp leaned over and extended his hand to Jared. "So do we have a deal, buddy?"

Jared laughed. "Not as fast as all that.

Let's take a walk, okay? Show me the rest of the town. I want to see more. Show me *everything*."

Tripp had arranged for Jared to spend the night in Lulu's vacant apartment. It was as eclectic and funky as the space downstairs — macramé wall hangings, rag rug, two patchwork quilts, one on the double bed and the other hanging on the wall — plus it had the advantage of the restaurant downstairs. There was no air-conditioning, but there was a ceiling fan overhead and another, a heavy old thing that seemed to have been lifted from some 1940s movie, on a table beside the bed. With the two sets of blades whirring, it was like a tropical breeze wafting through the room.

Jared tried to imagine himself in this place; it would be so different from anywhere he'd ever lived. Tripp kept stressing that it didn't have to be permanent. He was right: Jared knew he could easily sublet his apartment and Athena would no doubt handle it for him. But Lily — Lily could not be dispensed with so easily. He'd have to bring her with him. Or leave her behind. And at the moment, both of those choices looked pretty lousy.

# Twenty-Seven

Jared kept checking his watch on the plane back to New York. So far, he'd been in the air close to two hours; he had another hour of flight time left to go. The week in Gilead had been packed, meeting everyone from the mayor to the guy who ran the Pick 'n' Pay at the outskirts of town. He'd checked out the old school building and the library — perfect for condo conversion — the long defunct poultry-packing plant that would make great artists' studios. He envisioned green space — a park, a playground — as well as a theater and galleries. Maybe even a small museum, though that might be a stretch. Or at least at first. And he could see all of it coming together in some organic kind of community, a place people would want to call home.

The flight attendant came around with bags of pretzels, so he took one and tore it open. Eating helped pass the time; he checked his watch again. Now he was down to forty-five minutes. He shifted in the minuscule seat and crunched another pretzel. Despite Tripp's pressure, Jared hadn't committed to the job. He was definitely leaning that way, but he still wasn't ready. He had some unfinished business he had to attend to first. And none of it was going to be pretty. First up was Isabel. He'd been dodging her text messages ever since Labor Day weekend.

Just thinking of that phone call put him in a funk; he closed his eyes and kept them closed, a willed simulation of sleep, for the remainder of the flight. But once he was on the ground, he felt ready to take it all on. Back in his apartment, he dropped his bag, riffled through his snail mail, and picked up the phone. It was midafternoon on a Tuesday and Brandon was sure to be at work — a good time to call.

"Finally!" she said when she picked up. "You didn't answer; I was worried."

"I've been out of town. Louisiana."

"Louisiana! What were you doing down there?"

"I'll tell you all about it. But first — how are you? How are things with Brandon? He didn't touch you, did he?"

"No, no. It wasn't like that. I cried. *He*

389

cried. We both said we were sorry and that we would try harder." She paused. "I told him I wouldn't see you anymore. But that was a lie. I can't give you up."

"I'm glad you're okay," he said. "Things got out of hand that day. That's part of why I took off." Jared avoided responding to the second part of what she'd said by telling her about his trip and the job offer.

"Baby, that's great!" she said.

"It could be," he said. "I'm not one hundred percent committed to it. But I'm leaning that way."

"I meant great for us! My sister and her husband live right outside New Orleans. I go to visit her three or four times a year. And now that she has twins, I have a reason to go even more. I could see you when I'm down there; Brandon would never know. He wouldn't even have a *clue.*"

"No." Jared tried to make his tone as gentle as he could. "Not going to happen."

"Why not? What are you talking about?"

"We both know why, Isabel. What we've been doing, well, it sucks. Either you leave Brandon and we can see how it goes with us. Or else you stay — and I'm out of the picture. The guy who screws another guy's wife? I just don't want to be that guy anymore."

"But if I leave him, where will I go? What will I do? I can't support myself. I'd have to move out of the city, completely reinvent my life —"

"Exactly," he said. "That's just what you'd have to do. And then we could find out whether we have a future together — or not."

"I can't!" She was agitated and might have been crying; he couldn't tell for sure. "I won't!"

"I understand," he said. "But then you know this is good-bye, right?"

"You don't mean that!" she said.

"I'm afraid I do." And with that, he ended the call. He didn't know whether he wanted Isabel to leave her husband or not. But he knew that he was no longer up for the subterfuge.

Next he called Athena and arranged to meet her at Minty's at around six o'clock; he was not officially back in the office until tomorrow, and anyway, he didn't want to have this conversation with any of his coworkers around. He spent the rest of the day unpacking and sorting through his mail, both actual and virtual. At one point, he walked into the room Athena had helped him create for Lily.

Thanks to his housekeeper, the room was

immaculate, the soft pink quilt folded neatly in the crib, the toys and clothes and baby gear neatly organized and put away. It was like a photo shoot, a magazine spread — not a room where a baby actually lived. He left the room and closed the door on the way out.

"So, how was New Orleans?" Athena was already waiting for him at the bar, a glass of wine and a dish of salted peanuts in front of her.

"Not New Orleans," he corrected. "Gilead. And it was quite a place." He sat down and began to tell her about Tripp's offer. "I don't know if I'm ready to relocate. But if I do, I'll give you enough lead time to find a replacement."

"That's not going to be so easy," she said. "You've got the touch. People like you, Jared. The ladies like you."

"Sometimes a little too much." He took a swig from the beer he'd ordered.

"Meaning?" Alert, she put down her glass.

"Isabel Clarke."

"The little blonde and the windbag husband? You showed them the place on One Hundred Seventeenth Street?"

"I had an affair with her. The windbag found out." He touched his lip, healed now, but the memory was still there. "It wasn't pretty."

"If you weren't already telling me you're about to leave, I would fire your ass right now." She looked grim. "Though since you have a kid to support, I *might* have given you a second chance. Still, what a stupid thing to do! What the hell got into you?"

Jared stared into his beer. He didn't offer an explanation because he didn't have one to give. "Speaking of Lily, I'm not sure it would be the best thing to bring her down there with me."

"Best thing for her? Or for you?" Athena was sparing him nothing tonight.

"For me, I guess. And ultimately for her. Athena, I can't do it — this dad thing. I didn't know about her, didn't plan for her, and I can't deal with her. It's not like I don't care about her. But I can't raise her. Not now. And not by myself. But I know who could."

"The subway woman." Athena picked her glass up again. "Have you asked her?"

"Not yet. But I have a hunch she'll say yes."

"She might."

"Might? Are you kidding? She's crazy about Lily. She'd do anything to be with her."

"Only if she knew it was for keeps. You can't play with this woman's life, Jared. She lost that baby once. She's not going to take a chance on it happening again."

"It wouldn't." He finished the beer and signaled to the bartender for another.

"She'd need that in writing. You'd have to give up all parental rights and waive your right to seek them again — ever."

"Hey, have you been talking to her or something?"

"Of course not. I've never met her. I couldn't even tell you what she looks like."

"So how do you know what she'd want?"

Athena smiled. "In case you've forgotten, I'm a woman, Jared. And I know what *I* would want."

Jared took a handful of peanuts and chewed them slowly. He'd miss Athena if he left New York; she was hard on him and wouldn't let him get away with a thing, but he respected her for that.

"As long as we're in full disclosure mode, I've got something I want to tell you," she said. When he looked up, she said, "It's about Gabe."

"You two are tying the knot?" He wasn't actually sure how he felt about this.

"Not yet." She glanced away, a shy little smile forming on her face. "But we're headed that way. We're going to find a place together and see how that works."

"Hey, that's great!" He clicked the neck of his beer bottle to her glass. "I'm really happy for you." And, he realized, he was. Athena was a great catch; he hoped Gabe could see that.

"Thanks." She fiddled with the stem of her wineglass. "I wasn't sure how you'd take it. I mean, I think you know I always had a thing for you."

"I do know. And I'm sorry I didn't feel the same way." There, he'd said it. "But Gabe — Gabe is a good man."

"So are you, Jared," she said. "So are you."

On the way back to his apartment, Jared allowed himself to smoke a cigarette. The first puff felt great — a mini-high — and the second was pretty good too. But by the third, his lungs felt scorched and gross; he ground out the unfinished cigarette under his foot and threw away the pack he'd only just bought. Once at home, he went into Lily's room again. The board books on shelves that Athena and some of his other pals had brought — he'd never even opened them. He didn't really know which toys she liked best or which foods either. And he remembered, with mortification, the night he had left her in this very room by herself.

He'd never fully forgiven himself for his act; he probably never would. Lily may have been his biologically, but in every other way that counted, she belonged to Miranda Berenzweig.

# TWENTY-EIGHT

The next evening, Jared was sitting on Miranda's sofa, willing himself to relax. He had not been here since that night he'd almost stayed over, and the memory was still fresh. And the fact that they had not mentioned it since gave it an even greater power. But how to introduce the subject? Maybe she didn't want it mentioned; maybe she was eager to talk about it but was waiting for him to bring it up.

He looked to her for cues but received none. She offered only iced tea or sparkling water, not wine. Nothing to eat. And she did not sit down. Jared opted for the water. Lily was already asleep; Supah had taken her to a baby music class at the local Y and Miranda said all that stimulation had tired her out. "I can probably get her into the car seat without waking her." He noticed that when she finally did sit, it was not next to him but on a chair, several feet away. "And even if she wakes up, she'll settle right back down again."

"Fine." He was nervous and took a sip of water.

"She ought to sleep the whole way home."

"Actually, I wasn't planning on bringing her home."

"What are you talking about?" Miranda put her own untouched water glass down on the table.

"You know the trip I took? To Louisiana? Well, I've been offered a job down there. It's a really exciting opportunity, and I'm pretty sure I'm going to take it. But it's going to demand a big commitment from me, and I thought Lily would be better off staying here with you." She remained eerily still. "That is, if you want her."

"Want her? Of course I want her." Miranda became animated again, getting up from the chair and pacing the room. "But how? On what terms?"

"You could adopt her. She would be yours. She always has been, anyway."

"This isn't just about the job, then, is it? It's more than that."

"Way more." He breathed in and then out again slowly. "I told you: Carrie was a complicated person. A troubled person. Even if she hadn't died, we wouldn't have stayed together. So being hit with this out of the blue — listen, I tried to step up and do the right thing. To claim my baby girl. To raise her. But I can't. I'm not ready and I'm doing a shitty job of it."

"I wouldn't say that. You're being too hard on yourself."

"No, I'm not. You don't know the half of it." And to his own astonishment, he began to cry, hot, copious tears that felt as if they were being wrenched from him. Jesus. When was the last time he'd cried? His mother's funeral? He pressed his fingers to his eyes, as if he could make them stop. He couldn't.

"It's all right." Miranda was right beside him on the sofa, hand on his arm. "Really, it's all right."

"You know what I said before? About not knowing the half of it?" She nodded. "I want to tell you what I meant by that. I need to tell you."

"I'm not sure what you're saying." She moved away again, leaving an empty expanse of couch cushion between them. "Did you hurt Lily in some way?"

"Not intentionally. It was a sin of omission, not commission."

"Are you sure you want to share this with me? Because you don't have to, you know. We can leave it right here."

"I think it's better if you know the whole story." He used his fingers to wipe what remained of the tears on his face. "And I want you to hear it from me." Jared then told her about the much-anticipated date, the phone conversation with Olivia, the night in the hotel, the frantic messages the next day, the way he'd been upbraided — by the pediatrician, Supah, and Athena — and his ongoing remorse. "It's the worst thing I've ever done."

"That was pretty terrible." She spoke in a low, controlled voice. "Selfish, irresponsible, and, if anything had happened to her, criminal."

"I know," he said. "Believe me, I *know.*"

"But nothing serious did happen to her. She was fine, right? She is fine."

"Totally and completely fine. But it did something to me — kind of like a wake-up call. I'm not ready for her, Miranda. Not ready to be the parent she needs and deserves. At least not full-time. But you — you are."

Miranda was quiet for a moment before she replied. "Thank you for saying that."

"And there's one more thing. I owe you an apology for that night I was here before. I shouldn't have kissed you."

"I kissed you back." She kept her gaze

400

locked steadily on his. "We both wanted it. There's no one to blame."

"No." His respect for her was growing by the second. "I guess there isn't."

"But what about Lily? Did you mean what you said?"

"Yes," he said. "I did."

"What if you change your mind? I don't know if I can trust you."

"You can. I'm going to call a lawyer and start getting the papers drawn up. We'll have things to work out. I want to contribute to her support. And to see her on a regular basis. Maybe even some kind of joint custody arrangement?"

Miranda paused, and he waited while she thought it over. "I couldn't accept that," she said finally. "We could talk about visitation rights. But custody? No. I've already had my heart broken once; I won't risk that again. Either she's mine or she isn't."

Jared looked at her. She was so sure of herself. So steady. And she was right. "All right," he said at last. "I can understand that. Until it's all hammered out, Lily can stay here with you. It's what you want, isn't it?"

The radiant smile that came to her face made any doubts he might have had evaporate. "More than anything in the world."

# Twenty-Nine

Miranda carried Celeste — even though the papers had not been signed, she was calling her that now — by the handle of the car seat as she walked into the lobby of the small Upper West Side building. She clutched the handle tightly, as if someone might snatch it away; Miranda still could not believe that her daughter had come back to her. But Jared had honored his word, and her initial wariness changed into pure, undiluted happiness; she'd been flooded with it. Cascaded. Miracles did happen. She was living one.

But once the adoption was made official and the ink on the paperwork had dried, she realized there was something that had not been resolved, something that continued to eat at her. Geneva Highsmith Bales. Evan — who had not, to her great sorrow, returned her call — had given her the rudiments of the connection, but she still needed to fill in the blanks. Why had Geneva chosen such a devious, convoluted path instead of coming out directly with whatever suspicion or knowledge she had? She had to find out.

"Miranda!" Geneva had been surprised but not unfriendly. "It's nice to hear from you."

"Is it?"

"I heard the baby — Celeste — is back with you now." Geneva ignored the question. "It sounds like it's working out well for everyone."

"You could say that." Miranda was not sure how to best frame her request. "But I still had some questions. I was wondering if we could meet."

"Meet?" Geneva's smooth surface had been ruffled.

"Yes, meet. It would mean a lot to me." She paused, wanting to play her trump card to maximum advantage. "And in the long run, to Celeste."

The doorman called up while Miranda waited. When the doorman gave her the nod, she pressed the button for the elevator and waited. Was there anything that Geneva could say that would exonerate her in

Miranda's eyes? Doubtful. But here she was anyway.

Geneva stood in the open doorway; she must have been listening for the elevator. Dressed simply in an oversized white shirt, black leggings, and black ballet flats, she exuded the austerity of a nun. "I was afraid to see you at first. But now that you're here, I'm glad." She addressed Miranda but was staring at Celeste.

"Why were you afraid?"

Geneva shifted her gaze to Miranda. "Jared told me that he knew about my relationship to Caroline — and that you know too."

"I know," Miranda said. "I know, but I don't understand."

"Come in." Geneva stepped aside so she could pass. "We can talk more comfortably inside."

Miranda followed her into a living room whose walls were painted dove gray and whose floor was mostly hidden by a thick Persian rug that glowed with jewel-bright arabesques. Gingerly, she lowered herself onto the love seat, covered in pale yellow raw silk. She placed Celeste, still in the car seat, on the floor beside her. Poking at her back was a small army of obscenely stuffed pillows: tufted, tasseled, and embroidered, they seemed designed to prevent anyone from getting too comfortable.

"So here you are. Both of you." Miranda said nothing, but Celeste struggled to get out of the car seat so Miranda removed her and gathered the baby onto her lap. "Can I get you something?" Geneva was still standing, eager, it seemed, to dart off to the kitchen. Miranda shook her head. "Not even a glass of water?"

"Nothing," said Miranda. "I just want to talk. And then leave."

Geneva sat down on the chair right across from Miranda. "It's Caroline," she said. "You want to know about her. About us, really." Miranda nodded. "All right, then," Geneva said. "I'm going to tell you. But don't blame me if you don't like what you hear."

"I just need to hear it." Miranda looked down at Celeste. "Please."

"She was always different," Geneva said. "Even when we were little, I knew. Knew that something was, well, not wrong exactly. But not right."

"She was younger than you?"

"Three years."

"And what was 'not right' about her?"

"So many things. She was so pretty. And smart too — they skipped her a grade in school. But she was what my mother used to call 'high-strung.' That was a nice, Southern-lady way to put it. But it was more than that. She had these rages; she would throw things, scream, and threaten to hurt herself. Or one of us. My mother would take me into the bedroom and lock the door until she wore herself out. Our father had died when she was a baby, so she didn't have much help; she really didn't know how to cope."

"How sad," said Miranda. She shifted Celeste in her lap.

"Sad?" Geneva looked as if she were surprised to see Miranda sitting there. "It was *horrible;* that's what it was. *She* was horrible. And it only got worse."

"But why didn't your mother get her into some kind of therapy? It seems so obvious she was disturbed."

"My mother was ashamed at first. She didn't want anyone to know. Which was absurd because of course people knew. In first grade Caroline cut up the living room drapes in her best friend's house to make a princess costume. When she was eight, she hacked off all her hair. That same year, on a dare from some boy, she walked into her class at Sunday school naked. Naked! Imagine my mother showing up at the church supper after *that.*"

"But those were all signs of how troubled she was. Didn't she see that?"

"She thought it was her fault, something she'd done. Or not done. Or because our father had died. Did you know he drowned too? In a boating accident? Anyway, she did try to get help for her. From our pastor, and when that didn't work, she consulted with doctors all over the state. And then other states too: she took her to Atlanta to see one specialist and to Charleston to see another." Geneva picked up a large nautilus shell, one of a grouping that was arranged on the glass-topped coffee table, and began rubbing its smooth, pearlized surface.

"And there was nothing that helped?" Miranda was very aware that their roles had reversed; now she was the one asking the questions.

"Not consistently. By the time she was a teenager, she was on so much medication my mother had to type out a chart to keep track of it all. One day Caroline crumpled up the chart and refused to take it anymore. Said she couldn't bear the side effects: nausea, bloating, headaches, double vision — and those are what I can remember. 'I'd like to see *you* swallowing those pills,' she said to me. And do you know what I said?"

Geneva's eyes filled with tears. " 'If I lived with the kind of pain you live with, of course I'd take the pills! That's what they're *for.* ' " She pressed her palms together hard, in furious prayer. " 'I don't know who I'd be without my pain,' is what she said back to me. 'I wouldn't know myself anymore.' "

Miranda was silent. This was Celeste's mother Geneva was talking about, the troubled, tortured woman who had given birth to her alone and then left her in a subway station. What if this illness had been transmitted to Celeste? What if she grew up to suffer in the way that Caroline had? Miranda felt physically assaulted by the thought; her head throbbed like she'd been hit and her mouth was suddenly parched. "If you don't mind, I think I will have that glass of water."

"Of course." Geneva put the shell back in its place before getting up and heading for the kitchen. Miranda stood too, and with Celeste in her arms, began moving around the room. There on the wall next to the window was an oil painting she had not paid attention to before. Two young girls in high-waisted dresses, one blond, the other brunette. The taller of the two had her arm around the shoulders of the smaller girl; the gesture did not seem affectionate or casual, but grim and even desperate.

"You have her picture hanging here," Miranda said when Geneva had returned with the water. "Why?"

"She's still a part of me," Geneva said. "She always will be."

"I would have thought you wouldn't want to be reminded of her."

"It doesn't matter whether the picture is here or not. She's with me all the time anyway."

"Even though you shunned her?" She drank the water greedily.

"I know it seems awful," Geneva said. "Heartless." She walked over to the love seat and sat down. Miranda followed. "But I just got tired. Tired of trying to help, again and again, and to have my help spurned. She couldn't take the hand that was being offered to her. She didn't know how."

"When did you cut her off?"

"It wasn't all at once. After I graduated from college, I came to New York, but we stayed in touch. By that time, she had dropped out of college and was living in different places, but always down South."

"What about your husband? Did he come to New York too?"

Geneva seemed to flinch at the word *hus-*

*band.* "What makes you think I was married?"

"The wedding photograph — the one in the country club newsletter."

"It was a brief marriage."

"You still use his name." Miranda didn't know where she was going with this, but it was one of the facts Evan had presented her with, and it seemed, if not exactly relevant, then not without meaning either.

"Preston and I were very young. Too young, really. I was still in college. But we had to get married."

"Because you were pregnant?"

Geneva nodded. "And even though I could have had an abortion, my mother and Preston pressured me. It was — a mistake."

"What about the baby?"

"She was stillborn." Miranda bounced Celeste a little; she was getting fussy.

"I'm sorry." Miranda looked at Geneva's pale, drawn face and felt the first stirrings of pity for this puzzling woman.

"Preston and I — well, things kind of fell apart after that. I knew he blamed me somehow, like I was being punished for even considering an abortion. For wanting one — because I really and truly did."

"New York was a new start for you."

"Exactly." Geneva's color came back, and

410

she looked more animated now. "A clean slate. But I kept my married name. I'm not even sure why; maybe I believed that if I did, Preston might come back to me."

"What happened when Caroline got here? Did you let her live with you?" Miranda felt restored too; the water had helped. Celeste wouldn't become like her mother; Miranda would not let it happen. If she saw the signs — *any* signs — she wouldn't be ashamed, wouldn't hide behind the scrim of denial. She'd go to the ends of the earth to help her daughter. To save her, as poor Caroline had not been saved.

"She showed up in New York when our mother died. She knew where I lived and she sweet-talked the super into letting her into my apartment. I nearly fainted when I came home and found her taking a nap on my bed. But I let her stay — at least for a little while." Geneva was quiet, remembering. "It wasn't so bad at first. She could be fun; she could be charming. She had a wicked sense of humor. We used to laugh a lot. . . ."

"But then it changed." Miranda pushed one of the offending pillows out of the way so she could lean back. It slid to the floor, but Geneva did not seem to notice.

"No." Geneva shook her head. "It just

went back to the way it was before. The way it had always been. If I asked her to do the dishes, she screamed at me and accused me of being a scold, just like our mother. She stayed out until all hours and then woke me up when she came in. She let the tub overflow, left the stove on, and nearly set the place on fire with her smoldering cigarettes. A couple of times she even did light fires — intentionally. 'I just wanted to see something burn,' she said. She tossed garbage out the window, swore at the neighbors. Then there were the men. I once got up in the middle of the night and found her having sex with someone on the living room rug. And she could barely keep a job —"

"You supported her?"

"Yes. Almost the whole time she was here. She only worked sporadically."

"Doing what?"

"Well, she didn't have a lot of options. She wasn't cut out for waitressing or being a salesgirl — her moods were too unpredictable. And forget about office work. But I knew someone who owned a small modeling agency —"

"Caroline was a model?"

"Not a fashion model; she modeled parts — eyes sometimes. She had gorgeous blue eyes. Lips too. And feet! She had *the* most elegant feet: small, with high, fine-boned arches and very even toes. Not everyone has those, you know. They're very highly prized."

At another moment, Miranda would have burst out laughing. But this was not that moment.

"Anyway. Finally, I told her she had to go. But even then I was still involved; she'd have a fight with her landlord and I'd have to intervene. Or she'd run out of money for the fourth time in six months. So I'd go in and patch up whatever it was. It was only later that I cut her off completely. I had to. She had keys to my apartment, and one weekend when I was away, she came in and practically cleared the place out. Clothes, dishes, even furniture — gone. I didn't even try to find out what she had done with everything. Or why. I moved and left no forwarding address. When she called my office, I instructed people not to put the calls through. She was crazy, pure and simple. Crazy and hell-bent on staying that way."

"She was your sister. She had no one else," said Miranda. Couldn't Geneva have had her committed? Put her somewhere that she would have been safe?

Geneva was silent for a moment. "I don't expect you, or anyone who hasn't lived with

413

someone like her, to understand. She was my sister, but my sense of revulsion — and it really was that, revulsion — began to overshadow any love I might have had."

"You were angry," Miranda said, beginning to understand. "You still are."

"Yes, I was angry. I'm not proud of that," she said finally. "But I had reached the end — of my patience, my tolerance, of my everything. She used me up."

There was a silence in which Miranda tried to imagine herself in Geneva's position. "How did you put it together? About Celeste, I mean," she finally said. "Because you did put it together, didn't you? You suspected she might be your niece when you sought me out, flattering me and getting me to agree to the profile. It wasn't just that you saw the story and thought we would make good subjects. You had a plan all along."

"Yes," Geneva said softly. "I did." She looked down at her hands; they seemed to offer nothing in return.

"You still haven't told me how you were sure," Miranda said.

"Wait here," Geneva said. She went into another room and returned with a photo album.

As Geneva flipped through the pages,

Miranda caught glimpses of a fair-haired woman with a French twist, a big brick house, a backyard teeming with roses. Here, in these snapshots, was Celeste's heritage, her legacy, and her birthright.

"Look," Geneva said, stopping. There was a close-up of the French-twist woman holding a baby; on the baby's wrist was a tiny string of beads. The photo was black-and-white, but Miranda knew that the beads were pink and white glass, with black lettering. She had seen it before, the first time she'd seen Celeste. "That bracelet? My great-grandmother got it as a gift when my mother was born. It came with a layette — everything pink, white, and smothered in lace. The letters spelled out 'baby girl.' My grandmother kept it and gave it to my mother, who was saving it for when she had a granddaughter. I didn't even remember it until I saw that photo of Celeste on the news. She was wearing it."

"You suspected Celeste might be Caroline's —"

"Caroline had told me about Jared." Geneva went on as if Miranda had not spoken. "She was mad for that man. Head over heels. And the bracelet? She must have taken it earlier, before my mother died; I didn't find it with her things." Geneva's voice cracked then. "I wish she had told me about the baby. But I probably wouldn't have believed her."

"Jared didn't," Miranda said.

"She told him?" Geneva looked surprised. "He didn't mention that."

Miranda nodded. "On the last night he saw her. They had met for drinks at the Cosmo. He thought she was making it up. He was furious; he stormed out and never saw her again."

"She drove everyone away!" Geneva burst out. "She couldn't help herself, but that's what she did."

"I suppose that's true," Miranda said. "But to her, it must have felt like you were the ones pushing her away. Abandoning her."

"I know," Geneva said. "And even though I'm not sure I could have done it differently, it will haunt me."

"Why did you come looking for us, then? That's the really twisted part," Miranda said. "That's what I still don't get."

"Isn't it obvious?" said Geneva. "Guilt. Pure and simple."

"All right. So you were guilty. But what did you think you would accomplish by writing those articles? What was it that you wanted?" There, she finally had asked the thing that had been plaguing her most.

"When I first suspected that Celeste was Caroline's baby, I felt sick. *Sick.* It was almost like Caroline had come back from the dead to taunt me. Of course that wasn't true. But I couldn't stop thinking about the baby: what would happen to her? Where would she end up? I didn't want her; I didn't think I could handle having her. Still, I wanted her to be safe. Protected." She paused. "Loved."

Miranda was quiet.

"Then I found out you were trying to adopt her. I thought if I interviewed you and wrote the piece, I would be doing two important things. Learning more about you. And helping Celeste. Because the piece did help, didn't it? You got offers of diapers, food — things like that, right?"

"Yes," said Miranda. "I did."

"But when I found out about Jared, I changed my mind. Not about you — it was clear to me that you were a wonderful mother. But I knew that Caroline had loved him — at least as much as she was capable of loving anyone. And that she would have wanted him to raise their child. So I switched allegiances. In the end it didn't matter, though. You didn't fight to keep her."

"I wouldn't have won. But, more important, I didn't think I should. She was his child, after all. Who was I to take her from him? I loved her so much I was willing to let her go."

"You put her first. Not too many people would have done that. Caroline wouldn't have."

"Caroline couldn't have."

"No. That's right." Geneva stood and walked over to the portrait. Miranda got up and joined her. There was nothing in that enchanting child's face that forecast the sorry story of her life. Whatever she had read into Geneva's gesture was only because she knew its tragic end.

While Miranda was still looking at the portrait, she felt Geneva's touch on her arm. "Could I hold her? Just for a minute?"

Miranda hesitated. But as Geneva stood there, a supplicant in white and black, something in Miranda softened and she handed the baby over.

"She's so heavy!" Geneva exclaimed. She looked ill at ease — even burdened.

"She's big for her age," Miranda said. "Which is actually a good thing, considering her start in life."

Celeste began to squirm and reached out for Miranda. Geneva seemed relieved to give her back. "Do you think you could find your way to letting me see her sometimes?" she said. "Not often, not alone. But just once in a while."

Again, Miranda was silent. She let her eyes roam around the meticulously appointed room. Although she had not seen the rest of the apartment, she knew it would be governed by the same sense of order, the same loving attention to detail. And she also knew what it had cost Geneva to make this request.

"I'm not sure," she said finally. "I'll need to think it over." Geneva was on the outside of Celeste's life; she wanted to step a little closer to it, and Miranda was the one who could bestow or deny permission. It was, she realized, a terrible position to be in. She was ready to go; she had gotten what she had come for. Or as much as she was going to get. She strapped Celeste into the car seat and took her bag from its spot near the love seat. Then she moved toward the door.

"I won't call you." Geneva followed her and stood with her hand on the polished brass knob. "But I'll be hoping that you'll call me."

Miranda did not reply. She had come to judge, to excoriate and to blame. But what she felt now was less anger and more compassion. Geneva was damaged too — by her past, by the choices she had made, and by the burden of guilt she would always carry with her. She still had not said anything, but she reached for the other woman's hand and gave it one short, strong squeeze before she left.

# THIRTY

When Evan walked onto the set of the *Soigné* fashion shoot, he couldn't help but compare it to the last shoot he'd been on: yapping dogs, hissing cats, a rogue parrot, and yards and yards of pee-stained no-seam. Here, in this elegant Brooklyn Heights town house, the mood couldn't have been more different. Not only was the place itself posh by any standards — velvet drapes, massive crystal chandelier, enormous mantel in black, veined marble — but the mood was so subdued and even elegant. The smooth, creamy sound of Nat King Cole was issuing forth from a pair of speakers and, at the far end of the room, a long table had been set up with lavish platters of sliced fruit, a sink-sized bowl of yogurt, and a matching bowl of granola, croissants, and muffins; there was also coffee and hot water for tea.

Mario, who had asked for his help on this shoot, came up behind him. "Fashion

421

people like to live well." He paused to take a bite of a blueberry muffin. "And if you're in their orbit, that means you get to live well too." Evan had been friends with Mario since their days at Pratt, and when Mario's assistant bailed at the last minute, he didn't mind stepping in to lend a hand. The work wasn't too hard, and Mario had offered him a great day rate.

Evan began unpacking the lights, keeping an eye on the terry-cloth-clad girls — and they really were girls — who were having their faces painted by the makeup person. Not one of them was especially pretty, but as the makeup was applied, they became transformed, their features suddenly springing into vivid and compelling life. There was a red-haired, freckled one who truly did look like a kid, but when the makeup person got through with her, she was turned into someone at least a decade older — and decades more sophisticated. Those freckles reminded him a little of Thea, though Thea never attempted to cover them.

"We're going to start in the parlor," Mario said. "So you can set up in there."

The parlor had a long, lace-covered table, and the models were asked to sit and pose around it. They wore wispy, light dresses that looked like silk or, in one case, gauze;

although it was now October, the magazine was already shooting for a spring issue.

After Evan had positioned the camera, a medium-format Rolleiflex, on the tripod, Mario began with several shots of the entire table — the girls holding crystal goblets, the pyramid of fruit in the crystal bowl, the platters of petits fours, the enormous sprays of white lilacs, flown in from who knew where — before he began to focus on the individual girls. "Come on. Throw your head back and smile, smile, smile." He kept up a steady patter, cajoling them with his words, his compliments. "You're at a party; you're having fun, the time of your life. Let it show, sweetheart. Let it shine."

When it was the redhead's turn, Mario had her stand against the dark green velvet drape; her hair stood out like a blaze. In addition to her sliplike dress, she wore dangling earrings, a wristful of bangles, and a long scarf she wound in different ways around neck, shoulders, and arms. A stylist hovered nearby to make adjustments to her clothes and hair, adroitly stepping out of the way before the shutter clicked. "That's right. That's the way to do it!" The girl arched her throat and giggled; *click, click, click.*

Evan wondered if Thea had ever considered modeling when she was younger. She was very pretty, and she certainly had the body for it. They were lovers now, and he'd learned to appreciate that body, despite its not being the kind that naturally excited him. But she was fun in so many other ways. Since they'd started dating, they had gone rock climbing and Rollerblading. They were planning a white-water rafting trip, and Evan was looking forward to it. She was even taking trapeze lessons at Chelsea Piers, and although he declined her offer to treat him to a class, he did stay and watch. The sight of her long limbs stretched and flying through the air was exhilarating, and yeah, sexy. He didn't feel like he loved her, but he liked her a lot, and for now, liking was more than okay. "And this time, you picked one who's really into you," Audrey pointed out. He knew she was right.

Around noon, they broke for lunch. Evan went back into the first room and saw that the breakfast stuff had been cleared and consolidated to make space for the sandwiches, wraps, bowl of salad, and cookie plate that had been added. He reached for a sandwich — turkey with arugula and cranberry mayo on a ciabatta roll, just the kind of thing Miranda would have prepared. He also helped himself to a bag of sweet potato chips and a pickle. He still thought of her, often, though he tried to banish her image from the bedroom, especially when he was with Thea. He thought about Lily too. Were Miranda and her father, Jared Masters, a couple now? One happy little family? The thought still could make his stomach churn, so he tried not to think about it.

He was just about through with the sandwich when he was approached by a tall, blond woman in caramel-colored leather pants and a soft sweater of the same shade. At first he thought she was a model but quickly realized she was at least twice the age of the rest of the girls in the room.

"Evan Zuckerbrot?" she said, putting out her hand.

"I'm Evan." He shook her hand and swallowed; it was hard to talk with a mouthful of turkey.

"Courtney Barrett. I'm the accessories editor at *Soigné*. I don't usually show up at these shoots, but when I saw your name listed as the assistant on the shoot, I wanted to stop by."

"Nice to meet you." What possible interest could the accessories editor of this bigtime magazine have in him? He was just pinch-hitting here.

"I'm not here about the shoot," she said

425

as if she'd been able to divine his thoughts. "But I did want to talk to you. Can we go upstairs?"

"Isn't that off-limits?" he asked.

"Not to me."

Evan finished the sandwich and took a drink from the can of green apple soda he'd plucked from the table. Then, still carrying the soda, he followed Courtney Barrett up the handsome old staircase and into a room that was home to a pair of wing chairs, a low table, and a brass chandelier. "Please sit down." He did as she asked. "I'm sure you're wondering why I asked you to come up here."

"Yeah, I am. It all seems kind of mysterious."

"It's not really." Courtney smiled. "I just wanted us to have some privacy. I'm a friend of Miranda Berenzweig." She let that hang in the air.

"Did Miranda ask you to talk to me?" Miranda! He'd just been thinking of her. Evan took another sip of the soda.

"No, she didn't. And I think she'd be pretty upset to know that I was here, so I hope you won't tell her."

"Your secret's safe; I'm not in touch with her. But why did you come? We broke up."

"I know that."

"Do you know why?"

Courtney nodded. "She mentioned it had something to do with Jared Masters."

"Did she tell you she cheated on me with him?" He finished the soda.

"She told me everything. Even things you don't know yet."

"Like what?" Underneath his hostility, Evan was intrigued. Maybe there was more to the story than he'd realized. Maybe he was secretly hoping there was.

"That her father died."

"Really? When?" Evan thought of the game of checkers and the misplaced but nonetheless sincere affection shown to him by Miranda's dad.

"A few weeks ago. Here's another thing I'll bet you don't know. Jared Masters took a job in Gilead, Louisiana. He's relocating there for at least a year — maybe more. He signed over all his parental rights to the baby to Miranda."

"You mean Lily's going to be Miranda's? For good?"

"Celeste," said Courtney. "That's what her legal name is now. And yes. For good."

"Wow." Evan ran his finger around the rim of the empty can. "Miranda must be thrilled."

"Delirious is how I'd put it."

"Well, I'm happy for her. Really, I am. You can tell her that for me."

"Maybe you want to tell her yourself."

"I don't think that would be such a great idea." He waited. "I'm seeing someone else now."

"Oh," said Courtney Barrett. She looked like a woman who was used to getting her way and who was clearly surprised when she didn't. "I didn't know."

"Yeah, well, how would you? Anyway, I wish Miranda well, but things are different now."

"Are they?" Courtney said.

Uncomfortable under her direct stare, Evan stood up. "The shoot," he said. "They're going to be starting soon. I'd better get back."

The afternoon passed quickly. Nat King Cole gave way to Billie Holiday and Judy Garland. More food — cream puffs, napoleons — appeared late in the day. Mario chanted to the girls, *Rock it, shake it, work it, work it, work it.* They finished up around seven o'clock, and Evan stayed to take down the lights and put the rest of the equipment away. "Thanks for the help today," Mario said when they had finished and everything was loaded up in his van. "I owe you one."

"No, you don't," said Evan. "I was happy

to do it."

"That blonde who came looking for you? You know her?"

"Friend of a friend," said Evan. He wasn't going into it with Mario — not now anyway.

"I'm heading out for a drink," said Mario. "Want to join me?"

"Rain check?" Evan said. "I've got plans."

"The blonde?"

"Not the blonde," said Evan. "Blondes aren't my type."

Later that night, he was lying naked next to Thea. They'd gone out for a few beers and a burger at Anchor on Van Brunt Street and then back to his place. The sex had been particularly acrobatic tonight; she wanted to try all sorts of positions — stretching, bending, twisting. Evan wasn't really into it, but he went along for the ride. The novelty was appealing and it helped distract him from what was still missing with her, the thing he'd had so effortlessly with Miranda. Somewhere outside was a wailing sound.

"Is that a cat?" She propped up on an elbow.

Evan got up and went to the window so he could hear better. "I don't think so. It sounds like a baby."

"How annoying. I hope it doesn't cry all night."

"Babies do cry," Evan said as he got back into bed. "Comes with the territory."

"I know — that's part of the reason I've never wanted to go there."

"You don't want kids? I mean — someday?"

She shook her head. "I decided pretty early on it wasn't for me. I'm the eldest of five and helped raise my siblings. That's enough."

"Not even one? One baby?"

"No, Evan." She swatted him playfully on the arm. "Not even one. Anyway, we'd be idiots to have a baby."

"And why is that?" He tried to keep his tone light; he'd never told her about his — condition.

"Are you kidding? Look at how tall we are! If we had a baby, it'd be a giraffe."

*I like giraffes,* thought Evan, *Giraffes are fine.* But he just smiled and said nothing.

Soon she had drifted off to sleep, the sound of her light, even breathing gentle as a lullaby. Evan, however, remained stubbornly awake. Miranda's father had died. Masters was both out of the city and out of the picture. Celeste was now Miranda's child. For good. The thought kicked and danced in his head, making sleep even more remote a possibility. Finally, he got up and went into the kitchen. The first gray light of morning had begun to show at the window, and Evan sat down to watch as it grew lighter and lighter: the breaking of a brand-new day.

# THIRTY-ONE

Celeste was especially clingy on the morning of Halloween; when Miranda attempted to hand her to Supah, she wrapped her arms tightly around Miranda's neck and would not let go.

"She be fine with me. Go to office." Supah extricated Miranda from the baby's grip and then, when Celeste started to howl, bounced her in her arms as Miranda stood there in her coat, stricken with indecision. Leave now and assume that Celeste would be fine once she was out the door? Take the morning off and go in this afternoon? But that would be setting a bad precedent; much as she might have liked to stay home with Celeste, she did not, even with her father's money, have that luxury.

"Mommy will be back," she said as Supah attempted to distract Celeste with various stuffed animals. "We'll go to the Halloween parade and see all the costumes." Celeste batted the toys away and cried harder. Miranda left, the sounds of Celeste's wailing an awful echo in her head the whole ride into the office.

When she arrived, late and perspiring — the temperature had spiked and her wool coat was much too warm — she saw with some dismay that her desk was crowded with bottles of olive oil: estate-produced olive oil from the hills of Chianti Rufina, first-day-of-harvest oil from Spain, oil infused with orange, with cardamom, coriander, cumin, and cinnamon. They were doing a feature story on olive oil and she planned to have a tasting party later in the day, only she'd forgotten the loaves of bread she'd meant to pick up. Another thing to deal with.

Moving some of the bottles aside, Miranda cleared a place and got to work. Lunch was a yogurt at her desk; when her cell phone buzzed around two o'clock, she was tempted not to answer. Then she saw it was Courtney's number on the screen; the wedding was just a few days away and she sensed it might be important.

"Can you talk?" Courtney sounded very agitated.

"For a few minutes." Miranda looked at the layout she'd been considering, splashed across her computer screen, and the bottles of oil, which she had not even had time to bring into the office kitchen. "You sound upset; what's going on?"

"It's Fluff."

"Is he sick?" Miranda knew how much Courtney adored that odious little Pomeranian of hers.

"He's gone!"

"What do you mean, gone? Did he escape? Or run away?"

"No, it was Harris. You know he's never liked him."

"You've mentioned that. . . ." This was an understatement; Harris had an extreme aversion to the yappy little animal, and for once, Miranda was on his side.

"Well, this morning I had an appointment with the hairdresser, and when I got back, Fluff was just gone! I nearly went crazy looking for him until I found Harris's note. He said that he couldn't live with him anymore. The barking drove him insane, and this morning, after I left, he snapped at him. But that's because he was wearing those shearling slippers again!"

"The dog has a problem with Harris's slippers?" Miranda was not following.

"For some reason, the smell gets to him. So I told Harris he had to get rid of them.

But did he listen to me? No! Instead, on his way to work, he dropped Fluff at what he assured me was an *excellent foster home* and said that we could figure out what to do about him after the wedding. Right now, there isn't going to be a wedding because I'm ready to call the whole thing off!"

"Have you phoned Harris?"

"Only about fifteen times! He's in some meeting or other and *can't be disturbed.* I don't believe it for a second! I'll bet he just doesn't want to deal with me — and he's right because I am so furious I might set his office on fire!"

"Courtney, I know how angry you are —"

"Not angry! Enraged! Seething! And this isn't the first time he's pulled something like this."

"What do you mean?" Miranda was curious. Courtney had never indicated that there was anything wrong with the perfect guy she'd snagged; she praised everything from his Ivy League education to his taste in ties.

"He's an autocrat. Instead of discussing, he just decides. He gave a chair I like to Goodwill because he said it was uncomfortable. He dumps my junk mail; I know it's just junk mail, but still, it's mine to dump. He even got rid of a sweater whose color he said made me look wan — his word. And now Fluff — that's the last straw!"

"Why did you put up with it?"

"You know why." Courtney's voice was no longer angry, but small and sad.

"I do?" Miranda was confused. Certainly she had put up with plenty from Luke, but she'd always shared her misgivings with her friends; Courtney had not.

"Because you're not the only one feeling a little desperate; my clock is ticking too, Miranda. I wanted to get married, start a family, and so does Harris. And there are so many things I do love about him. . . . But now I don't know. I just don't know. I think I should tell him the wedding is off."

A few months ago, Miranda might have cheered at that statement. But where would that leave Courtney? "Listen. I want you to promise me — and I mean *promise me* — that you will not do anything until I call you back. You need someone to help you through this, and I've just been elected."

"I want Fluff; he had no right to take him." She was crying now.

"No, he didn't — at least not without telling you first. Now, just sit tight."

She got off the phone and sprang into action. First, she sent a group e-mail postponing the olive oil tasting until the next day.

436

Then she called Harris — she still had his number — and when she was told that he was in a meeting, she went into Sallie's office and told her she'd have to leave for a few hours. "Personal crisis," she said.

"Not the baby?" Sallie looked worried.

"No. Not the baby. But something urgent that just can't wait."

Then, leaving her coat but grabbing her bag, she hurried downstairs, flagged a taxi, sweet-talked the security guard downstairs by saying she had a surprise for her fiancé — one of the attorneys — and did not want to be announced. Then she took the elevator to the twenty-first floor, where Wickham, Stephens and Grotstein had their offices.

"Do you have an appointment?" asked the receptionist.

"No, but it's an emergency. Tell him Miranda Berenzweig is here to see him."

"I'm sorry, but he left very clear instructions — he was not to be disturbed."

Miranda tried to read the woman's face, but it was opaque. "Fine." She turned and settled herself on the leather sofa at the far end of the reception area. "I'll wait."

"He might be some time."

"That's all right." Miranda picked up the copy of *Architectural Digest* from a pile that sat on a table. "I'm in no hurry."

Miranda went through all the issues of *Architectural Digest* that were on that table, and then she moved on to *Vanity Fair.* When she had nearly gotten through the second issue, three men in dark suits emerged from behind a closed door. Harris was one of them. Miranda stood, sending the magazine sliding to the floor. Hastily, she picked it up and walked right over.

"I need to see you," she said quietly. "Now."

"Miranda, hi. I'm afraid this isn't a good time —" He looked nervously at his companions, both of whom seemed just a little too interested in what might be about to happen.

"Yes, it is. In fact, it's an excellent time. Is there somewhere we could talk that's more private?"

Harris looked wretched. "I suppose so." He turned to the other men. "You go ahead without me; I'll catch you later." Then, to Miranda, "We can go into my office, but it's got to be quick."

Miranda said nothing until she was seated on the other side of his wide mahogany desk, door closed quietly behind him.

"Is this about the dog? Did Courtney send you?"

438

"No, and it's better that I came without her — you wouldn't want her here now."

"I guess it wasn't the best way to handle it —"

"You mean kidnapping her dog when she was out? No. I'd say that was about the worst way. She's about to cancel the wedding — that's how mad she is."

"She wouldn't." Harris looked anxious, though.

"Oh? I wouldn't bet on that. When's she's angry, Courtney is a force of nature."

"Don't I know it." Harris rubbed his forehead with the heel of his hand. "But the dog is a menace, and Courtney just will not hear it. From day one, that animal has had it in for me — snarling and snapping all the time. And then there's the peeing on the floor, the sofa, even the bed; and the chewing, but only my things: shoes, my favorite cashmere scarf. Did she tell you it almost bit me today? I just couldn't take it anymore. I knew she'd never agree, so I brought the dog over to my aunt in Forest Hills. She lives alone in a big house with a yard and she loves dogs — even psychotic ones like Courtney's. It's the perfect environment for that miserable fur ball."

"Did you tell Courtney how you felt about the dog?"

"Did I tell her? Of course! She just stone-walls me. She even wants to take the dog on our honeymoon; can you believe it?"

Miranda could. "I know that dog could try the patience of a saint. But how you handle this issue is a blueprint for your marriage. You can't just make a unilateral decision, especially about something that's so important to Courtney."

"She can visit the dog anytime she likes; my aunt would be so happy to see her."

"Have you listened to one word I've said? This isn't just about the dog; it's about how you and Courtney are going to make a life together." When Harris was quiet, Miranda continued. "Come on — you're a lawyer. You were trained to negotiate."

"I was also trained to cut through the crap, and Courtney has been dishing out plenty of that. But maybe I should have tried harder to get through to her. I'm used to just taking action; it's just how I operate."

"That might work in a courtroom. But not with your wife-to-be."

Harris studied his hands; his nails were bitten way down, a small vulnerability that Miranda found almost endearing. "I'll go to my aunt's after work and get the damn dog. But only on the condition that she acknowledges we have a problem and is willing to confront it."

"It sounds like Fluff needs a professional evaluation."

"What do you mean? An animal behavior expert? A pet therapist, for Christ's sake?"

"Actually, yes. We interviewed a pet therapist for a story on canine acting out a few months ago and he was pretty insightful. I'd venture he'd say Fluff was used to being Courtney's main man before you came along and now he has to share her and adjust to a new environment — all at the same time. The dog doesn't know how to be around you. Will he be dominant? Will you? That might explain the peeing too. There's even a name for it: submissive urination. It means he's trying to ingratiate himself with you."

"Well, it's not working." But Harris did smile. "I guess it couldn't hurt to consult someone; could you get me the name of the person quoted in the article?"

"I'll even send you the article to read." Miranda let that sink in before making her next suggestion. "And maybe it would help if you two saw a couples therapist a few times; it might help in coming up with better ways to deal with conflict." Listen to her: Social Work 101.

"I should call. She's been trying me all day."

"Do that, and when you're through, I'll talk to her." Miranda waited while Harris made the call. At first, he did almost none of the talking; Miranda could hear the shrill sound of Courtney's voice on the other end of the line. But eventually she let Harris talk and he touched on the major points — therapy for dog, therapy for them, no dog on honeymoon. By the time he handed the phone to Miranda, they had already made plans for the trip out to Forest Hills later that day.

"You're good?" Miranda asked her.

"I'll be better when Fluff is back home again; I'm going to call Harris's aunt so I can talk to him."

"Courtney, you cannot talk to a dog on the phone."

"Why not? He'll recognize the sound of my voice; he always does."

"If you say so."

"Thank you, Miranda. I think you're right about the couples counselor, and I'm going to make an appointment as soon as we're back from the honeymoon. Harris said he's on board with it."

"I know. I've been right here with him the whole time."

"Of course you have. You're the best."

Miranda said good-bye and handed the phone back to Harris. "Okay, crisis averted — at least for now."

"Thank you, Miranda."

"You're welcome." She stood up; what time was it anyway? She had to get back to the office.

"So how's it working out with your baby girl? Courtney says that the adoption is being finalized."

"It is and I couldn't be happier." *Except if I had a partner — like Evan — to share it with,* she thought. But though she was feeling more kindly disposed toward Harris, she wasn't about to share that. She took her bag and left.

It was almost five o'clock when she walked into her office; she saw that the bottles were gone — someone must have taken them to the kitchen — and in their place was something shrouded in purple and turquoise tissue. What was it? She lifted out a small costume comprised of felt, satin, and a few real feathers in the tail — Celeste's Halloween costume. She had totally forgotten! The crew in sewing had made it and Celeste would be the most adorable peacock in the Park Slope Halloween parade — if Miranda could get home in time to take her. She stuffed the costume into her bag, grabbed her coat, and rushed out the door. This was Celeste's first Halloween and Miranda wasn't going to miss it.

Pushing the stroller down the hill toward Seventh Avenue, Miranda couldn't stop looking at the costumes that flitted, trotted, and cavorted by. Along with the witches, ghouls, and monsters, she saw children dressed as mermaids and Barbie dolls, as dragons, a Lego piece, and an iPhone. A family dressed as flowers and their baby was dressed as a bee; another baby was costumed as a chicken with a pair of yellow rubber gloves as feet. She'd always gone to the parade as an observer, to gather ideas for the magazine. But today, with Celeste in her own costume, she felt like a participant.

On the avenue, the crowd grew thicker. The merchants handed out candy to the parade-goers, and the Häagen Daz store on the corner of President Street was giving out coupons for free ice cream cones. Had it been colder, she would have saved the coupon for another time. But the balmy temperature made the thought of eating ice cream irresistible, so Miranda stopped in for a single scoop of coffee in a sugar cone. She knelt down and let Celeste have a lick;

Celeste clamored for more, so Miranda let her eat the rest of it, soggy, leaking cone and all. When the cone was gone, she cleaned the baby's face with one of the premoistened towelettes she always kept in her bag. "Your first Halloween with Mama," she said to Celeste, who was now pulling at a tail feather. "Isn't it fun?"

"Mama!" Celeste put her sticky hands on Miranda's face. "Mama!"

This was the first time Celeste had used the word directly in connection with Miranda; before, she'd been making *mmmm* sounds quite randomly. But her meaning now was clear: Mama meant Miranda. She knew. She *knew*.

Later, as the parade wound down, Miranda ran into Heidi, a woman she remembered from the food co-op. Heidi was pushing a child in a stroller too; he was dressed as a fireman, though he had his red hat in both hands and was chewing on the visor.

"Auggie and I are going to stop in for pizza; want to come?" Heidi took Auggie's hat and put it back on his head.

"Sure." Miranda followed her inside Roma's Pizza. Over the slices the women dissected and fed to the children — a bit of cheese, then a bit of crust — Heidi told Miranda about a regular single mommy's group she was organizing.

"Sounds great," Miranda said. "I'd love to join."

By the time they got home, Celeste was asleep in the stroller. Most of the peacock feathers were gone; there were crumbs in her hair and her face was streaked with tomato sauce. Miranda managed to get her inside and into her crib without waking her; she'd bathe her first thing in the morning.

Then she opened up her laptop, knowing that what she was about to do was a bad idea. She also knew that she was going to do it anyway. Although they had broken up and he had not responded to her phone calls, Evan had not unfriended her on Facebook, and it was his page she opened now.

It was from Facebook that she'd learned about his new girlfriend, Thea. Miranda had hated her instantly. She was impossibly thin, the sort of woman who subsisted on celery and lettuce; a carrot or some shredded beets were probably what she considered a big splurge. And she was annoyingly athletic, as evidenced by the pictures of the two of them rock climbing, Rollerblading, and, most shudder inducing of all, camping. Miranda loathed few things as much as she did camping and saw no reason, after all the progress made by civilization, to spend a night outside on the cold ground, a hapless target for insects, wild animals, and a whole range of other natural disasters.

Evan and Thea did not seem to be living together, but he certainly looked smitten with her. No wonder he had not returned her calls; he was in love with someone else. Miranda started at the expression on his face. She recognized it quite well; it was the way he had once looked at *her.* She hated herself for scrolling through the recent posts, yet she was unable to stop. Here were Evan and Thea bowling. Bowling! Also playing shuffleboard and windsurfing. The pictures galled her. How had she been so adroit in articulating the problems between Courtney and Harris and so utterly dense about her own romantic life?

Enough. This pity party was over. She navigated away from Evan's page and turned to the more neutral realm of e-mail. But there was a decidedly not-neutral surprise waiting for her: a message with the subject line *Wie gehts?* It was from Luke.

Miranda had not heard from him in more than a year, and just seeing his name sent her stomach into freefall. Quickly, she scanned the message and then read it a second time, more slowly. The art scene in

Berlin had proved to be less stimulating than he'd envisioned. His work was being met with the same polite indifference there as it had in New York. Also, the city was unfriendly, the weather bad, his job in a bar dead end. And Liesel, the cute little *fräulein* he'd followed across the ocean, had dumped him. He'd never given up his place in Brooklyn, only sublet it; he decided he would be moving back. Maybe they could pick up where they'd left off?

I realize I treated you shabbily, Miranda, and I am truly and deeply sorry. I didn't appreciate your loyalty and depth, the way you fed not only my body — I'm still tasting your spaghetti alla carbonara, your spiced mocha nut cake — but my soul too. You believed in me and that's worth everything. Can you ever forgive me? I promise we could make a new start of it. A new beginning.

A new beginning. Had this entreaty come a year or even a few months ago, Miranda would have leaped at the chance. Luke, with his perpetual air of entitled, even proud dissatisfaction, his touchiness, his moods, his lofty pronouncements. Luke, who could reduce her to a quivering puddle of Jell-O with a single heated kiss. Luke, whose lazy sidelong glance completely undid her. Luke wanted her back. The irony of it. The sweet, *sweet* irony. She let herself savor it before she began to compose her reply.

I'm sorry to hear things didn't work out for you in Berlin. That must have been hard. Maybe you'll get that new start back in New York; I sincerely hope you do. But it's going to be without me, Luke. I've moved on and I no longer want to rekindle what we had together. And if things pick up for you, I'd really appreciate the return of that money you "borrowed" when you used my credit card. I won't say stole, because I want to believe better of you. Please don't disappoint me — again.

Miranda was not the same woman Luke had so cavalierly left behind. She had been changed — by Evan, by Jared, and most of all, by Celeste. She hit SEND without any hesitation. Then she turned off the computer and went to bed.

Lying in the dark, she did not think at all about Luke, whom she had banished from her mind with the ease of a keystroke. Instead, all her thoughts coalesced around Evan. Those eyes of his. Those enormous hands that had touched her — and Celeste — with such surprising delicacy. The attentive way he looked at the world, the way he listened to her. But this was futile; she needed to stop. *I won't think about him,* she told herself. *I won't.* And with a vigorous punch to her pillow, she rolled over and willed herself to sleep.

# THIRTY-TWO

On the following Sunday morning, Miranda woke early and sat up straight in bed. It had rained heavily the night before, leaving a brilliant autumn day in its wake. Opening the window, she poked her head out and squinted into the sun. The bright sky and clear air seemed like good omens. Somewhere in Manhattan, she knew Courtney was rejoicing. Then she heard a sound from Celeste's room. "Mama!" Celeste called. "Mama! Mama!" *That's me,* Miranda thought happily, and hurried in to fetch her girl.

Several hours later, they were both dressed and ready to go; Miranda had called a car service and was waiting in front of the house. Mrs. Castiglione was standing outside with them, a thick plaid coat zipped over one of the three housedresses she typically wore.

"You both look lovely," she said. "Let me

take your picture."

Miranda handed over her phone. She did love the dress she'd eventually settled on. Bea had chosen a forest green silk sheath, to set off her hair, and Lauren had opted for a similar dress in midnight blue. Miranda wanted the dress in gray, but the raw silk somehow leeched the color from her face. "I have an idea," Solange had said, and she brought out a bolt of shimmering gray satin, the color of pewter. "What do you think? I can make up the same style using this." The result — an elegant, simply cut dress in the most sumptuous of materials — was perfect. And Solange used some of the leftover fabric to fashion a matching frock — that was the only word to describe it — for Celeste.

Mrs. Castiglione handed Miranda the phone as the car pulled up. "Have a wonderful time," she said, pulling the coat more tightly around her small frame.

"Thanks!" Miranda put in Celeste's car seat and climbed in next to her.

The car sped up the hill, past Grand Army Plaza and up Eastern Parkway before stopping at the entrance to the Brooklyn Botanic Garden. She would be the only one of the four friends at the wedding without an escort; Bea and her restaurant manager had gotten pretty serious and were looking for a place together. Had Evan still been her boyfriend, he would have accompanied her. But he was not. She was going to enjoy the day anyway; she had a personal stake in it.

As Miranda was paying the driver, she saw several other wedding guests milling around the newly designed entrance. Miranda didn't care for that entrance; it was too modern and seemed at odds with what was beyond the gate. But the garden itself, with its meandering paths, manicured flower beds, and expanses of green, was one of her favorite places in the city. She picked Lauren out of the small crowd, Sophie and Max right beside her. Toting the car seat, Miranda hurried over as fast as she could.

"Sophie, you are going to make such a wonderful flower girl!"

"Mommy says I have a very important job."

"Your mommy is right," said Miranda. Celeste started kicking in her seat.

"She's so cute," Sophie said. "Can I touch her?"

"Hold out your finger and she'll grab it," said Miranda. Sophie complied, and when Celeste grabbed her finger, she giggled.

"You can play with her after the ceremony, okay?"

"Okay!" Sophie hopped from one foot to the other. Then Lauren took her by one hand and Max by the other; Lauren's husband, Dave, came up beside them and they all walked into the garden. They stayed on the main path until they reached the Palm House, the grand, domed glass conservatory; in the waning autumn light, it was lit like a castle.

"Pretty, pretty, pretty!" sang out Sophie as she loped around the circular fountain that stood in front of the entrance.

A classical quartet was playing Bach as Miranda walked in, and once she'd hung up her coat and stowed the car seat, a slender girl with ballerina-straight posture introduced herself as Jordan and asked if Miranda wanted her to take Celeste to the room set up for all the children.

"That would be great," Miranda said. "I'll stop in to check on her." She attempted to hand the baby over, but Celeste buried her face in Miranda's neck when Jordan reached for her.

"Maybe I'd better go with you," Miranda said when Celeste lifted her face and turned, coyly, toward Jordan again. This time, she let herself be picked up and taken away. As Miranda stood watching them go, a waiter stepped up carrying a tray of glasses filled with white wine. "May I offer you a drink?" he asked.

"You certainly may." Miranda took it and began to circulate. There was Lauren and her husband, Dave, and there was Bea, with her restaurant manager beau; she looked like a sprite, all her crazy hair barely tamed for the event. Miranda's own long hair had been done up in a loose topknot, and she wore pearl-drop earrings that had belonged to her mother, along with her grandmother's triple-strand pearl choker.

"Isn't it beautiful?" Bea raised her glass and gestured around the space; small lights twinkled above the guests, and the setting sun was turning the panes a brilliant orange.

"Courtney's finally come to appreciate this much-maligned borough," said Miranda. She raised her glass in a toast. "Here's to Brooklyn weddings!" They all drank to that. More waiters had begun to circulate — with wine, with appetizers — and there were various tables of food toward which people had started to gravitate. Miranda decided to head for the crudités first. On her way, she was offered baby lamb chops, crab cakes, and toasted coconut shrimp. She accepted only a single shrimp; there would be so much more to eat later on, and she didn't want to fill up now.

The shrimp was succulent; maybe she would have just *one* more; she downed the last delicious bit and was looking for the waiter who had produced them when she ran right into the last person she had expected to see tonight. Evan! She was still holding the shrimp tail and wished desperately to get rid of it.

"Nice to see you, Miranda." Evan, who did not look at all surprised, had the advantage.

"Who invited you?" Her cheeks were starting to flush. Surreptitiously, she dropped her hand to her side and let the shrimp tail — along with the greasy, balled-up napkin that held it — fall to the floor.

"You did." He seemed to be enjoying her discomfort.

"*I* did? Are you crazy?"

"Your invitation said plus guest, didn't it? Well, I'm your guest."

"This is the first I'm hearing about it."

"I could use a drink," Evan said, and from his lofty height, he was able to signal to a waiter, who quickly materialized with a tray. "How about you?"

"Definitely," Miranda said and reached for the proffered glass. She'd already had one, but if there was ever a moment when she needed a second drink, this was it. "So how are you?"

"I'm fine." He seemed to consider the contents of his drink as integral to his reply. "Listen, I heard about your father and I'm sorry. He was a sweet man."

"Thank you." She sipped again; the drink was nearly gone. "Who told you that anyway?"

But Evan didn't answer; he swiveled around, surveying the room, before turning back to her. "I heard about Celeste too. That's wonderful. Really wonderful. You must be so happy."

She drained her glass. "I brought her with me. She's here tonight."

"Can I see her?"

Miranda nodded. "Later. After the ceremony." Who had the advantage now? She didn't know for certain who had been feeding Evan his information, but she could guess. And clearly he was as interested in keeping tabs on her as she had been in keeping tabs on him. Then, across the room, she spotted Courtney's mother, whom she hadn't seen in more than a decade. "Will you excuse me?" She handed her empty glass to a passing waiter. "There's someone I want to say hello to."

"Sure." He remained unflappable. "Catch

457

you later."

Walking quickly away, Miranda was aware of his eyes following her. God, but she was grateful to have made her escape. Courtney must have found him somehow; found him, invited him, and never breathed a word to Miranda. What if she had known? Would it have changed anything? How strange: she'd been tracking Evan for weeks, carefully following his every electronically documented move, but now that he was actually here, she'd wanted only to get away from him.

She chatted with Courtney's mother, younger brother, and some assorted cousins she'd never met but had heard plenty about. She managed to avoid Evan for the rest of the cocktail hour — after Courtney's family, she moved on to other mutual college friends and one of Courtney's colleagues who actually had worked at *Domestic Goddess.* But she was aware of him the entire time. If he'd come to see her, why wasn't he making more of an effort? Apart from that initial greeting, he had not approached her again. Disconcerting. And just the slightest bit hurtful.

Soon it was time to file into the even larger, central room — also glass paned — for the wedding ceremony. Miranda sat with the wedding party in a designated area off to the side. She would be walking down the aisle with Peter, one of the groom's attendants. They'd met for the first time last night. Evan had found a seat near the back. In case he wanted to bolt? But didn't he want to see Celeste?

The musicians had moved into this room and the strains of Pachelbel's Canon began to fill the space. Miranda and Peter stood, and he nodded. It was time. They began their decorous walk down the aisle toward the altar, decorated with a crimson cloth and strands of bittersweet, tiger lilies, goldenrod, and tiny, jewel-like rosebuds. Even though Courtney had shared the details of the decor with her, Miranda was not prepared for the actual sight of the thing and moved toward it as if toward some glowing oasis. Would she ever walk down an aisle where the man she loved waited? It did not seem likely. But that was okay. *She* was okay.

Down the aisle came Lauren and Bea with their escorts. Courtney's mother followed, accompanied by her brother. Sophie performed her task with great enthusiasm; some of the red rose petals ended up in her hair and one landed right on her nose. The little ring bearer accompanied her solemnly, the bands of gold balanced on a red velvet pillow. Next was Harris with his parents and, finally, Courtney, on the arm of her favorite uncle. She really did make a striking bride, and the assembled guests murmured appreciatively as she slowly walked toward her groom. But Courtney seemed unaware of them; she was utterly focused on Harris. During the ceremony, she kept looking at him, and when it was time for the kiss, she had to duck a bit because even in flats she was taller than he was. Something about this — the awkwardness in this picture-perfect moment — struck Miranda as the best, most authentic moment of the entire ceremony; her eyes welled.

On the receiving line, Courtney was alternately beaming and hugging. When Miranda reached her, she whispered, "Love you," in her friend's ear. And then, "What's with Evan?"

"Love you too," Courtney said before the next well-wisher moved in. She ignored Miranda's question.

Miranda made her way to the dinner tables, which had been decorated in a similar fashion to the altar; the tablecloths and napkins were red, and the centerpieces were clusters of tiger lilies, red rosebuds, and goldenrod, into which acorns and pinecones had been woven. As she sat down, she saw the place card right next to hers read Evan Zuckerbrot. Courtney had struck again.

Evan sat down just as the salads were being served. But because they each had table mates on either side, it was impossible to exchange more than small talk. There was a break before dessert, and as Miranda got up to check on Celeste, he followed her.

They went down a flight of steps into the room where Jordan and another girl were attending to the kids. Max had dozed off on an armchair while Sophie and a few others were coloring with crayons. Plates of partially eaten food were scattered around, along with glasses of juice, one of them spilled. She spied Celeste in a playpen that had been set up in one corner. As soon as she saw her, Celeste called out, "Mama" with evident joy. Miranda lifted her up so Evan could see her.

"Look at you!" He turned to Miranda. "She's grown so much. And she's talking now."

"*Mama* was her first word. It's pretty much her only word. But still."

"And the matching dresses — love it." He took the ever-present camera from his shoulder and held it up. "Do you mind?"

"No. Knock yourself out." Miranda stood patiently while he snapped several photo-

461

graphs but could not understand the point of all this. Why had he come? He was in no hurry to tell her. Evan was different, she realized. There was something more self-contained about him. More remote and less open. The slight reserve made him seem more appealing somehow. Sexier. It was an unsettling thought.

"I'm going back upstairs." She kissed Celeste on the forehead and handed her to Jordan. "They'll be cutting the cake soon." Evan didn't say anything, but he followed her to the room where an elaborate, three-tiered cake had been set up on a crimson-covered table. Courtney stood next to Harris, a knife in her hand. Miranda watched while she made the first cut, extracted a slice, and fed it to him. There was a cheer and a server deftly took over. Waiters began circulating with trays of champagne, and guests were drifting back to their tables, where platters of truffles and cookies had been set out.

"No cake?" Evan took a bite of the piece on his plate.

"Not now." Miranda scanned the room. A band had replaced the quartet and was tuning up; soon the music — and dancing — would begin. "Let's get out of here." She took Evan by the hand and led him away.

"Where are we going?" He was still eating the cake.

"We can take a walk," she said. "In the garden."

For a moment she thought he would say no. But he set down his plate. "All right." They retrieved their coats and stepped out into the night. The sky was filled with puffed, charcoal-dark clouds through which the moon — not quite full — peeked. She turned to Evan. "Why are you here?"

"I told you: I'm your plus one."

"Evan, stop it! You came here for a reason, and I want to know what it is."

"Courtney invited me; I didn't want to turn her down."

"Courtney! When did you talk to Courtney?"

"That doesn't matter. The point is I'm here. You're here. It's been a while. I thought maybe we could talk."

"Fine." She was getting mixed signals. Was he here because he wanted to get back together? Or to say a final farewell? "What did you want to talk about?"

"Well, I could tell you that it broke my heart when I found out you'd slept with Jared. That I loved you. Because I did. And I loved Celeste too. That I thought — hoped

— we could be together. The three of us. A family."

"I didn't sleep with Jared. I *told* you that. You just didn't believe me." Now he was the Evan she knew and remembered. The Evan she had — and how foolish she was for not realizing it sooner — loved all along. But he hadn't finished. He was still talking.

"I didn't tell you about me, Miranda. There just wasn't the right time or the right opening."

"Tell me what?"

He looked so pained that she almost wanted to say, *No, it's all right. Don't tell me.* But he seemed to need to tell. Whatever *it* was.

"A couple of years ago, I found out that I couldn't have kids. The motility of my sperm is, like, nonexistent."

"What are you talking about? When did you even try to have a child?"

"I don't want to go into all that now. But it's been weighing on me ever since: how I would explain it to someone — if there were someone to explain it to. How she would react. All of it. And then you came along. I fell for you right away. And then when I met Celeste, well, it seemed perfect. It wouldn't matter if I couldn't father any kids of my own. Because we'd already have her; she

464

would be mine too."

Miranda was silent. He'd offered her a precious gift and she had not properly cherished it; was it too late to claim it now? "Evan." Miranda's voice was uncertain. "You said *loved*. Past tense. You *loved* me. You *loved* Celeste." The wind had come up and was blowing the hair into her face; impatiently, she pushed it away. "Do you still love us? Do you still love . . . me?"

"There's someone else now."

"Oh." Facebook-generated images of Thea — rock-scaling, oar-wielding, tent-pitching Thea — burned across Miranda's mind. "Well, then, I guess there's nothing left to say except that I hope you're happy with her. Very happy." She began walking back toward the conservatory, moving more quickly with every step. Behind her she heard Evan say, "I'm sorry, Miranda," but she didn't turn. What for? To see his pitying look? Better not to have that be the last image from this mortifying conversation.

Reaching the glass doors, she pulled one open and stepped back inside but did not head back to the party, where the sounds of the music had grown louder and more boisterous. Instead, she went down the stairs to fetch Celeste. She would call a car; no one would notice if they slipped out now.

The strains of music grew softer and more subdued as she moved away from them. Miranda's evening was over, and it was time to go.

# Thirty-Three

Evan wove through the New Year's Eve crowd in Times Square wearing a down jacket, ski hat, and scarf, but even though the temperature was in the single digits, he wore no gloves, not even the ones whose fingers he'd snipped off himself. Anything on his hands was an impediment; he needed his fingers, cold as they were, to be able to react to the unfolding pageant as the boisterous group waited for the ball to drop.

He stopped, attention caught by the group of young women all wearing the same glitter-encrusted hat, and he stood depressing the shutter as the girls laughed, talked, and in the case of one, swayed to music that only she heard, courtesy of her earbuds. Then someone attempted to muscle past them, and the whole mood shifted. Evan turned his eyes elsewhere and kept moving.

He'd been photographing the New Year's Eve scene for about a dozen years, and he looked forward to it every time. He loved the raucous energy of the crowd and the visual juxtapositions created by the faces and the bodies, the signs, the billboards, and the flashing lights. And then there were the costumes — despite the bitter cold, he saw sequins and stilettos, poufy dresses and miniskirts, glasses whose frames were made from the digits of the new year, novelty hats and sweatshirts. The camera could capture it all.

What was different this year was that Thea was with him. He'd told her she didn't have to come — it was sure to be noisy, crowded, freezing and, since he'd be preoccupied, not much fun. None of this daunted her. "I'll be your shadow; you won't even know I'm here." And it was true: she kept out of his way, leaving him free to work.

As the clock approached midnight, the mood amped up. And when the giant, glittering ball was released, the crowd chanted out the seconds as it descended. Ten, nine, eight . . . A roar erupted when the ball touched down; there was a lot of kissing, and one girl tossed big handfuls of confetti into the air. The tiny flakes rained down all over the shoulders and heads of those nearby, creating snowlike patterns on the dark coats and jackets; Evan snapped quickly and, he hoped, deftly. When he finally brought the camera away from his face, there was Thea, ready for her own New Year's Eve kiss.

He stayed a little longer to photograph, and then they wended their way to Gallagher's, an old Irish bar he liked on Forty-fifth Street. The place was crowded, but they were able to find a spot near the back. "Your hands are like ice." Thea took his palms in hers and began rubbing. "You'll get frostbite or something."

"I'm used to it," he said. He realized he was starved; shooting could do that to him.

Over hot toddies — it was too cold for champagne — and baked clams, they toasted the new year and made plans for the next day. "Mike and Gaby invited us to an open house tomorrow afternoon; I thought we could stop by," said Thea.

"Mmm." Evan was noncommittal. He'd met Mike and Gaby before and had not liked them — she was coarse and loud; he was a backslapping jerk. A party at their place was not something he was looking forward to, but he didn't want to disappoint Thea.

"I said I would bring a six-pack or two; she knows better than to ask me to bring any food!" Thea popped a clam into her mouth. A few bits of confetti had settled in her coppery hair, and her cheeks were still pink with cold. She was pretty, she was fun, and as Audrey had pointed out several times, she was *really into him.* So why did he feel so remote and lonely?

They ordered another round of hot toddies and the corned beef hash that Gallagher's had probably been serving for the last forty years. It wasn't a great dish, but it was a familiar one and Evan ate quickly, wondering how Miranda would have rated it. Ever since he'd seen her at the wedding, she'd been on his mind. Her father had died; the adoption was going through. She was very much alone in the world, raising Celeste by herself, but she'd seemed undaunted and even content. Jared Masters was not part of her world, at least not the way Evan had envisioned after seeing her with that damning mark on her neck.

"Are you okay?" Thea asked. "You seem kind of quiet."

"I'm fine," he said. "Totally fine."

They went back to her apartment, but by this time, it was so late and he was so tired — the adrenaline rush of shooting had wound down — that he begged off sex.

"That's okay," she said cheerfully. "Tomorrow is another day." She kissed his nose and went to sleep. Evan lay beside her. He thought of that morning when Miranda had come to him after her shower, dropping her towel as he reached for her. He loved sex in the daylight, with everything made so achingly clear. And she'd been so beautiful that day. All days really — he never got tired of looking at her. Miranda had kept insisting that she hadn't slept with Jared; maybe she was telling the truth. And even if she *had* slept with him, he could understand now how easy it would have been to succumb to that temptation — the baby, the father, the whole package neatly tied up with a bow.

Next to him, Thea shifted and turned; her slender, even bony, back, was facing in his direction and he stared at it. He wanted to love her, he'd tried to love her, but he did not love her. And he did not think he could begin another year struggling to find or manufacture what just wasn't there.

February in Gilead felt like spring; Jared was in his shirtsleeves, the light jacket he'd considered this morning left hanging on its hook by the door. Today he was helping the fledgling small-business association throw a luncheon; there were four members and they had invited other local small-business owners as well as those in a twenty-mile radius. The idea was to encourage some of these outliers to relocate to a designated stretch of Gilead's now-defunct main street; reduced rents, low-interest loans, and tax abatements were just a few of the enticements being offered.

The luncheon was taking place at Lulu's, and Jared had spent a good part of the morning helping her get the place ready for the buffet; together they had pushed the tables together, covered them with her collection of vintage embroidered cloths and various swaths of fabric, set out glasses, dishes, napkins, and cutlery.

"You don't have to do this stuff," said Lulu. Her dreads had popped loose from the scarf that covered them. "I can get Pedro or Jean Paul to do it."

"I don't mind." He moved a stack of dishes from one side of a table to another. "It's fun, actually."

"Must be different from your big-city days."

"Not as different as you think. I did my fair share of staging apartments before the buyers came through."

"Staging?"

"You know: rearranging or eliminating furniture, putting some flowers in a vase, lighting a scented candle — grapefruit or

472

pine are always winners — opening the blinds to show off a good view or closing them to disguise a bad one."

"Did you like it?" She had gone into the kitchen and returned with a tray filled with mugs, no two alike.

"The staging?"

"No, all of it. Living in New York, being part of that life. I'm guessing maybe not, because you're here, right?"

"I'm here." Jared looked around. The place looked good — not sophisticated or chic, but homey and welcoming. And the smells emanating from the kitchen — Lulu was serving a shrimp chowder, fried catfish, and banana cream pie, among other things — well, they were as good as anything in that Big old Apple he'd left behind. "I'm here and I like it just fine."

Lulu's cell phone chimed a few musical notes and she paused to answer. "Hello, baby." Her boyfriend? "That's all right. Sure." She paused, listening. "That sounds great, baby. Great. You be a good boy now. Mama loves you." She clicked off and glanced in Jared's direction. "That was my son, Nicky."

"How old?" asked Jared.

"Eight. He lives with his daddy and I only see him on weekends — at least for now."

"It's complicated?" Jared thought of Celeste; he was planning to call tonight to check in and see how she was doing. He hadn't seen her since he'd come down here in December, but he'd been in regular touch with Miranda.

"In a word — yes." She began rolling the cutlery — knife, fork, spoon — into the napkins. "You have any kids?"

"A baby daughter." He fished his phone out of his pocket to show her a picture. "But she doesn't live with me because —"

"Because it's complicated." She smiled. "I know." Lulu arranged the rolled-up napkins into a wide fan shape and glanced at the clock — shaped like a black cat with a tail that moved as it ticked — and said, "They'll be here soon. I'd better see how Jean Paul is doing in the kitchen."

She was right. At the door was Marybeth, the owner of a stationery store that specialized in letterpress and handmade cards. She had a small following already, and hers would be a great business to lure into town. Jared ushered her inside. "Wait until you try some of Lulu's popovers; your mouth will think it's gone to heaven."

Marybeth smiled. "That's why I'm here. Lulu's got a reputation, you know."

"Well, we're hoping you'll like it enough

to decide to stay."

Jared followed as she made her way toward the back table, where the platters were being set out by the waitstaff. In the center was the tureen of spicy shrimp soup; he could smell it from here. Lulu was certainly pulling out all the stops.

The rest of the invited guests started coming in after that — fabric store owners and ice-cream makers, the weavers, bakers, lighting designers, and potters. Each small, many artisanal, and all exactly the sort of businesses to attract shoppers, strollers, potential renters or buyers — and in so doing, resurrect the moribund street. Jared was in his element here, talking up the avenue, the town, and the entire enterprise. He had no time to eat, which was a damn shame, and was able to get in only a few sips of Lulu's limeade.

When the last guests — a couple with a small garden supply business they were currently operating from their house in the next town over — left, the tables were pretty much decimated. A lone wisp of a popover sat in its napkin-lined basket; the soup tureen was empty, as were most of the platters. Jared was hungry and reached for what was left of the popover. But the day was a big success — he'd hoped for five to six new members to sign today and they had actually gotten ten. At least three were considering relocating and had scheduled appointments to look over vacant spaces and discuss terms.

"You'll need more to eat than that," Lulu said. "Hang on; let me see what I can rustle up in there." She went into the kitchen and came back with a small bowl of soup and a plate that held a slice of the catfish, sautéed greens, and a baked sweet potato. "The pie's all gone, but if you're still hungry after this, I think I have some rice pudding left."

"Thank you." Jared sat down on a chair. "This looks delicious." He picked up his fork and glanced at Lulu, who was still standing. "Join me? It's no fun to eat alone."

Lulu pulled up a chair and sat down next to him. "How old is your baby girl?"

"Almost a year. Her birthday is March twenty-second." He didn't say that her exact birth date was not certain — no one knew if she had been born before or after midnight on the morning Miranda found her in the subway station — but they'd had to pick one for the birth certificate.

"Does she live with her mother?"

Jared didn't even hesitate. "Yes. Yes, she does." There would be time to explain the finer points; he planned to ask Lulu out to a movie or something. Though she was hardly the sort of woman that he usually went for, he liked her — he liked her a lot. And he wanted to hear more about Nicky and about all the complications that resulted in his living with his father and not with her. It was those complications, he decided, that made things interesting.

# THIRTY-FOUR

"Out!" Celeste clamored. "Out!"

"All right, sweetheart. You can get out." Miranda knelt in front of the stroller, unbuckled Celeste and, taking her hand firmly, set her down on the sidewalk while she attempted to push the stroller with her other hand. Bundled into her fuchsia snow-suit — it was a Saturday morning in March, and although the light looked like spring, the air was still nippy — Celeste teetered along happily. Now that she had just started walking, she wanted to walk everywhere, all the time, even when it would have been so much more convenient for Miranda if she stayed in the stroller.

A man with a big, shaggy dog ambled by; Celeste lunged, and Miranda grabbed her just in time. The dog looked friendly, but who knew? He might not appreciate the onslaught of one small, fuchsia-clad girl. "Woof!" Celeste said, tugging at Miranda's hand as she attempted to follow the dog. "Woof, woof!"

"Yes, that's a dog," Miranda said. "Dogs go *woof.*" Had she thought having a baby was exhausting? Well, that was only because she hadn't experienced life with a toddler yet. And with Celeste's first birthday coming up next week, toddlerhood was right around the corner.

Miranda led Celeste into the party store on Seventh Avenue. She had planned a birthday celebration at Baby Space on McDonald Avenue in Brooklyn, and she was going to order the balloons — Celeste loved balloons. "I'd like two dozen," she told the young girl behind the register. "And can you mix the colors — some pink, some red, and some white?"

"Sure thing." The girl began writing the delivery information on the order pad. Miranda was about to take out her wallet when she looked down to see that Celeste, though still holding her hand, had discovered some brightly colored jelly beans in small plastic bags at her eye level and was just about to yank down the entire display.

"No touching, honey." Miranda quickly scooped her up. In response, Celeste began to wail. "Sorry," said Miranda to the girl, raising her voice above the sound. She dug into her bag to find her credit card but succeeded only in dumping the contents onto the floor. Wallet, keys, phone, a package of Life Savers, several crumpled tissues, and a handful of pens landed in a heap near her feet; a tube of lipstick rolled off and stopped several inches away.

"Hey, let me help." The girl came out from behind the counter and began picking everything up. Miranda opened her wallet, paid for the balloons, and hustled Celeste — still wailing — out of the store. Once they were outside, her despair evaporated and she began tugging on Miranda's hand again, eager to wander off. They came to the bagel store; Celeste was a big fan of bagels. Miranda bought her a cinnamon raisin bagel with cream cheese; she knew the cream cheese would end up everywhere, but it was worth it because Celeste would tolerate being in the stroller while she ate.

With Celeste contentedly chewing the bagel, Miranda was able to finish the rest of her Saturday-morning errands. She ran into someone from the Zumba class she'd recently started taking, and also Heidi and Auggie, who was in his stroller napping. "We'll see you at the party next week." Heidi adjusted Auggie's blanket to cover him better. "I haven't been to Baby Space, but I hear it's great."

"It looks perfect for their age group." Miranda debated whether she should try to wipe the cream cheese from Celeste's chin now or wait until they got home. "No bigger kids to contend with."

"Soon these guys will be the bigger kids," said Heidi. "Auggie is just growing like crazy. He wears something once and the next time I put it on, it's too small."

"This one too," Miranda said fondly. "But since she's the birthday girl, I bought her a new dress for the party and I don't care if she only wears it once."

"Of course not," said Heidi. "A first birthday is a real milestone."

"Yes." Miranda looked at her daughter; white flecks of cream cheese were now dotting her face and she was patting her hair with a cream cheese–smeared hand. "It certainly is."

Back at home, she cleaned Celeste off and put her down for a nap. That was one of the upsides of her new insistence on walking: she tired herself out and succumbed to long, luxuriant bouts of sleep. Then Miranda quietly left the room, picking her way around the cardboard boxes whose number was increasing by the week. Much as she loved her apartment in Mrs. Castiglione's house, she and Celeste had outgrown it. So with the money her father had left, she'd put a down payment on a proper two bedroom in an elevator building on Eastern Parkway. The apartment was well proportioned and light, but it was in terrible shape; Miranda would have a lot of work to do. It was a daunting and even terrifying task, but Jared had strongly encouraged her to make the move, and he'd already connected her with a contractor who was a personal friend — and who would give her a good price on the renovation.

While Celeste slept, Miranda went over the details of the party. The guest list included all seven of the children from her single mommies group — along with their mothers — as well as Bea, Lauren, and her husband and kids. She'd invited several people from her office, Mrs. Castiglione, Supah, and, of course, Jared. Courtney and Harris were out of town and Sallie couldn't make it, but it would still feel festive.

Something was nagging her. Evan. Though she hadn't seen him in some time, she still had faith in his connection to Celeste. Those photographs he took. The way he'd looked at her, held her. He belonged at this party as much as anyone. And without stopping to second-guess her decision, she quickly shot off an e-mail to invite him.

In her obsessive replaying of their final conversation at Courtney's wedding, Miranda kept fixating on the sentence he'd said about not being able to father children. She knew he had not been married before, so how would he have found out? And why hadn't she pressed him for more information? As it was, she was left with a mystery. She also replayed the moment in which she'd asked if he loved her and seized upon the fact that he had not said no — not in so many words. He had said there was someone else. But not that he no longer felt anything for her.

Well, she wasn't going to sit here and go over all this — again — or wait for his reply. She got up, made a cup of tea, allowed herself to be distracted by cleaning out her kitchen drawers. Was there a reason she had three can openers? And really, her knives were so dull they wouldn't cut Wonder Bread. Organizing was one of those easy-to-put-off but ultimately satisfying domestic chores. And when she returned to the laptop, there, as easy and as casual as could be, was Evan's response: *Thanks for the invite. See you on Saturday.*

She stared it for several seconds. He'd

spent months ignoring her messages and now, just like that, he'd answered. What could it mean? The brightening hope his words engendered was immediately dimmed by her next thought: Thea. She had not said anything about her, but what if he brought her along? Miranda would not allow herself to ask; the question was almost craven. No, she would have to believe he'd arrive solo. And if not, she would have to deal with it.

Celeste woke Miranda early on the morning of the party. "Mamamamamama," she crooned from her bedroom. She'd pulled herself up and was hanging on the crib's railing with both hands, and when she saw Miranda, she stamped her feet in a tiny flurry of excitement.

"Up you go." Miranda hoisted her in one arm.

"Up!" said Celeste; she had taken to echoing the words Miranda spoke to her.

After bathing her, Miranda put Celeste in the smocked dress with the Peter Pan collar. The label read Bonpoint, the children's shop on Madison Avenue, but Miranda had found the dress — pale pink with tiny, star-like red flowers — at a thrift store on East Eighty-fourth Street for a fraction of its original cost. In the same store, she had also bought a pink, stretchy headband with a bow on one side. It looked darling on Celeste's soft mass of hair, but Celeste kept yanking it off, and after a few attempts, Miranda gave up. Then she deposited Celeste in her crib while she slipped into the fluid, dark red jersey dress she'd bought for the occasion; after all, it was a milestone for her too.

Bea came with her car and drove them, along with Mrs. Castiglione, to Baby Space; the two women entertained Celeste while Miranda made sure everything was ready. The balloons had arrived and so had the tea sandwiches; Supah, Miranda saw, was already there, and she went over to give her a hug.

"Big girl today." Supah beamed. "This for her." She handed Miranda a box wrapped in metallic pink paper and a silver bow.

"Thank you, Supah." Miranda put the box off to the side, to be opened later. Then she saw Heidi and Auggie come through the doors, and Max and Sophie too, with Lauren right behind them. She went to retrieve Celeste and set her down in the enclosed baby ballroom, where dozens of plastic red, yellow, and blue balls filled the space; Auggie joined her, along with three other members of the mommy-baby group Heidi had started. Celeste slapped at the balls with her open palms and laughed when she sent them flying; the party was in full swing.

After the visit to the ballroom, there was a ride on a "train" whose cars were all stenciled with cartoon characters and many trips down a baby slide. Auggie had a minor tantrum and Heidi had to take him off for a little while to settle down, but Celeste seemed to be the life of the party; every time Miranda looked at her, she was smiling.

Over the sandwiches, cornichons, and fruit salad, Miranda mingled with the guests. She spent a long time talking to Jared, who had flown up from Louisiana. "You've given her such a great day," he said. "You're giving her a great life." Miranda absorbed the praise quietly — she had transformed Celeste's life, just as Celeste had transformed hers. This last year had not been easy, and at the start of it, she could not have predicted its direction, or the unfamiliar paths she would take to arrive at this surprising new destination. And now here they were, mother and daughter, united by accident but bound by love.

After the meal, they opened presents: a plush teddy bear and a baby doll, two puzzles, a busy box, a set of blocks, a whole slew of dresses, pajamas, and other things to wear. Courtney and Bea helped Miranda dispose of the wrapping and put the gifts off to one side. "Are you ready to serve the cake?" Lauren asked when everything was cleared away.

"Didn't I tell you? There isn't going to be a cake."

"No cake? What are you talking about it?"

"Come on." Miranda started walking. "I'll show you." And she led Lauren to the kitchen area, where, on three trays, were thirty-six cupcakes, each one covered with a cloud of marshmallow frosting, sprinkled with shredded coconut, and capped by tiny 1's fashioned from pink marzipan.

"Oh!" Lauren said. "Did you make these?"

"Not this time. They're a gift from Alan Richardson, cupcake king. *Domestic Goddess* is doing a story on him and we've become friends."

"Well, they are perfection." Lauren helped Miranda carry the trays into the main area, where they were greeted with a chorus of oohs and aahs. Then Miranda lit a single candle — pink, of course — and they all started to sing.

When the song was over, Miranda turned to Celeste. "Now you blow, sweetie pie."

"Bow," said Celeste; the letter *L* was not yet in her oral repertoire.

Miranda demonstrated and Celeste, eyes

fixed on her face, puffed her cheeks in imitation and blew. Together they vanquished the small flame and everyone started to clap. Miranda handed Celeste to Jared as she began handing out the cupcakes.

"Let me give one to the birthday girl." Jared was still holding Celeste, who was reaching for a cupcake.

"Of course; just see if you can keep her from getting it in her hair, okay? I have a feeling marshmallow is going to be *very* sticky and *very* hard to wash out." She handed him the cupcake, and when she looked up, there was Evan, trademark camera on his shoulder. And as far as Miranda could tell, he was alone.

When Evan saw her looking at him, he smiled and raised a hand in greeting. Miranda returned the smile and kept handing out cupcakes. No one else seemed to register his arrival, and he remained on the periphery, camera held up to his eye, shooting quietly and unobtrusively. Miranda had been taking photographs all day with her phone — snapshots, visual notes. But Evan's photographs aspired to so much more; she hoped she'd get to see them.

Finally, everyone who wanted one had a cupcake and Evan made his way over. "Hey,

Miranda." He leaned down and kissed her on both cheeks. How very European. "Good to see you."

"It's good to see you too," she said. "It was nice of you to come."

"It was nice of you to invite me. I didn't want to miss Celeste's first birthday."

While they talked, Miranda registered how good he looked: new haircut, black turtleneck, black leather jacket. Like one of the Beatles. Only taller. She was about to say something else when she felt someone touch her elbow. Jared.

"I think you should take her." He handed Celeste to Miranda. "She's been doing that *mamamamamama* thing."

Miranda positioned Celeste on her hip and introduced Jared to Evan. She could feel Evan scrutinizing him, looking for signs — of intimacy, of erotic connection — but she knew he would detect none. She and Jared were in a good place now, and Miranda would never again allow anything to jeopardize it. Jared moved away, distracted by another guest.

"Celeste is looking great." Evan smiled down at the baby. "She's gotten so big. And her face has changed a lot. I might not have recognized her." He covered his eyes and began a game of peekaboo. Every time he emerged from behind his fingers, Celeste emitted a little yelp of delight and tugged on the bright red balloon clutched in her fist. He turned to Miranda. "I have a present for her." He took his backpack off, reached inside, and handed Miranda a tissue-wrapped package.

"Thank you." She jiggled Celeste, who was getting squirmy. "But maybe you should open it — I've got my hands full."

Evan opened the package and held up a small hand-knit sweater and matching hat — both had blue and white nautical stripes, and the sweater sported a red fish on its front and red buttons in the shape of anchors.

"How adorable!" Miranda fingered the fine, soft-gauge cotton.

"I was thinking about the knitting challenge," said Evan.

"Knitting debacle was more like it. It was sweet of you to remember."

"I remember a lot of things." He paused. "Is there somewhere we can talk? Somewhere a little more private?"

Before she could reply, her attention was caught by a sharp popping noise. "What was that?" Miranda looked wildly around. Did someone have a *gun*?

"Look!" Evan pointed upward. A balloon

had drifted too close to the ceiling vent; the sharp corners of the vent caused it to break.

"Oh!" She laughed with relief. Just a balloon. But then another balloon popped and another. Celeste, startled, let go of her balloon and up it went.

"No!" cried Miranda. Evan jumped, trying to grab it, but he missed by seconds. The balloon drifted up and over and then — *pop!* Just like the others. Celeste's eyes followed its doomed progress, and when the balloon burst, she began to squall, beating her feet against Miranda's chest and reaching vainly for the balloon.

"We'll get you another one." Evan darted off in pursuit of another red balloon, but when he presented her with it, Celeste refused to be mollified. And her crying had started a chain reaction. Now several other children were crying too. The remaining balloons were in a cluster in the corner, their strings hopelessly snarled; Evan attempted to unknot them.

"I think this party is winding down." Miranda wiped Celeste's damp face with a napkin; Celeste twisted away.

"I hope I'm not too late, then."

Miranda turned to see Judge Waxman, unexpectedly elegant in a leopard-print coat. She had sent the judge an invitation but had not gotten a reply. "You came!"

"Of course I came." Judge Waxman pulled off her gloves and looked at Celeste. "This is one of the happy stories; I don't see too many of them in my line of work."

"You wouldn't think so from looking at her now, but yes, it is a happy story." Miranda looked at the child she'd found that night a year ago: robust, thriving, darling — and wailing her head off.

Judge Waxman smiled. "I have something for her." She handed Miranda a small, flat package wrapped in gold paper. "I'll even tell you what it is: a copy of *Anne of Green Gables.* It's always my gift of choice when the recipient is a girl."

"I loved that book." Miranda touched the gold-embossed cover. "I must have read it ten times. Thank you so much."

"A story about an orphaned girl who finds her true home seems especially apt, don't you think?" Judge Waxman asked.

"Yes." Miranda clutched the book tightly. "It is."

By this time several of the other mothers with their own crying children in tow came over to say good-bye; Miranda asked Bea to bring Judge Waxman a cupcake — the last of the batch.

"Do you want me to take her?" Evan had

walked back over to Miranda. "So you can start cleaning up?"

"I don't know. She's still kind of fussy."

"Fussy? Who's fussy?" Evan reached for Celeste. "Are you a fussy girl?" He made a silly face, and after a moment, Celeste tilted back her head and laughed. "That's what I thought. No fussy girls here. Not a one."

While Evan entertained Celeste, Miranda started gathering up the dirty paper plates. Lauren's son, Max, was now sobbing because his sister had eaten the last bite of his cupcake; so she needed to get him home; Bea had left for a rehearsal. Finally, everything was done and Miranda went to retrieve Celeste. Evan was bouncing her on his knees; he had managed to untangle a white balloon from the cluster, and Celeste now held it in her hand.

"Thank you for distracting her," she said. "And for coming too. It was really nice of you."

"No problem." He was looking at Celeste, not her, so his next words were a surprise. "I have my car; can I give you a lift?"

"Sure." She tried to act as nonchalant as he was. "That would be so nice." And convenient too — she would not have to call a car service.

They piled the gifts into the trunk and

strapped Celeste, still clutching the balloon, into her car seat. She was asleep in about three minutes, and the balloon, untethered now, floated to the front seat, where Miranda snatched it before it could obscure Evan's vision. They were quiet on the drive back, and when they got to Miranda's house, Evan found a parking spot right out front. "You take her up and get her into bed. I'll deal with everything down here."

"All right." Miranda carried the sleeping child and her balloon upstairs into the apartment. Celeste's head pressed against her shoulder, a solid, grounding weight. Miranda was able to ease her gently into her crib; then, propping the door open, she went down to help Evan with the gifts. "Thanks. For everything." She was nervous, but so what? She wasn't going to let that stop her from seeing this through. "Do you want to come in? For a glass of wine or something?"

"Why not?" He followed her inside and sat down on the sofa. Miranda brought them each a glass of wine; he sipped his as he looked around. "What's with the boxes? Are you moving?"

"I am; the closing is at the end of the month."

"Good for you." He took another sip of

wine. "Where to?"

She told him about the place on Eastern Parkway with its doorman and its big windows, its scarred floors and blistering paint; then they both lapsed into an uncomfortable silence. He was the first to break it. "So how come you invited me to the party?"

"How come you decided to show up?"

"Touché." He set his wineglass down on the table and leaned back against the couch cushions. "I'll just come out with it. I've been lonely and I missed you; I missed you a lot."

"I missed you too." Miranda chose her words very carefully, not wanting — or daring — to give everything away all at once. "But I thought there was someone else."

"There was, but that's been over for a while. And anyway, you can be lonely even with someone else — if she's not the right someone else."

"This person, she wasn't the right someone?"

"No." Evan held her gaze. "She wasn't. But you, Miranda — you are."

"What about Jared?" She had to ask.

He moved closer to her. "What about him?"

"You accused me of cheating on you with him; you refused to believe me when I told you it wasn't true." The white balloon had drifted in from Celeste's room and now bobbed overhead.

"I should have had more faith in you, Miranda. I'm sorry."

She looked at him; he was utterly sincere, and she had to meet that sincerity in kind. "I can't say that I wasn't attracted to him because that would be a lie. And I don't want to lie to you. But whatever I felt, it was — transitory. He was not the right one. He never was. No, the right one was you — *is* you: you were meant for me, Evan Zuckerbrot." Then she waited, for several tense, awful seconds, until he pulled her close and kissed her. This was where she wanted to be. This was where she belonged. Why had it taken her so long to figure that out?

# EPILOGUE

Geneva had started driving before it was actually dawn, and now she could see a thin silver line of light at the horizon that grew wider and brighter as she sped along. A container of coffee sat in the cup holder and next to that, a bran muffin, taken from the motel's complimentary breakfast bar and wrapped in a paper napkin.

Outside the car's windows were the chalk and sugar maples, the yellow birch and the pig buckeye she recalled from her childhood; Geneva had spent eight years as a Girl Scout, and she'd learned to identify the flora and fauna of her native state. It was April, and everything was in lush, glorious leaf. The scenery was starting to look familiar now; she remembered this stretch of road. She drove up to the gates of the Eternal Springs Cemetery and parked in the adjacent lot. Then she picked up the bag that had been sitting on the seat beside her and pocketed the muffin; she might get hungry. From here, she remembered the way easily. Her father had been buried in this place, and her mother too, along with various other Highsmith relatives. The bag bumped awkwardly against her thigh as she walked, so she ignored the handle and cradled it in both arms.

Shortly after Caroline's death, Geneva had claimed the body and had it cremated. The ashes had remained in an urn on the top shelf of her closet; she had been waiting for spring. Now that it was here, she had brought the ashes down to be buried in the family plot. It was the right thing to do.

The cemetery was impeccably kept — the winding paths swept regularly, the trees and shrubs neatly trimmed. The sky was fully light now, and there was a soft mist over everything. Geneva continued down the path, making a right turn and then a left. There was her father's stone, and next to it, her mother's. Caroline's, newly raised, was right beside them. In front of it was a freshly dug hole, perhaps two feet wide, and leaning against it was a shovel, just as she had requested. Good.

The director, Mr. Emberly, had not wanted to do this at first. But he knew her, and he knew her family; eventually, he relented. "It's not at all regular policy," he'd said several times during their conversation. "Please don't tell anyone I made an exception for you. And please, get an early start; I'd rather you kept this between us."

Geneva walked up to the stone and laid her hand on the marble surface. The inscription was simple: name, dates of birth and death, and these words: daughter, sister, mother. She sat down and pulled out the muffin. Birds twittered nearby, and she recalled the litany of names she'd memorized as a Girl Scout. Some of these birds were probably in the trees right above her though she was not sure she could identify them any longer.

She took a bite of the muffin. Gluey, cold, and stale. The birds wouldn't mind though; she began breaking it into bits and sprinkling it on the ground. Instantly, they began swooping down, first one and then a bevy, pecking and hunting in the grass for the crumbs. Most were brown and gray, but then a cardinal appeared, and, being so much bigger than the others, scared them off. But when Geneva reached into the bag that held the urn, even the cardinal fluttered away.

The etched brass vessel, ordered from Stardust Memorials, gleamed in the soft morning light. She had peeked at the ashes when they first arrived; they were not ash-like at all, but gritty and coarse — more like broken crockery. And they were surprisingly heavy. Their weight, added to the not-insubstantial weight of the urn, made it hard to handle, and it landed at the bottom of the hole with a small thud. "I'm sorry," she said aloud. Was she talking to Carrie? Her mother? Miranda Berenzweig? It could have been any of the above because in some way, she owed each of them an apology.

Then she picked up the shovel and began to fill in the hole. Not a difficult job, but she still worked up a slight sweat while completing it. Next she unwrapped the seashells that were also in the bag and began setting them in front of the tombstone, the largest, the pearly nautilus, right in the center. Next to the nautilus she placed the conch, then all the rest: nacreous, striped, whorled, beaded, and studded. The shells were part of the collection she rotated in her apartment; Caroline had always been drawn to them, and Geneva could remember her picking up a shell, running her fingers along the surface, pressing it against her ear. The shells Geneva was leaving behind today were her most beautiful, most unusual, most arresting. They were an offering. Or a penance.

Once she had finished, she sat on the grass as the mist slowly burned away. The birds returned, only this time the pack of mostly brown, gray, and whites was joined by another more vivid specimen: the Eastern bluebird. She identified him — she knew it was a male — in an instant, not only because of the Girl Scouts, but also because she had helped Caroline do a project on Eastern bluebirds for a grade-school science project. Her sister had been largely indifferent to the discipline of doing the research or assembling the facts. But Caroline had drawn a meticulous and haunting rendition of the bird, bearing down on the colored pencils until she'd complained that her fingers ached from the pressure and she'd snapped the points of the pencils. Underneath the drawing she had lettered the words *The Bluebird of Happiness.* Geneva had tried to get her to change it.

"That's not a scientific designation," she'd said. "The teacher will take points off."

"But it is the bluebird of happiness," Caroline insisted. The lettering remained.

Geneva held very still as she watched the bird, the feathers on its breast a rusty red, the head and wings an impossible, vivid cerulean. Delicately, the bird searched for the crumbs; for a moment, it regarded her with a bright, black eye. Then it flew away. She got up, dusted off the seat of her pants, and headed toward the car. It had grown considerably warmer, even hot, and she peeled off her cardigan, tied it around her waist, and reached into the bag, now empty except for a crushable straw hat that she set on her head.

On the way out of the gates, she saw a family — mother, father, boy, and towheaded little girl. Carrie had been that kind of blond. Geneva thought of their summers at the beach, Caroline growing more sunkissed by the week, hair gone nearly white from the long, bright days. How she'd loved the beach, the water; what an irony that she, who had been such a good swimmer, had drowned.

When she reached the car, Geneva got in and switched on the ignition. Something made her look up, and there it was again: the bluebird, perched on the overhanging branch of a maple tree. It was only when the bird flew off a second and final time that she turned on the air conditioner and put her foot to the pedal.

# CONVERSATION GUIDE
# YOU WERE MEANT *FOR* ME

## YONA ZELDIS MCDONOUGH

This Conversation Guide is intended to enrich the individual reading experience, as well as encourage us to explore these topics together — because books, and life, are meant for sharing.

# A CONVERSATION WITH YONA ZELDIS MCDONOUGH

*Q. Was there any factual basis for this story?*

A. Yes. My good friend Patty Grossman told me about a man who had found a newborn on a subway platform, brought the infant to the police, and then continued to follow the case. No one claimed the infant and the family court judge suggested that he foster the child with the goal of adoption. He did, and now the baby is a teenager and happily living with his two dads in New York City. Here is an instance in which so much could have gone wrong — resulting in another ruined, wasted life — and yet, instead, everything went right. I loved the hopeful aspect of this story and wanted to turn it into a story of my own. I am by nature an optimist and love to find stories that affirm my optimism.

*Q. Did this novel tap into any fantasies of your own?*

A. Absolutely! I'd always wanted a third child, and would occasionally allow myself what I called the "found baby fantasy." What would I do? How would I respond? I think I would have reacted very much as Miranda did.

*Q. Do you feel women are your core audience?*

A. I do and I love writing for them. Yet since I often include strong male characters and male points of view, I would love to be able to reach a wider audience that included more men as well.

*Q. You've chosen two male protagonists along with one female voice. Why did you choose this structure?*

A. Having those three voices creates a triangle, and triangles are essentially unstable shapes. From a dramatic standpoint, that instability is interesting and potentially exciting because of the tension it creates. Miranda's affection and attraction hovers between two men; which one will she choose?

*Q. How do you choose the professions of your characters?*

A. I like to select professions that I either have some familiarity with (so the work lives of my characters will seem believable) or that interest me enough to do the necessary research. In Evan's case, I drew on the experiences and insights shared with me by my husband, Paul McDonough, who is a photographer and has used a Leica — the same camera Evan uses — for years. I love and admire my husband's work, so Evan's profession is a kind of homage to him. I chose real estate for Jared because it's a field that has always held a certain appeal for me. The buying of a home is so deeply personal, and says so much about who we are and what we long for. It's also an area that allowed Jared's particular qualities — his easy charm, his affability — to shine, so I thought it would suit him. In Miranda's case, I felt comfortable with the world of publishing and magazines; I made her a food editor to give it a slight twist and because it gave me the chance to write extensively about cupcakes!

*Q. Can you talk about Geneva? She is an important character but an elusive one.*

A. She was a challenging character to write because much of what she does is devious and deceptive. And yet I understand her and her motivations. Having a family member with mental illness can be very draining and exhausting. Geneva's feelings about her sister are not necessarily nice but I believe they are accurate.

*Q. What does a typical writing day look like for you?*

A. When I am in the zone, I might start work before breakfast, cup of coffee by my side. I break for a late breakfast/ early lunch around eleven o'clock and then it's back to work. I have to stop to make dinner, and often go to the gym late in the day or in the evening. Now that my children are older and I don't have to be up early to get them off to school, I can stay up very late and work if I want. I like those evening hours best; fewer interruptions and the night like a long, deep pool I can dive right into.

*Q. In addition to fiction, you write nonfiction and you write for children too; how do you balance those three different kinds of writing?*

A. I actually find it works out very well because each kind of writing taps into a different part of my heart, soul, or brain. If I am stuck or stalled on one manuscript, I can turn to another. Hopefully I will have better luck with that, and if I do, the confidence that success inspires spills over into the other project and gets the process going again.

Q. *What's next on your horizon?*

A. I am working on something now that is a bit more challenging for me. It involves an interesting — and tragic — bit of New Hampshire history and will contain bits of a novel within a novel. Also, there is something in the plot that requires me to write a poem or two. I love poetry and, like Wallace Stevens, believe that "poetry is the supreme fiction," but apart from some rather pedestrian attempts in college, I have not written in the form. I'm excited to try it; fortunately, the character who's a poet is not all that skilled, so my amateur efforts will suffice just fine.

# QUESTIONS FOR DISCUSSION

1. Do you think Miranda's decision to adopt Celeste was impulsive and ill considered? Why or why not?

2. What do you think of Jared's decision to give up his child? Was it for her sake or for his own?

3. Has anything happened in your life that you believe was "meant to be"?

4. Have you ever done something that a friend did not support? If so, what happened? Was the friendship made stronger as a result or was it damaged?

5. What do you think about Miranda's attraction to Jared? Should she have succumbed? Why or why not?

6. Why do you think it takes Miranda so

long to appreciate what Evan has to offer?

7. How do you view Geneva's behavior? Are her actions reprehensible or comprehensible?

8. What are some of the differences and similarities in Miranda's relationships to the four men in the novel: Luke, Evan, Jared, and her father?

9. How much sympathy did you feel for Carrie?

10. Does Miranda change and grow in the course of the novel? If so, how does that come about?

11. What makes someone a good parent? Is Miranda a good parent? Is Jared?

# ABOUT THE AUTHOR

**Yona Zeldis McDonough** is the author of five previous novels and the editor of two essay collections. Her fiction, essays, and articles have appeared in *Bride's, Cosmopolitan, Family Circle, Harper's Bazaar, Lilith, Metropolitan Home, More,* the *New York Times, O, the Oprah Magazine,* the *Paris Review,* and *Redbook.* She lives in Brooklyn, New York, with her husband and two children.